A Saint from Texas

Edmund White

BLOOMSBURY PUBLISHING
LONDON · OXFORD · NEW YORK · NEW DELHI · SYDNEY

BLOOMSBURY PUBLISHING
Bloomsbury Publishing Plc
50 Bedford Square, London, WC1B 3DP, UK
29 Earlsfort Terrace, Dublin 2, Ireland

BLOOMSBURY, BLOOMSBURY PUBLISHING and the Diana logo are trademarks
of Bloomsbury Publishing Plc

First published in Great Britain 2020
This edition published 2021

A catalogue record for this book is available from the British Library

ISBN: HB: 978-1-5266-0044-8; TPB: 978-1-5266-0043-1; PB: 978-1-5266-0047-9;
EBOOK: 978-1-5266-0045-5; EPDF: 978-1-5266-4453-4

2 4 6 8 10 9 7 5 3 1

Typeset by Westchester Publishing Services
Printed and bound in Great Britain by CPI Group (UK) Ltd, Croydon CR0 4YY

MIX
Paper from
responsible sources
FSC® C020471

To find out more about our authors and books visit www.bloomsbury.com
and sign up for our newsletters

To: Giuseppe Gullo

What had men ever done, to deserve so much beauty and grace?

—Elif Batuman, *The Idiot*

Paul Valéry said to André Breton that he could never compose fiction
because he was incapable of writing the Balzacian sentence
"The marquise went out at five o'clock."

I t all changed in the 1950s when our mother, Margie Ann, died and Daddy married a lady nine months later and brought her back to the little house on Elm Street (Daddy called them "e'lums") in Ranger, Texas. Ranger in those days was a ghost town; the wells had run dry twenty years earlier. Just a dirty old rag stretched across the entrance to the town saying, RANGER—OIL CAPITAL OF AMERICA, and we really had been an oil capital for twelve years. Miss Bobbie Jean, Daddy's fancy lady, declared she was no ghost, and she wasn't going to sit in a broken-down ranch house with swamp coolers instead of ceiling fans.

She was a Texas gal herself, from dusty Denton, where her father had been a math professor and written *Mental Arithmetic* and three nigra joke books. He was the most boring man in the whole world, she said, and he spit chewing tobacco into a spittoon and told endless jokes about colored folks. When someone asked why he was a professor, not a farmer like his brother, he said he wanted a job out of the sun. That was supposed to be funny. His brother, the farmer, was the nice one and he had typed up his life story, "I Sure Am Happy."

No one much liked the math professor. He'd collar a guy while rocking out on the open-air porch of Brown's Hotel in Mineral Wells, Texas, where he was taking the cure, and chaw and spit and pause. "Did you ever hear the one about—" And off he'd go. I guess he was smart. He used to tell us he was smart.

Boring. He was the most boring man in the world, with his lean face, his brown teeth, and his sun-creased neck. If an ant had crawled across that neck he would've broke his leg. He could tell you how to get up to one-hundred-digit numbers and all in your head. Boring. He was so proud of his mental arithmetic skills. All the men back then wore suits and ties and hats. His suit was brown and shiny and too big for him (double-breasted when he was a single-breasted man), and his tie loud and floral. His porkpie always tipped way back like he was younger than he looked, maybe a reporter in a 1930s talking picture.

Now, Bobbie Jean, who'd had a quickie Reno divorce from her lying, no-count (but handsome by all the pics) first husband, had done a little snooping around and found out that Daddy had millions in oil money socked away in Farmers–First National Bank in Stephenville, Texas, though we lived in that ranch house with the peeling paint and the swamp coolers, a black-and-white television with a screen no bigger than a third-class porthole and strips of colored plastic across it, green where the grass would be at the bottom, blue at the top where the sky might be, pink in the middle for the faces.

Well, Miss Bobbie Jean made Daddy throw out that old TV on the street and the swamp coolers quickly followed. She had big ceiling fans brought in, which would suck air through the windows if you left them open just a slit. A giant color Motorola was installed, a whole family entertainment center, and Daddy was sick when he saw his electric bill quadruple. Before you knew it she'd got herself a candy-colored Cadillac convertible and she'd traded in Daddy's rusty old Packard, which we called Bouncer, for a black Cadillac sedan that rode as smooth as a hearse and had cigarette lighters in each of the four door ashtrays, as if the corpses needed a light; the lighters were lit up from underneath so you'd never mistake where they were in the dark and they glowed with red coils when you pushed them down and held them up to your cigarette tip.

My sister and I were twins. Our mother had named us out of a movie fan magazine, Yvonne and Yvette, but she was so ignorant she said our names "Why-Von" and "Why-Vet." By the time we both knew better we liked them and wouldn't say them proper. We were fourteen and real Texas beauties with our blonde hair, tiny ears, long legs, and high breasts, though our real mother made us cover them up with extra-large blouses. That was 1952 and we even wore girdles to church, though we were skinny little things and our hips were no bigger than a boy's. Must have been hard to find girdles that narrow, but Mommy special-ordered them through Bacon's Dry Goods Store.

All that changed under Bobbie Jean. She made us say our names in the proper French way and corrected our old relatives who mispronounced them—"I'm sorry," Bobbie Jean said, "but we're not that country." She bought us tight sky-blue sweaters and threw away our girdles. She drove us to Dallas (not a long ride) and outfitted us at Neiman-Marcus in the latest grown-up Paris styles, but we felt like freaks in our New Look Diors with the cinched-in waists and long wide skirts, prancing around Ranger, when all the other girls in high school were wearing puffy skirts with cute poodle decals or tartan kilts fastened with giant safety pins. We had on high heels while they were bobby-soxers. The girls were so hypocritical—they'd finger our thin wools and heavy medieval leather belts and say, "My word, ain't you all spit and polish?"

As if our Diors weren't bad enough, Daddy put us through another scandal. He'd been shacking up for years with this pretty but pudgy fake blonde matron from Merkel, Texas. Once a week she'd drive her powder-blue Cadillac into town, pass the Piggly Wiggly, and park on one side of the road, and Daddy would drive his new hearse and park it on the other side. Exactly at high noon. Everyone saw them but nobody cared.

Well, Bobbie Jean minded and moved in on them like a farmer bagging wasps. And they never tried another rendezvous after ten whole years of sin. Bobbie Jean shot ten bullets into the tin ceiling of their room with her little Miss Derringer pistol, silver and with her initials on it. I did not say "tin," I said "tin." They weren't skinny folks neither and they pulled their sheets up over their robust bodies like Roman gods in a fountain. They were terrified! Bobbie Jean didn't say a word, just walked away, blew across the working end of her pistol, and gave a big tip to the astonished old desk clerk. Bobbie Jean sent that lady packing for good back to Merkel.

I took an interest in all this, of course, but sister Why-Vet was totally indifferent. She was in her own world a million miles away. She was a bookworm, even though I told her that "books are only good for pressing

3

to our breasts and propping them up." She didn't like that kind of talk. She would wrinkle up her nose like the Christian girls at school wearing their "purity rings" did when they heard nasty words. Or she'd just look away, as if a shadow on a wall or sunlight on a silo was more interesting than the future and reputation of our whole entire family. She was strange that way, our Why-Vet. We were identical in body alone, down to the least little mole, like a bug squashed on a bleached linen sheet, on our right sides, but in spirit—Lord! In spirit we were in opposite land. At least until we got older.

We had our bunk beds, everything pink and tidy as a virgin's undies, and by the glow of our cute little hamster night-light, we'd talk about . . . oh, life and love, and I'd bring up boys but she never did. I thought she might like girls, but she never looked at the naked girls in gym class and seemed unaware of everyone's breast size, though bet your bottom peso most girls that age *are* aware, painfully aware, are they *ever*!

I liked to read women's magazines and stuff, especially about European nobility and Paris fashion, but Why-Vet brought home so many heavy books from the Andrew Carnegie Public Library that the librarians got mad at her until they realized she was helping their circulation numbers, which they could point to down at City Hall, the one where they found a hundred-year-old toad still alive buried between the bricks. Why-Vet would make herself a little picnic lunch and go out to the edge of town under an old creaky windmill, with its rudder turning as the wind shifted, the blades rattling as they turned. She'd find a nice cool mott of wild oak. She'd sit on the ground there for hours in her Dior and read and read. Heavy books, too! All of Shakespeare and Homer. Lots of Pascal.

We had an aunt Bunn who lived in Bluff Dale, Texas, who'd taught elocution in high school and she coached Why-Vet on how to lose her East Texas twang. "You do not say 'hay-uh' but 'hair,' in one syllable, and it's not 'may-um' but 'ma'am.'" Aunt Bunn lived in an itty-bitty house her daddy had built, with no heat but a single Franklin stove. She had a big white chenille bedspread on a rosewood double bed and lots of little pillars she'd knitted covers for, cute little kittens and rabbits. Yvette soon sounded like a no-gut Yankee, as bland as Quaker Oats. She had a pretty enough voice. She was a pretty girl, no denying that, but her fire'd been dialed down to a pilot light. Yvette was so smart she made the debate team in our little high school. Our school motto was just three musical notes: "B sharp, B natural, but never B flat." Isn't that cute? Anyway, Yvette was immediately made the captain of the debate team and she won every match until she was best in state. My, Daddy was proud; he was a strangely competitive man. Yvette didn't even like debating, having to argue pro and con free trade, because she said Plato dismissed those shenanigans as mere sophistry and an orator should argue only what he or she knew to be true.

Bobbie Jean quarreled deep into the night with Daddy. She wanted to move us all into Dallas. She said we could come to Ranger for weekends, it was that close, but she was surprised Daddy wanted his girls growing up in a played-out ghost town with barely five thousand inhabitants and not one suitable suitor. "Your girls are millionaires and sm-a-art! My, are they smart! You'd stunt their fine minds here and get them hitched to bucktoothed farmers in coveralls and cow shit on their boots, pardon my French. These girls deserve some nice, polite, well-spoken gentlemen. Yvonne should have a debut and Yvette should go to a top-notch place of learning like UT at Austin, she's that bright. Boy, is she bright. You know how proud you were when Yvette took All State. You remember how you wanted her to get a varsity letter, how you said brain was better than brawn? They're my girls, too, now, and I'd feel I'd let them down if they didn't have golden opportunities—golden! Platinum!"

Daddy said, "They're sweet little things but in Dallas they might get uppity. I've seen them spoiled little Dallas gals."

"You have not," Bobbie Jean exclaimed. "You don't know anything about Dallas! You couldn't even find Neiman-Marcus or the Adolphus Hotel." And then Bobbie Jean went off into a long complaint about how the head waiter at the Baker Hotel refused to sell her a drink at the bar after a long day of shopping. "He said, 'I'm sorry, ma'am, no single women here at my bar.' Then he had the nerve to say, 'We gotta present a moral image to the world,' as if I was a common streetwalker looking for business."

She rumbled on and on until Daddy got impatient and brought her back to the issue at hand (clever strategy on her part!).

Bobbie Jean was very clever. She invited Daddy's mother along, a dowdy farm woman with a huge mono-bosom and swollen legs, a woman who read out every street sign as we passed it on the highway. If she approved of someone she called her "precious." If she disapproved she said, "Bless her heart," as in, "She eats a box of chocolates a day all by herself, bless her heart." She scarcely ever censored a thought, no matter how dull, inconsequential, or childish. She'd make such dopey remarks that the real estate agent asked in an aside, "Has she been like this for a long time?" with a look of concern that made Daddy mad.

We headed right for Turtle Creek and looked at houses in the $250,000 category—Renaissance palaces and adobe haciendas and an update of Versailles (which the salesman pronounced "Ver-sales"). He wasn't much— smelled of Brylcreem and wore a wristwatch, which Daddy thought was sissy, and had a mustache, a sure sign of a weakling or criminal, Daddy said.

We looked at a mansion with a circular portico. "Dang, it's nice if you want to live in the White House," Daddy said, and I could tell he was impressed but didn't want to show it. For the White House even his mother got out of the Cadillac and after she stumbled on her thick legs sealed in supportive hose through the Great Hall—or was it the Lincoln Bedroom—she said, "It's precious, well, I declare." When Daddy whispered, "How much is this national treasure?" the salesman (who was smoking a cigarette, which Daddy also thought was sissy) whispered something to him, and Grandma held her hands over her ears, since ladies weren't supposed to know about money. Money was "common."

We were shown the four bedrooms, the five bathrooms, the dining room, all carved mahogany and gilt eagles, the basement rec room that extended the length of the property. Namaw, as we called Daddy's mother, couldn't manage the stairs but an elevator was found for her. If she wasn't sure if something was precious she'd describe it uneasily as "different." The elevator was "sure different." She had a rural fear of sounding overly impressed by something urban, which she laid to rest by calling it dismissively "different," thereby acknowledging both the strangeness and the banality of anything new.

When Bobbie Jean said the price sounded reasonable, Daddy cursed her with a disgusting word that begins with *b* and ends with *h* and Namaw

6

said, "Why, P.M.,"—Daddy's name was Peter Martin Crawford—"no reason to talk ugly about such a precious house." She laughed her mirthless country laugh. "I'm going to have to wash your mouth out with soap, P.M." He flushed dark with rage.

They went on to look at the Alhambra, Sanssouci, the Palazzo Vecchio, and who knows what else—every bathroom, every double oven and warming tray, every winter garden. Ver-sales was being sold fully furnished. The owner had bought Louis the Something chairs and had them copied one and a half times larger, then he'd thrown away the originals. We were shown how the fireplace in the "salon" was insulated behind glass and was guaranteed not to give off heat and could be lit even in 103-degree weather. Poor Daddy, he must have had considerable in the bank but the idea of squandering so much on the house—why, who knew where it would all end? He was worn out with all the fancy historical labels (we even saw a moat and a portcullis and Daddy had to ask what they were); finally he said, "Haven't you got anything up-to-date?"

Namaw had to use the ladies' room but Daddy refused. He wanted to get this all over with, like it was a tooth extraction, and Namaw squealed, "Why, P.M., you'd have me relieve myself in my shoe," but in the end she got to use the toilet in one of the houses we were inspecting.

Yvette was practically comatose from all this house-viewing and when asked her opinion, she mumbled, "Any sort of shelter will do, won't it? Most of humanity is exposed to the elements, which obviously isn't fair." Everyone looked stunned by this bleak reminder of how vain and empty were these disputes of Ver-sales versus the Alhambra, this discontent with just four bedrooms and two glassed-in fireplaces roaring away in August. I couldn't help but think of the Fisherman's Wife and how she lost everything because she wanted to be the equal of God—until the magic flounder got fed up and returned her to her hovel. Yvette would've been happier in our Ranger, Texas, hovel with the three chickens out back, once including her favorite, Biddy Scratch, and the Concord grape arbor over the pathway, the grapes often sizzling in the heat into cracked miniatures of themselves, and the grasshoppers we'd catch. They'd wriggle dry as sticks in our closed fists before we released them. We'd carpeted the garage and we'd sit there in green-and-white metal chairs and sip iced sweet tea. When our real mother killed Biddy Scratch because cousin Brewster was coming to Sunday dinner, Yvette cried for days, especially because chopping Biddy's head off was a bloody mess and Biddy ran, headless, all over the yard, scaring the bejesus out of us all. If a poor old Negro woman would come to the door with a tin pail asking for food or beer, our real mother would fill her pail with good vittles but send her to work mopping the kitchen linoleum or dusting the living room, where we never went; it was like a museum or a funeral parlor family grief room with its horsehair couch, yellowing lace antimacassars, big freestanding radio with the cloth face over the speaker, and the carpet with faded roses.

Bobbie Jean really knew how to play Daddy. She'd figured out that as a teenager he'd suffered because his parents were the poorest people in town—and Weeping Hills was one poor town, cut off from the world with only one radio for five hundred people and only one copy of one newspaper that would arrive in town once or twice a week. Daddy says he can remember that when World War I ended they didn't know it for a whole day, until an old farmer came running over the hills shouting, "Kaiser Bill is done for!" No one ever visited except some little salesman who'd come by twice a year selling salt and needles and a special kind of cough syrup that'd drive the ladies crazy. The town couldn't keep a doctor or a dentist because nobody had any cash money to pay them with. And Daddy's folks were so poor, they ate for dinner what was called Martin's supper, toast soaked in bacon drippings. They couldn't afford anything; their house was falling down and hadn't had a lick of paint for an age. That kind of poverty is humiliating, even in a godforsaken one-street town like Weeping Hills.

Our Daddy always wanted to be a big shot. When he was in college for two years in San Marcos, he had to work all the time and even take off one semester to break rock on the state highway. Then, later, he got himself elected to the state government in Austin, but there he earned only six bits a day and four went to room and board. He found other jobs but they were hard as hell and he never could get ahead of his debts until an acre he owned in Ranger, Texas, came in with oil, black gold, and for ten good years he was saving nine-tenths of it. Our poor mother had to break her back washing the sheets once a week in the bathtub, though Daddy bought her a mangle to wring the water out before she hung those heavy sopping things on the line. He refused to hire a woman to help with the ironing or the cooking or the housecleaning. He thought Mama was a healthy woman and should work. He would expect her to polish his boots and wait on him. "Sugar," he'd say, "mo' pie." But then she died of TB and exhaustion at forty-nine, and while he was in mourning Daddy read the diary she'd kept all those silent, uncomplaining years. He wrote in the margins, "Poor Angel!" and "What a varmint," when she mentioned him. He read page after page of how he'd offended her, even left her covered with bruises, and he wrote, "This man is a monster! My poor baby, how I tortured you!" He could see how his whole myth of a happy marriage was crumbling in front of his eyes. Usually Daddy was cocksure—or so insecure he had to prove his way was the best way, the only way, and everyone around him must be envious and an enemy. But this time he sat up late every night listening to sad country music on the radio, all about cheating or broken hearts, and he read and reread Margie Ann's diary. He was always talking but now he was silent, like a big parade balloon slowly deflating till it was small enough to slip into a hip pocket.

One morning he locked the diary and put it away and buried the key beside the grape arbor. I imagine that's why he bowed down to Bobbie Jean's least wish: he was repentant and she was hard where our mother was soft. She knew what she wanted, whereas Mama was always dithering, fixing to find out what *you* wanted.

And then Bobbie Jean kept hammering on about us girls, how we deserved every opportunity money could buy, how we'd lost our mother, whom Daddy had worried and worried into an early grave, how I deserved a debut as lavish as the Hope Diamond and precious Yvette had the right to a first-class education in Greek and Latin and French and Texas history and domestic science!

Six months later we were living in the Turtle Creek White House, with its columned portico, though the lot wasn't that big, nobody's was. Bobbie Jean hired a cook and a maid but, boy, was she mean to them! They were colored girls and she paid them tiny salaries. She called the cook Pinky—maybe that really was her name—and Bobbie Jean gave them some sort of dog food to eat. They didn't eat what we ate, which often enough was steak, big well-done steaks, the way country people like them. You never saw a farmer eat a rare steak. Yvette could barely swallow hers. One day Miss Yvette didn't touch her blackberry cobbler and later Pinky told her she'd eaten it. "I never tasted that cobbler before," she said, "though I've been fixin' it since I started working at twelve." I couldn't be bothered, I knew there were lots of hungry people in the world; when we wouldn't clean our plates Bobbie Jean would say, "Remember the starving Armenians," but I doubt she could even picture them and never went to bed hungry herself. Yvette wrote a paper for our fancy private high school, our young ladies' academy, Hockaday, on the Armenians and uncovered all those horrors, how the Turks had made them walk through the desert without food or water until they dropped like flies or something. Yvette really did remember the starving Armenians. And the Jews who died in the ovens and Lord knows what else—I didn't want to think about all those poor people, it just made me sad.

Daddy had a great big collie. He called him Ole-Boy and said he was his best friend, and he had that big smelly thing sitting right at the huge mahogany dining table under the biggest chandelier you ever did see, Bohemian crystal, and Daddy would give him little bites of steak, though he'd make Ole-Boy beg for it with his big, imploring eyes and his upraised nose. When someone said collies weren't that smart, Daddy said, "That must be why we get along." Yvette learned how to give most of her steak to the dog when Daddy wasn't looking, though Daddy got suspicious (and a little bit hurt) when his best friend sat by Yvette instead of him.

Finally Yvette announced she'd become a vegetarian and Pinky served her extra helpings of peas and carrots and grits and Ole-Boy went back to Daddy's side. Yvette's dislike of meat made Daddy mad, and he talked about how they'd been so poor when he was growing up he'd get an orange for Christmas, that was all he'd get, and he'd hoard his orange till it turned blue and was rotten. He was so ashamed of his daddy he'd sass him and wouldn't mind him, that's what Namaw told me. She was proud of him that he lived in the White House now, but he'd been lucky with oil only for ten years, nothing to brag on him about, plenty of folks were oil-rich, half the families in Turtle Creek.

I overheard Yvette once in the next room when she was studying with a friend, Duke. They didn't know I was nearby and listening. He said, "I'm so bewitched by you, Why-Vet," and I knew he must've been reciting some script or something, using a word like "bewitched."

"Oh, come on, Duke. You can sweet-talk my sister. We're identical twins and she likes you so much."

I could've strangled Yvette for saying that, especially when he remarked, "She's different from you. She's brassy. She's forward. When she's in that little skirt doing her cheerleading . . ."

"Yes?"

"Well, she *sprawls* when she sits on the gym floor."

I was seeing red and almost barged in then and there, but I wanted to hear what Little Miss Muffet would say. She didn't say anything. Finally she whispered, "Let's go back to our equation."

"Why-Vet, I'm so bewitched by your perfume. It's as sweet as you are."

"Oh," she said. "I'll give you the rest of the bottle. Then you can put it on your hand or your pillow—"

"I don't want to *wear* it myself," he said indignantly. "I am bewitched by everything about you, your eyes . . ."

"If I could I'd dig them out and hand them over to you." She said it so simply, almost childishly, that I believed her. Perhaps someday she'd really do it, though I knew she liked to read and write and she "liked the look of God's world," as she said. She needed her eyes.

I was about to make my presence known when I heard Duke begin to moan. He was breathing hard and gasping and whispering, "Just touch it, just touch it. Don't you like it? Touch it! Out of . . . the kindness . . . of your heart," and now he was breathing like a steam engine pulling out of the station. "Oh, Why-Vet, if you only knew how painful it is for us fellows, we get blue balls, they hurt so bad, just touch it, Why-Vet, or lick it just there where that clear juice is dripping out."

"Please, Duke, leave me be. Put it away. I'm sure Why-Von would lick it, but I don't want to. Duke! For the love of God!"

"Just hold it in your little hot hand, please, Why-Vet, it hurts so bad. You always want to help people, you don't like to see other people suffer."

Yes, I thought, the sore limbs of the old and poor and afflicted, not some big red poker like yours, Duke Willens.

"Don't, Duke, don't!" And I thought I could hear them wrestling.

And then I coughed loudly and sang out their names: "Yvette, Duke, aren't you done with that old math yet? I brought you some nice cold iced tea, just the way you like it, Duke, Lipton, three sugars, and cut lemon, here I come!" And I rounded the bend and there was Yvette, her dress yanked around and her hair unpouffed, and there was Duke, red-faced, sweat on his forehead, clutching his lap. I could see something poking out. I walked over to the window, pretended to look out, adjusted the air conditioner to high, and did everything very slowly. "Oh, I forgot the tea, silly me, now y'all come with me, come with me into the east wing and Pinky will bring it out with some nice Toll House cookies."

I marched ahead, but when I looked back there was Duke Willens, zipped up but with a big old thing poking his pants with a wet spot soaking the linen just to the right of the zipper. My, I thought, that's an abnormally big one. It would scare even me.

Just before bedtime Yvette kissed my hand, which she *never* did, and whispered, "Thanks!"

"What for?" I asked.

"For saving me."

I just smiled and patted her shoulder. I wouldn't want to be saved from Duke Willens. Why, he was the most popular boy on his school team and his folks both sang in the Turtle Creek Baptist Choir. They were lovely people, though Duke's fat sister was stuck-up and Duke oversexed.

Yvette was a brilliant student. Daddy had to find her a special tutor in Latin and Greek, which she learned extra-fast because she wanted to read Plato in the original and the Greek tragedies and Cicero's *Treatise on Friendship and Old Age*. She picked up Spanish anyway tutoring José the gardener's kids in English and math. She loved tutoring children, but she said she had no desire to give birth to her own.

"But why not?" I asked. That girl kept me stumped, though we were identical.

"That's not my destiny," she said.

"How do you know that? I don't have a destiny. We're only teens."

She just smiled, her eyes unfocused, as if she'd just ridden through a car wash, the windows being scoured in a deluge.

She heard from José how Mexican people were staggering across the desert, sleeping on the sand, skipping meals, and broiling in the sun. That broke her heart. I'd catch her crying her eyes out. She started sleeping on the floor and refused to eat. She got so skinny her monthlies stopped. Daddy was furious but silent and drove her to the doctor's.

The doctor was a fake Texan, actually from New Jersey, but he wore cowboy boots and a ten-pound belt and a blue shirt snapped shut with pearl pressure buttons, and he had long white hair to his shoulders like Buffalo Bill. White chest hairs poked out of his shirt between buttons. His office was meat-locker cold. He took a friendly, avuncular approach. "Well, now, young lady, you'd be a lot prettier if you ate. Look at your twin—as pretty as a Texas bluebell, everything a cowpoke would dream of on his lonely cot."

I was sitting just beside Yvette and she set her jaw in a real ugly way and wouldn't meet the doctor's eye—and seized up when he said "cow-poke" in a loud, grinning, fake-Texas way. Everything he was saying was wrong and I felt sorry for my sister. He was talking to her as if she were three years old. "Now, you do me a little favor, will you? Be a good girl and eat your Wheaties in the morning and your daddy's steak with biscuits and gravy at night." I wondered if Yvette would begin to retch.

I could feel what she was feeling. After all, we were identical, right? But Lord knows I didn't want to keep her company down her lonely path.

I wanted to have fun! I wanted to be popular in school and belong to the Crowd, which is what we called the neat kids. I thought with our money and my looks and smarts I could go far—I could be captain of the cheerleaders. Why, I could even be the homecoming queen. Now that I've risen so high and even become a baroness, you might could smile at my social ambitions as a teen, but that's all we could dream of in Dallas in the fifties! Our yearbook motto was: "Not on the heights but climbing."

I served on every committee back then; I was a top majorette baton twirler. I'm afraid I avoided Yvette, who grew so thin she looked all peaked and flat-chested and green and stopped peroxiding her hair and cut it all off like a boy. I can still picture her scurrying across an empty lot, her books pressed to her flat chest and her skirt nearly falling off her hips.

Just to give you an idea of how different we were, our Namaw gave us each a record player for our birthday. I was always listening to Top Ten tunes or country music, but Yvette was playing day and night Bach's *The Art of Fugue*. To me it sounded like those old-fashioned IBM punch cards chattering to one another, but Yvette said it was "sublime" and like an "X-ray of God's brain."

At that point she was still a Baptist like the rest of us. Daddy didn't hold with any other denomination and didn't want us to date or socialize even with the Presbyterians, say. What would he have said if he'd seen Yvette sneaking off to Christ the King Catholic Church? ("Go, Crusaders!") When I asked her if she didn't get sick of praying (for she'd made a little altar in our room and was bent over it night and day), she said Bach didn't get sick of his dozens of cantatas. I remember she was always listening to *Weinen, Klagen, Sorgen, Zagen* (Weeping, Lamenting, Worrying, Fearing), and she found that music written for the third Sunday of Easter—and those sentiments—electrifying. "No one ever got tired of that music," she said, "because it was inspired by God. A hundred ways of saying Christians must suffer in this world and embrace death so we can join Our Lord." Her devotion (and her simplicity) gave me chills. I didn't want to hear about embracing death, which seemed years and years away, practically invisible, completely foreign to our young bodies being irrigated with blood and hormones, these pulsing warm bodies still growing and blossoming.

I became best friends with Jane Beth Smith, whom I met at school. Yvette had always been my shadow, because different as we were, we were identical. I always needed to be with her. As children we played house together and made up words and had imaginary friends, "Crêpe Suzette" and "Tom-Tom-Tony." If we were apart a whole day I'd feel lost and start crying for my Yvette. It really felt like a big ache in my stomach.

I guess you could say she was my security blanket. But now something healthy and vital in me was drawing me away from Yvette.

Jane Beth's daddy had bought her a yellow Corvette and we rode in it all through Turtle Creek and Preston Hollow. We'd go to cheerleader practice and Jane Beth helped me through my moves and even taught me at home how to follow in slow dancing. She'd play the boy and lead me through swirls and dips. She gave me my first grown-up perfume, Je Reviens, and she taught me how to paint my toenails opalescent pink—why, she even taught me how to inhale! Lord, I coughed myself silly the first five times I tried it but then I got a taste for it and we bought ourselves some Virginia Slims.

Her parents were never around, thank God, and we'd drag boys back to her place and dance and make out and smoke every afternoon. We were pretty wild but we drank only beer and we never let the fellows get our panties off, though once or twice I took off my bra. Once a guy did get a finger in me.

Yvette spent her afternoons creeping around Christ the King or tutoring little Mexican children in English. She would concentrate so hard—she thought concentration was a form of prayer. She wanted to do factory work but I guess she couldn't find any. Anyway, she wasn't a union member. And who ever heard of an Anglo rich bitch working on an assembly line?

She told me she and the priest had some knockdown drag-out fights. When I asked her over what, she clammed up.

"Over what they call the mysteries? Virgin birth? The resurrection?"

Yvette's eyes went all wide on her, and her forehead? She got the crease of sincerity the way she does. "Oh, no," she said, as if she were taking an oath, "I believe in the mysteries, every last one," and I'd seen her literally enraptured by the crucifixion. She had an itty-bitty cross on her altar and she could . . . *contemplate* it for hours with her tears flowing.

"What you crying for?" I asked one day.

"For how he suffered for our sins."

"I don't have any sins, personally," I said, "except asking Daddy twice for my allowance one week and lying I'd lost my money purse, but that was just to get extra money to buy y'all Christmas presents, so it was a good deed after all."

She put her arms around my waist and kissed my cheek and then turned up her nose. "Ooh-ee, you smell of cigarettes!"

"Don't tell Daddy. He's always saying, 'Don't drank nor smoke,' and he promised me a thousand dollars on our next birthday if I stayed pure."

"He never made that promise to me," Yvette said.

"He knows you're not the wild one," I said.

I wasn't really that wild, except compared to Yvette. Yes, I kissed boys, I even drank beer and smoked Virginia Slims, but I always stayed alert. I knew that in our high school a girl can get labeled a slut if she lets a boy stick fingers in her. Oh, and those Dallas boys sure knew how to sweet-talk a girl, promising love eternal and the secrecy of the tomb. But there were no secrets. If a girl let a boy defile the holy temple of her body (just a finger up to the second knuckle), the guy would be on the phone that very night crowing about what a *whore* that Betty Sue (or that Yvonne) was . . . you see, the Crowd, the popular kids, had to stay in and study at night and not everyone had a TV and anyway the shows were mostly boring and there were only three channels. So we phoned one another. I had my own telephone line because my parents got so mad the phone was always busy. And I ran up hundred-dollar charges! A hundred dollars in those days was a fortune. But Daddy looked the other way, better his little girl was home jabbering rather than riding around in some boy's car.

Even the boys called one another, all the fellows on the football team. And they called girls, too. I had a list of forty-two names and numbers and I'd work my way through that list every three nights normally, unless I got a real *juicy* call, usually from another girl, and that might take *hours*.

So if a girl let a guy in, well, that night he would be telling all his guy friends, who'd relay it on to their guy friends. "Did you hear that Betty Sue let Deacon get up to the second knuckle? Yeah-huh. And she must've liked it, too, because she was as wet as a bloodsucker, he said, and she even touched him through his jeans. He swore on his mother's life and a stack of holy Bibles. She got all flushed in the face and was gushing like a fountain. She's not going to say no to our star quarterback. Well, she *is* still a virgin, but not for long."

I tried to get Yvette to boost her popularity by making some calls, but she was no good at it. The whole trick was to keep it as light and trivial as gossamer and Yvette was incapable of that. She called it "silly chatter" but I told her Meg Stevens, our English teacher, had said "silly" had originally meant "blessed," "innocent," and it changed over the centuries to mean "simple" or "ridiculous." Anyway, these girls, like Betty Sue, who talked about Peter Pan collars or Tab Hunter, could turn their talk into real art. They never got serious, it's true, but there was such delicate wordplay, such innuendo, while sounding technically innocent—well, that was *pure* intelligence devoid of content, and I, who've heard all the most brilliant badinage of Paris salons, should know frivolous but famous for its froth. I've been at the very heart of Paris *frivole* for thirty years.

I heard Yvette trying but within seconds she'd sunk her ship. "Spinoza says we shouldn't lavish on animals the love we should reserve for human beings. The Church says animals don't have souls—"

"Well, my Anna," the girl sputtered, naming her poodle, "has more of a real soul than most of these zombie *Christians* around here." She said "Christians" with deep scorn. "They're all like the Thing," she said, referencing a popular horror movie released six or seven years previously.

They chitchatted about everything and nothing, but it was brilliant chatter, I was sure, and I could guess from her end of the conversation that Yvette was being led in discussions of the thick white socks versus the thin white socks, whether Brenda Lee was a heartbreaking singer, how a girl could keep a boy she didn't like from slow-dancing up her leg: things that Yvette had never even considered before.

After she hung up she said, "You wouldn't guess from eavesdropping on *that* conversation that we have but one life to lead and if we're lucky it will land us in immortal, loving arms."

"I see," I whispered, "you have a crush on God."

That night in bed I tried to figure something out. When a boy was with a girl, a real sweetheart, someone he loved with the whole rush and sincerity of adolescence, his first love, an almost religious outpouring of his evangelical heart, was that the moment he was being honest? Or was it when he was laughing with his friends (I'd overheard them) about his beloved's "juicy cunt," how it "smelled like tuna left out in the sun," how it was only a matter of days before she would be going "all the way," how he'd say "Yes sir, I'm going to be shucking the hairy clam"—was that when he was being honest? Which was it—the troubadour in love or the cynical pussy-hound?

The next evening I asked Yvette what she thought, what with all her book learning. "So many people are hypocrites," she said. "Every well-heeled man who walks past a vagrant and says to himself, 'He'd just buy booze if I gave him a handout.' Well, who wouldn't get drunk if he were homeless, hungry, and in rags? I'd get drunk, too. Or every white woman who fires her maid for sassing her, though she knows perfectly well her colored girl cooks better, cleans better, and cleans up better then she can or does. For every kid who mimes hobbling behind an old man on a cane, though he can certainly imagine growing infirm and—no, he can't quite imagine dying, because no one can. But we can all feel ourselves sluicing through time like a keel through water. We can all feel the scandal of having an immortal soul chained to a dying animal. We are meat-covered spirits." She paused and stuck her little finger in her ear—we had pretty ears, small and pressed to the skull, intricate as a bird's wing—and she said, "So a boy's first lesson in betrayal is calling his one true love a filthy cunt. What's that song from *South Pacific* about having to be taught to hate?"

I interrupted, "Daddy knows that show. He won't let Bobbie Jean play the record. He says it's against God's will to mix the races and he starts talking about the sons of Ham."

"God," Yvette said quietly, almost modestly, "God has nothing to do with Daddy's prejudices." She lowered her eyes and blushed, as if she were bragging on her real father's riches. Her heavenly father, you might say.

Every time I'd neck with a boy, I'd look at his intriguing eyes, his almost girlish features, his slender body, and I'd think, This is my enemy. He may chew Dentyne gum to sweeten his breath, he may douse himself in Old Spice to disguise his rankness, he may hand me a love poem he's copied from an album of hit ballads and pretend it's his, but he's a traitor, he will soon be talking about the hairy clam and its stench. Both boys, horribly enough, may be the real ones, equally real. The gentleman and the traitor. They're able to live in the same host body with the contradiction—they don't even see it.

~

I was tired of Yvette. She'd always draw a lesson out of every situation. I wanted a real friend, one who loved the same sexy movie stars like Tab or Troy Donahue, who read the fan magazines, who wanted to go shopping at Neiman-Marcus for hours and hours, who would smoke a Kent or a Virginia Slim at a lunch counter with me while sipping a cherry Coke. Jane Beth was that friend. She'd recently moved from Fort Worth, where her daddy had something to do with Leonard Brothers Dry Goods store (she's a born shopper), and lots and lots of real estate. Downtown real estate was valuable, though the value had dipped, she said, because of "white flight," all the "nice" white people moving their offices to the suburbs. Even so, she told me the family accountant had warned her that she had to spend a million dollars a year just to keep up with her stock earnings or something. She may have been lying to me, but Jane Beth wasn't a liar. It didn't make sense to me; I got only two dollars a week in allowance and had to earn money babysitting. The following summer, when I had a driver's license, I'd earn good money driving the bus for the retarded kids.

My, how Jane Beth and I would talk on the phone for hours! She'd complain about her folks, how her daddy was so religious he wouldn't let her go to the movies on Sunday and how her mother was so stupid we called her Dull Mull. I'd complain about my father being so cheap I had to pay for my own clothes or wear my cousin Dottie's hand-me-downs, all yellow under the arms from perspiration. Bobbie Jean, now that she'd established herself as wife and our mother, had stopped buying us designer clothes—or any clothes at all. I saved and saved all my money so I could buy two short-sleeved cashmere sweaters, one royal blue and the other dusty rose. I wore one almost every day. I'd say to Jane Beth, "Can you believe my daddy makes me work? To learn the value of the dollar? I've got news for him: the dollar is practically worthless."

We'd talk about Jane Beth's brother, Jim, whom we called Jelly, and she'd complain how Jelly never went outdoors or played sports, no wonder he was so flabby and pale, he'd just bake and sew. Then I'd complain about Yvette, whom we called Saint Why. I'd make fun of her idea of conversation, all Spinoza and Day Cart, and her horrible clothes and her flat chest and her bad breath from not eating and her always sneaking off to Christ the King. Daddy would say he could understand why Klansmen hated old Catholics and Jews and niggers, how the world would be a better place without these three groups. Since Daddy didn't have a regular job and an office, he had a lot of spare time to devote to his hates. Sure, he'd climb up on a ladder in his old clothes and unclog the gutters or he'd go crazy with his power saw in the basement, trying to make a bookcase for his wife, but it came out all spindly and *bancal*—how do you say *bancal* in English? "Precarious," "wobbly," "bandy-legged"? "Wonky"! I have to look up some French words now to find out what they mean in English. Sometimes there aren't equivalents. Like how do you translate *quand même*? "Seriously"? Or *frileux*? "Susceptible to the cold"? Of course, Daddy had some old relative he admired who was a Klansman. Daddy'd always tease us for saying "Cue" Klux Klan instead of "Coo." He'd laugh and laugh; he never did have a sense of humor like other folks.

Jane Beth said the Klan wasn't all bad, they were pledged to protect white womanhood, which made her feel safer. I thought she was crazy but said nothing. Jane Beth's parents were rich, really rich—at least, they had twelve bedrooms and eighteen bathrooms, an indoor swimming pool and what I thought back then was a snazzy decor, all Western with leather chairs designed by a saddlemaker complete with a big horn and dangling skirts, wagon-wheel chandeliers and branding irons turned into andirons. In the basement stood a massive carved wood bar with mirrors advertising beer labels from the last century—and of course there were swinging louvered doors admitting you into the saloon. Oh, and a player piano cackling old-fashioned Wild West tunes. Her daddy had even bought Tom Mix's original cowboy hat and a photo of Mix on Tony, his horse. There were brass spittoons everywhere, which made me think of the boring math professor, Bobbie Jean's daddy, but they were just there as authentic "accents" (no one spit in them). In the yard out back they had a custom-built outdoor grill. You could've smoked half a cow on that baby. Remember, this was before such things were common. Of course, the whole house was air-conditioned with ducts disguised by log cabin *boiseries*, if you can imagine such a thing. There were dehumidifiers in every room, but they weren't hidden. They looked like friendly little robots. The maids dusted them every day, that's what Jane Beth told me.

During our interminable phone calls, we bad-mouthed our parents for being so selfish and such hicks. We also complained about our teachers, how hard and unreasonable they were, and how no girl needed to know her quadratic equations anyway.

We had dates but no steadies. I didn't mind, except I wanted to be popular, but how could I with no boyfriend and such horrible clothes? I would even have considered going out with Jelly, though he was so skinny (I bet he weighed less than me) and he knitted, at least he was a guy.

Real guys sort of scared me, though I'd made out for hours with that nondescript Luther, president of the Math Club, who always had food stuck in his braces and didn't seem to know about deodorant.

We never, ever talked about it, but when I'd stay over at her place, Jane Beth and I would fool around. That's right: with each other. Two girls, that's right. She had much bigger breasts than I, though they had icky hairs, just two or three, near the nipples. But down below she was pretty clean. In the dark we'd finger each other, and that's how I had my first orgasm. It was pretty gentle, like one of those lights nowadays that gets brighter and brighter until it dims. I mean, it didn't tear me apart the way it does now. We'd kiss, but with our eyes closed and always in the dark and we'd never talk about it.

One night at dinner (pork chops and baked apples), Daddy said, "Why-vet, I heard tell you've been lurking around some old Catholic church, King of something. Are you fixing to become an old Catholic? How'd they recruit you?"

Yvette turned bright red. She put down her fork and looked Daddy in the eye. "I'd never join the Catholic Church."

Bobbie Jean piped up, "Why not?"

Yvette said, "I'm not worthy."

Daddy got real mad then. He said, "Look here, young lady, you were brought up a Baptist and that's that. You're a hardshell Baptist and I don't want no back talk. I'd spank you like I used to and send you to bed without your supper—"

Bobbie Jean interrupted again with a sly smile, "Except she'd like that, P.M." She'd started calling Daddy P.M., just like his mother did. I'm not sure he liked that. He suddenly started tugging on the Kentucky string tie he wore laced through a little black bolo tie on which was a pink jackass bucking, his rear legs kicked back. Daddy liked to look ordinary, even ridiculous, especially when our fancy friends dropped by. He thought we'd all gotten too big for our britches—yes, that's what Texans said back then: too big for your britches.

I looked at poor Yvette. I felt sorry for her. Usually I was a little envious because Daddy favored her—she was such a good student and made him proud. Since she and I were identical he had proof positive that I wasn't living up to my potential. But now I felt real sorry for her and I wondered who'd ratted on her. We didn't even know any old Catholics, but maybe one of the maids had seen her at Christ the King and snitched to Bobbie Jean. Daddy disapproved of everyone; Jane Beth was a Methodist and Daddy couldn't leave it alone, he'd bring it up with Jane Beth, ask her if her folks were teetotalers who refused to dance or bet on horses.

"When you said you didn't want to go to church no more," Daddy said to Yvette, "I thought you wanted to sleep in on Sundays. Or maybe you'd lost your faith studying all that chemistry and physics and biology. I figured they'd talked you into evolution."

"No, Daddy, it has almost nothing to do with science or even theology," Yvette said. She was blinking really fast, the way we both did when we were saying something unwelcome to our listener.

"Do you like all those old Catholic gewgaws, then? The satin and the holy water and the incense? Men in dresses? Well, I'm not going to have it. No daughter of mine is going to swallow all those lies and take her orders from Rome."

"I'm an independent thinker," Yvette said in such a small, little-girl voice that it was hard to take her seriously.

"What is it—have you fallen for some Mexi boy? Do you go to that church because your sweetheart's an old Catholic?"

"I don't have a boyfriend," Yvette said. I could feel what torture this interrogation was for her.

"I almost wish you did have a boy—at least that would show you were normal. Not some damn vegetarian and Catholic, starving yourself half to death and stinking of incense like some damn R.C."

Bobbie Jean said in a low voice, "Now, P.M."

The maid came in to clear and everyone went silent. We always did that, usually because we were talking about something "cute" Pinky had said that day. Bobbie Jean announced as soon as we were alone, maybe to change the subject, "You want to hear the most preciousest thing Pinky said today? Today she said she was afraid of plugging in the Hoover because she was afraid of being 'electromocuted.' Isn't that the most preciousest thing you ever heard? Electromocuted. Don't that beat all?"

I smiled a sickly little smile and Daddy laughed out loud—he just couldn't stop guffawing—but Yvette looked at us all stony-faced.

Daddy said, "Can't you even laugh at something funny, Goddammit, Why-vet, or does it have to be in Latin to tickle your funny bone?"

Now Yvette looked terrified, as if her face were no longer hers to do with as she pleased. Or her thoughts.

After dinner I went straight up to our room. I thought she'd be sobbing but she was sitting there, glassy-eyed. It was worse than tears. It was hopelessness. I touched her on the shoulder, her little shoulder. At first she was startled, then she reached up and patted my hand. I said, "What did you mean you weren't worthy to join the Catholic Church?"

I thought those superstitious monkeys would be lucky to snare someone as smart and sweet as my Yvette, someone so solid and good, if weird. It may sound strange to call her weird now that she's on her way to becoming a saint, but you have to remember, I was just a Texas girl and nothing is more conformist than the teenager who longs to be popular—all the more so in Dallas back then!

"I'm not kind enough, my faith is wavering, I like to debate with my priest instead of just believing. It's all about belief! Belief is inarguable. And I'm not in a state of grace."

I said, "I guess Daddy would be happy that you argue with the priest."

"I pray for all of you every day," she said. "Not that you'll change or even come to accept me as I am. But that you might find some peace—or feel God's grace."

"Do you think only Catholics can feel God's love, God's grace?"

"No," she said slowly, quietly. "I'm not sure what I think. I know I feel bad about having said to you some boys are hypocrites. So am I! I'm the biggest hypocrite."

I said, "Daddy must rub your fur the wrong way"—that was an expression I learned from Jane Beth—"with all his bossiness."

"I guess he thinks we're still small children, easily hoodwinked. We must try to understand him."

"Why?" I nearly shouted. "Why on earth? He makes no effort to understand us."

"We must love the Christ in Daddy. Charity isn't based on reciprocity. What did Marx say—'From each according to his ability to each according to his needs'?"

"I hope you're not drifting toward Communism," I said, feeling stupid.

"Our Lord was close to a socialist. At least he was mainly concerned with the poor."

It made me queasy when she said "Our Lord." I wanted to say "Their Lord." I wasn't sure her Lord was the same as mine. I couldn't wait to share all this—Daddy's anger and Yvette's calm—with Jane Beth. Things didn't quite seem real until I talked them over with Jane Beth.

Daddy grounded Yvette every Sunday. He didn't want her sneaking off to Christ the King. Of course, he didn't realize old Catholics celebrate Mass every day and several times a day and that she'd become a regular.

CHAPTER 2

When I was seventeen I started planning my debut. Bobbie Jean hadn't met a lot of "the good people," as she called them, and I think she was planning to social climb through me. She hired Honey Mellen, a "party planner," as she called herself, although we called her our "society coach." The fiction was that Bobbie Jean and I were too busy to look after the million and one details involved in coming out, though the truth was we didn't have Honey's little green alligator-skin book of names and numbers, we didn't know who to invite or the right florist or photographers or musicians or caterers. But Honey knew, she knew all about that—she also did weddings. It's funny, weddings and debuts are all about getting a girl hitched to a man or at least in the right marriage sweepstakes, but both events involve women alone. Whoever heard of asking a man his opinion? At least in Texas, if not in France, women decided the kind of lace, the length of the train, the tiny buds in the tightly bound bouquet, the church, the preacher, the bridesmaids' dresses, the reception and its hors d'oeuvres, hiring Lester Lanin's real orchestra and some rinky-dink local band to fill in during the breaks, even if they knew how to play only "Tenderly" and Johnny Mathis's "It's Not for Me to Say." We all liked Mathis. He was Texan. Sort of.

Bobbie Jean told Honey the sky was the limit price-wise. She wanted her Yvonne to be properly launched in society. She and Bobbie Jean decided on the theme for my dance, "Venetian Night," at the Brook Hollow Golf Club, complete with gondolas and men dressed in tights and straw boaters singing "O Sole Mio," and a Bridge of Sighs, two-thirds as large as the original, and a campanile-shaped pizza oven.

Honey must have been in her forties, but energy! And she wore the trapeze look from Neiman's, natch. Her hair was thick and wild, turbulent actually, and peroxided a platinum blonde. She wore nearly black lipstick and matching nail polish (she called it aubergine, though at that time I didn't know that meant "eggplant"). She drove a red Cadillac convertible with fins out to here and she always kept the roof down. When it was raining she drove faster, honking all the slowpokes out of the way. She played loud colored music on the radio, music from Memphis, she called it race music. She wore a very strong perfume, dizzying really; I think it was an attar of roses, meant to be diluted to eau de cologne, but she used it full-strength and old ladies at concerts complained about it ("a real invasion of our privacy," they muttered). She was always laughing loudly and jangling her costume jewelry bracelets, a dozen of them, bangles like a slave girl's, as if she were on Benzedrine. She never finished a sentence but constantly interrupted herself with some new extravagance. She was never catty and never bad-mouthed her other clients, much as I tried to lure her into a good chin-wag. She was as discreet as an agent or a psychiatrist, which she was for all of us, I suppose. She always started out brimming over with excited enthusiasm for my ideas, no matter how dumb, but the way she shepherded you back to a more original concept—and the way she made you think it was your own—was truly astonishing.

Middle-class people imagine the privileged and social are bored and negative and languorously disapproving, but the truth is they're bubbly, almost frothing with enthusiasm; you'd swear they were on speed. Everything is "fabulous" or "inspired" or "titanic." If they're English they say "brilliant." If they're French they say something you'll never find in any dictionary: "*Sublissime!*"

Honey was a social engineer. She thought Bobbie Jean and I should belong to the Shakespeare Club, to which all these rich menopausal biddies belonged, though most of them were old cattle money and not common oil money like Daddy. We said, "Sure, why not?" to the Shakespeare Club, which was limited to just a hundred old ladies. The first half of the meeting was devoted to a play. Our week it was *Cymbeline*, which I'd never heard of. Whenever some old bag would say something cautious about Simpline, Bobbie Jean started murmuring assent like she was in church—"Mmm-hmm, tha's right, um-hum"—and the other ladies would look at her as if she'd farted loud and nasty. Then we all had coffee and an iced cake, mint-green icing over chocolate with jujubes stuck all over it. Then I saw too late there was no place to piss (a lady never pisses in public) so I crossed my legs tight and willed myself dry. At this point, it seemed, they usually heard reports on theatrical events in San Antonio (cultural capital of Texas at that time, home to the Alamo) or Chicago or New York or even London, but that day, I don't know why, all the world's theaters were dark, so Mrs. Everett ("Minnie") Wilson decided we should play Shakespearean charades and the question she chose, which she whispered to me, was "Ill met by moonlight, proud Titania." The first thing I did was blush poppy-red. I'd never heard that quote before, had no idea which play it came from, and didn't have the foggiest who Titanium was, but wasn't that a kind of metal?

I decided to convey "ill" by playing sick. One of those hags on my team said, "Sleepy? Tired? Sick?" And I made inviting gestures like I was landing a plane on a carrier. "Ill?" And another old biddie exclaimed, "Ill met by moonlight," and I shrugged and smiled, still clueless, though all the old chickens started cooing with cultural rapture.

Bobbie Jean whispered, "What just happened?" And I just blitzed my way through with a knowing smile, too cultured for words. I did guess "To be or not to be" when Mrs. Phipps held up two fingers, then pretended she'd been stung. Honey was delighted, jumping up and down in her seat with such glee that I checked to see if she'd wet herself. I was glad Bobbie Jean didn't let out a rebel yell. On the street, Honey exclaimed, "You girls are absolute geniuses. Everyone is so impressed!"

"What is titanium?" I asked, but Honey batted my arm like I was just fooling with her. Of course we asked Yvette as soon as we got home. She said, "*A Midsummer Night's Dream*. Titania and Oberon." She had a way of dispensing information simply and without proprietary condescension, as if all that mattered was the right answer.

Yvette needed to get glasses; I was afraid I was next, but nope. Yvette read so much more than me. She chose the cheapest army-issue tan plastic glasses. Her hair had grown out into bushy black curls on either side of her thin face, not blonde and sleek like mine. So that's what I'd look like, I thought, if every beauty parlor in the world shut down.

Bushy eyebrows.

Daddy accepted that Yvette wasn't going to make a debut; one glance at her in her man's suit, tan glasses, and bushy hair, it was obvious. But Daddy wanted her to attend my Venetian Night at the golf club and my luncheon party at home in the White House. Jane Beth had finally decided on her theme—"the Paris Café"—and her folks were going to hire Edith Piaf, the real Edith Piaf, to sing "La Vie en Rose," and her rose bill alone would cost more than three Cadillacs. Now that we'd both selected our themes, everyone could get to work—the designers, the gown tailors, the bakers, the florists, those who'd create the invitations (a gondola for me, the Eiffel Tower for her, on little silver plates), and the invitation printers. Jane Beth's mother, who made her debut in Tyler, Texas, wanted her daughter to choose her old theme, "Gone with the Wind," but Jane Beth declared, "No, ma'am! No Confederate soldiers for me!"

When Daddy brought up Venetian Night with Yvette, she smiled and said, "I could come as a Moorish boy servant. Or as an eighteenth-century castrato."

"A what!" Daddy almost shouted.

"Castrati were male singers whose voices never changed because—" She held up two fingers and mimed, "Snip, snip."

"People actually did that to those poor little boys?" Daddy asked, fuming, grabbing his crotch uneasily.

"Now, P.M., we do that to steers all the time," Bobbie Jean said, wiping her lips with a heavy damask napkin. She must have been tromping on the servant's bell under the carpet because Pinky came flying in. "Yes, ma'am?"

"You can clear, Pinky," Bobbie Jean said generously, as if it were a favor she was granting. "And don't stack! Run the plates up your arm like a real waiter, or otherwise make several trips. And never scrape one dish into another. Remember, serve from the left and clear from the right."

"So how about going to the dance, Yvette, and this time as a *girl*, a white woman?"

"I don't know how to dance," Yvette said. "And you know how awkward I am. I pity the poor boy who tries to lead me."

"We can get you lessons, huh, Mother?" Daddy'd started calling his own wife Mother.

"We sure can, P.M. There's that nice Conchita Benson with the castanets and the hair extensions and those big brass hoop earrings."

"Well, line her up, Mother." He cocked an eye at Yvette. "Okay by you, pal?" When he spoke to her he lowered his voice, as if it were a secret, and Yvette blushed whenever he called her pal. I wondered what was up between those two. He seemed to approve of her for all sorts of things I couldn't get away with—approve, or grumble affectionately. Her little-boy clothes, her bushy black hair, her bad eyes, her tutoring little Mexican children in math and English, her anorexia and vegetarianism— *tout un programme*, as the French say ("the whole kit and kaboodle," we say, whatever "kaboodle" might mean). He never called me pal.

"Mother" hired Conchita Benson, who drove herself out to the White House in her battered old Chevy. As usual she was wearing her heavy terra-cotta makeup, her murderously red lipstick, her cowcatcher eyelashes, her piled-up hair, her big black castanets with the lacquered red mouths strung together with rawhide, her gunboat high heels, her form-fitting, ageless black sheath dress molded to her flat stomach, flat breasts, and cello hips. She was also carrying a record player designed to look like a powder-blue-and-maroon-striped suitcase. I was peeping through the upstairs window in the Lincoln bedroom. She rang our bell with one of her long red nails, checked her watch, and waited. Pinky answered the door and half-curtsied to the tall lady, made taller by her high heels and hair extensions. She was led up to the ballroom, where Pinky said she installed her record player and fox-trotted experimentally around the room. She pulled a pair of washed and mended white gloves out of her big black purse. She sat perfectly straight on one of those spindly gold chairs up there, deliberately fragile (as Daddy said, "We don't want those old biddies to get too comfortable up there and miss their bedtime").

Finally a sheepish Yvette materialized in her little black suit and sneakers, with a volume of Kant under her arm in case there was an idle moment.

"Well, I'd ask you to wear this extra pair of white gloves," Conchita said, "but I can see they're way too big and wouldn't go . . . with your . . . clothes. For the next lesson I suggest you wear a long dress so you can get used to it—kicking the train out of the way, lifting the front when climbing stairs, gathering it up in your left arm when waltzing. Holding it correctly for your Texas dip."

Yvette said softly, "I'm just attending, not making a debut, and I'll be wearing a tuxedo."

Conchita expressed her alarm with a quick, nervous clacking of her castanets. "Tuxedo? This is your sister's debut and you'd become the only subject of conversation if you wore a *tuxedo*. I can understand wanting to blend in and that can be done with a sweet little blue organdy gown. You can buy one right off the rack. White gloves, a gold cross around your neck, and dahlias in your straightened hair."

"If you promise I'll pass unnoticed like that."

I'm sure Conchita was surprised by her easy victory. "Good, that's settled. And Yvonne will be so relieved that you've made a wise decision." Yvette reported all this to me at bedtime.

Then the dancing class began. "I'm going to show you the basic fox-trot," Conchita said, and rattled her castanets sharply (as if to call everyone to order).

She reached down, flexed her long legs, and grabbed Yvette by the waist. Conchita led her forcefully, counting, "*One* two three four," and they pranced across the shiny parquet, full daylight flooding down through the high windows. "We must've looked," Yvette told me that night, giggling all the while, as we lay on our stomachs, both of us smelling of toothpaste, "like a praying mantis and an ant, black and tiny, all head and eyes. '*One* two three four.'"

"How did you do?"

Yvette shook with laughter. "Horribly. I was horrible. You know how awkward I am. And no sense of rhythm. She kept saying, 'Just relax. Let me lead,' and her hand, though gloved, was digging into my side, forcing me into a box step." She whooped with laughter. "No, she really looked like a mantis, her hair piled up, standing on those heels, towering over me. Don't mantises snap their victim's head off?"

"Their victims are their husbands."

"I must have looked like a tiny, edible husband with my bushy hair, my suit, Capezio flats, very edible."

"Are you going to try again?"

"Wednesday at four. Do you think Pinky would drive me to the store to buy a cheap formal?"

"Sure. I'll ask Bobbie Jean to let her off for the morning."

Pinky drove her old Buick, sitting stiffly upright as if she were trying to get her driver's license. Yvette sat beside her, playing with the hydraulic window, up and down, up and down. A white family in an old Town & Country station wagon, the kind with the wood sides, pulled up right next to them at a stoplight and gave them the worst stares.

Then some drunk teenage boys with D.A.'s, in a ratty old convertible with Oklahoma plates and a broken exhaust pipe dragging along on the pavement and casting off sparks, drove by real slow and one of them shouted, "You two dykes? Don't you know it's 'gainst the law for a white girl to eat out a nigger?" Then they hee-hawed with laughter. "Hey, Whitey, you the husband? You dress like a drag king in your man's suit."

"Hell," one of them asked the other, "what the hell is a drag king?"

"A big ol' bulldagger in a zoot suit. Hey, Whitey, like that Brillo pad pussy?" Then they laughed, sped up, and turned the corner.

"I tol' Miss Bobbie Jean this was a bad idee," Pinky said. "What if they don't let me in the store?"

Yvette had tears in her eyes, not of embarrassment but of shame. "Let's go home," she said. "I'm so sorry, Pinky."

"Jes' the way the world is," and she shrugged and headed home. On the bus, even the *school* bus, there were little signs over the seats; on one side it said COLORED, on the other WHITE.

That night at bedtime Yvette told me the whole story. "I'm so ashamed of my naivete, putting Pinky in that position. I'm so ashamed of our world, where such things exist." Yvette must have prayed for an hour that night. The next day she joined the NAACP and gave them all the money she'd saved—$231. I'd have to drive her to her meetings. She didn't have her license yet, and I wouldn't have trusted her with one, clumsy and awkward and nearsighted as she was.

Bobbie Jean went with her to get a dress, not a cheap one off the rack, which is what Yvette wanted, but it was blue organdy, by a Paris designer, and after twelve lessons Yvette did learn the box step and how to gather her train for a waltz, though I think Conchita got pretty bruised in the process. Of course, we didn't take Yvette to a colored girl's beauty salon but the beautician did use burning hair relaxant for Negroes on her kinky hair. First they applied a thick coat of Vaseline to her scalp to protect it, then this sulfur-smelling relaxer to her hair. It was a dull, thick cream color and they left it on for half an hour. Then they rinsed it all out, the Vaseline as well, and trimmed and styled her hair and dyed it my shade of blonde, though my hair of course was shoulder length, with a soft bouncing curl, and hers was just an itty-bitty blonde cap—she looked like Tweety Bird but, just think, I'd convinced my identical twin to be the same shade of blonde as me! Then, of course, we had to scare up a date for her and at last Honey located a real nerd, as much an egghead as she was, as untanned and as lacking in muscle tone. He had tails but they were his grandfather's or something and hung huge and gaping on his bony little shoulders. He had a stiff collar and white tie and a white piqué vest and in his coat pocket a white silk handkerchief. His tails were shiny with use.

His name was Edward Coffee, I kid you not, and he was more of a science nerd than a Christian nerd. The Coffees were an old family by Dallas standards, but they lost their money trying to grow cotton in the Hill Country and now they had a little jewelry shop on a side street, where Bobbie Jean, just to be nice and diplomatic, bought a brooch of white gold and pink gold, tied like a bow with a pale blue lapis lazuli haunting the center, an eye with cataracts. Edward didn't seem to want a date any more than Yvette did. I was robust and tanned in my Dogaressa white gown with sparkles all over and the fabric draped over one shoulder, whereas Yvette looked like a skinny, pale little child in her organdy tube. She was wearing a very tight foundation garment with no panties so she could sit and piss without undressing, and boy, she was scandalized by the no panties. We said no one would know she was hanging free inside that tube. How would they get in there to check it out? She was so skinny she had no tits and had to be sealed into that dress with gummed tape. Honey did it all. It was as intricate as an expensive face-lift. Yvette trundled along in her flats inside that dress, just speeding along in her blue carapace.

Bobbie Jean had offered Edward a glass of champagne. He didn't dare refuse and they sat there, Yvette in her taped tube and Edward in his gaping tails, running his finger under his collar, for an uncomfortable ten minutes of silence. Yvette, being a bookworm, had prepared to be "interested" in the best Texas way in her date by scanning a book on electrical engineering (Edward specialized in ham radios). She asked him what his "handle" was, and, rather disconcertingly, he said, "Wifebeater." I mean, that's how he identified himself on the airwaves. Once that was established, they withdrew into silence. Edward had brought her a wrist corsage, a large purple flower. She fixed it to her thin, starved arm.

After the ordeal of the drink, Edward stood and led the way out to his pickup truck. Yvette told me she wanted to say something shockingly honest, something that would clear the air, like "I hear your family is poor and ashamed of it," but I'd steered her away from that particular conversational gambit. Yvette's tube was so tight around her shoes that she couldn't climb up into the cab of Edward's truck and he had to put his hands on her skinny buttocks and push. My party, which was at the beginning of November, was very glamorous, what with the illuminated boats in the water and the singing gondoliers and the pizza-oven campanile and the bathrooms concealed in a scale model of the Doge's Palace and a billiard table plunked in the middle of the Bridge of Sighs for the older men who wanted to play rather than dance. The winding lane to the porte cochere of the golf club was lined with 200 hurricane lamps, and Honey had paid men in hacked-off red velvet sweatpants and white silk stockings to keep all the candles lit because the one constant in Texas weather, from the Panhandle to the Rio Grande, is *wind*. It's always blowing hard in Texas. Inside the club we'd re-created one-third of Piazza San Marco, including of course Caffè Florian, but what really made it all zing were the flowers. Honey had emptied every greenhouse west of the Mississippi—40 dozen gardenias, a blanket of bride's roses, smilax for days, 150 sprays of white stock, 1,500 bouquets of white freesia. It smelled like a rich man's funeral.

I swanned around and danced with maybe fifty guys. What some people don't realize (I certainly didn't at the time) is that whereas the debutantes are very few and very rich (there were only eleven in my year), the boys are numerous and of various castes—virtually any guy who owns evening clothes. The idea was to have three times more boys than girls so they'd cut in on every deb as well as dance with their mothers. The only problem is that some of the boys were fairly present-able fortune hunters or they were much older and sort of beat-up. I guess they were veterans of the war, still unmarried, still studying on the G.I. Bill.

One of the tall, blond, square-jawed guys who cut in to dance with me said, "Hey, I'm Greg Martins. Don't y'all live in the White House? Funny old place. My aunt May used to live there all by herself after Uncle Pete died. She never could get the ovens to work. And it's strange not having an indoor pool—doesn't the real White House have one? Or did they fill that in to make the room for the press corps?"

"My," I said with a giant smile, "you sure know your D.C. You must have lived there."

"A bit. My grandfather was a senator from Mississippi and he got me a job one summer as a page."

"I declare."

Luckily just then Harry Hopkins cut back in. He was my escort, a smiley guy fixing to bust out of his tails.

"Thanks for rescuing me," I said.

"Poor Greg," Harry said with a grin. "All that money and those looks and no one likes him. He's the president of the Bachelors' Cotillion." I think he meant the Idlewild Club, the men who'd selected us debs. "They say he has a private room in the pool house here and takes some of these young bachelors out there for sex."

"Oh," I said. "That can't be true, Harry Hopkins. You just made that up." He smiled and didn't say anything, but for the next ten minutes I couldn't get that image out of my head, one penguin on top of another and both male! Pumping away. I never was so disturbed but then that sexy tennis coach cut in. He said, "I tried dancing with your sister but I'm all black and blue now. She can't dance worth a darn."

I laughed and said, "She says so herself, though Conchita gave her twelve lessons."

"All I tried was the box step."

I laughed again. "*That's* the one she knows, bless her heart."

I spotted her across the room near the vases of white stocks. Her date, Edward? He was holding her at a respectful distance and was steering her around to a slow ballad, but, poor thing, Yvette has two left feet. I must say she was a good sport, her hair straightened and peroxided, her blue organdy gown almost falling off her skinny torso, the idea she had no panties on—Lord! How she must have hated that! Only for the love of a sister.

Our daddy cut in and I danced with him to "The 12th of Never." He was a pretty good dancer but it was odd to feel his breath on my bare shoulder. He'd had a lot to drink and was slurring his words. "Are you happy?"

"Ecstatic!" I said. "Bobbie Jean looks lovely."

"She's happy as a pig in shit," Daddy said. "All these stuck-up high-society bishes are inviting her to this club and thas. How do you think Yvette's holding up?"

"What a trooper!" I said. "She's being good as gold."

"Mostly," Daddy said, "but Bobbie Jean overheard her talking to the colored help in the kitchen, asking them why they don't organize in a damn union. Born troublemaker!"

"That's just Yvette being Yvette." We both smiled.

Dawn was already breaking when the waiters brought in scrambled eggs, coffee, and toast. They'd opened up the Magnolia Room, where all the tables were set with peach-colored cloths, matching napkins, and more smilax. The orchestra members were yawning and packing up their instruments. The horn section looked particularly gray in the daylight, all that puffing. The coffee smelled wonderful!

Each woman was given a goodie bag with a big bottle of Chanel N°5 in it and a silver tray engraved with the invitation. The boys got Canoe cologne. Some of the women couldn't wait to open their bottles and soon pockets of perfume were competing with the rich coffee smell. Everyone was smoking, especially some of the more sophisticated girls.

I saw Greg Martins slip in and a moment later the handsome little Howard Clay. They went their separate ways—guiltily, I'd say. They both had red lips as if they were wearing lipstick. They'd loosened their white ties, which were dangling across their shirtfronts. Maybe their fathers had tied them hours ago and neither of the boys knew how to retie them. I looked long and hard at Howard; I'm sure he was the "wife" in bed with that big manly Greg. I was fascinated.

After endless farewells my escort found my wrap and steered me to his green Pontiac, which the valet had just pulled up. Harry was a live wire and a fun date, bristling with extra energy, his eyes always moving nervously behind his glasses as if he were watching a speeded-up ping-pong game. He loved to gossip but understood that I, as a "nice girl," could only go so far. "Did you catch sight of that disheveled Greg Martin and his little Howard?"

I just put my finger over his lips, though I was dying to hear more.

When I went upstairs to our room in the White House, I saw Daddy in the hallway looking confused. I said, "Why, Daddy! I'm going to help Yvette out of her dress—and help her to burn it, probably."

"Don't. Let me help her. And why don't you sleep somewhere else?" His voice sounded choked and I could guess how serious he was, just as you can tell how drunk a man is when he fails to walk a straight line.

I was alarmed. "No reason for you to bother, Daddy."

"It's no bother. I want to touch base with Yvette after the ball—which must've been a trial for her."

I felt protective of Yvette and was willing to risk Daddy's ire. "I'm not sure it's appropriate for a grown man—"

"I don't give a damn what you think!" He shouted in a whisper, pushing me roughly aside. He let himself into our room and I sank to the floor, stunned. I'd seen him angry before, usually about suspected Communists, but he'd never cussed *us* out. Was he just drunk? Why had Yvette never told me about . . . Daddy? Was Bobbie Jean in on this too? I couldn't bear to think about it. Was ours the strangest family in the world?

I went down the hall, out of sight. I must have fallen asleep there on the floor in the hallway. I thought I could hear the sound of a belt clinking, of the mattress wheezing, of a muffled cry, but I felt helpless. I could feel only an immense pity. I know I cried myself to sleep and thought this night marked both the high point and the low point of my life. The carpet I slept on smelled new (it *was* new). It was plush and had been recently swept and still smelled of electricity.

Much later I saw Daddy come out of our room, his hair and clothes all in disarray. In a heartbreaking voice, he said as he looked back into the room at Yvette, "Sorry, pal." I had an impulse to run to Yvette and comfort her, to hold her in my arms, to coo soothing words. But what if Yvette was covered with shame and the only fire burning in her was indignation?

My father had done "everything" for me by giving me a spectacular debut, the high point of the season, but I hated him now for what he had done . . . to *us*.

CHAPTER 3

M y sister and I were driving down to Austin that September for our freshman year at the University of Texas. We drove past empty fields of scorched grass dotted with cactus. We passed a big century plant, a mountain laurel, cedar elms, palo verde. It was a real scorcher that day, and my new Buick didn't have air-conditioning. But it was a convertible and halfway there we decided to lower the roof. It was so much fun to see it retract and collapse and disappear into its slot just above the trunk. It jerked and groaned. The sun was punishing, so bright and hot, we'd had absolute *years* of drought that ended in 1956, but the landscape was still dry. I thought the sun might lighten my hair and deepen my tan; it left Yvette so sunburned she had to sleep between wet sheets for two days in her dorm room—I'd plum forgot she didn't have a starter tan and was always white as a ghost. Later her arms and neck peeled—brown patches of dead skin that lifted off to reveal tissue as pink as bubble gum.

We were assigned dorm rooms. Daddy said he'd buy an apartment off-campus for us but freshmen had to live in the dorm. That was a rule. I ran around signing up for Texas history and secretarial skills like typing, which I already knew how to do, and home economics with a specialty in baking. I wanted to take Human Sexuality but Daddy wouldn't hear of it (Daddy said he thought premarital sex was the Devil's handiwork).

Yvette, whose room was just down the hall, signed up for Introduction to Philosophy 101, Music Appreciation from Bach to Ferde Grofé,

English Literature 407 from Chaucer to Larry McMurtry, and Quantum Physics. She was considering majoring in religion but she heard the course Comparative Religions was nicknamed "the faith breaker," and that put her off. What she really loved was anything medieval, especially Gregorian chants and Luca Marenzio's madrigals. She would listen to them on the turntable she brought down with her from Dallas; it was a birthday gift from Namaw. Yvette wore the same clothes every day—cowboy boots and a denim skirt and a man's cowboy shirt. She had three of those skirts and seven of those shirts, all identical. She had let her hair grow in black and kinky again. She was neat and clean. She said, referring to the dorm cafeteria, which everyone else complained about, "I don't mind what I eat as long as it's always the same thing." I think she got that line from one of her favorite philosophers. Don't ask me who; I don't do names after six o'clock.

I took one course in French history and it ignited all my longings for another life, a noble life, one that was rooted and flourishing. Texas seemed nothing more than a tumbleweed blowing across an arid field. I wanted a castle with walls ten feet thick. I wanted historic jewels. I wanted a titled husband, not some heavy-drinking cowboy with a mustache and piss-soaked jeans. I wanted the people around me to be polite and deferential, gentle and respectful.

I knew a bunch of girls from our fancy high school, Hockaday. We were all determined to get into Tri-Delt, the Theta Zeta chapter. We were all white and blonde in those days (I see from the alumni magazine they still are!). The girls were so sweet you could have a diabetic attack after ten minutes with them. But also playful. They'd answer the phone: "Delta Delta Delta. May I help you help you help you?" You had to demonstrate a "broadened moral or intellectual life"—which meant not going "all the way" and choosing the occasional "brain" (but only if she was pretty) to keep up the house average. The girls had a strange way of shrieking with excitement and stamping their feet and embracing each other when they ran into one another, even if it was the third time that day. When we became exhausted we'd stare at one another's feet and exclaim, "Cute shoes!" I can still hear that breathless talk ringing down through the decades. At the oddest moments, like when I'm walking down the Quai d'Orléans or waiting for my guests at my favorite table at Voltaire, or when the house lights go down at the Opéra Comique and the curtain hasn't risen yet and the only light is coming through the blue windows in the boxes. Sometimes it will get stuck in my head like a *rengaine*, "Cute shoes! Cute shoes!" What's *rengaine* in English? I must look it up. An "earworm"?

I rushed hard with some of my friends. Two of my classmates posed with me, our arms describing a giant Delta. Wishful thinking at that point, of course, because we were just hoping to be selected. Our chapter had been founded in 1912 and our motto was "Steadfastly Love One Another." *Now* women like one another, but back then they'd as soon stab you in the back, though they all played honey-sweet. And most of them were *rich*—enough to fart through silk all their lives.

I was selected because I was blonde and white and a Dallas deb. Our house was pretty; we called it the Delta Shelta. I was excited because I knew that all the big men on campus (BMOC), like those on the football team, wanted to date Tri-Delts. Oh, those guys treated us like little sisters, so respectful; they'd drive down to Laredo, get drunk, and fuck fat whores, two men at a time, spit-roasting the girls, but with us Delts butter would melt in their mouths. A Sigma Nu told me that during their secret initiation ceremonies the men, hooded like Klansmen, took a pledge to protect white Southern womanhood, and most of the frat guys I knew back then actually subscribed to that kind of creepy pledge. Sure, they'd kiss us for hours and their hands might stray below the waist in the dark make-out room, but we Delts knew how to stop that kind of funny business.

I tried to get Yvette to rush a minor sorority. "Why don't you try the Kappa Alpha Thetas? Someone told me the chapter was close to being suspended for bad grades and public drunkenness—they're really desperate for someone sensible and with brains."

Every sorority was so eager to keep up their grade average that they'd recruit rush girls with easy majors—education, not engineering. At Austin the competition to get into a top sorority was so fierce that I hired a "rush consultant" (Honey recommended her). You might think a rich beauty who'd made a Texas debut like me would have no problem getting into the Tri-Delts. But I wasn't a legacy. At one afternoon ice-water tea, I'd worn open-toed shoes, which I later found out was a real no-no. No white shoes before Easter or after Labor Day, no velvet after February 14. No gold in the summer, just silver. Lots of "Yes, ma'ams" and "No, sirs." No dark meat in the chicken salad, plenty of mayonnaise, no weird curry powder. Everyone can be divided into "trash" or "quality." Never chew gum in public and never smoke on the streets— that's trashy. Put a paper doily under the finger bowls. Be sure to "sparkle" all day long and with men turn on the "charm." Learn to recognize that the three biggest insults are "sweet" and "nice" and "interesting" (pronounced "innarestin'").

Jane Beth, who was also rushing Tri-Delts, told me her grandmother had been a Louisiana Tri-Delt. She dressed me for the next event, the Courtyard Cookout. She told me that they were looking for girls capable of "unselfish leadership," which meant volunteering for charity work. I visited some children with cancer in the Austin Hospital; Tri-Delts were especially committed to juvenile cancer and were raising money through a Sincerely Yours letter-writing campaign. I knew that Yvette was tutoring Mexican children at the local church. I wondered if I could pretend I was the one doing that—or maybe that was a controversial charity. I asked my rush consultant, Sue-Ann, and she said it would be best to avoid anything that might involve dark people. Stick with cancer, she said, though I pointed out there were only three afflicted kids in the whole hospital right now and one was nigra. She made a little face and pulled her bobby pins out and shook out her full mane of blonde hair. "Concentrate on the other two," she said. "You'll get no points for loving colored folks. And never let me hear you say the N-word. Say 'Negro' or 'Colored.' Our top girls are never prejudiced." She bit her lip, lowered her head, raised her eyes, stared at me thoughtfully to make her point as dramatic as possible.

Pledge day came early in the semester—and I got in! I was so proud to be a Tri-Delt that I plastered two crests on my car window, but then Jane Beth, who also got in, told me that decals were considered tacky in Austin. I scraped them off.

The best church for quality people was Episcopal, but I had to go to a Baptist one or Daddy would've had a cow and docked my allowance, just when I needed it most to buy little gold fish for the Tri-Delt president's charm bracelet and to make a significant donation to the St. Jude fund for cancerous children. I needed money for gas also, since I wanted to drive to all the football games our guys were playing within five hundred miles. As the coach said, we should all work to make a university our team could be proud of. Football games were the biggest events in our campus life and we worshipped these gladiators. I would've been in awe of any of those cute boys—well, "cute" isn't the right word for these hulking, lumbering death machines. If I met one, he could do anything he wanted with me, I swore. It was only normal for a Texas girl.

One morning (it must have been in November) I was twirling the radio dial, looking for some of that exciting race music, when I heard on the local news a classy Yankee bass voice saying, "We interrupt our broadcast to report that, well, something like a miracle has occurred right here on Congress Avenue near the Capitol building. A Ford pickup truck, driven by Mr. Orville Teddlie from Bluffdale, Texas, ran up over the curb onto the sidewalk and rolled over a Mexican child, Hector Colimas. I can hardly tell this in a normal voice. Well, a young woman—I'm getting all this over the phone from our reporter, go on, Maybelle, tell me—a young person, a Miss Yvette Crawford, a UT freshman, single-handedly lifted the vehicle a foot in the air and the child's mother was able to pull him to safety. And, Maybelle, is this girl a big strapping farm girl? No, you say she's a little biddy thing—well, Lord, how on earth did she do that? She doesn't know herself? But she felt this superhuman force? Was she related to little Hector? No, you say she's an Anglo. Folks, this is an amazing story, an eighteen-year-old white freshman girl, a puny little girl, has saved a Mexican boy! Yvette Crawford has saved Hector Colimas." Suddenly a jingle interrupted the broadcast. "Now, have you ever wondered how to wash your delicate underthings, your Luxables?"

I snapped the radio off. Lord, next they'd be advertising wood-burning barbecue at Golgotha or breast cancer at St. Agatha's.

But I ran down to Congress Avenue looking for Yvette and I found a weeping group—two slender young Mexican men in straw cowboy hats and jeans and a mother (maybe she was the grandmother) in a blue rayon skirt holding on to a little boy, all of them sobbing and clamoring and saying Hail Marys in Spanish.

Where was Yvette?

One of the slender young men who could speak English said "an ambulance took her away." She was at Brackenridge, he said, which I'd never heard of, but I jumped into a taxi and surprisingly the man got in with me. I wasn't sure if the (white) driver would object to a Mexican riding with me but he didn't seem to notice. Maybe he thought I was taking my gardener to the emergency room. That's where we were going—the emergency room. The Mexican man kept saying, "She's a saint, *santa*. It was a *milagro*," which I figured out later meant "miracle."

There she was in the emergency room, waiting impatiently, still not "observed." She looked blue and tiny under the harsh neon lights in her little-boy clothes, with her bushy hair and big black glasses. She was hugging her knees but she jumped up when she saw us. The man took off his straw hat and went to his knees and kissed her feet. She looked to one side in embarrassment and pulled him up, saying, "For pity's sake."

"What happened? Did you really lift an entire car off a child and save his life?"

She rubbed her hand across her face and shook her head slightly, as if awakening from a bad dream. "I—I really don't remember." She smiled and held up her feeble arm, making a muscle. "It seems highly unlikely."

"But I saw it with my own eyes! It was a miracle. You saved little Hector Colimas." Yvette touched his bare brown arm with her tiny hand; she didn't want to disabuse him of a crucial belief but didn't subscribe to superstitious nonsense either. She looked confused, as if she'd just stepped in a puddle with one foot and on a live cable with the other. She had that *scorched* look and I thought that something serious had undoubtedly happened to her.

"Are you feeling all right?"

She nodded. "Let's get out of here." We both knew it was against the rules to walk out.

The Mexican man asked her to bless him. Yvette looked around in real embarrassment, I suspected. She shook her head no, and we went back into the infernal heat. The asphalt was melting and I saw someone's sandal half-buried in the tar.

Two days later there was a nasty letter in the Austin newspaper: "We never did like no Catholics round here. Thank God there's the Klan to defend us against these foreigners. But now they're trying to stir up trouble with our wetbacks. Them Catholic priests with their incense and holy water live off the backs of poor people; the people eat tortillas and the priests eat cake. Yes you can always fool them Mexies with meer-cles." It was signed, "a Baptist nabor." I thought it was clever of the editors to leave in the bad spelling—showed just what kind of white trash we were dealing with.

I dashed off an angry letter to the paper on my Tri-Delt stationery: "Dear Miss Nabor, I'll have you know my entire family, including the meer-cle worker, my sister Yvette—we're all Baptists, though educated ones. Yvette never claimed to have performed any miracles; we Baptists don't have saints, in case you forgot (back to church with you!). And I don't care what priests eat! Signed, A Baptist Sister."

They printed my letter and a couple other pledges congratulated me, but our Tri-Delt president, while sharing a Co-Cola with me and smiling, said it was better to avoid all controversy. "A Tri-Delt never argues about politics or religion and never mentions money or sex."

Things died down. I was still puzzled by what had really happened, but Yvette just said mysteriously and with a smile, "God moves in strange ways." Was she being ironic? I found out later that people were leaving plastic flowers on the sidewalk where the miracle had taken place (real flowers just died right away in the Texas heat though they were ever so much nicer). They also had left big pink and blue candles that smelled like sweet bubble gum. The Catholics were always relighting the candles and crossing themselves; I watched them from half a block away for nearly a half hour.

I had my own pearl-encrusted key to the Tri-Delt house and we pledges were guaranteed a date, a fraternity pledge, every night. My, it was exhausting but exhilarating. It was all arranged by our officers and the fraternity leaders. Because I spoke well, had gone to the right girls' school and the right summer camp and made a Dallas debut, I was popular.

Sometimes my date was a jock, rarely a brain, usually a "good guy" (heavy drinker), and once in a while a "face man" (handsome). All the fraternities thought they had to have face men in the mix; I thought it was amusing that these guys, who pretended they were so straight they were blind to male beauty, could actually pick out a looker if need be.

I never knew what the evening would bring. Some guys would invite me to a keg party that was so noisy I knew nothing more about my date at curfew time than I had at seven thirty, when he came to pick me up. Some guys would drive me to an open-air barbecue place in the hills for a piece of blackberry cobbler. Sometimes we'd go to a bowling alley and I'd always let my date win, though I could ace the game, really. My sorority "big sister" had warned me against showing more skill or knowledge than my date.

If we sat in a coffee shop on the Drag, I knew that the boy, with his nascent mustache, which looked like a streak of coal dust, and his West Texas drawl, was feeling homesick or lonely and wanted to tell me about his drunk Lubbock father who flogged him as a child if he was scared to dive into the deep end. Brian, a Sigma Chi I dated, worshipped his father, said his dad had an airplane, owned a ranch, could break a wild horse, and could even ride a bronco in a rodeo; he was a Baptist deacon, a real estate millionaire, and a "good ole boy" who'd been on the UT football team, the Longhorns, under the legendary coach . . . but here I stopped listening. It was boring listening to a guy who was obviously lying—worse, lying to himself. Brian evidently hated his father, a he-man sadist, but there was no way to cut through all that deception, so I just smiled and said, "Gracious me, your daddy sounds like Superman. You are one lucky son." Brian just stared at me, wide-eyed, tears welling up. When he lit our cigarettes his hand was shaking. I pitied him, but I pitied myself more for having to swallow so much bull crap.

Between dates and the occasional class and a retreat out to a local dude ranch called Christian Faith and Life Community, I scarcely had a moment to myself. All my clothes smelled of Lone Star beer and cigarettes. I'd given up Kents and Virginia Slims and become a Pall Mall girl, which I pronounced "Pell Mell" because that sounded more British. Like I said, I loved everything British or Continental. Pinky would drive down every week to pick up my dirty laundry and deliver fresh, pressed blouses—she even ironed my underwear and my sheets. Sometimes I'd watch TV with my "sisters" (*Dragnet* and *The Ed Sullivan Show* were my favorites, though I also liked *Your Hit Parade*). Whenever I did these normal things, I'd picture my twin disapproving of me wasting my youth, my life! But over lunch on the Drag she said earnestly, "I don't disprove of anyone or anything except war. I love you."

I teared up and said, "Why, I love you, too, Yvette."

But she added chillingly, "I love Christ in you and with the tenderness of the Blessed Mother."

I laughed and felt ashamed of the tears in my eyes. "Waiter, another Lone Star, please. So you've gone over to the old Catholics after all, have you? Or what are you, a Communist? Some folks say you're a Communist. A Catholic Communist?"

"I'm an anarchist," she said, "not the bomb-throwing kind or the enemy-of-the-state kind. I just believe people should govern themselves."

"That'll never happen!" I exclaimed merrily. "You can't even get two Tri-Delts to agree on a place for lunch."

"I should visit you in your sorority one day to see what it's all about," Yvette said, as if to show she loved the Christ in me and didn't think herself better than me. But I dreaded a visit from her, so skinny, her hair bushy and black, her eyebrows untweezered, her clothes so masculine. What if she told the girls she was my twin? Would they just laugh in disbelief? Could I convince Yvette to say she was my *little* sister?

Oh, I knew even then that Yvette's way was the serious one, but I didn't want to get serious just yet. I liked dating a different man each night, feeling an erection through gabardine trousers, letting Tom, Dick, or Harry lean his hot cheek on my breasts in their wired brassiere, laughing and speeding out to the Hollow, where a few fast kids bathed and sunbathed nude.

I knew it was a shallow life, one that could lead only to disappointment, to loneliness, to an understanding of how empty these worldly pleasures are, this unholy alliance of charity work performed by girls of the highest status, this conflict between the inclusive and the exclusive.

I wanted to be a rich woman in Junior League doing charity work for little white cancer victims. I prayed God to let me be young while I was young, to walk in the rain holding a quarterback's powerful hand under the glow of the campus tower, lit orange to celebrate our latest football victory. I wanted to squeal and stomp with the other Tri-Delts, to feel a big masculine hand inching up inside my skirt and stopping dead, frustrated, turned back at the fortress wall of my foundation garment, though one golden hair was poking out, and just on the other side of that unyielding molded rubber I was a hot liquid mass, a magma of molten lava. I knew I'd cool off, reform, turn sensible—but not yet, oh Lord, not yet! I knew real youth was expensive, afforded only to the privileged, that to drive into the night with the top down in a pretty scarf holding one's peroxided, perfumed hair in place, that to snuggle while parked, looking at the full moon, and to talk about one's painful childhood or boring debut, to joke about one's lesbian psych professor or airheaded roommate from Natchez—that this frivolity was priceless and that my duty was to be happy. Eventually I wanted a husband and children—an aristocratic husband whose worth was guaranteed by a long noble lineage, children finer than their mother. Wars and poverty and crippling physical labor and sickness, a spotted face and a grotesquely ballooning stomach—all this suffering was on every side and probably lay in wait for me, but not yet, oh Lord, not yet; for the moment I was among life's elite.

CHAPTER 4

I asked Yvette what she did with her free time. "Be interested in others" was the Tri-Delt rule. Once I wouldn't have had to pretend to be interested in Yvette, I knew what she was thinking without asking, I felt the same menstrual cramp at the same moment, but now I was intimate with my sorority sisters, with Nan, Kelly, Page, Anne, and Rhonda. I laughed and cried and squealed with them and whispered about how to keep marauding male fingers beyond the panty line.

"I'm studying Spanish with a tutor," Yvette said, "so I can communicate with the Mexican students I'm helping at St. Austin's. It turns out I'm not bad at languages."

"Oh, that's so good to hear," I cried. "Want another Co-Cola?"

"Sure. Why is that good to hear?"

"Here I am—Miss Egotist—but if my twin is quick to pick up a language—"

"Yes, it must be genetic," she said with a smile. "A good ear for the accent. What language do you want to learn?"

"French!" I said. "I want to move to Paris. I'm crazy about fashion. I want to move to Paris and work for Monsieur Givenchy. And maybe be a noble."

She cocked her head to one side. "Well, we all need to be clothed, especially in cold weather. And nobility begins with the soul."

I wanted to kiss her for making an effort to be agreeable and understanding, but I needed to point out that there was a world of difference between functional clothes and fashion. I smiled weakly. "Any beaux?" I asked. When she looked blank, I said, "Any young men you're dating?"

"I have several male friends on the *Observer*." I forgot she worked for the campus paper. "I get along fine with them."

"Have you ever been kissed?" I thought I'd surprise a confession out of her.

She looked out the window, drew some Co-Cola through her straw, and whispered, "No." Then she squared her thin little shoulders and said in a more definite voice, "I know and respect that woman was meant to comfort man, to help him, to be bone to his bone, flesh to his flesh, to bear his children and kiss away tears—but that's not for me. God wants something different from me."

"Do you really believe in God?" I blurted out. "I mean, we all do, but do you really?" I believed in God during rush before I pledged, I believed in God the night before my debut, I believed in God that time the car skidded clear across the turnpike and faced the oncoming traffic, I prayed on my knees the night I wanted Buzz to invite me to his prom, and he did! But I'm not in touch with God on a daily basis.

"You're enjoying being natural, you don't want to be supernatural, everything's going your way but if you ever feel the need to cast off the natural woman in you and to let the supernatural live—"

"Then *what*?" I asked sourly, wearying of this freak, my sister.

"Then you know how to call on God. You've already called on Him for the things you needed—"

"Needed and *deserved*," I said, maybe a bit petulantly.

"Yes, you know where to find Him. He's waiting patiently for you."

"Do you believe in the Devil, too? And in Hell?"

"I believe in Hell because it's doctrinal," she said with a smile, "but I don't think anyone's in it."

I couldn't wait to get back to the Tri-Delt house where three "sisters" (the fun kind) were watching *As the World Turns* on TV and eating unbuttered popcorn. When I got there, Jane Beth had her hair in curlers as big as frozen orange juice cans and she was wearing a peony-pink silk nightgown with a cocoa-colored lace waist and a gathered bust. Good enough to eat! She was glued to the television screen but patted the empty spot on the sofa next to her. As soon as I sat down she swiveled her lovely legs onto my lap and, still not looking at me, passed me the popcorn. The show was the usual: a weepy organ, the threat of the criminal brother skipping bail, the adulterous couple, the niece who snitched on them. There weren't even any cute guys, just middle-aged men in suits, with forlorn voices, and a corny old gramps with an Irish brogue.

During the Oxydol commercial, Jane Beth finally looked at me and smiled. "I just shaved my legs. Aren't they heavenly smooth? Wish they weren't so plump."

I stroked her thigh as if testing out its smoothness. I said, "You're not plump, Jane Beth, just edible," but she wrinkled up her nose in irritation and indicated with a sideways jerk of her head the other two girls. Okay, what I said was weird, maybe, but not indiscreet until she reacted guiltily. She did look like a Valentine's box of chocolates, with her cocoa lace and pink—foil? Glistening with shattered light. Silk?

We hadn't made out, Jane Beth and I, since we'd joined the sorority. But I had discovered how to pleasure myself, which I did at least once a day. I could do it quietly, in the john or even in my bunk bed without the girl in the upper bunk noticing. Anyway, she was always studying to be a civil engineer or something and was at her desk with bright lights and a protractor deep into the night. Lord, I was so glad I was studying baking!

When I was bringing myself to a muffled climax, it was then I discovered I liked girls, not boys. Or if not girls, at least Jane Beth. I could caress her lovely breasts in my mind, giving them breasts a release from the brassiere like blancmange coming out of the mold and wobbling. Of course, the perfectionist in me wanted to pull those two or three hairs on her nipples. And I could feel that warm juicy slot between her legs, those lips of life! When you're young and letch after someone, you assume she must be feeling the same thing, too—but what if she isn't? What if she's outgrown these pubescent pleasures and is now feeling genuine, oceanic ecstasy only with her Herbert? What if you made the wrong move and she looked at you with disgust, with horror?

Yvette's success with Spanish impressed me and made me courageous. I copied down a number for a French tutor on the church bulletin board. She was called Pauline, which sounded saucily authentic to me, and I pictured her, all fingerless black lace gloves, matching parasol, bangs, and white lipstick.

We met at Schultz's Beer Garden and I spied her right away: long straight hair that she kept shaking out of her eyes, flats, dark clothes, transparent skin, unsmiling even when I hailed her by name. She didn't look at all like a cancan dancer but rather like an existentialist, a Juliette Gréco. She stared at me as if I were some unrecognizable animal or an ugly guy harassing her or some impertinent stranger. I tried to dial down my big Tri-Delt smile. "Pauline?" I asked, and you never saw such a minimal nod, more a facial tic than a nod. "I'm Yvonne," but I said it wrong, the "von" like the German *vahn* instead of the French way to rhyme with "fun." She drank me in with her huge, heavily made-up raccoon eyes, though the rest of her face was scrubbed clean. "*Asseyez-vous*," she said, making a mock-courtly gesture with her hand. Not until later did I learn about French politeness, that every native was embarrassed by their manners and made fun of them. French women, even or especially the *gratin*, were always saying that things made them "shit" (*ça me fait chier*) or that men and women were stupid "cunts" (*cons*)—as if this gutter talk proved their sincerity and made up for their seventeenth-century formulas ("*Je vous en prie*"). I didn't even get that right away, but I did understand that there were no rules governing the baldest curiosity (Pauline stared and stared), and that every polite gesture had to be performed buffoonishly lest one seem stiff and old-fashioned.

It wasn't indifference that guided her but deep exhaustion, a total abnegation of enthusiasm, which was so at odds with Texas pep.

I asked her, "So why are you here on the forty acres, in Austin?"

She said, sighing, almost groaning, "I'm here working on Virginia Woolf's papers. For some reason they are here in the Airy Rensome Library."

Oh, I thought, that's her cute way of saying the Harry Ransom.

"I'm comparing her to Nathalie Sarraute, a French writer you've probably never heard of."

"You're a hundred percent right there."

"Why do you want to learn French?" she asked, as if it were Swahili. Or as if I were unworthy of it.

"Fashion!" I said. "I want to work in fashion."

"Not in those sneakers, you don't—just kidding!" She touched my arm with her hand as though smoothing the part she might have burned. "I have an aunt—*enfin*, a sort of *cousine*—who works for Givenchy."

When I beamed my Tri-Delt smile, she said, "You know Givenchy?"

"And how! I adore him."

"Do you know him personally?"

"Oh, no. I just love his work."

"My *cousine* is his public relation." She looked strangely smug at her specialized vocabulary. "Of course, Givenchy are being only snob because she's a species of countess or something."

"My word, your cousin is a countess! Isn't that like royalty?!"

"Not really. But she is a good species of countess . . . if you care about silly old things like that." I figured that by "species" she must mean "type." Now I know she was translating "*espèce*," which is slightly contemptuous. I guess it's what today we'd call a humble-brag.

"You've got to teach me French." I paused and then asked suspiciously, "Does that mean you're a countess, too?"

"Oh, no. That is too stupid! When I had my *rallye* the invitation called me a *baronne*—first I'd heard of it."

"Golly—is that like baroness? You're royalty, too! It must be so, so wonderful being a baroness: that's what I long to be. Through marriage, of course."

She sighed and shrugged, but I could tell she was pleased.

"I think it's great you're working even though you are a baroness. That's very American of you."

She held up her index finger and tick-tocked it back and forth reprovingly. "*Là*, there you are very mistaken, my friend. I am very, very poor. Many of us old *régime* aristocracy are very poor." She smiled primly.

"Old regime?"

"Here's a lesson. The *ancien régime*, repeat after me: *ancien régime*."

"Ancient regime."

"Ha-ha, not bad."

"What does that mean?"

"You've heard of Lewis Sixteen? Or Mary Antoine? Head chop-chop?" And she mimed with her right hand a guillotine falling.

"Oh!" I said. "Marie Antoinette and King Looey the Sixteenth?"

"You're very *cultivée* for an American."

"I went to a good school."

"In New York? Boston?" she asked encouragingly. But when I said "Dallas," she made a face and informed me, "That is in Texas," as if it were an open-and-shut case, a bad one.

Little did I suspect, but Pauline would be my *entrée* into a whole new world, the world not of Paris fashion but of Paris aristocracy. I would take conversation lessons from her three times a week for three years. I never learned to read or write and after all these years I still write French "like a cow," as they would say, but I learned to speak with a perfect accent, even a perfect *r*, and I acquired a big, if not huge, vocabulary, except when it comes to the technical words of a glazier, say, or a chimney sweep (though I learned that the "little chimney sweep"—*le petit ramoneur*—had a very dirty meaning and most *ramoneurs* were considered Gypsy thieves who would clean out your hole—and house).

It turned out I had my sister's gift for languages, though my French is better than her Spanish ever was. Maybe because Pauline was so rude about my slack-lipped Texas accent, I was cured of it in a matter of months, and to this day Parisian friends who know my exquisite, idiomatic French are astonished when they hear my mushy Texas English. I used to have in Paris an answering machine in which I said my message in both languages: "*Je vous prie de me laisser un message après le signale sonaire*; please leave me an itty-bitty little message when you hear the bip." I'd say I rose a whole social class just by switching languages, not to mention my advantageous marriage.

I brought Pauline home for Thanksgiving. Daddy thought she was very pretty and smart. She adored Yvette, whom she considered a "real person," and she accepted Daddy as "amusing," which I realized later conveyed a very limited approval. I constantly pumped her for an insider's information on fashion and the French aristocracy. Those were my two great passions, though they were only side interests for Pauline. But she could see how I snapped to when she mentioned my subjects, and maybe she began to pad them out (in a plausible way, to be sure) once she discovered they could be used pedagogically.

Now three decades have gone by. We have CNN here in Paris and the other day someone called and told me to turn it on. There was a middle-aged Mexican man with a thick mustache. The legend on the screen identified him as Hector Colimas, the little boy my sister saved in Austin that day, her first miracle. Of course, I knew my poor deceased sister had already been named a Venerable and the Vatican was right now deciding whether or not to make her a Blessed. Mother Cabrini and Elizabeth Ann Seton were the only American female saints, I believe. I was so depressed seeing what an ugly man Hector had become. He was being interviewed about the "miracle" right here in Texas, as he said, that had led to her being named a Venerable. The altar in Austin looked like a jukebox.

CHAPTER 5

For my spring semester abroad I arrived at the big old-fashioned apartment of Pauline's grandmother on the Avenue Mozart (she'd taught me to say "Moh-Zar," not "Moht-zart" as we pronounce it—correctly, I might add) with seventeen pieces of luggage and an extra taxi. For the door on the ground floor Pauline had given me the "code," whatever that was. I saw a panel with some numbers and punched them and wedged my hatbox in the heavy wood door, lacquered teal blue and adorned with a heavy round brass knocker. Though I'd tipped them extravagantly the drivers had just dumped my bags on the sidewalk. I moved them all into the building's big entrance hall, which had rather dirty black-and-white tiles and smelled of fish (cod, as I later learned, since the concierge was Portuguese and ate nothing but bacalao). She looked suspiciously out through her lace-curtained window and disappeared. Wasn't it her job to help me?

The elevator was big enough for only two people. I decided to haul everything up in three trips to the fifth floor and the entrance to Mme de Castiglione's apartment (in French with two p's, *appartement*). When I got everything up there I sat on my suitcase for three minutes till I stopped perspiring, then rang her bell. I didn't expect her to hug me, exactly, but I did expect her to greet me in slow but precise French with a formality and a certain warmth.

Instead she looked at my mountain of matching Vuitton luggage, put her hands on her hips, and snarled, "*Mais non! C'est impossible! Vous exaggerez, ma chère.* You have rented only a *chambre de bonne*, a maid's room one floor up, and you can never fit all that—" She made a wide, despairing gesture and tilted back her head, lips downturned.

"This is not the Ritz. Oh, *non*, full of *American* clothes, no doubt."

Still clucking like a broody hen, she gave me a key to my room and said, "I'll see you at eight for dinner," then slammed the door. I sat down on my biggest suitcase and sobbed. But I decided to be peppy and happy, like a true Tri-Delt, and within three minutes had pulled myself together, carried all my bags up in three elevator trips, found the right door, and let myself into a maid's room with a sink, no toilet, one window, a room no bigger than my closet in Dallas, the narrowest bed I'd ever seen with the thinnest mattress and just one coffee-stained blanket and a pillow, which, if you peeked under its crisp white pillowcase, you saw had turned tobacco-yellow with years of sweat. Other people's sweat. There was no closet and no armoire, just three wire hangers stuck into cracks in the wall. Everything smelled of old copper wire—or was that roach spray?

I discovered the toilet behind a curved door halfway down the stairs. It had a bare bulb, nothing to sit on, just two scored ceramic tiles on the floor, where you were supposed to place your feet, squat, and let fly into a stinking hole in the floor. The whole thing was no bigger than a phone booth. I couldn't see any trace of toilet paper, though some scraps of a newspaper—*Le Figaro*—were probably intended for mopping up, which might have been okay if you had a bidet, which I didn't. I assumed the shower was in Mme de Castiglione's apartment.

No, the whole thing was impossible! I would rent a proper hotel room nearby where I could leak in comfort and hang my clothes and bathe but I would *pretend* to live here so I could still have my total immersion in French (if not in soapy water) and eat French food and participate in the life of impoverished aristocrats. Tomorrow I'd get my hotel room while Madame was out and tip two bellboys to move my luggage. And get myself some great croissants (I'd researched a patisserie across the street called La Flûte Enchantée). Next door there was supposed to be an art nouveau hotel with green glazed tiles and the inevitable dragonflies (*libellules*).

Something built by Hector Guimard, the man who did those wonderful old noodle metro entrances under the fanning pebbled glass awnings.

It was only six o'clock, so I decided to go out for a walk. I was in a very tight skirt and bright colors and high, high heels. It took me a moment to realize I had to push a button to release the front door.

Everyone looked at me oddly, the men with interest and the women with disapproval, or was I just being paranoid? Although it was January, the air was surprisingly warm and pregnant with moisture, as if it might rain at any moment, stop the moment after—and it wouldn't really matter except to my hair. I looked around for the Flûte Enchantée—and spied it! And it was open. I walked in and queued up behind four rather dowdy older women and rehearsed what I would say, but the other customers looked at me and one even clucked, whereas a saucy teen behind the counter pretended he'd just touched something hot with his hand, hissed, and shook his fingers in the air as if to cool them off. In my best French I said, "*A crescent, s'il vous plait*," and the cheeky teen scrunched up his face in confusion and the man behind me said, "*Elle veut un croissant*," and tipped his hat. I smiled. The boy said,"*C'est trop tard, y'a plus*." The man translated (very loudly), "NOT MORE." I smiled my thanks. When I finally chose a coffee-cream pyramid called a "nun," *une religieuse*, the clerk waved his hand impatiently, as if I were a fly, and then pointed to the cashier. "PAY NOW," the nice man said.

When I finally returned to my room, I devoured my creamy nun, hoping it would spoil my appetite, since the food was bound to be as austere as my room. I made sure in the cracked mirror that my mouth showed no signs of pastry. I opened my one window and lay down on my sagging bed and stared at my ceiling, which was low and had beams buried in the plaster, rough-hewn supports that looked surprisingly primitive in prissy ol' Paris. The bells were ringing in several neighborhood churches and the breeze had turned cold. It was January 20.

When I went down to dinner after taking a maid's bath at the sink (washing under my arms and my neck, my heine and my cooze) and applying fresh makeup and lots of perfume, Mme de Castiglione greeted me at the door, invited me into the shabby salon, indicated where I should sit on the couch, introduced me to her other boarder, Justine Goldwasser, a name she pronounced with an obvious emphasis on the last name, as if to indicate I must avoid saying anything anti-Semitic, which she was implying might be my first impulse in polite conversation.

Justine, I learned after I posed a few questions (Mme de Castiglione later taught me that questions were considered rude in France), had grown up in Zurich. Her first language was Swiss-German though she assured us she was also fluent in "real" German. She was a sullen girl with dirty hair and a dirty face, dressed in an almost laughably anonymous way. She said she wanted to learn French and English, since she was obliged someday to take over the management of the family "palace," which I learned must mean a luxury hotel in the Alps.

Mme de Castiglione, holding herself erect on the edge of her chair, said, "This is the last occasion we speak English—to welcome Madamoiselle Cravfjord."

"Crawford," I corrected.

"Yes," she repeated, "Cravfjord. This is the elegant French pronunciation. Would you like an aperitif?"

"Don't go to any bother."

"I wouldn't. Elegant French people drinks an aperitif before their souper."

She stood, poured me a thimbleful of sweet vermouth, and handed it to me. I smiled but her face was blank, or rather *composed*, like a salad of cooked vegetables pressed and shaped into a dome. "Thank you," I said. "*Merci.*"

She said nothing back and I assumed it was inelegant to answer, "You're welcome," though I learned later the tacky French-Canadians say, "*Vous êtes bienvenu,*" a horrible Americanism. The real French might ironically mime doffing a plumed hat and mutter, "*Pas de quoi,*" making their compatriots smile at the antique foolishness of it all.

"And you?" she said, turning to Justine. "As the Italians say, 'What beautiful thing have you did today?'"

Justine ran a hand through her bushy hair and shrugged. Was she rude or shy? I wondered.

"*Eh bien*, I have been busy searching the black fabric. See!" Madame de Castiglione pointed to a pile of bunting. "I will put it in the window tomorrow. January twenty-first is when his majesty Louis the Sixteenth was beheaded. For us it is a national day of *deuil*."

"Mourning?" I asked. "But I thought France was a republic with a president."

"*Hélas.*"

"I looked you up in the encyclopedia," I said brightly. "They suggested you weren't ancient regime at all but that the countess of Castiglione was Napoleon the Third's mistress."

"My poor Yvonne," she said. "I never thought I would be discussing my own genealogy—which goes back to the Crusades—with a Texane—oh! How amusing!" And she laughed mirthlessly. "We're having *pas mal* of work to make you a lady. Now our aperitif is finish we go in to dinner." She smiled, showing her bad teeth. "First lesson. Do not talk so loud. Here in Paree we say there are two bad accents—the American and the Cantonese. Mademoiselle, you must lower your voice. Also no loud clothes—but that is tomorrow's lesson." Wearing her dirty old sweater (*sa petite laine*), a blouse yellowed with age, a straight black skirt, and worn-down spool heels, she led the way into the dining room, which was brightly lit ("So we can see our food"), the table outfitted with a patched white damask cloth, matching napkins and an array of forks (the tines turned upside down), two knives—one big, one small, the blades facing out—a soup spoon, and, above the plates, lying horizontally, another soup spoon, all describing, it seemed, some obscure Masonic symbol. The utensils looked from another century, with heavy baroque handles. Three glasses of different sizes, faintly etched with worn gold swirls. The tableware was the only sign of a now-vanished wealth.

"I don't know where to begin," I confessed in what I hoped were more moderate tones.

"Yes, we're a long way from Dallas," Mme de Castiglione said primly. I wanted to knock her in the puss. "Start from the outside in. And sit up straight, your back not touching the chair, both hands on the table."

"In Dallas—" I started to explain.

"We're not in Dallas, *heureusement*." She spooned out a watery soup with a ladle from a tureen. She poured a minuscule glass of white wine, which tasted like turpentine.

"What heavenly celery soup," I lied.

"It's a classic *soupe de légumes*. But we don't comment on the food. It's assumed that the cooker made it; of course it's good. If you are offered seconds you may say, '*Merci*,' which means no. You may add here, 'But it is delicious,' or better, simply, 'It is very good.' In aristocratic families the way you hold yourself at table is extremely important; it say everything about how you were elevated. I know in America you eat soup from the side of the spoon, but in Paree from the tip." And she demonstrated the proper method, like swallowing a liquid medicine. I wanted to ask why, but I knew it was as senseless as challenging the rules of grammar.

"Where were you brought up, Madame?" I asked, wanting to show a Tri-Delt interest in the other and shift the subject away from table manners.

"You must never ask that of a Parisian. It suggests they might have a provincial accent. And you must not ask them what they do for work. What if they don't work? Many of our best families have never worked."

"What *do* you talk about?"

"The movies. That's safe. Your upcoming holiday in Thailand or Granville, a seaside resort at Normandy, two hours from Paris. Or other people's sex scandals."

"You can talk about sex?"

"Of course! *Histoires de cul*, ass stories, sex stories, considered very gay and *osées* and amusing. Sex but never money." I eventually learned that if Americans talk about money to avoid talking about sex, the French discuss sex instead of money. I was thoroughly confused. I had never been at a loss for words before, but now there was a long silence, which I broke by asking, "Are there any good movies playing at the moment?"

Madame said complacently, "I wouldn't know. Since I am widow I do not go out except to play *bezique* with my friend la princesse de la Tour du Pin."

Justine roused herself and said, "It's what you call 'peaknuckle'—is that how you say 'pinochle'?"

"That's just how you say it!" I exclaimed agreeably. On a roll, I asked of Madame, "Do you play with a group of senior citizens at a community center?"

"I go to the *hôtel* of the princess. It's a game for two people."

"Oh, she has a hotel? Here in the neighborhood?"

"Now we will eat delicious *topinambour*."

Justine said, "Ugh. Jerusalem artichokes."

Madame stood. "Or rather you will eat them. I repose me. *Bonne nuit*, Madamoiselle Goldwasser, *bonne nuit*, Madamoiselle Cravfjord."

"*Bonne nuit*, Madame de Castiglione," we said in chorus, half-rising from our chairs.

After she glided out of the room, Justine said, "This shit is not eatable. This is the third night she's served this *scheiss*. It's what people ate during the war. My father pays for real food. Meat!"

"So," I said, "what's the deal with Madame?"

"Spanky?"

"Pardon?"

"That was her nickname in *le monde* before the war."

"She was known as Spanky?"

"They were all Anglophiles. She was very Mer-Mer. That's what they call the upper-crust, named after the Merovingian dynasty, one of the earliest."

"Christian?"

"They claimed to be descendants of Jesus Christ—but did Christ have children?"

"Search me. Maybe a brother or cousin. So she was very snazzy, our Spanky?"

"Lord, yes. Dressed by Jacques Fath. Her grandmother was a favorite of the Bourbon pretender to the throne, Henry the Fifth. Now they all make a fuss over the Orléans pretender, the comte de Paris, who lives in Morocco because he's forbidden to live in France. Forgive me, I'm studying French history, so I'm up on all this crap. As recently as 1870 his grandfather was offered the throne, but he refused to wear the cockade because that was a symbol of the Revolution, so they withdrew the offer."

"Are there many of these royalists over here?"

"Better say 'monarchists,' or else they want to shit. No, not so many. Some are not aristos at all. They worship Joan of Arc, all of them. And that moron Louis the Sixteenth and that silly dyke Marie Antoinette. There are some Bourbons in Spain, friends of Franco, no doubt. Some monarchists favor them over the comte de Paris."

"And Spanky?" I asked. "Did she collaborate with the Nazis?"

"Not at all. She's a war hero. She and her husband were both in la Résistance and sent off to concentration camps. Her husband died there but she survived. Two of her uncles were killed in the camps as well."

"What does she do with herself all day?" I said, not wanting to admire her. "Drink tea with other old bats?"

"No, she works as a volunteer nurse at the local hospital."

"Why on earth?"

"It's part of her whole Catholic bit. The hospital is Catholic, of course, and she empties bedpans and pushes wheelchairs—six hours a day. And she's in her eighties."

"I declare," I said—I don't think Justine knew what that meant; she scrunched up her face as if she were a car in a car wash. "She must be very pious."

"Oh, she is. She has a life-size statue of the Virgin Mary next to her bed, smiling down at her as she sleeps. And a prie-dieu in the corner. And she goes to Mass every morning on her way to the hospital." I thought she'd like my sister more than me.

Justine added with a conspiratorial smile, "In French they call these ladies 'frogs in the holy water.'"

"That's rich. How do you say that in French?"

"*Des grenouilles dans l'eau bénitier*, I think. I'm not sure. My English is much better than my French."

The next day I managed to move into a suite in the hotel next door. I tipped the bellboys handsomely. I took a long shower until the hot water ran out. I waited for the cistern to heat up again and I washed my hair. Then I decided to stop by American Express to cash another check; I got the hotel switchboard to connect me and I asked for directions. Rue Scribe behind the opera house. I tried to hail a taxi and a nice older woman, very neatly dressed in a suit, cape, and gloves, explained in English that I had to walk a block to a taxi stand and wait my turn. Why did everything have to be different?

With my money from American Express in hand I entered a grandiose café and was shown to a little round pink marble table surrounded by bad florid paintings of blowsy women with pink tits framed by acres of carved gilded wood. The second half of the menu, to my surprise, was in English; then I realized that the only other customers at eleven in the morning were other Americans. As I heard their flat, boring voices I thought I'd never escape the curse of being born on the wrong side of the Atlantic. Why wasn't I created as a French countess? I asked God, as if he were a master of heraldry or the editor of the Bottin (as the French called their high-society Blue Book). It seemed so unfair to be a big-boned, big-toothed American bimbo, head empty of thought, heart full of banality, with sloping shoulders, pockets heavy with lucre, and a ready smile (too ready). A stylish French couple, perfectly turned out and heavily perfumed, elegantly unsmiling, came in with a little girl of five or six, who chattered gaily until her mother shushed her. The child lowered her head and shut down. When she became voluble a moment later, the mother said, "People are looking at you!" as if that were the worst fate imaginable. People—at least me—*were* looking; I returned my eyes to my *café crème*. Using an exaggerated theatrical whisper, the child chattered on and I thought, How unfair she can speak French and I can't!

I was morose for a full six minutes and then decided, in the best Theta tradition, to pick myself up and become practical. I gave myself three assignments: (1) learn fluent French; (2) become a French aristocrat; (3) turn haughty. Tomorrow I would figure out how to do all three. I knew I was smart enough—I had only to look at my identical twin, who was brilliant! I was young, rich, beautiful—and a Texan, which Pauline had told me the French thought of as "fun," except she made the same mistake most French speakers make and said "funny." Anyway, more amusing than a dour Bostonian or a transactional New Yorker. Texas had an air of fantasy about it, of cow-punchers, barbecue, and unimaginable riches. It was gushing with oil; Texans were loud, proud, and exhilarating, eager to buy the best, whether it was a jewel, an Old Master, or a titled husband.

As I glanced out at the opera house, which looked to me like a Victorian inkwell, I thought of that ambitious, social-climbing young man at the end of Balzac's *Père Goriot*, which we read in Miss Smithers's French 301, the guy who looks at Paris lying at his feet and says, "It's up to you and me now"—"*À nous deux, maintenant.*"

CHAPTER 6

True to her word, Mme de Castiglione would converse with us only in French. Luckily, she spoke clearly and slowly and said the same thing in two or three different ways. I gathered she was shocked that I had moved into the hotel next door; the concierge had snitched on me. I had already rehearsed what I would say and had even looked up a few words in my dictionary. I reassured her that I would still pay my full amount and that I treasured her hints (*clins d'oeil*) about French manners and morals and language, and that I hoped to still take my evening meals with her. I think she got it, though she was still puzzled by my extravagance and the rejection of her hospitality. No other "guest" (*invitée*) had ever done such a thing. I conceded that I was a spoiled brat (*enfant gaté*) and we exchanged a wintry little smile.

I suspect she admired my resolve and simplicity. She told us that true elegance was being completely "natural." At least I think that's what she said; I couldn't vouch for it. I had to master my irritation that she insisted on speaking this hushed, nasal language of her own when she could speak English perfectly well—or perfectly *enough*—like everyone else. She was marginally more cordial in French than in her spiky English, though perhaps not as sincere. After a long life of speaking French she had accumulated a huge mass of rolling, ready-made phrases, whereas in her pidgin English she had to invent words to fit her thoughts, and frustration handicapped her slightly. I found out later she didn't consider English (despite Shakespeare!) a real language but rather a sort of creole born out of German and French. Besides, the English didn't have an academy to determine which words were acceptable and which were *not*. Shakespeare, all right for the great characters (Lady Macbeth), but the plays didn't observe the unities or the necessity of having all the action offstage. We drifted into debating Shakespeare versus Racine; Madame clearly preferred the chiseled passion of Racine and his chaste vocabulary. As for Shakespeare, she liked him only in opera form—Gounod's *Roméo et Juliette*, Verdi's *Falstaff*, *Hamlet* by Ambroise Thomas, in which the text had been sorted out by Alexandre Dumas. I thought I acquitted myself fairly well in French, that my three years of conversation with Pauline had paid off, but I felt I had to pour every thought into an electric mixer and break down all the pieces of bright fruit into a brown broth. I won't speak of our dinner—the Jerusalem artichokes had been recycled in a soup. I filled up on a very crusty baguette, but then Madame said (in French), "I can't sit here if you eat one more slice of bread and destroy your lovely figure (*votre belle ligne*)."

I decided I liked Mme de Castiglione. She was a survivor, a war hero, an example to us all. If I talked too loud, she'd clamp her hands over her ears. Or she pretended there was an imaginary porthole between us and she was wiping away the ocean foam with circular motions. When I asked her why she was doing that, she said, "I've discovered that if girls become too excited, this calms them down." As promised, she gave us a lecture on what a lady (*une dame bourgeoise*) could wear. Definitely not loud colors (*clinquant*) or anything garish (*bariolé*), and nothing showy (*voyant*). She kept me busy strumming my dictionary. "A lady should be neat and very, very clean, impeccable, and if she's too poor or old to be fashionable then she should try to be unnoticeable, anonymous. Just as a real lady should have her name in the newspaper only twice—at her birth and at her death."

"And when she gets married?" I asked gaily.

"Never," Spanky said, and shuddered.

After Madame took her leave, Justine said, "I'm starving! We can't eat soup like water and nothing else."

"Come with me to the hotel and we'll order hamburgers. My treat."

"But Spanky doesn't want me going out at night," Justine wailed. "And I'd have to phone her and wake her up to get back in."

"Oh dear. You must ask her for a key." She'd given me one—was Justine staying in the apartment? Later, I discovered Madame had given her bedroom to her paying guest and she herself was sleeping on the tattered red silk couch in the study.

"Ha! Today I wanted to take a bath and she told me I owed her twenty francs for each bath and not to use too much hot water, not above waist level."

I didn't want to be drawn into a conspiracy of bad-mouthing Madame. Besides, I felt guilty about breaking the no-English rule. I just touched Justine's shoulder and slid past her. "*Bonne nuit,*" I whispered, pulling the apartment door shut behind me, pressing the button that turned on the timed hallway lights (the *minuterie*), and summoning the elevator. Once outside it was cold and damp with the constant drizzle the French compare to spit (*crachin*). Enormous white clouds were hanging over the sleeping city, like egret plumes over a black sultan. I hurried up to my hotel room, ordered a hamburger rare (*à point*) from room service, and began to review my wardrobe, selecting anything somber and wrenlike— *bref,* ladylike. That's what I'd wear to Madame's tomorrow; she'd promised to teach me how to tie and drape a scarf (which I'd buy tomorrow *chez* Hermès).

The next evening I told her gleefully that my new teacher at the Alliance Française was Mme de Rochefoucauld.

"Rochefoucauld?" she said with asperity. "They were nobodies in the eleventh century."

And the Crawfords? I thought. Indentured shepherds in Aberdeen, probably, struggling with the Black Death.

If Madame disapproved of my conversation teacher as an upstart (*arriviste*), she liked my sober clothes (gray suit, ecru blouse, hair up in a brioche) and, as promised, gave me very precise instructions about tying my Hermès scarf.

For dinner we had *oeufs en murette,* which turned out to be poached eggs on toast with a red wine sauce (the sauce contained onions, bacon bits, and mushrooms). There was even a tiny leaf of frisée lettuce with its own vinaigrette. After Madame retired, Justine explained that she'd complained to her father about the Jerusalem artichokes and he'd phoned Madame from Zurich and gently reproached her. He ran a luxury hotel, after all, and knew how to deal with difficult old women.

"Good work!" I said. "*Bon travail!*" but I wasn't sure you could say that.

Every night I retreated to my hotel room with the strangely shaped, asymmetrical, art nouveau windows, the amber overhead lamp made to look like a dragonfly's swollen belly, and the twisting tendrils of rosewood scrolling across the walls. Everything resembled a fever dream of an expensive swamp. Televisions already existed back then but not normally in a Parisian hotel room, though there was one downstairs in the lounge, a little black-and-white thing that surrendered at midnight to a test pattern. I would order an old-fashioned and sip it gratefully while watching ironic blabbermouths showing off on-screen (I understood only one sentence in four, but by my second drink I imagined I was comprehending everything). When I finally fell in bed asleep, sometimes with the lights on and fully dressed, I was so exhausted from trying to fit in with these accursed foreigners that I passed out and awakened thirsty at three A.M. before properly undressing and returning to bed.

I suppose Madame was pleased enough with the way we "held" ourselves at the table and conversed in our stiff, banal fashion right out of an Ionesco play that she invited her nephew Adhéaume de Courcy to stay over for dinner. It was the last week of January, when distant relatives dropped by with their New Year's greetings. He had brought a little box of *marrons glacés*.

At first I thought he must be homosexual, he had such graceful manners and yet seemed so reserved. His face was a mask of indifference— cold and inexpressive—except when he bent to kiss my hand (without touching it with his lips, I noticed). I had no idea what he was doing and he had to grab my right hand and raise it.

He was beautifully dressed in a very subtle black watch plaid with a silk pochette and a harmonizing but not matching tie (things that match are vulgar, I was told). His suit struck me as too tight, but later he told me he had flown back and forth to London for Savile Row fittings (this was long before the Chunnel). He was rather short, slender, in his late thirties, with sandy curly hair and big bluish-green eyes, the color of a house finch's eggs, and a hawklike nose (in fact his face was avian or, as he would say, "heraldic").

He spoke English to me until his aunt corrected him and insisted on French. I asked him (in French) where he'd learned to speak English with an English accent; he shrugged and said, almost impatiently, "In England, naturally." Then, possibly realizing he'd been brusque, he explained, "French adolescents are sent to England in the summers to learn the language. Unfortunately I went with my sister and we spoke French all the time. I had better luck with German, since I lived in Vienna alone."

He was nice enough but rather cold (much later I realized he was determined to display *sang-froid*). All the boys I knew in Texas (except ruffians and other zircons in the rough) smiled a lot and leaned into a conversation with a pretty girl; Adhéaume struck me as rude (or a faggot, though the faggots I knew back home were extremely cordial).

"Is it your sister who works for Givenchy?" I asked, hoping to establish a contact.

He sighed and said, "Yes, painful as it is for me to admit. Of course, she's more a hostess than a shopgirl (*midinette*)."

"Why is it painful?" I asked, genuinely puzzled and worried that I hadn't understood.

"The *noblesse* isn't supposed to work. It's a great source of shame."

"But why? I'd kill to work for Givenchy. He's a genius."

"That's a big word for a *fournisseur*," Adhéaume said. Justine smirked and Madame looked blank (perhaps her hearing was bad).

We went in to dinner. The first course was segments of lettuce tied with string and cooked in chicken broth, I think. The second was delicious chicken breasts and potatoes Anna (sliced thin and baked in butter). The dessert was *riz à l'impératrice* (a tasty rice pudding with almonds and raisins). The cook shuffled out resentfully with each dish and slammed it on the table. She was fat, in a greasy apron, and probably underpaid or unpaid. Madame is really putting on the dog for her nephew, I thought.

She and he talked over something about an ailing relative, but it went on too long and Justine and I were excluded, so after a while I asked her what she'd done that day. She shrugged in her rude way. I told her I'd bought three white silk blouses that had enormous wide jabots attached and she said, "Very hard to keep clean." I wanted to say, That's why I bought three, but I resisted and just smiled. I could feel my period coming on and my innards cramping up. I had a headache and felt weak. The horrible cook brought out demitasses of burned coffee and Madame suggested we take them to the salon.

We'd barely taken a seat there when Adhéaume said to me, "Perhaps you'd like to come with me to a meeting of the Knights of Malta. You'd find it very Vieille France and *folklorique*. It's in two days. We've taken over the entire Opéra Comique. It's very *rustre*." (Which I later looked up. It meant "boorish.")

"Gladly," I said (*"volontiers"*).

"I'll pick you up at eight," he said, taking his leave, kissing his aunt on two withered cheeks and bowing to Justine: *"Enchanté, mademoiselle."*

Before I could slip away Madame told me what an honor it was, going to the Knights of Malta evening. "You have to have six aristocrats among your eight great-grandparents to belong," she told me solemnly.

Snobs, I thought, all homosexual. All poor. The Opéra Comique sounded amusing at least.

Adhéaume was only half an hour late, which was early for a Parisian, I discovered. "Oh, what a day!" he exclaimed, by way of excuse, I suppose. He was dressed in white tie with an elaborate medal on his lapel. In Dallas I'd have asked all about it, pretending to be interested, but I'd already learned not to ask questions of the French. I was in a long blue wool skirt and one of my new white silk blouses under a long blue military jacket. He seemed pleased with the way I looked.

We took a taxi to the Opéra Comique, which was a heavily ornamented white lozenge in the middle of a small square. It was in the style of the 1890s, a period that I came to love for its questionable taste, its heavy gold ornaments, and its sentimental paintings of gods, satyrs, and naked women, often frankly pornographic, with alabaster skin and delectable nipples, like desserts made of whipped cream topped off by strawberries. In the grand foyer upstairs many tables were set up for dinner under two huge chandeliers and ceiling scenes from operas I didn't know.

The hall was already crowded with men and women in evening dress, many of them blond and blue-eyed (those Norman ancestors!) and many of them surprisingly noisy and vivacious for French people. Now, all these years later, I understand that the Knights of Malta were uninhibited in the presence of one another—and proud of their countrified manners and regional accents, all of which attested to their lives in far-flung châteaux. Only once a year did they assemble in Paris for one of their drunken routs, full of back-slapping, heavy teasing, and faces dilated with drink-broken capillaries. Except for their clothes, height, and faces reminiscent of Jefferson's, and their boorish self-confidence, I might have taken them for a convention of farmers, the Knights of Columbus in Findlay, Ohio, rather than the Knights of Malta in Paris.

Adhéaume made no effort to introduce me to anyone, though he did say to several people, "You know Yvonne," and they bowed slightly and I lowered my eyes. I didn't know what they were saying to one another and I'd learned that the eyes inevitably give away one's confusion. We were all drinking flutes of champagne that the waiters, curiously dressed in wigs, brocaded coats, and knee stockings, kept serving when they weren't offering warm canapés of blue cheese and something chewy. A bare-shouldered lady at the entrance had told us we'd be at table five. As a costumed majordomo passed by ringing a gong with a cloth-wrapped mallet, we found our way to our table. Adhéaume inspected all the place cards and switched two—"She's a terrible bore," he said in English. Then in French he muttered, "The man to your right is a famous wit and a Communist duke—we call him the Red Duke. You'll like him." I didn't want a wit if that meant puns and wordplay. I wanted a dullard who spoke clearly and liked women.

As it turned out the duke was very jolly, spoke English, and soon was pinching my thigh. He was about seventy-five, I'd guess, had sapphire-blue eyes, a ready smile, and endearing ways. He told me that he'd lived in Texas in his twenties and was never so happy. Why? Oh, managing a family agar factory. "Have you ever heard of agar?"

"Algae?"

"No, it's even duller. It's used in food to thicken things, like candy. It's used to make dental impressions. Oh, it has a million uses, all of them excruciatingly tedious. The Japanese had dominated production but during the war we needed to develop our own. The thing was discovered by a French, who was some sort of ancestor . . ."

The duke, who was named Henri and had a slight Texas twang, asked me if I liked France.

"I love the people! They're so friendly, just like folks back home. I love everything except the food."

Henri frowned. "You can't be serious."

"Like take this gray, wobbly thing we're eating that tastes like old rabbit. Is it agar, too?"

"Of course not. It's foie gras."

"What's that?"

"It's duck liver paté."

"I guess we don't have that in Texas."

"It's illegal in Texas."

"Why?"

"It's made by force-feeding a duck till his liver bursts."

"Eew . . . That *should* be illegal."

"We eat lots of strange things, we French. Tripe, the second stomach of the cow. And tiny . . . periwinkles, which we take out of the shell with a straight pin. Pig's trotters. Kidneys in mustard."

"We like a good pig in Texas."

He put his small hand on my pubis. "And we love Texas pigs."

"I declare," I said, lifting his hand and putting it back on the table. "Now I can understand why the French keep their hands in full sight."

He laughed. "You're very droll. I like you."

I winked and said, "It's mutual."

"Now we all have to talk to the person on the other side. You must come to my château in Bourgogne with Adhéaume, of course. I promise to make a Texas barbecue, Yvonne."

I thanked him and turned to the person on my right, a prince who couldn't speak English and had a putty-colored hearing aid. He was very old and seemed bent over by his order, a white enameled cross that looked like something he might have inherited from his grandfather (it was chipped and fissured). He understood after a while that I was American.

I asked him to explain to me what the Knights of Malta were. He spoke at length in a very faint voice, but I gathered it was a Catholic order founded during the Crusades in the eleventh century to provide hospitals to knights wounded in battle with Muslims. He said there were only fifty "professed" knights (*profesés*, that is, those who'd taken vows of poverty and chastity), but that there were about twelve hundred Knights of Malta altogether in the world. It was a sovereign nation that printed its own stamps and money and had embassies in most countries; it was also the only nation with no territory (I thought of the Panthers and the Palestinians). Its head-quarters were in Rome and the pope was the titular head, though the knights had their own prince with the rank of cardinal. I must confess that Justine, who'd studied the Knights, confirmed the next evening what the prince had told me.

"But tell me, Prince, most of these men look like rich roués—how can they have taken vows of poverty and chastity?"

The prince laughed and said he didn't think any of the professed knights were here tonight.

"Is it true you have to be a noble to be admitted?"

The prince looked embarrassed.

I said, "Forgive me for my American questions. We're not very discreet, are we?"

He seemed charmed by my apology, smiled, and tried to speak but choked on his *tournedos Rossini* (a little steak with more of that wretched foie gras smeared on top) and I waited quietly, hands in lap, while he struggled to spit it up, making terrible sounds and drooling long thick streams of saliva. I felt terrible but thought it best to do nothing. Adhéaume leaped up and started to beat the old man on the back, but the prince waved him away. He went on struggling, but I could tell he was still breathing in and out and I knew from my first-aid course at school that that was a sign he'd survive. At last he settled down, though he was very pale and his eyes were moist. He tried to speak in a ghostly whisper but I put my finger to my luscious lips and he nodded and smiled, coughed some more and drank a sip of water.

At last he could speak normally (albeit faintly) and he said, "I'm not sure any of the professed are here tonight—it can get pretty rowdy and the tickets are expensive. Oh, there's one! You see that little bald man at table three? That's the comte de Saint-Esprit. He's taken vows."

"Is he a monk?"

"No, a knight."

"That's so glamorous."

The prince looked at me quizzically, like a hen who's hard of hearing and isn't quite sure she's heard a mating call.

True to the promise of *une soirée rustre*, at first a few guests, soon almost all, broke into throwing bread pellets at one another. Some knights were standing on their chairs and taking aim. The poor little professed knight seemed to be a special target. Adhéaume was dancing on his chair and ululating; he'd pulled his shirt out and we all had a glimpse of gray belly. I was afraid his chair might break. He was obviously *bien arrosé* (drunk).

After a dull crème caramel, the bewigged majordomo went past again, pounding his muted cymbal, this time to move us into the theater. Adhéaume had mopped his face with his napkin, arranged his clothes, and came panting up to accompany me.

For me the most magical moment at the Opéra Comique is after the houselights go down and before the curtain rises, when the only visible things are the small blue windows in the door of each box seat, light coming from the corridors behind. The big audience is reduced to a black, breathing, rustling, perfumed mass unseen but alive in the faint fairy lights, the blue squares. Though they are square, not round, the windows make me think they're portholes and we're at sea. Then the curtain goes up to discover a stage brilliantly lit, the dust swirling festively in the draft. Unfortunately we were treated to a male chorus from Offenbach's threadbare *La Grande-Duchesse de Gérolstein*, "*Piff, Paff, Pouf*," sung by General Boum. Since it was only forty seconds long, we had it twice. Luckily a real female singer came out and sang the sprightly words, "*Ah! Comme j'aime les militaires*" ("Oh, how I love soldiers"). When she let out the scored mouse squeaks, the merrymakers in the audience and onstage all burst into thunderous applause. Next a man in a black supplice with a white Maltese cross inscribed on his chest came out wearing a long purple robe and a velvet collar, blue on one side and red on the other.

"What does that symbolize?" I whispered to Adhéaume.

"The purple because his family has been in mourning for Our Lord since the First Crusade, the blue for Our Lady, and the red for Golgotha— he's the warden of his family chapel in Wittenberg."

"You have Germans here?"

"German, if you insist. I think of him as a little bit cousin."

There were many speeches and toasts, as champagne was passed again and again, in the theater itself. I was very eager to get home. I thought, I hope the knights left a big deposit to pay for all the broken glass and booze-soaked red plush and the live cigarettes tossed carelessly on the *strapontins* (the folding seats at the end of rows for an overflow crowd). I'd estimate there was $10,000 worth of damage. Not to mention all the breadcrumbs trampled into the carpets.

"Let's go," I said to my date.

"Had enough?" He smiled enigmatically around his cigarette holder. I was living in both languages and translating feverishly and had a bad headache, or was it just linguistic fatigue? "Let's go," he whispered in English. "Do you feel like you've just spent an evening amongst the Hottentots?"

"Ancient, titled ones." Despite my disappointment and weariness, I still felt I'd passed muster with the rarest of rare birds, the titled French.

CHAPTER 7

About a month later, early in March, I received a letter from Yvette. It looked very bedraggled, had been mailed in mid-February, and bore stamps from Colombia.

Dear Yvonne,

I miss you terribly and think of you constantly and finally am setting my lazy self down to write you.

Here I am in Jericó, Colombia. As you know, I've never felt worthy of being baptized and received into the Church but I'm living in the convent of the Missionary Sisters of Immaculate Mary and Saint Catherine of Siena here in Jericó. It is an order founded by the blessed Laura Montoya y Upegui not so long ago; she worked with the Indians here in Antioquia, about 100 km from Medellin. We're hoping she'll be made the first Colombian saint before long! She's already a Venerable. Soon a Blessed.

You'd love this town! It's so typical. I'm sitting in the town square. Children—children of all colors in shorts with glossy black hair—are playing noisily all around me. There are many little stands selling things to eat. One sunburned lady, almost a midget, is hawking candy and chewing gum. Another lady, with long, lank hair, who looks indigenous, is selling something stuffed with *dulce de leches*. A donkey is plodding down the street pulling a cart with big black automobile tires. The adult men wear big cowboy hats, but straw ones, and square shoulder bags made of palomino hide. We're high in the hills but palm trees are in the valley below and pines up above; the weather is perfect, the temperature of the Garden of Eden, one imagines.

Many of the houses are just one story high, but those that are two stories have balconies behind a grill of curved wood spindles. The people like bright colors—bright green doors, dark blue walls, pistachio façades. There are birds-of-paradise planted on the other side of the square. In the wilds outside town you sometimes see the bright plumage of a small parrot. There are sixteen churches in town. Right beside me is the rather ugly and recent adobe cathedral. Much prettier is a nearby church with sky-blue vaults, the Immaculate Heart of Mary. On top of a hill is a huge white statue of Christ, his arms extended to bless the whole countryside. There are many small streams in the immediate vicinity. On Saturday night the campesinos get blind drunk on aguardiente, a clear alcoholic drink that looks like vodka; I stay safely at home after sunset on Saturday while the men stagger around town like zombies. Luckily, the people are very sweet and humble—and sober!—the rest of the week. It's probably sinful to say so, but many of them are ugly—limping or missing teeth or tiny and deformed. Our convent has a lovely inner garden lined with white columns; the roofs are all green tiles, overlapping like the scales of a pangolin. The people speak Spanish very clearly, but I'm constantly learning about their social customs (you must be going through the same thing in Paris). I know you're not a believer, but you're a kind, generous person and our rather controversial bishop says that you don't have to be Catholic to be saved. (He draws the line at Masons, whom he won't bury in holy ground.) I include you in my prayers twice a day. I can go a week or two without speaking a word of English, though soon I'm going to start to teach our bishop English. He wants to be included in the church dialogue everywhere!

Someone nearby is strumming a guitar. It's really lovely here—you must visit some day! Of course, it's a simple, unsophisticated world compared to Paris, I imagine.

I've been very inspired by our bishop, who really embraces the poor of our region. The rich landowners detest him and accuse him of being a Communist, which isn't true (Communists are atheists, after all). But he loves the poor as did Our Lord. His critics say he has a hidden agenda and a hatred of the wealthy; he's involved in a dispute with the papal nuncio, which journalists have caught wind of and have completely distorted in the press. Although the bishop, Oscar Geldbach, is dedicated to the poor, he loves all of us sinners and prays for us all constantly.

What is my day like? I usually awaken at about four (probably the same hour when you come home from a ball and go to bed). After I tidy up, I kneel on the hard tile floor and pray for two hours. Just after terce (around nine A.M.) I begin tutoring the village children in Latin and, in the case of one little boy who wants to be a priest, in Greek; math (up through plane geometry) is something I also teach, as well as philosophy. I wish I knew something they might actually use, like leather-working or animal husbandry—maybe I'll go back to school to learn them. I have some mundane tasks at the convent, including gardening and washing the tile floors and polishing the silver articles used on the altar during Mass. I enjoy gardening so much that I've asked the Mother Superior to take away that task; I prefer something duller and more painful. Something the other sisters complain about, like husking endless ears of corn for our tortillas. I embrace every job with true joy.

For a long while Mother María Concepción was very harsh with me. I suppose she distrusted me because I'm American and won't be baptized. She's always pointing out some tile bit I didn't wash (you know how shortsighted I am). Once I clumsily tipped over a ceramic pot of suds and broke it. Mother María whispered, "What else do you expect from a rich American?"

At first I thought her constant disapproval was unfair and cruel, and I prayed to God to open her eyes—but the only result was that God turned away from me, hid His face with His hand, and my spiritual life became arid as a desert. Then I understood that Mother María wanted me to embrace my work for the Sacred Sisterhood with all the care and attentiveness of which I was capable. And in my heart of hearts I still suspected that I was special, that I was a sort of tourist who could always go home rather than a traveler who had no place to return to except Heaven. Moreover, about that time I begged God to send me to Hell, since no one there worshipped Him; even in Hell I could adore Him so that he would look down on the map of the universe and see at least one point of light in Hell. I'm in love with affliction; I could not ask God to raise me from Hell, which would be an offense against His infinitely tender Love, which has made me the gift of affliction.

Actually, that's an idea I stole from Saint Thérèse of Lisieux, the "Little Flower"—stole or it resonated within me. I also liked her goofy idea (she was fifteen when she wrote it down) that she could be a toy to amuse baby Jesus, a little ball; he might toss her aside as distractible children do and forget all about her—and then, spying her one day under the curtains, rush to pick her up and play with her again and again. I'd like to be the baby Jesus's ball. But you must think I'm crazy! Or that I've become simple-minded (Saint Thérèse was a bit dim). For most people I don't exist—I'm the barren fig tree. I do love the sweet naivete of Saint Thérèse. Some people say she was fat and stupid.

I usually attend Mass every day and usually I communicate daily (I had to get special permission from Bishop Oscar since I am not a Catholic). You can't imagine how happy that makes me! It occurs to me each time I take the host on my tongue that in Heaven, He will feed me directly (but I promised myself that I wouldn't go all crazy pious on you).

I think of you during my prayers every day, how you have submitted to a discipline as well, to learn a complex language and a whole new set of subtle customs, how you mayn't eat too much and must endure endless fittings during which couturiers stab you with their little straight pins, how you must always smile even when you have one of our horrible migraines, how for the moment you're friendless, transplanted from our blowsy, comfortable Texas with all your sorority sisters to a stern, austere Paris, still suffering from wartime shortages and committed to a rigorous code of hints and manners. You're a quick study but even you must feel overwhelmed sometimes by how *muted* every ironic word must be, how *loaded*. At least that's how I remember your friend Pauline (isn't it her grandmother you're staying with?). Of course, that's racist to say—I'm sure the French are fundamentally like everyone else, if we can even generalize about "the French." My job is not to love everyone for himself but to love the Christ in every person.

My bishop is Swiss but, in spite of his name, French-speaking from Geneva and not German from Zurich. Bishop Oscar is very quiet but very loving, in his fifties, I suppose. I gather that when he first arrived on this continent he was quite conservative politically and theologically, but in the fifteen intervening years he's become "radical" in the original sense of returning to his "roots," i.e., to the roots of Christ's message, especially in the Sermon on the Mount. He sees how brutal and selfish the big landowners can be, how influential they are with the police, the government, and even (alas) with the hierarchy of the Church. Whereas Bishop Oscar started out obedient in all things, now he gives weekly broadcasts from the cathedral and often touches on questions of social equality. He does so only in conformity with Christ's love of the poor and his distrust of the rich; in all things he obeys Christ's vicar and Peter's heir, the pope. Bishop Oscar has undergone the spiritual exercises of Saint Ignatius Loyola, a four-week training that I myself am participating in, halfway through. One of the crucial methods is imagining everything about Our Lord's life, the places he preached, the people he met, the Marriage at Cana—how it looked, smelled, how the wine tasted, what his cloak felt like to the lips when kissed. The sound of sheep bells or a horse trotting. It's really like Stanislavski's "sense memory," and you can't imagine how vivid all these precious subjects of meditation become! As you recall, Stanislavski taught his actors not to attempt to re-create the emotions of the past but to remember in hallucinatory detail the sensory surround of each moment. He thought if you can remember the sights, smells, sounds—then the elusive feelings will come flooding back. And that's more or less what Saint Ignatius taught, too.

It's great to have a road map toward sanctity—and to have Bishop Oscar as my spiritual advisor. Interestingly, Saint Ignatius Loyola warned the spiritual advisor not to be too strict with the postulant and not to dictate to him or her the "right" way. Left to his own devices he might come up with something new or at least more fitting, more appropriate. Not that Bishop Oscar needs to be warned to be kind. And Saint Ignatius Loyola does instruct the postulant not to harm his health through excessive fasting or long vigils (necessary wisdom for me, who is so greedy for suffering—or what Saint Teresa of Ávila calls the "delectable pain" God visits on believers).

Am I in love with Bishop Oscar?

As you know, I've never felt the slightest carnal desire, though of course I recognize it is a legitimate, God-given appetite if it is blessed by marriage and indulged in strictly for procreation. If children are the natural fruit of marriage, then it is also true that unbridled passion can be the most destructive human sentiment. I say "unbridled," because I'm thinking of the chariot allegory in which Plato conceives of the charioteer as the intellect guiding two horses, one representing reason and the other concupiscence; the charioteer's job is to control both horses.

But as you know, the nuns think of themselves as "brides of Christ" and even wear wedding rings; they are usually very proud of their spouse and their parents are delighted with their son-in-law (don't think I'm mocking anyone; I'm just trying to speak as vividly as possible). So even this spiritual version of serving God is marital.

I never think of Bishop Oscar as a man. Or rarely. Once on a very hot day I caught a whiff of his underarm odor (that sounds silly) and I thought to myself only a man could smell like that, like a brackish pond. It wasn't desire I felt, but rather a kind of animal recognition bordering on repulsion. Then I prayed and thought of the great physical sacrifice a healthy man still in his prime must constantly make to be celibate (I'm guessing chastity must be easier for a woman. Maybe not). I've heard that if women forego sex for a long time they forget about it, whereas men become more and more tormented.

No, I don't think of Bishop Oscar as a man except insofar as I picture a man when I pray to God. He is witty, charming, playful and wise, sustaining, strict. I've never met a person more enlightened or kinder. Like me, he agrees that the poor are dearer to God than anyone else and that our highest mission should be to serve them.

Which brings me to a problem. As you know, you and I have considerable resources. I'm tempted to spend everything I have on the indigenous population who live in the rain forest, who die young from hunger and disease, who do not even wear clothes, who are gentle and naive but far from being "saved" or even baptized. Their life expectancy is forty. But if I give them my millions, will I destroy or at least distort their culture? I pray constantly for guidance.

Daddy and Bobbie Jean are threatening to come down here. You know how strangely attached he is to me. Maybe that's why I turn to Bishop Oscar like a flower to the sun; I feel safe with him. Maybe Daddy has caught wind that I might do something foolish with my fortune. I made the mistake of talking to Daddy's banker when I was back in Dallas last Christmas. Bankers are not as discreet as priests.

I love you, Yvonne. I know I once offended you by saying I love the Christ in you, which is true, but I also love you as my sister, my twin.

CHAPTER 8

I was thrilled and troubled by Yvette's letter, by her way of anticipating every thought of mine, every objection and assent. It worried me that she'd give all her money away to some flea-bitten perspiring *priest* and I was glad that Daddy might put a stop to that sort of foolishness. It was obvious she was in love with Oscar. I wondered about her crush on "Father" Oscar, given her horrid past with our real father.

Jericó sounded ghastly, with its magenta walls, mules sashaying past, and men and their male shoulder-strap purses (firemen and cops in Paris—tacky men like that—carry male purses because their trousers are so tight and pocketless). And all those nuns on their knees at four A.M. I thought at least she was comparatively safe in that village—but what about all those drug smugglers? I'd heard cocaine came from Colombia—was it a bit like novocaine? People said it wasn't addictive. It just gave you crazy energy.

Adhéaume began to drop by regularly at his aunt Spanky's for her horrible dinners. Even Mme de Castiglione remarked on how singular it was. "He's always been devoted to family—it's almost a cult with him. But we have much more brilliant family members than I—women who still tend a musical salon or a monarchist one. Women who can still attract a François Mauriac or Iannis Xenakis, the great Greek composer. We had the Daudets till recently (they died). You mention Hemingway—I met him! No, I never read him but he was a very nice man. Poor when

I knew him, but handsome—as handsome as Boni de Castellane." We loved our Spanky.

Adhéaume always had something amusing to say or report. He was in Amsterdam to see a Vermeer show and came back with a complete canal's worth of miniature Dutch blue china replicas of tall, skinny houses. He had a woman in veils who smelled of cigarettes come by one evening to read our tarot cards (she could see an aristocratic marriage in my future, which I must confess thrilled me). He often accompanied Spanky to morning Mass, but he was usually still in evening clothes with a wilted flower in his lapel. He knew everything about seventeenth- and eighteenth-century French furniture and never stopped talking about *goût* (taste, not excretions or "goo"). He had very precise evaluations of people, especially women: "She is an exquisite beauty, fundamentally shy, coldhearted but theoretically devoted to her friends." Or he could say, "Madamoiselle Morgan, a little heavyset, was very elegantly dressed, with a pleasant, healthy face, an overwhelmingly good constitution, a purposeless busyness, a lively curiosity about everything, more receptive than creative. She didn't get along with her father. Her mother adored her. Her brothers resented her independence." If he thought a woman ugly he'd say she looked like a toe without a nail.

He took me horseback riding. I wasn't so sure about an English saddle; I was used to hanging on to the knob of a big old comfortable Western saddle, but my thigh muscles were strong and I had a good "seat." I think Adhéaume was pleased. I had a very Baptist cousin come visit me. She was rich, lived in the Panhandle, her family had invented a cure for blackleg, something cows get, and Adhéaume took us to La Tour d'Argent. She insisted we three hold hands to say a blessing before we ate our bloody ducks; that must have been a first for him and La Tour d'Argent ("Dear Lord, bless the bloody birds we are about to eat and bring peace and happiness to my beloved Why-Von and to her nice French friend. Amen").

Cousin Dorothy was horrified by his offer to serve us wine, but in her best coquettish Texas way, she slapped his arm with her gloves, laughed, and exclaimed, "Oh you! The very idea!" Luckily he understood his faux pas instantly. The French have a sort of social gyroscope that orients them very fast. After lunch he invited us to the Musée Gustave Moreau, once the artist's private house; the first floor, where the family lived, is divided up into tiny rooms chockablock with heavy furniture, but the studio, up above, is tall and all glass and sunstruck. Moreau had his sketches put between panes of glass on a spindle that opened like the leaves of a book. Cousin Dorothy, always smiling and dressed in baby blue, looked at them suspiciously; her smile never faded but I saw her mood darken when she looked at the lurid paintings, thick with impasto. "Here, Dorothy," Adhéaume said, "you'll like these biblical scenes—Salomé dancing with the head of John the Baptist or Judith decapitating Holofernes . . ."

"I declare," Dorothy said. "I wish they weren't in *my* Bible."

She was staying in Hotel le Bristol in a suite, a room for her maid and another for her two Scotties. She invited us up to her room for an iced tea, which came with mint leaves poking out of the top that she cast aside. Adhéaume played with the dogs, Sir Walter and Bobbie Burns, though I could tell he was too fastidious to really enjoy their yapping and licking and constant circling about; Bobbie even peed a bit and a drop landed on Adhéaume's church shoes (later he had his shoes handmade in London; he always said you could tell a gentleman by his shoes).

But he was very well behaved. He chitchatted with Cousin Dorothy in an instantly improvised version of that horrible Texas custom of "visiting." He asked her about her plans to visit London and Berlin and where she'd be staying (Claridge's and the Kempinski). Of the former he said, "They have a great high tea and it's five minutes from Bond Street," and of the latter he said, "Best swimming pool in Berlin. Every starlet has her bikini session there," and once again Dorothy playfully slapped his arm and said, "Oh, you!" I could tell she didn't like him. I just knew she was sitting there thinking, And he's sure as heck a Catholic, too. I knew Adhéaume would sooner die than be dull and she'd sooner die than be risqué. She could talk about the weather for hours; his mother had taught him it was vulgar to say it was too warm.

He began to advise me on my clothes. I wondered if he was gay or just French. I resented his advice but I was clever enough to recognize it was good advice. I wondered how a *man* of all things could have such an eye for hats, gloves, shoes, jewelry, and how to put together an ensemble down to the perfume. He liked me to wear honeysuckle, or *chèvrefeuille*; I wondered which mistress it reminded him of. He said all American perfumes smelled like bubble gum.

"Taste" he thought of as his strong suit. His was very conservative, "blue chip," as I said. He was infernally picky; he could spend two hours at Puiforcat choosing a serving spoon. He wouldn't wear a tie that didn't come from Charvet or eat a peach that wasn't from Hédiard. You know I'm not religious, but something Protestant in me rebelled against all this materialism disguised as elegance.

We "motored" to the South of France and the Var, a Texas-size trip of eight hours, from Paris. We were going to visit Henri, the Red Duke, who'd remembered his invitation and made it a second time. The château was lovely, at the top of a landscaped hill above the village; the houses were like children clinging to their mother's hoop skirts, the walls around the castle. When we arrived on the gravel path, eight liveried footmen minus the wigs, thank God, were lined up, four and four, on each side of our car. The American in me wanted to say howdy to each of them, but I followed Adhéaume's example and reserved my smile for the duke, who trotted out and kissed my hand like a dunking bird sticking his felt beak in a glass of water—except no touching with the lips (Adhéaume later explained that it was bad form to kiss a lady's hand outdoors, but his point seemed odd, given that we were already on the Duke's grounds).

The château had a large square part that was sixteenth century and an adjoining eighteenth-century tower, far more graceful, with wonderful plasterwork tendrils in bisque against a pale-blue background, all curved, of course—it was our tower. The duke had placed me on the second floor and Adhéaume on the third. "Of course, it's Liberty Hall here, and you can circulate freely." He winked naughtily at me. "Breakfast in bed, but only after you pull the rope beside your bed. No surprises—this isn't a French farce. In the morning do you like café au lait and croissants and orange juice?"

"Yes," we said in chorus and the majordomo nodded and left the room. Another, younger servant, timid, afraid to look us in the eye, delivered our luggage and slipped away, as insubstantial as a cloud in trousers.

When we were alone, I said to Adhéaume, "Shouldn't we have brought a house gift?"

"*Pourquoi? Très mauvais ton, les cadeaux.*"

And that was that. With him there was no use saying, "But in my country," since he despised every country except France. He thought he was doing me (and all Americans) an enormous civilizing favor to teach us French ways; no cultural relativism here. Years later in Istanbul we had only crossed the threshold into the world's largest covered bazaar before he said, "There's nothing here. Let's leave." I insisted we look around and in fact we found a small gated bazaar in the very center that was full of antiques and curios and jewelry, where Adhéaume bought some lovely hand-painted Ottoman water glasses.

Eventually I figured out that since the *gratin* endlessly visits one another for country weekends, no one should bring a gift. A bottle of wine? An insult to the host's cellar. A book? Possibly, if one has written it. A lovely piece of Sicilian pottery, if sent afterward with a bread-and-butter note (*une lettre de château*). And of course a handsome tip to the servants.

Communist he may have been but Henri was very harsh with the servants, constantly muttering reprimands about the table service ("Forgive me, but he's new and a total oaf"). The oaf was the same shy boy who'd brought up our luggage. I sneaked a smile at him.

The duke was proud of his English and with reason. I was delighted to be speaking my own language—so restful. And it gave me a chance to be funny, which I loved, and which wasn't yet possible in my rudimentary French. At dinner—a cucumber salad and cold pheasant stuffed with apricots, and a peachy rosé—I was seated in the place of honor, to the right of the duke. There was a Frenchman, small but bristling with virility, and his American wife or possible ex-wife, an actress I'd seen once in a Truffaut film, a strawberry blonde "in the flower of age," as the French refer to people in their fifties. She was slim, simply but beautifully dressed, radically "lifted" ("Her face was butchered," Adhéaume said later), heavily sunscreened. I liked her right off. She touched my arm as we went in for dinner, as American women will do, and I hoped we could gossip later. The conversation was in English but typical of social people in that it was all about schedules and other people's sex scandals. ("She told him he could say anything in his memoirs except that they *didn't* make love—after all she was keeping him." "Venice in September, of course, Gstaad for Christmas, Tangier in April—with lots of side trips to London for clothes and shows." "Carlo said he would give her anything for Mme de Pompadour's gold microscope and she said, 'All right, send me your boyfriend, the baron, for a night,' and he said, 'Fine,' and he did but the only problem was that the baron fell for her and became her full-time live-in lover. *Flûte!* Carlo was furious.")

I was dying to get the American actress, Helen, alone, so after dinner when we moved into the library to drink thyme *tisane* out of a bamboo-sleeved thermos and tiny Chinese cups, I installed myself on the love seat and patted the place next to me, staring at her. She turned around as if I might be looking at someone behind her. When she realized I was inviting her to join me, she shrugged slightly, smiled, and came over.

"How nice to meet an American!" I said. "We're pretty thin on the ground here. Where are you from, Helen?"

"California. Sacramento. Actually, right after the war I was *Miss* California. That's when Édouard found me. He fell madly in love with me and proposed within two weeks, so that's how Miss California became the Princess of Foix."

"Doesn't that beat all? Where is . . ."

"Foix. F-O-I-X. In the Pyrenees. And you?"

"Dallas."

"Oh. Actually, I'm divorcing the prince."

We each stared at our hands and she asked, "So how do you know Adhéaume?"

"Mutual acquaintance. His aunt."

"Spanky? She's a character. Are you rich?"

"Yes."

"Watch out. No wonder she introduced you to Adhéaume."

I was on the verge of bristling, but I was too curious. "Watch out for what?"

She looked up to make sure no one was in earshot. "He thinks he's God's gift to womanhood. Worse, he has a mission to educate American women in the finer things of life. Your money for his taste. His ability to 'compose,' to 'arrange.' But he's a good guy. Harmless."

"You seem to know him very well," I said, sucking a swizzle stick caked with sugar.

"We've all known each other for donkey's years, as the English say. What are you doing over here?"

"It's my junior year abroad."

"As a broad, I always think it should be."

"I'm very innocent," I said with a smile.

"You're on the second floor and he's on the third?"

"Yes."

"Expect a visitor."

"You speak from experience?"

"I'm very innocent," she said.

I felt even lonelier than before. It's as if I were a dog and spotted another but on closer examination it turned out to be a cat.

It disturbed me that Adhéaume might like me for my money alone. Daddy's wasn't a famous name like Rockefeller and there were lots of poor Crawfords, so Pauline must have done some research, which seemed so craven. The cliché was that Americans were materialists and it was true we took serious money seriously, but most of us couldn't be bothered to be fortune hunters. Maybe the rich in Texas ended up with the equally rich, but that was just how social life was organized. In France, it seemed people tried to put together "amusing" evenings (one actress, one admiral, one academician, one axe murderer if he'd written a book about it), which was much more fun but exposed people to *les interessés*.

As the brandy flowed, Adhéaume sat closer and closer on the striped love seat. When I caught Helen's eye, she winked. I hated that we were so predictable, like those smartphones today that always finish your message for you—correctly. "I had such a"—(next word: "wonderful") (next word: "evening") ("with you")—and thus your most sincere sentiments are predicted automatically. He leaned close and said, "Don't trust Helen. She has an evil tongue. I once rejected her."

"I should clear up one thing: I'm not going to marry you."

"Then don't," he said without changing color or hesitating.

"Besides," I added, "you'd want me to convert to Catholicism."

"I see you've been thinking it over."

"But I don't want to convert."

"And I wouldn't want a *Baptist* baronne. I didn't realize you were so dogmatic."

"It's harder to get divorced if you're Catholic."

"Why would you contemplate divorce before you're even married?"

"I'm very practical. Daddy might know he's going to buy a new Cadillac but he'd still test-drive all the new Lincolns. Realistic, as you say in France with such pride."

He made a puffing sound, as the French do when stymied. "Not too romantic," he said under his breath. "Test-drive . . ."

I didn't see him for a week and I realized my Paris life was dull without him.

Helen had given me her number but sounded vague when I called. "It's just that I have so much to do these days," she wailed. "I have a charity event to plan. It's the children's ski holidays and we're all off to Verbier. And after that Édouard's planned an annoying little holiday in the sun in Marie-Galante, the last thing I need. Édouard likes it because it's a *département* of France and everything's the same, the news, the postage stamps, the money, and you don't have to go through immigration and you can speak French."

"Where is it? I thought you were divorced."

"Guadeloupe . . . In the Caribbean. We are getting divorced. But we see each other for the children's sake. Actually, I'm looking for a new husband."

"Oh."

"I long to see you. In March, probably. *À bientôt*," she whispered, as a well-bred English girl might trail off with a soft, soprano, slightly anguished "Bye . . ."

Spanky never read the press but, just by coincidence, she left the society page of some newspaper lying around—and there was Adhéaume's picture, dancing with the young princesse de Polignac in the château at Maisons-Laffitte, and in a group shot with an American, Jacqueline Bouvier, and in another picture at a costume ball dressed as a "hippy" with J. P. Morgan's great-grandaughter "Bob," as the straw man from *Le Magicien d'Oz*. "She looks like a rather dangerous lesbian," I said to Spanky.

"Possibly," Mme de Castiglione said. "Men are excited by lesbians, I've heard." I liked the dopey way Spanky could play dumb as co-conspiritor as well as deny her racy past at Le Chat Noir, or was it in Montmartre? I wondered if pretending to be stupid was just a way of trapping me (and my millions) more easily.

"I think they're exciting," I said. She looked puzzled, as if she hadn't heard me. Answering the question she wanted me to pose, she said, "Adhéume is quite the lady's man."

"What does he *do* with his time all day?"

Spanky shrugged and turned her lips down like a crowned dot, the musical mark for a prolonged pause. "Well, his day doesn't start till noon, I suspect. His mantel is littered with invitations, which courtesy demands he answer somehow. I don't think the poor man has a secretary. Then he probably has a two o'clock lunch somewhere. And that goes on till four thirty. The wine makes him sleepy and he has a nap. Often he goes to an auction; the other day he found a self-portrait by Caruso, dated 1905, signed. Authentic. He paid only ten francs for it. Worth thousands. It seems Caruso was a good artist and would draw self-portraits for friends. Then Addy has one of these *répondeurs automatiques* and he's plagued with all these messages from frantic girls."

"Tell me about this Jacqueline Bouvier."

"She's nobody. Poor, though she claims to belong to the *noblesse d'épée*, but they were actually shoemakers or something in Lyon. She lived here for a while, to be polished (*peaufinée*). Stylish, good French, snobbish, though her face is too wide and her eyes are too far apart. No money."

"What kind of nobility did you mention?"

"My poor darling. We must begin at the beginning, I see. Before the Revolution there were two main kinds of aristocrats—of the sword and of the robe. The sword nobles were very ancient medieval knights like my family, the only ones who had the right to wear a sword. The robe nobles weren't real—they had bought their titles."

"And after the Revolution?"

"Napoleon gave fancy Ruritanian titles to his brigands—*noblesse d'empire*. But no one takes them seriously. How do you say in English? Thugs?"

I began to obsess about Jacqueline Bouvier. She had a wonderful smile and seemed to know how to wear clothes. Someone who knew her said she had a very faint, baby-doll voice—irritating, but men like that (look at Marilyn Monroe). And her name sounded more regal than Yvonne Crawford. I was sure there was money buried somewhere behind that bland, wide face. I heard her stepfather was an Auchincloss—weren't they somebodies? Spanky had a thick book called a Bottin for all the European nobility—their heritage, castles, siblings, current addresses. I wish we had a Blue Book for all Americans: their net worth, first marriages, addresses, nicknames.

When I saw a second newspaper photo of Adhéaume and Mlle Bouvier with the gilded youth (*la jeunesse dorée*) of this season, I went wild with jealousy. I asked Spanky for Addy's phone number and she wrote it out for me, a chilly little smile on her lips.

"Hello, Adhéaume, it's me, Yvonne Crawford."

"Why, hello, Miss Crawford. Forgotten your French already?"

"I don't have many chances to practice it these days."

"What can I do for you, Miss Crawford?"

"You said your *cousine* works for Givenchy? Could you take me there tomorrow afternoon and tell them I want to buy several couture dresses?"

"My *cousine* isn't there every day—she's more of a hostess than a *cadre*—what's that in English?"

"Employee."

"I'll call you right back."

Five minutes extended into ten, then twenty. I wondered if Spanky for some reason forebade all incoming calls on the same principle that caused her to have the hallway lights on a dangerously short half-minute timer. My dearest ambition was to be in the Bottin.

Thirty minutes later Adhéaume telephoned to say that we were expected at Givenchy's at four thirty. "I'll come by to fetch you at four," he said in English (there is no French equivalent to "fetch"); I noticed with regret how little time he was devoting to socializing with me.

I felt as insignificant as I had when we moved from Ranger to Dallas, a hick with strange turns of speech (I remember saying "I might could" and eliciting peals of laughter), fancy grown-up clothes, no car of my own, a weirdo sister. I felt that Adhéaume had given me a chance, but that I'd somehow failed and now I was cast back into obscurity. I was determined to be unironic with him, polite, nicely dressed, grateful. If I didn't ingratiate myself this time I'd end up conspicuously defeated at Mme de Castiglione's table each evening, eating Jerusalem artichokes with the unlovely Justine and turning in early. Perhaps the worst of that was waking early and having an endless vacant day to face. I'd learned how to nurse a café au lait while flipping through *Allo*, to walk along the Seine on the Left Bank and look at all the books and prints at the *bouquinistes*, to end up across from Notre-Dame at Shakespeare and Company with its English-language books and periodicals (I'd talked once to an American poet there named Ferlinghetti, one of those beatniks, he'd made clear). Then I'd stroll up to the Café de Flore, have a salad and a Coke—and it would still be only twelve thirty. A little window-shopping at expensive stores (*lécher les vitrines*) and a taxi home for a nap. Then awaking at three, there were still five hours to fill till the gloomy, inedible dinner. Oh . . . and there was a school visit to the Louvre area and an "advanced" French class.

I would go to sit in the park and read a bit—I'd never read so much!

Today I had a simpler problem—how to rekindle Adhéaume's interest and to dress appropriately for Givenchy. I wore very luxurious silk underwear, nice black spool heels, one of my silk blouses with the sewn-on foulard, and a dark pencil skirt and matching jacket with a gold brooch. Chic but understated. If only I had time for "unbrushing," but I would have to tease my hair out myself. A black leather purse from Hermès.

I kept rehearsing things to say to Adhéaume, and then pushed my cobwebby speculations away from my face; I'd always done well by being spontaneous in the past. If I started parsing out everything, I'd end up paralyzed. Better just to chatter away. No one expected anything more from a Texas girl. It was strange how he'd gotten under my skin.

And there he was, right on time. I ran to the door, then pulled myself up short and tried to appear casual, though I said, wanting to dose out sincerity, "I'm delighted to see you."

"Really?" he asked, frowning, as if I were going to cause him more pain.

It was raining. We got out of the taxi in a glamorous part of Paris I didn't know yet. We were just a block away from the Hotel George V, he said, and over there was the Champs-Élysées. I liked this area at first glance, the rich nineteenth-century part, the one that "went" with the Ópera Comique, though it was far away, the one that was built when Paris was at its height of wealth and power if not of "taste." Of course, everyone thinks her or his taste is the best, by definition, but I wouldn't swear by mine.

"Isn't Givenchy some sort of count?" I asked.

"They're Venetian. Made tapestries. Were ennobled just before the Revolution. I guess he's some sort of marquis. Protestant. Artistic— grandfather who designed sets for the opera. You should marry him, you wouldn't have to convert. Though you might have to convert him—he likes men."

We entered the vast, marble-lined, underfurnished lobby and were escorted up the curving stairs by an unsmiling, elegant, chatless young woman, tall and painfully thin. We went up only a floor and were met by Adhéaume's cousin, Nathalie, who kissed both of my cheeks though she held her body at some distance so we wouldn't touch. She whispered, "*Enchantée*," pulled away, and smiled. "Right this way," she said, and she led us into a room large enough for two ranks of twenty chairs on each side and ten at the end. A large white-cloth runway ran down the center. All the front-row chairs were occupied by pudgy, badly dressed older women; there was an ashtray on a white stand between every two ladies. Only three clients were smoking but the air was thick with smoke. The second rows on both sides were empty. The room had a sort of canine odor—it must have been all the wet furs.

We found our seats; Nathalie just perched on hers as if she might fly away at any second. The same five models paraded slowly past in different clothes, walking down the white runway, stopping, twirling, wearing hats and white gloves, sometimes sunglasses, always long costume necklaces. I imagined these fashion shows were weekly events for the rich out-of-towners (mostly American) who could afford couture. Nathalie handed me a white square of cardboard, with HG in small gold letters, and a pencil, I suppose so I could write down which dresses I liked. She whispered, "You could choose two day dresses, a simple black dress for cocktails, maybe an evening dress or two." I wondered why the models didn't hold numbers the way they did in Dallas at Neiman's. They'd even talk and smile in Dallas and say, "Oscar de la Renta, two hundred dollars"— and we'd scribble down numeral five or six, all the while eating our crustless chicken-salad sandwiches or smoking or drinking white wine or Cokes. Here the ladies had partially shrugged off their fur capes, wore worn-down (éculés) shoes and boxy suits, murmured to their neighbors, and rarely glanced up at the models. At the end, Givenchy himself came out and all the ladies applauded, though their gloved hands didn't make much noise. He was as tall as de Gaulle, wore a white chemist's coat and a dark tie, had lovely thick hair. He went up to (I guess) three treasured customers then came over to us. He ducked toward my extended hand and said in good English, "Did you see anything you liked?"

"Everything! You're a genius."

Oddly enough he blushed and said, "*Bonjour, Adhéaume.*"

"*Bonjour. Excusez-moi, deux instants.*" And Adhéaume went over to Jacqueline Bouvier. Why hadn't I noticed her before? She was entirely in Givenchy, including an alpaca jacket the color of diluted Pepto-Bismol, a tiny hat the same color, white gloves, and a black dress. They greeted each other with big smiles, Jacqueline and Nathalie waved to each other across the room, Adhéaume bowed quickly and returned to my side.

"I hate you," I said in English.

"Maybe," Givenchy said in French to Nathalie, "Mademoiselle Crawford can make an appointment to come back to have paper patterns made of her and a wicker model of her exact size so we won't have to waste her time with fittings, except the last *essayages*." Then in English, "I'm afraid my staff is exhausted today after the *défilé*."

"Of course."

"Thank you for understanding. So kind of you. Nathalie can list the dresses you liked and make an appointment for another day that will be convenient to you. *Au revoir*, Adhéaume," and Givenchy went over to greet Miss Bouvier.

"I adored the pink suit with the brown hat that looked like unpotted soil," I said.

Adhéaume put me in a taxi and sent me home alone. Nathalie had accompanied us to the taxi stand. Again, two kisses. I thanked her and said she mustn't linger or she'd catch cold. I was furious.

When Adhéaume proposed the next evening, I accepted, though I didn't love him. I'd never loved anyone; I wasn't sure I believed in love.

CHAPTER 9

Dear Yvette,

Guess what? I got married! Of course, I understand why you couldn't come.

My husband is the Baron Adhéaume de Courcy, whose family goes back to the First Crusade. He's ten years older than us, very handsome but not tall, deals in antiques, wants children, he's my landlady's nephew. I'm very happy! Remember how I always wanted to be a French aristocrat? Well, now I'm a baroness. I'll be listed in their Blue Book!

Givenchy made my wedding gown—an Empire bodice with 120 white beads, a wide white silk belt, a ten-foot train carried by two of Adhéaume's adorable nephews, six and eight, and the ring bearer was another relative, this one nine. The church was *huge*, baroque, St. Roch on the Rue Saint Honoré near the Louvre; it was filled with white calla lilies (I wanted carnations but the French associate them with death). We had a small orchestra that played something by someone called Vivaldi, a forgotten Venetian priest now coming back in vogue. There were a hundred guests, mostly Adhéaume's friends, a very handsome priest; this particular church has been through a lot and there are even bullet holes in the façade from when it was sacked during the French Revolution. Saint Roch is the patron saint of people who've been falsely accused and of dogs (a dog saved his life). But you probably know your saints by heart! The reception was a sit-down dinner for fifty at the Ritz in a private dining room—guests could choose filet mignon or lobster thermidor. Lots of champagne.

Daddy paid for it all. He gave me away. Givenchy dressed Bobbie Jean in a royal blue dress and wove pearls into her hair, which was all swept up off her neck. Daddy wore a dark business suit he bought at Lanvin (Adhéaume went with him). They couldn't get that not everyone spoke English. I think Daddy liked Adhéaume more than he might have just because his English is so good (though he and I always speak French, of course).

We had lots of interesting guests. One, Aimery de Lusignan, is the direct descendent of a mermaid and the King of Jerusalem; he is a great guy, a polo champ, and lots of fun. Daddy said he never met so many highfalutin folks. I pawned him off on a family friend, a Communist called the Red Duke, who once lived in Texas and sounds like a good old' boy—you'd love him. They had a lot in common and talked for hours about agar, whatever that is. I didn't dare tell Daddy he was a Communist; you know how worked up he gets about "pinkos." I'm not so sure Bobbie Jean was happy. She was under the impression that Europeans are still living in poverty in bombed-out hovels. She was shocked to discover so much luxury and thinks the "frogs" and "wops" are pulling the wool over American eyes and taking advantage of us with the Marshall Plan. I tried to tell her she's only seeing the *gratin* with us, that the "peasants" are in rough shape. (I'm still not used to calling people "peasants," but I don't know how to translate *paysans*, and besides, everyone likes them, peasants are respected as the backbone of France, though of course they're dirty and uneducated.) Adhéaume thinks of Daddy and Bobbie Jean as something like peasants; he's shocked by how naive they are.

Addy wanted me to join the Church but I thought that was hypocritical to do just for the sake of convention; of course, he thinks it's for family (he's *very* family-oriented) and I've agreed if we have children to raise them Catholic, which here just means baptism, catechism, first Communion, Easter, marriage, and funeral. Nobody ever goes to church or talks about the pope or anything; Addy says they weren't even allowed to read the Bible till 1905, but that can't be true. They're very fierce about the separation of church and state, except the aristocrats, who pretend to be pious but know nothing about Jesus, whom they call Christ. So that we could get married in church I went through the motions—baptism, first Communion, and confirmation—but believe me I had a big reservatio in petto about the whole rigamarole.

My bridesmaids were all relatives of Adhéaume, except Jane Beth was my maid of honor; she was a darling to come over. Givenchy dressed them all in heliotrope with little silver tiaras and Daddy footed the bill except for Jane Beth's, who's richer than all of us. When we saw each other at the airport (I went out to meet her plane) we stamped and squealed ("Jane Beth, oh my God, I can't believe you're here in Paris") and she looked down and said, "Cute shoes," and I cried a little for my lost youth and Addy made fun of us for screaming and acting like kids and making a spectacle of ourselves (remarks I did *not* translate for Jane Beth, you can well imagine). She and I have had so much fun doing all the tourist things (Versailles, Eiffel Tower, Notre-Dame, three-star restaurants, shopping). I took her to the Galant Vert on the Île de la Cité and she loved it but was vexed they didn't understand what a "doggy bag" was and wouldn't give her one for her extra pork chop.

Well, I lost my virginity on my wedding night and it didn't hurt at all. Thank God it was Addy; he was so gentle and romantic and kept calling me his little pigeon. I didn't mind it. You'd be surprised, I didn't bleed much, just enough to satisfy him I was a virgin. He was very sweet and his thing wasn't too big, not like that awful Duke Willens, but it looked big because in Europe they're not circumcised. I don't think I could get to like it, but it wasn't bad. You guessed I always had a crush on Jane Beth, but she's no longer up for it; she said she'd "outgrown" it. Hmnn . . . Anyway, Addy believes in separate bedrooms, which is good (he snores) and when he sees me I want to be at my best (teeth brushed, eyelashes on, hair combed, perfume fresh); I can't bear to have people see me after eight hours of sleeping. You know how some people order breakfast to their hotel rooms and use that as an alarm to wake up? Not me! The poor bellhops . . . Really squalid.

For our honeymoon we didn't go far, just to Provence, which is nice and warm in May, full of flowers. An aunt lent us her farmhouse just outside Saint Rémy de Provence on a huge piece of property. It was sort of primitive with a polished wood cage, a food cellar (eighteenth century), high on the wall to keep the food away from the mice but just for show, though the kitchen wasn't all that modern either. I had a nice breezy room with my own bathroom (functional) and Addy was next door with lots of religious sayings on the wall and framed sheet music in funny old French (Provençal). He said it's terribly important by someone called Mistral. There's a swimming pool, but Addy says it's just a *bassin* for animals and it's *so* cold because it's fed by a *source* (spring). My French is really getting fine-tuned, though Adhéaume's relatives mainly talk about one another and whether their marriages were "good" (meaning high-born or rich). At least they all speak clearly and slowly, sort of like educated Texans, except in French of course. Bobbie Jean and Daddy came down for two days but stayed out of our hair (Bobbie Jean had a guidebook and wanted to see Avignon, which got three stars). Daddy was grumpy because he couldn't wedge the big Cadillac they rented through the narrow streets and it was even worse in Arles, where they had to park and *walk*! You know how they hate to walk. And Bobbie Jean complained about what she called the "French food," though I offered to get them itty-bitty steaks at the butcher's.

Sometimes I feel lonely, specially in the morning. Addy says soon I'll have friends of my own and we should be sure to go to the Fourth of July party at the American embassy in Paris. I thought I had made an American friend, Helen, at the Red Duke's château but that friendship fizzled on the vine. It used to be I mostly made friends with men, but as a married woman that would seem tacky to me, though the French *gratin* expect you to take lovers. I imagine Addy wants me to wait a bit till I'm preggers (wants the bloodlines to be pure).

I guess you're not lonely. You have the bishop. The nuns. Our Lord. Your pupils.

It's fun living in another culture, isn't it, but I'd hate to die in France. I miss Texas. My sorority sisters. You.

Addy thinks I'm a sentimental fool. Ungrateful bitch. But I don't think French people have friends except school chums (if the chums have become a success and live in the sixteenth arrondisement) or family members, whom they don't much like but are loyal to. Condemned for life.

He's sort of mad at me because he didn't realize Daddy put our money in a trust and we can't touch most of it till we're thirty. He never asked and I never told. Well, at least I can be sure he'll stick around for a few years. Cynical? No, I'm happy, but Addy thinks the world owes him a living. He's mad as a cat in a bath because his grandfather spent all their money on chorus girls; he even sold some of their ancestor's tombs, recumbent statues and all, to the Cloisters in New York City. And his father ran after the women, too.

We came here for our honeymoon, I figured out, because he wanted to show me a castle that used to belong to his family. The grounds are beautiful, though the revolutionaries stove in the roof and pillaged it and it's a complete ruin now. But Adhéaume wants to restore it. The ancestors who weren't sold to the Cloisters are buried there. It has eighty-seven rooms—oi! We'll have to go into debt but Adhéaume won't hear of waiting a bit. He's already lined up an interior architect. But we'll have to fix the roof first, and there are miles of it, all very special tiles, dark red and only slightly sloping, originally made in the Tuileries (get it?) but there's still some place Addy knows. (He has all the *bonnes adresses*, as do all French people, they keep them in little notebooks, Mme de Castiglione even has addresses for saddles in Ireland!)

Yvette, I think of you all the time. I think you should join the Catholic Church—how else are you going to become a saint? A "society priest" (yep, we have them in France) told me that to be named a saint, it's like anything else, you need people with money and influence lobbying for you at the Vatican. Nobodies (at least unrepresented nobodies) don't get beatified. Certainly not non-Catholics. Politics plays a part. Is a saint meaningful for our times? Different from the others? He told me that when there was a separation of church and state in 1905, the pope tried to regain ground soon after in France (the oldest daughter of the church) by naming a French saint, Saint Thérèse of Lisieux—a sort of consolation prize. She died so young and did so little they had to attribute a posthumous miracle to her (pushing back a German tank in World War I).

Hope you're not falling for that sweaty bishop with the German name.

Love,

Your sister, Baronne Yvonne (rhymes)

Adhéaume bought us (with my money) a beautiful big apartment just two blocks from the Arc de Triomphe on the Avenue Foch, the most expensive street in the world. It used to be called the Avenue de l'Imperatrice, as Adéaume explained, named after Empress Eugénie, but then it was redubbed for a World War I hero. It's the broadest street in Paris and is planted with hundreds of flowers and exotic trees, meant to serve as a royal road for the belle époque beauties in their carriages between the Arc de Triomphe and the Bois de Boulogne, where they all go to see and be seen, as the elegant men trot past on horses, sniffing their scented *mouchoirs* (the men, not the horses). The Rothschilds live nearby. We have a ballroom the size of a football field. Our very first dinner we had twenty-two guests, with a liveried footman behind each chair (hired for the occasion). The food was indifferent, but people expect that of aristocrats. Good cooking is considered bourgeois. The only cheese permitted was odorless, tasteless goat cheese, but best of all (classiest), Adhéaume told me, is no cheese at all. We drank champagne before and during the meal *à la russe* and people smoked like the Russians between courses. Nothing afterward except coffee or herbal tea (brandy is for drunks). You can see, I've learned a lot—a lot of trivial nonsense. A good hostess takes a newcomer around to the other guests and says, "Philippe is an art historian at the Louvre and Janet is an American, Philippe is an art historian at the Louvre and Henri is a retired banker who collects African sculpture, Philippe is an art historian at the Louvre and Madeleine is a great niece of Anatole France who has just redone her house in the seventh . . ." People think it's intrusive or unnecessary (since everyone knows everyone already—theoretically), but they're actually grateful to be handed a topic.

I could see Adhéaume must have been running up astronomical bills on credit, using my good name and the myth of Texas oil millions; he certainly didn't have a franc to his name. Daddy does have millions but not in oil so much now; recently he's invested in downtown Dallas real estate and owns several blocks of office buildings and has put up his very own suburban galleria all rented out to high-end shops. I think Bobbie Jean is the real power behind the throne. She's the greedy one.

Suddenly one day my French was good enough that I understood exactly what Addy was telling his friend Guillaume as they smoked horrid cigars in the next room. Addy didn't know I was measuring a couch in the pink salon for a new summer slipcover and that I could hear them guffawing like schoolboys.

"It's how to be married?" Guillaume asked, with a laugh in his voice.

Addy actually laughed. "Claustrophobic."

"But at least you have no more money worries (*ennuis de sou*)."

"It's not true. We're living, rather grandly, on credit."

"*Et les amours?*"

"*Je suis fidel.*"

"*Pas vrai!*"

"*Plus ou moins.*" (He laughs.)

"But you always liked the little ladies."

"My Texane is enough for me."

"Are you joking?" ("*Sans blague?*")

"I want sons. Then she'll be mine forever. I perform my matrimonial duties in a very regular way, three times a week."

"And the other four nights?"

"I'm not as obsessed as you."

"You're kidding." ("*Tu rigoles.*")

Then they started talking politics and I slipped away unheard and unnoticed.

Then she'll be mine forever—those words sounded ominous: cynical, selfish. My heart was pounding. I thought, Maybe I'll start taking the pill. How to convince him I don't want to be penetrated three times a week like a broodmare? He pretends to be romantic before and after, but it's pretty unconvincing. I can tell he's performing his "duties," as if that's all it takes to keep me quiet and footing the bills. He probably thinks he's doing little me a favor by filling me with his noble sperm.

The next few nights I kept my door locked and at breakfast he looked disgruntled. Finally he whispered when the maid left the room, "You don't want sons?"

"They might be daughters."

"One of each, okay?" But he pretended he was talking to a child: "Shall I explain to the little one how babies are made?"

"No need. But I haven't been in the mood (*état d'ame*)."

"Unless you're having your period (*tes règles*), you have no right to deny your husband—not in the first year of marriage."

"Who says?"

"I say."

"Oh, the Autocrat of the Bedroom," I said, but he didn't catch the allusion, too American. Like most French people of the period who'd passed the baccalaureate he knows a few standard works by consecrated French authors (usually in *précis* form), but almost nothing in English (except Shakespeare, whose *Hamlet* was read in the Gide translation). That was fine with me, since I'm not a book person and reading is appropriate only for trains in my opinion. Why read if you can do anything else?

Adhéaume has constant plans to buy beautiful paintings and furniture from the past. Every antique dealer in Paris is willing and eager to tell him about the wonderful eighteenth-century *commode* that had just come on the market. ("Yes, the old Marquise Belleboeuf finally died and her son Geoffroy wants to sell all this gloomy old stuff, as he calls it, and replace it with rubber and steel furniture and those big horrid Arcimboldo paintings he collects of vegetable people. Of course, nothing could be more exquisite than the Belleboeuf collection of old furniture—including a door lunette painted by Fragonard, very characteristic of a girl on a swing and a boy pushing her, staring at her panties all pink cheeks and silk trousers against a backdrop of a huge exhausted stone Silenus, in case you didn't notice the eroticism. These items will never come up for sale again; they'll be grabbed by a Cleveland museum and how much more *sympathique* to keep them in France with a Courcy," and here he moved in for the kill, "who will know how to *arrange* them.") Addy was certain that that was his strong suit—an eye for composing.

He had agents scouting "buys" or "attractive possibilities," as he would say; it was really like a private postal service in some earlier century. If he heard of an "important" Gobelins tapestry showing Louis XIV on horseback pointing toward a Batavian haystack he'd just conquered, the victory described eloquently on a scroll just beside him, the words written by Racine, no less, who was the official court historian—that's all Adhéaume could think about, though he had no place to put all his treasures. That's why it was absolutely essential we start restoring the family château; that tapestry would be *éclatant* in the Great Hall just as the Coromandel lacquered screen would be perfect for the baronne's wardrobe.

His other obsession was his own clothes, which were bespoke, made for him on Savile Row. He was endlessly plying the English Channel for hats at Lock's or shirts at Turnbull & Asser or suits at Gieves & Hawkes. His jackets always looked tight on him, as if they'd run out of that kind of fabric—a "popinjay," isn't that what they call such gentlemen? That degree of narcissism doesn't match with any Texas idea of manliness; can you imagine John Wayne fussing over collar width, suit sleeves that unbuttoned and rolled back, trousers that "broke" just so over his cowboy boots? No rear vent, so that he looked like he had a duck ass? Detachable celluloid shirt collars?

He was absurdly demanding with the servants. The furniture must not lose its patina through sacrilegious polishing. He sent the woman who does our ironing for "lessons" with the Spanish ambassador's wardrobe mistress, who knew how to turn out a shirt to perfection. Geneviève, our maid, was very humiliated. He gave the cook vague and confusing recipes for "those tiny pigeons with cream and mushrooms" he'd once tasted at the Duchess of Alba's table; he thought the pigeons had to be spit-roasted first, but he wasn't sure. She just made the usual dish *à la grande-mère* and he declared it a "triumph."

I suppose I should talk, the hateful way I treated Pinky back home, sowing my bed with bread crumbs from late-night snacks, leaving my soiled clothes scattered about, teasing her about mispronounced words. But at least we said "Please" and "Thank you" and gossiped about her only behind her back, whereas Adhéaume would complain about how backward the Auvergne was and how greedy and beady-eyed were

Auvergnates right in front of Geneviéve, as if she couldn't understand French. Even more insulting, he'd usually switch to English the minute she entered the room and back to French the instant she left it, thereby underlining, I suppose, what an eavesdropper he thought she was.

After my Givenchy clothes were ready at last, Addy wanted me to wear them every day with jewels, purse, hat, and shoes he'd selected after endless consultations with his *cousine*. He expected me to throw away all my old clothes, even nice things from Oscar de la Renta. He allowed me to keep my mink but wanted me to shorten it to a three-quarters length. When I objected to giving my Texas clothes to Geneviève, he said, "You Americans have closets bursting with clothes and none of them fit. They're in loud colors, cheap materials, and they're usually too old or too young for the individual, too dressy or too casual. You see something nice on someone else and you think you can look like that if only you dress like that, forgetting that that dress is for teenagers or women with smaller butts."

Thanks to Addy's thrice-weekly conjugal duties and my animal health, I was soon pregnant. After I missed my period the second time I told Addy.

I make fun of him now that he's no longer alive, but I must admit at that moment he was perfect. He knelt beside me and held me in his arms and said how happy he was. He called me his little pigeon and then little mother and he actually had tears in his eyes. I fell in love with him for the first time.

I was so happy, feeling something inside me growing, something ancient (related to crusaders) and brand-new (my baby). Addy told his mother, who made an appointment with the family gynecologist—a man, of course. He'd been to dinner once and I'd heard him say, "I work where other men play."

Being American, I marched right into his office and took off all my clothes; when the nurse came in she said in broken English, "But miss—I mean, missus. *Madame la baronne*, the Frenchs were—were?—this little robe," and she presented me with a paper gown, tied it at my nape and lower back, leaving my buttocks hanging out, then handed me up onto the examining table, sheathed in clean paper, and put my raised feet in the stirrups. I felt ludicrously pornographic, like one of those red-assed estrous baboons in the zoo who are always "presenting."

The doctor came in, robed, gloved, and smoking a cigarette. He gave me a curt "*bonjour*," then tore a hole in my paper smock at vagina level. He inspected my organ carefully, his breath, even filtered by the mask, warming my nether parts in a disagreeable way. He was still smoking. He touched my vagina and lingered over it. Then he listened to my belly with a stethoscope (this was all before scans).

"You're having twins," he said, lighting one cigarette from another. "Your vagina definitely reveals you're pregnant and you must be at least nine weeks pregnant since I can hear the heartbeat. Or rather two heartbeats. Do you have any twins in your family?"

"My sister and I are twins. Identical."

"I can't determine if they're identical or fraternal now, but they are twins," he said. He took a deep breath, and, as if casting aside his professional role for a friendlier one, he said, "Congratulations!" Holding his cigarette between his lips (the smoke was burning his eyes), he eased my feet out of the stirrups and I sat up. Suddenly I liked him much more than before, as if we were intimates, not patient and doctor. I felt waves of gratitude toward him, as if he'd been the one to induce my pregnancy. "I assume you'll be the one to tell the baron."

Of course, I thought. Did he imagine I was too modest to mention pregnancy to my own husband? Sometimes I felt we were living in the nineteenth century. And yet it seemed acceptable for everyone to have lovers. If I chose one, I thought, it would be a woman. I wondered why all men weren't heterosexual and all women lesbian. Women were so beautiful, and everyone seemed to agree. Their skin was so soft, their hair so lustrous, their lips so pouty and adorable, their breasts just begging to be cupped. In society women's charms were constantly on display, which seemed so unfair, since so few of us were allowed to touch them. I was certain I could never fall in love with a man for more than a day. Who wanted a man, with their rough beards, their big, awkward hands, the charcoal squiggles on their chests, the barbed wire encasing their legs like fishing waders, their big yellow feet with dirty blue nails, the hair on their backs, their nipples like dried currants, those absurd penises that were always poking their wet, dripping noses in everyone's business, their leathery ball sacs carrying unevenly hung balls like back-up ammunition, spare cannon fodder? And the *smell* of all this heavy equipment compared to a woman's daintiness? And men's blunderbuss assertions compared to a woman's delicate coquetry? I love the girlishness of girls, their feline independence and playfulness compared to the male canine way of grasping you with their front paws and mounting you, wiggling till they spurt, their penis impossible to extract.

Compare Grace Kelly and James Stewart in *Rear Window*. She is so appealing—fashionable, her eyes startling, her jawline clean, her movements ravishing, her voice caressing—that anyone would prefer her with her full bust to his pale, scrawny body, his scarcely expressive face (all his acting is in his glances up through his eyebrows), his dull, droning voice; if someone hadn't tried to forgive all that leaden immobility and drawling and that unappetizing appearance by dubbing it "masculine," the poor man would never be allowed to touch, much less kiss, such a dazzling, pivoting divinity. Everyone, man and woman alike, should be enamored of Woman! I thought the doctor, despite professional ennui, must be enthralled by this flourishing Texas woman (*épanouie*): me!

Being pregnant made me miss my mother, who'd been dead so many years. I wanted her by my side to help me through the nausea of morning sickness (Adhéaume's mother, as the offspring of Crusaders, couldn't tolerate signs of weakness). To whom would I turn? Yvette was unreachable in the hills of Colombia or the jungles of Venezuela. Bobbie Jean had never had a baby, was too selfish to help me—and, besides, didn't really like me and wouldn't travel. I asked my gynecologist if he could recommend a nurse.

"But why? You don't need a nurse. In another week your nausea will go away. Try to take a nap every day and don't run in the Bois de Boulogne" (he laughed his way through a phlegmy smoker's cough).

My only confidante was Geneviève, the maid. When she wasn't busy cleaning or mending or ironing or running errands, she'd come into my room after knocking, mutter "*Madame la baronne*," sketch a curtsy, and sit beside me on the love seat, but only when I insisted. She was very good for my French. She'd grown up near Montoire-sur-le-Loir (*not* the Loire, a different river). Her parents were peasants; she had six siblings. She was the second oldest. Her parents made goat cheese, grew hay for the animals, had a huge vegetable garden, owned a tractor (which Geneviève had bought for them with two years' wages), owned an old Renault 5; her older brother restored the tile roofs of barns in the area. Her middle brother grew sunflowers on the land his grandfather owned but was too old to farm; the flowers would raise their golden crowns and then he'd starve them for water until they turned black, could be harvested, and the seeds pressed for oil. He was in love with a local girl but was still too poor to marry her. It seemed he would inherit the grandfather's cottage and land when he died; then for sure he could marry. His fiancée was from a richer family and studying to be a nurse's assistant in Vendome.

"How far along is she in her studies?" I asked.

"Christine's in her last year and will graduate in June. It's just a two-year program."

"Maybe she could come work here during the last months of my pregnancy."

"She knows a bit about how to be a midwife (*une sage-femme*). I wonder what my brother would say, but if I watched after her and she lived with me it might be all right."

"And you?" I asked. "How did you end up here?"

"I have an aunt who cooks for the baron's mother. After the young baron married your highness (*votre altesse*), she 'placed' me in your household."

"Oh, please, I'm not an *altesse* but from a family probably very much like yours, except my daddy first struck it rich from oil, just pure luck, nothing else. Does your aunt like working for the baron's mother?"

"Yes, of course," Geneviève said quickly, blushing. She wasn't used to lying.

When I repeated a few things about Geneviève's family over lunch, Adhéaume said, "I wish you wouldn't talk to the servants . . ."

I pounded the table. "Then who should I talk to?!!"

"Don't shout. You mustn't get upset in your condition."

"Geneviève is my only friend."

"How sad (*comme c'est triste*). I'm afraid she's already taught you some vulgar expressions."

"What! Vulgar like dirty?"

"No, vulgar like common (*populaire*)."

"*Tant mieux.*"

"I can't have the mistress of my castle speaking like that."

"*My château*, you mean."

"See what I mean? Only a fishwife (*une poissonnière*) would say that."

I leaped up from the table, went into the kitchen, and told Geneviève that I would take my coffee in my room. When she arrived with a cup of chamomile ("grandmother's pipi," as I called it), I objected and she said, "The baron's instructions. He said it would calm you down for your nap."

"But I don't feel like a nap!"

Poor Geneviève looked startled into helplessness; I imagined her instinct would be to shrug, but she dared not lest it seem disrespectful. I couldn't help but feel like a horse, a multimillion-dollar Triple Crown winner, owned by a corporation and that could be put out to stud for more millions. *La baronne* must not become anxious, *la baronne* must rest, the rich Texas *baronne* must give birth to rich Courcy *baronettes*. Don't argue, just eat your hay and let us groom you till you foal. I'd heard about these new tranquilizers, Miltown, that would stun you into submission.

I wanted an abortion.

Not really. I felt my womb was filling up and I was about to bring two children into the world, twins like my beloved sister and me, solid Crawford brambles grafted onto prizewinning roses, like those at the Bagatelle, with names like Lady Jane Grey, saffron yellow and as large and drooping as a dying butterfly. If I'd married the wrong man—a spend-thrift, unloving, snobbish popinjay—at least I'd have my noble children to keep me company. With Yvette I'd never been alone; our identical genes communed with each other mystically, but I'd lost her and we were growing apart. Now I'd have my own babies, and though Kahlil Gibran (whose *The Prophet* Jane Beth had given me on my twenty-first birthday) warned, "Your children are not your children" but more like arrows you've shot into the surrounding darkness, nevertheless I thought of them as life companions, little friends I'd never lose.

One advantage of being *enceinte* is that Adhéaume thought he should stop having sex with me after the first trimester. He had some Gothic superstition that if the twins were boys they would be born homosexual if they became too familiar with their father's penis, if they worshipped it as much as their mother did. Besides, the ecstatic pleasure supposedly ripping through my bloated body might induce a miscarriage. The little mother must be coddled, kept warm like a broody hen, oiled, and massaged.

Luckily Christine did come to work for us as I became mountainous. Adhéaume thought I shouldn't go out into society after I began to show. He thought it wasn't proper, not *comme il faut*. I didn't mind staying home with Geneviève and Christine and watching television while the baron went out to his clubs (the Jockey Club, the Automobile Club) or to visit his mistresses. I didn't really know about the mistresses, but I understood that Addy couldn't bear to be alone. He'd sooner die than read a book. To literary people he always talked about a novel he'd dipped into once and only once. When I suggested he watch television with me in my room, he said, "I couldn't bear to watch the same programs my servants were looking at."

I valued what was cozy, but I was told coziness was as boring as innocence, whereas he prized what was "distinguished" or "magnificent." I quickly learned the supreme importance of the *non-dit*, what was left unsaid. He liked grandeur, I liked simplicity.

If he'd been a Texan we would have hashed out his infidelities, starting with the conviction that what he was doing was wrong. Since he was part of the *gratin*, it was assumed that marriage was for dynastic reasons alone and fidelity was for *ploucs*, or "hicks," or the pious or the seriously undersexed.

I hoped that since I was spawning twins, his family ambitions would be satisfied and he would leave me alone with the children and the maids. He wouldn't be attracted to me until my vagina healed and I'd regained my figure. Now that I was so pregnant and wearing giant smocks and running constantly to the bathroom, he couldn't bear the sight of me.

He'd enter my boudoir off my bedroom, and, seeing us "girls" (*les meufs* in *verlan*, the slang that spelled everything backward), he waved his hands in front of his face as if to erase the image of three women sprawling and giggling. I was happy for the first time in Paris, happy to be with other young *meufs*, happy to be free of the toxic, scheming Courcys and Castigliones, happy to be hatching my two giant golden eggs, happy to be watching terrible TV programs and having the maids explain the soap opera plots. I was learning how to be an average French woman in France while Addy attended auctions and came home exultant about buying a forty-two-piece set of Sèvres that had once belonged to Madame de Sévigné.

"It would be fun to have an Italian-style fight," I said, "and to smash it all against the wall. How much did it cost you? Ten thousand dollars?"

"Add a zero."

I gasped. Since he spoke English alone in front of the maids, I had to translate everything for them into my newly fluent French; Addy said I was acquiring an Auvergnate accent, which was terribly vulgar.

I was careful never to criticize the baron in front of the help, tempting as that might be. We could laugh at anything and everything but not at the baron de Courcy. I saw his august personage through their lowered eyes for a moment and felt a new, if fleeting, respect for the "quality."

It didn't last long. I smelled the mistress's Shalimar on his hand, saw that she'd been feeding him his favorite *croissants au beurre* in industrial quantities and that his tush was getting more and more cherubic in his tight, bespoke trousers; they were splitting at the seams. We were both swelling; it was a bit like the "freshman fifteen," the extra pounds a college girl puts on once she is away from her mother's watchful eye.

I suppose there was something squalidly gynecological about a harem of three young women idling and, in my imagination, licking *loukoum* and ingesting drugged sherbets as they sat out a dynastic pregnancy. The eighty-seven wives of a Persian king who happened to prefer boys—those obese ladies grew mustaches or glued them on, coaxed one wide eyebrow across their faces, ate gluttonously, and showed off their delights in ballet skirts without panties, not really sure how to rekindle his interest (they hadn't found the right way).

When we weren't watching soap operas or variety shows (most of the French singing stars seemed to be elderly), we were flipping through *Paris Match*; the girls told me that the royal family of Monaco had an exclusive contract to cook up a new scandal every month to be reported and photographed by the magazine. Nothing could keep us from giggling for long. Christine gave me long massages with heated baby oil. Following the most modern practices she'd just learned, she had me doing stretching exercises to remain in good shape (*en pleine forme*).

Eventually my gynecologist, smoking all the while, delivered my twins. Addy said he was "allergic" to blood and might faint, so I didn't see him until I was bathed and holding the babies in my arms. He dropped in an hour late, brought white roses, inspected the little girl and boy as if they were prize pigs, told me of the arrangements his mother had made for a wet nurse from the Morvan and of his dismissal of Christine, who wouldn't be needed anymore.

"You what! You dismissed my darling Christine? How dare you," I said indignantly with my last energy.

"We don't need her anymore, my beloved."

"*You* don't need her. She was my friend and helped me during most of my pregnancy."

He laughed with his little sneer. "May I point out that *Madame la baronne* is no longer pregnant."

I brooded and at last said, "I hope you gave her a handsome bonus at least."

"Bonus? Why ever would I do that? You're too generous with the servants. She was well paid, got to see the Eiffel Tower, and was *blanchie et nourrie* (her clothing was washed and she was fed) at my expense for months."

"*My* expense," I growled. Then I remembered something. "I'll get her address from Geneviève; I promised Christine money for her dowry to marry Geneviève's brother."

Adhéaume made that puffing sound of exasperation. "First you'll have to find her. I dismissed Geneviève as well."

I burst into tears and sobbed and sobbed and the nurse had to rush to take the babies from my arms. I assumed they were being bottle-fed in the room next door. Adhéaume sneaked away, always the coward. Undoubtedly he was rushing off to another auction. Somewhere in Paris there must have been a magnificent desk by Boulle of rare woods and gold fittings for sale for just the price of two downtown city blocks in Dallas. Or a selfish woman willing to trade her pussy for a tiara.

We'd squabbled over the children's names. I wanted to name the little girl Yvette after my sister and the boy Paul after my father. Those were both recognized names at the *mairie*. It turns out that if you were Irish and you wanted to name your children Deirdre and Cuchulain, you couldn't. In those days, at least, there was an official list of saints' names and only those were legal in France. Not for France, any of those poetic one-of-a-kind names chosen by black Americans, like Nakesha, as a unique handmade identity, a sort of haiku label, a magic ring. If you were Muslim, your son became Joseph, even if you preferred Karim or Abdellah. If you were German, your little Greta became Marthe.

"Yvette," Addy said, "is an accordionist's name."

Addy and his mother held out for Ghislaine for the girl and Foulques for the boy, medieval family names. "And what will their nicknames in America be? Gristle and Fuck? Fuckface?"

"Why would they have American nicknames?" Addy's mother asked, genuinely puzzled.

"They might want to go to university there. American schools have a very lively campus life."

"That will never happen," the old baroness said. Addy had told me that when he was a child she'd given him a very short list of acceptable playmates. She was very snobbish, he said with a smile, as if it were a virtue.

The wet nurse arrived from the Morvan the next day and started to feed my babies right away, one on each breast. My own breasts were so full of milk they hurt; if one of the babies cried (it was usually Foulques), the milk would spurt out of me, which Addy thought was distastefully "primitive."

The wet nurse was very young, a bit stupid, nineteen at most, with hyperthyroid eyes and lips so swollen they were always parted; for some reason they reminded me of her swollen breasts. Apparently she had just had a little girl of her own, whom she farmed out to a neighbor lady who was also nursing an infant. That way she could come to the big city and feed my babies. Her name was Marguerite, which Addy said was perfect since it was a name for a cow.

She knew I was a foreigner and she said (in French, loudly and slowly), "I don't speak English."

I smiled and said, "But we're speaking French."

She panicked and wagged her finger to mean no. "*Pas d'anglais,*" she said repeatedly, louder and louder. I suppose she'd never spoken French with a foreigner before, not in her village of fifty souls in the Morvan.

Spanky came by to inspect my piglets, stared unsmilingly straight ahead with unfocused eyes when I tried to introduce her to Marguerite, informed me, as if we were alone, that the people of the Morvan were so poor that they had been wet-nursing since ancient Roman times and were good at raising cattle and foundlings (*les enfants abandonnés*).

Marguerite, I think, was reassured when she heard Spanky and me speaking French (though Spanky's clipped, nasal French sounded to her a bit "Mexican," as she later told me). She asked Spanky where I was from and Spanky, just to be mischievous, said, "Auvergne." Marguerite nodded sagely—she'd suspected as much; the Auvergne sounded like another country to her far from France.

Spanky also engaged a trainer for me, male of course, *un professeur du sport*, who came every day to the apartment for an hour's exercise to help me regain my figure. Addy said that we should both go on a diet and that for two weeks we'd eat nothing but cabbage soup, morning, noon, and night—as much cabbage soup as we wanted. His valet, he said, had hinted it was time. On top of that Addy took a membership at the *salle de sport* at the Ritz, where they had a pool in the basement. Addy could do the sidestroke. Addy's mother explained to me more intimate, genital exercises I could do to tighten my twat for her son. Right out of a Sophoclean tragedy, I thought. I was deeply offended.

I missed my girls from Auvergne and was still seething that they'd been dismissed without my knowledge. Addy's mother turned on a ten-watt smile when I asked her how to contact Geneviève, and said nothing. My greatest joy was my babies, my twins, who for me had the charm of being

French aristocrats and little Texans. When I was a child I'd get cranky if I went more than three hours without seeing Yvette; now my children had become my perfect companions. I could spend hours holding them and looking at them, though Marguerite was always hovering nearby in case they needed to be fed. My milk was slowly drying up and that turned me sad, as though that made me less of a mother. Sometimes I broke down and cried. Were these the postpartum blues? I knew that all my life I'd been ruled by hormones, that reputedly the female brain was different from the male, but I'd never been conscious of the obvious oppressive reality before I'd had these extreme mood swings. I found them humiliating, as if I were entirely governed by my ovaries, which could bewitch my brain into inventing sad sentiments. When I was despairing, holding my babies comforted me. I thought it was my job to comfort *them*, but here I was absorbing their calming beta waves.

When I said to Addy that I hoped he was writing down all his expenses for me to go over, he exploded and said, "Talleyrand accused the English of being a nation of shopkeepers; he'd probably say Americans were stingy card sharps." He stroked his chin. "When Napoleon asked Talleyrand what America was like, Talleyrand said, 'The United States has thirty-two denominations, Sire, and just one recipe.'"

"Unlike the French," I said, "we actually are religious. We believe in God and Jesus."

Addy hooted his scoffing laugh and said, "Like your crazy sister."

"My crazy sister is on her way to becoming a saint. You may have had crusaders in your family, but my sister will be a consecrated saint."

"We have lots of saints."

CHAPTER 10

Dearest Yvonne,

You were so wise in your letter, which took five weeks to arrive here, when you urged me to join the Church officially. I've now done so, have been baptized anew, been catechized—and now can receive Communion every day without anyone's permission. As you know I never was a joiner (no Girl Scouts, no glee club, no sorority) but the Church is different, since it is an extension of Our Father in Heaven, the social expression of His will on Earth. It's a community that extends horizontally across the continents and vertically through the ages: a cross! In any event it exalts and humbles me at the same time—exalts because it teaches me how to throw off the Old Woman and how to embrace the New; humbles because I am only one of many, not like the egotistical Protestant who believes that each man is his own priest but, instead, like the obedient Catholic who is guided by the holy priesthood founded on a rock (Saint Peter).

I was instructed at every step by Oscar, my Swiss bishop. I almost said my "angel," since sometimes it feels as if he really and truly has descended from above to help his weak sister Yvette. I feel his vast white wings enfolding me, his hand on my elbow as I travel through the dangerous valleys of doubt and sin. Since we were girls we were always taught to respect and defer to men, but that convention was difficult for me to obey since, in my outlandish pride, I judged most men inferior to me—less analytic, more boastful, less well read, stubborn. But Bishop Oscar truly is more intelligent than I, and wiser. He's read most of the Greek and

Roman classics, knows his Saint Thomas Aquinas by heart—and you'd be shocked how quickly he's learned to speak, understand, and read English at my timid instruction (he has to insist I correct him, which I do now but always with tears in my eyes, as if I'm breaking a covenant or something). You'd laugh—he has a slight Texas accent! We always speak in English together; he says it's our secret language.

With the nuns and the children I tutor I speak Spanish, of course, and all modesty aside I've become quite fluent and have difficulty in understanding people only from other regions. (The Argentinians say the word for street, *calle*, which we pronounce as "cah-yeah," as "cah-jay.") This will sound like pride but the other day I had to show my American passport to someone to prove I wasn't Colombian.

As you warned me (indirectly), I have become overly attached to Bishop Oscar. I find everything about him adorable—the little hairs below his lower lip that his razor misses, his long but powerful hands when he works in the garden pulling weeds or training vines, the rank, doggy smell I used to complain of, his long, sunburned nose. I am especially moved by these words in *The Imitation of Christ*, which I read every day:

"Love is watchful, and whilst sleeping still keepeth watch; though fatigued it is not weary, though pressed it is not forced, though alarmed it is not terrified, but like the living flame and the burning torch, it breaketh forth on high and securely triumpheth. If a man loveth, he knoweth what this voice crieth. For the ardent affection of the soul is a great clamour in the ears of God . . . Enlarge Thou me in love, that I may learn to taste with the innermost mouth of my heart how sweet it is to love, to be dissolved, and to swim in love . . . Love is swift, sincere, pious, pleasant, gentle, strong, patient, faithful, prudent, long-suffering . . ."

When I read these words once to Oscar while he was decking the altar with flowers for Easter, he looked embarrassed and blushed. He recommended that I reread Cicero on friendship—a sort of love, to be sure, but less mystical, less delirious. Cicero argues that we can be friends only with virtuous men, since they would never ask us to do anything unpatriotic and at no time would we find ourselves torn between loyalty to a friend or to the state. He says that talking to a true friend is like talking to oneself—everything is understood in the intended way. Cicero reminds us that friends can grow apart, which is specially painful because of their former intimacy. It's all rather dry except when Cicero tells us that friendship is the greatest pleasure. I think that's what Bishop Oscar wants me to keep in mind: that friendship is the greatest earthly joy and that we can befriend only the virtuous.

I'm now a novice in our order of nuns and since I've joined, Mother Superior is much kinder to me. She was always kind, in truth, though her methods were sometimes acerbic.

Do you remember how I "saved" the life of little Hector Colimas in Austin? I always doubted that I could have actually performed that feat, but now they're ascribing another miracle to me. In the local infirmary there was a young indigenous woman, a mother of three, who was diagnosed with renal cancer that had spread to her lungs. She asked me to touch her with my hands. I did so and recited a Hail Mary and two Our Fathers. It seems that two months later the doctor declared that an X-ray showed the tumor had nearly disappeared. Now when I walk through the streets with another nun on some errand, people often kneel and ask for my blessing.

I feel like a total fraud! I'm delighted that Maria Crossifissa is recovering, but I'm embarrassed by all the fuss, especially since I'm only a novice. I was afraid some of the older nuns might be envious, though no one seems to be, thank God. On the contrary, they feel I've brought prestige to their convent. I quizzed the attending physician closely and asked if there were any scientific explanations for this spontaneous regression.

He said, with a certain tremulous deference, that Maria had had a large kidney cancer with metastases to the lungs. After the kidney with the cancer was removed because the patient was in pain and had blood in her urine, the metastases in the lungs also disappeared, perhaps due to a boost in the immune system—or to a miracle. I smiled and said, "I would bet on the immune system." He added, "It might come back. X-rays aren't all that accurate."

"Let's pray she stays healthy." And so far she has. The people who ask for my blessing call me Mother Yvette, which sounds silly since we're still in our twenties (though I do have a certain maternal width of the hips, probably from our starchy diet). I intend to fast, not to be thin but as penance for my many sins.

But speaking of sins, look how selfish I am! I've asked you nothing about your husband or your glamorous Parisian life. Isn't it odd how we're twins and one of us is becoming a nun and the other has become a French baroness? It's as if, discontent with our dull, empty past lives, we've run in opposite directions—you toward whatever is best in this vale of tears, the bounty and excitement of Paris, and I toward a nearly unnoticed rebirth in God's love in a remote Colombian village. In Catholic terms you are the best of the "Old" Woman and I'm the worst of the "New," i.e., reborn in Christ.

Not a day goes by that I'm not besieged with doubt. If you think of it, everything the Christian believes is preposterous. The Virgin Birth. A human God. Miracles. A new religion or a reform movement in Judaism? A man who dies for our sins—what does that even mean? The Resurrection after three days in a shroud in a tomb. And on and on . . . Not to mention the uncomfortable parallels with other Middle Eastern religions (but here I'm not too strong in my learning)—the virgin birth connected with Astarte, the resurrection of Osiris, the expectation of the Hebrew Messiah, miracles galore in every desert faith . . . Of course, no sooner do such thoughts occur to me than I hear the Devil chuckling somewhere nearby. He even tried to mislead Our Lord.

It's not that it's easier or more peaceful to be a believer. I'm not a Christian because it's more comfortable. I'm a Christian because I *believe. Simply believe.* Just as we know the air is to breathe, food is to nourish, and water to drink, in the same way I have an instinctual appetite for God, a need to fill myself with His love (or wrath, even His silence). Just as I think, therefore I am, in the same way I am, therefore I believe. God's love is an act of generosity on a scale as large as the universe, just as our love for Him is a tiny, fragile act of generosity. Cicero writes: "We don't practice generosity in order to secure gratitude, nor do we invest our gifts in the hope of a favorable return. Rather, it is nature that inclines us toward generosity. Just so, we don't seek friendship with an expectation of gain, but regard the feeling of love as its own reward."

My friendship with Oscar feels like a Ciceronian if not Catholic ideal. I've taught him English and he's taught me to live in the shadow of the Cross, to strive to be the least of all and the servant of everyone. In the Cross is peace and perfection and freedom from torment; in the Cross is the desire to be despised by all. I want to be meek in the face of universal scorn, to be "counted as a fool for Christ," as *The Imitation* puts it. I want to hate my soul in this world that I might keep it in the next. I know I am a stranger to other human beings but a kinsman and friend unto God.

Have you had children yet? Is your marriage sacrosanct and fruitful? I hate that the mails are so slow.

Daddy is very suspicious of Bishop Oscar, as if (in Daddy's words) he wants to cheat me out of my fortune and hand it over to the pontiff "so the pope can buy another uranium crown" (he means the platinum crown that the pope has sold to help the poor). He thinks the religion is all "a bunch of hooey" designed to hoodwink the credulous and pacify the poor (not Daddy's words, but you get the gist). He thinks the Latin and the bells and incense and hocus-pocus of the wine and bread are meant to stupefy the masses; he claims when he and Bobbie Jean cruised up the Nile he visited some of those ancient Egyptian temples and said in the innermost interiors were holy altars cast in shadows and sacred pools stocked with crocodiles. "It's all a bunch of hooey, sweetie, not God, not Jesus, but all these pagan gewgaws. The Old Catholics are no better than the pharaohs. They just have holy water rather than tubs of crocodiles."

I'm going to be ordained as a nun next spring if you and your husband want to come. I know I wasn't present for your wedding, so I certainly wouldn't mind it if you couldn't. Resentment isn't my strong suit, and I'm all about forgiveness. Daddy and Bobbie Jean will be present (he's still against the Church) but I'd feel somehow safer if you were here, too. I hope Daddy doesn't treat us to an outburst.

Your loving twin,
Yvette

No, I thought, my marriage isn't sacrosanct but it has been fruitful. After I regained my figure and did all the exercises for my vaginal muscles,

Adhéaume slept with me once after two bottles of vintage champagne of a strangely yellow color and a dinner of caviar, chopped egg yolks, and sour cream served on still-warm and peeled new potatoes. We didn't stuff ourselves. Addy gave me a lovely diamond bracelet—more a *cuff* of diamonds than a bracelet. He accompanied me to my room with his arm around my waist. For the few days before that I'd found a sealed letter from him beneath the bud vase on the tea tray after my afternoon nap. He wrote that he was too "shy" to say out loud the outrageously pornographic things he was imagining doing to me, but he could spell it all out on the page. A prolonged anal kiss was the least of his fantasies, the only one I'll confide. Before our caviar and champagne supper I'd taken extra care to wash thoroughly down there.

But once we were in bed he wasn't nearly as daring in reality as he was in his epistolary ravings. He fucked me in the missionary position. When he pulled out, he said, "I couldn't feel that much."

I said drily, "That wasn't entirely my fault. Roger wasn't fully at attention."

He stormed out to his own room, wrapping his sky-blue monogrammed robe about him.

After that he left me alone. No more letters. No more jewelry. No more amorous attentions. Just as well. The letters had embarrassed me, the jewelry I'd paid for, and the lovemaking had left me indifferent, *voire* irritated. Did he think twins were enough to make me his forever?

I reveled in my babies, especially since I didn't have to feed them, change them, or "put them down" (the awful American expression that is also used for shooting lame horses). They were brought in in their matching lace dresses for an hour each morning to giggle through peekaboo games and to grip my index finger, to smile with a senile old man's vagueness, to make preverbal babbling sounds, and suddenly to turn red like peppers on vitamins or apoplectic psychotics and scream. Instead of lithium the wet nurse fed them milk with her back slightly turned to me to conceal the awful mammalian reality. My own breasts, though slowly shrinking, were still bigger than usual. One time Addy touched one breast while I was dressing, made a lapping sound, and said "mnam-mnam," which is their "yum-yum." I wasn't really offended, but

I thought that's how humorously/unconsciously he thought of me, as a nourishing ruminant.

My babies were my refuge. They looked at me and even smiled. I was convinced that I could already see that Ghislaine was rebellious and Foulques sweetly compliant. I asked Marguerite if she could detect these differences but my interrogation rattled her—and she merely shrugged. When I tried to pursue this line of questioning, her attention withdrew like a frightened turtle's head. Unlike my darling Auvergnates, she was stupid. Unimaginative. Half-dead with normality.

Addy invited an attractive couple to dinner, Georges and Sally du Pic. He was young and skinny and not too clean, though in a nice suit slightly too big on him. I wondered if it was one of Addy's old suits, the ones he contemptuously called store-bought. It was cashmere, which meant it didn't hold its shape too well and it was too warm for the surprisingly hot June night. Sally was even younger and had yellow hair and black roots. She had on a stylish dress, the sort you could buy cheap at Le Mouton à Cinq Pattes after the designer label had been torn off (*dégriffée*). I wondered where Adhéaume had found them. Sally was American and he obviously thought she would please me; don't get me wrong, I'm really not a snob, but they weren't our sort. Addy always says innocence bores him, that the loss of innocence is a major American theme and makes our movies and novels so dull. "If you're innocent," he says, "get deflowered in the first chapter and get on with it."

But Sally and Georges were a little too deflowered; they were wilting and had lost their petals. They were so pale and thin. They smelled slightly like a washcloth that had been left in the heat to mildew. I wondered if they were heroin addicts, gamblers, prisoners, thieves. Sally kept swiping calculating glances at my diamond cuff. Finally I touched it and said, "It's a pity they're not real"; after that Sally stopped looking at it.

She said she was from Lawrence, Kansas, had met Georges there at the university, where he'd been studying civil engineering and she'd been majoring in pharmacology. He was from Annecy, in the mountains, not far from the Swiss border. His father was a minister in the church of Zwingli. Oh, you've never heard of Zwingli? He was a Protestant from Zurich, I think.

"How did you meet Adhéaume?" I asked.

She giggled and said, "He didn't tell you?"

"No."

"We met him just two blocks away."

I turned and saw Addy had locked eyes with Sally and had raised a warning finger to his lips, which he lowered the instant I looked his way. He pretended he was scratching his lip.

"We met him on the Place Dauphine. You know people go there for wife-swapping? *Les échangistes?*"

"I think I've heard of it," I lied, smiling. Adhéaume launched into a long disquisition on the wine, how he'd discovered twelve bottles in the cellars of an uncle's château in the Dordogne and realized they were prewar Bordeaux; he hoped they didn't taste of the cork (*le bouchon*).

"You were saying?" I said to Sally.

"So we have a huge old Buick. We live in it, truth to tell. Sometimes we park it in the Place Dauphine and lock the doors, turn on the over-head light, and make love."

"How amusing," I said. "In the nude?"

"Of course. Would you make love in your clothes?"

"Never," I said encouragingly.

"You'd be surprised how many gents gather around and like to watch."

"I'll bet."

"Sometimes they're breathing so hard and jerking off so furiously while we're going at it that the windows are all cloudy with breath. When we drive off and park in the Cité des Fleurs, we get out and find *buckets* of sperm on our fenders."

"How exciting!" I exclaimed. "And Addy was one of your spectators?"

"He's a regular. We're there three times a week around midnight and he's always there, so well dressed and always smiling, wearing a nice felt fedora and silk scarf; one night we unlocked a door and said, 'Hop in,' and he did, which is most unusual, believe me, but we wanted to know him."

"How nice," I crooned. "And now he's invited you to dinner."

Georges squinted at me and murmured, "I hope you're not too shocked."

"Not at all," I said serenely. "But you've barely touched your food. Are you vegetarians?"

"We don't eat too much," Sally volunteered. "We never do."

"What about dessert? I have a coconut crème caramel."

"We both have a sweet tooth," Georges said, and for the first time I noticed several of his teeth were missing, though they were usually covered by his long upper lip.

Once we'd tucked into our pudding, I asked, "But how do you survive? Paris is an expensive city."

"Well, Addy has been very generous with small amounts of money and Georges receives a minuscule allowance once a month to stay out of Annecy. Different gentlemen we've met allow us to take showers at their place, wash out our undies, which we collect a day or two later, and even spend the night on the couch when it's really cold. Most of Addy's money goes to repairing and fueling the Buick. If we're desperate I turn a few tricks, but Georges doesn't like that, he's so possessive."

"Men are like that," I said with a smiling complaint in my voice. "Have you ever turned a trick with Addy?"

"Are you kidding?" she said. "You know him. He likes just to watch."

"And touch?"

Georges said, "Sometimes he likes to stroke my buttocks, *mon cul quand j'enfonce* Sally."

"Oh, yes," I said, bluffing, "he likes that."

"Should I open another bottle?" Addy asked. "It's a different vintage. A little impertinent burgundy. I'll call for new glasses. Of a sweet Château d'Yquem? Or champagne."

"Let's stick with the red," Sally said, "and we can use the same glasses." She'd pushed aside all pretense of being an oenophile; she just wanted to get high.

Georges said, "I like people who are a little perverted. No blood, no shit, no pain, I always say, but everything else is fine."

I smiled and said, "That's what I always say, too."

"Sometimes we go to a nice little *échangiste* club right off the Rue Saint-Martin. Ladies get in free and so do I if I'm with Sally, but single men have to pay a hundred francs and their first drink is another hundred."

"But it's a solid investment," I said, "if you like to watch or knock off the occasional woman . . . or man."

"I wouldn't know," Georges said. "I never touch a type, though I don't mind if he touches me, but not my sex, *ce n'est pas permis*, that's for the *meufs* only."

"You have to have your principles," I added cordially.

I told them I had a headache, red wine always did that to me. Sally asked if I wanted them to join me and maybe give me a back rub, but I declined, whispering very girl-to-girl that it was that time of the month, though it wasn't.

Sally said, "Georges says no blood but I don't mind it."

I stood, took each of them by the hand (I couldn't bear to kiss them, as if they were infected, though I blew a kiss at Addy). "But don't let me spoil your fun. I'm sure Addy is roaring to stroke Georges's buttocks." I swirled away and double-locked both bedroom doors. When I couldn't sleep I tiptoed into the nursery, saw Marguerite asleep and snoring in a frightful many-colored nightgown of a slippery synthetic fabric and my adorable Ghislaine (who coughed slightly) and my brave little Foulques, both of them in matching white gowns and white knit booties, Ghislaine on her back and Foulques on his side. I bent down to kiss them each on a cool cheek and hoped I didn't reek of wine. Foulques stirred in his sleep and raised his tiny hand with the seed-pearl fingernails, as if a fly had troubled him. I thought, Maybe Addy and I are foul, but at least we've produced these angels, as rasa as any tabula.

The next day at breakfast I said ironically to a sheepish Adhéaume, "I hope your friends approved of me."

"I thought you'd like Sally, since she's American."

"And a part-time whore?"

"You always exaggerate (*tu exagères toujours*)."

"Did they stay on? I hope you were able to clock in some butt-stroking time."

"No reason to put too fine a point on it. Pity you had a headache."

"I hope you had a chance to hose them down first. They rather smelled."

"All right. I won't invite my friends to dinner."

"But Adhéaume, I thought you liked women, aristocratic women, or just rich, refined, educated, beautiful women, I didn't know you had a weakness (*une faiblesse*) for mud (*la boue*) or for male ass (*le petit cul d'un homme*)."

"Really, Yvonne! You go too far!"

"I'm just worried about your health. How do you know they're not heroin addicts—"

"I'm afraid of needles."

"Or riddled (*cribblé*) with syphilis?"

"I don't touch their genitals."

"*Yet!*" I emphasized.

"You won't sleep with me."

"Now I certainly won't. I can't trust you. I hope you can be satisfied with just two heirs, a boy and a girl."

"So you release me?"

"Like a big fish. But into a clear stream, not a mud bath, one would hope."

"I mean from my vows?"

"You've already broken them, I notice. Surely two little Courcys are sufficient to hold me forever, as you put it."

As if to prove his power over me, Addy began the restoration of his family château, which turned out to be a bottomless pit to fill with my money. Although I had an allowance of several hundred thousand dollars a year, all of my accounts were overdrawn and the tradesmen's bills came in every day. The newspapers were commenting with sly pokes and even my most discreet acquaintances would pause and raise an eyebrow when Addy's name was mentioned. The servants must have also been gossiping about it, since they often broke off their intense conversations and blushed when I walked in. I found out some of them hadn't been paid, an omission I corrected.

I didn't really care at first, though if I thought about it for a moment anxiety would creep over me like a skin rash or ivy. Daddy, who'd been brought up poor, always worried about money, even after Bobbie Jean convinced him to invest in Dallas real estate and he became seriously rich. He worried about "white flight" and what he called "unreal estate," though the French think there's no safer investment than in stones (*pierres*) and they seem really talented at perpetuating the "patrimony." For the French the stock market is what's precarious; Daddy thinks so, too, and doesn't trust anything except gold bars in the wall safe.

Daddy monitored my checking and saving accounts, which were in both my husband's and my names. He'd write me little warning notes on stationery he'd had printed up: FROM THE DESK OF PETER MARTIN CRAWFORD . . . He'd say, "What the hell is your husband spending a *fortune* on? You'll soon be bankrupt and tell him not to count on me no more to fill up them coffers, that count no-count of yours. Glad to hear the twins are happy and healthy. From the photos they look as cute as the dickens, especially that little girl of yourn." Daddy always was partial to little girls; when he was sixteen and she five, my aunt Bunn told me, he used to play with her hole. He'd make her sit on the fence and he'd stick his finger in and jiggle it. She liked it, she said. Her little female hole, not the dirty one. I'll never leave him alone with my children.

Adhéaume was busy rebuilding his family château, Quercy, in the Var. Those were our closest moments, when he'd excitedly discuss his plans and unroll the architect's drawings. I'd make a big pot of his favorite blackberry tea, which he drank with lots of sugar and which exuded the syrupy smell of the dunes on the Lido. The color returned to his cheeks, his drawl hastened into a trot, he couldn't unscroll the plans fast enough, so great was his enthusiasm. He was convinced, I'm sure, that he was restoring not only the château but his place in history. He talked about those ancient kings of France as if they were cousins he'd played with just yesterday and for whom he harbored a certain schoolboy contempt. Hauteur was his strong suit, but it was almost appealing if it was joined with excitement. He was excited that after years of sneering at everyone and envying them their good or middling fortune, he and his family once more counted in the great world (i.e., in France, the only *monde* he took seriously). Of course, he admired the English, their foul mouths and willfulness and eccentricity—the result, he'd always explain, of a country gentry rather than the nobility of the court, as in France. "We're always currying favor whereas they don't give a damn" ("give a damn" he'd say in English)! Did he entirely admire the surliness of the English? Perhaps he liked their independence, but he preferred the eternal politeness of the French, which often concealed a barb in its silky tail.

Addy loved his own geneology; working alone, spending many days at it, he traced out his family tree and made ten copies. When his aunt, the countess of Beaulaincourt, saw it, she said slyly, "You've left off Adam de Courcy and Eve de Courcy!"

Addy was thrilled to re-create the family château. He must have had a whole army of craftsmen working there—as many as fifty at times, perhaps more. It had been built originally in the late Middle Ages and in the Renaissance; Addy hired skilled painters to gild the galleries and ante-chambers. I used to imagine I could hear the drumbeat of cleated metal boots on the stone staircases and on the tiled floor of the *salle de gardes* as armored knights rushed in (Addy carefully restored the tiles from an extant scrap in one corner). He took me on a tour of the château. From the slits in the thick walls, darkened by the centuries, where archers once stood and shot their arrows, I could look out at the sun-dried fields, the barely trickling river—more a brook than a river—the evening volleys of starlings and the glaring white gashes left in the dust by the plaster quarries.

The library, with its gilt mottoes exclaiming from the cornices, VIVE LE ROI! VIVE LE ROI!, was lined with bookshelves behind ornate doors painted in faded blue with scenes of lanky shepherds and saucy peasant girls. Weirdly, the shelves displayed hundreds of bound volumes from the eighteenth century in English! And in German up to Schiller and Goethe. Not a single volume in French. Addy explained that an ancestor of his, Adalbert de Courcy, was a tremendous bibliophile and had agents buying up everything in Weimar and London, though he couldn't read either language.

Addy was very solicitous of his army of workers (or thought he was) and was always saying an encouraging word or providing them with a *coup de rouge* from a local vineyard. He had an easy way with them, acquired from dealing so much with game wardens, no doubt. One of his pet projects was re-creating a majestic marble fountain fed by allegorical figures representing the five continents—an Asian man with an elephant, a hooded Arab with a camel, a European knight with a horse, an Australian woman with a kangaroo, and a big-breasted American squaw with an alligator—all streaming water from mouths and even nipples! The arms of France surmounted it all. Addy was determined that all these masterpieces would someday be sold to collectors rather than museums, which he considered art cemeteries. Unfortunately tastes have changed and just as the price of rare stamps has gone down because fewer people collect stamps now, in the same way this sort of "colonial" art is less in fashion than formerly. When I first arrived in Paris, people still talked about the Paris Colonial Exposition of 1931—the fountain would have been perfect there!

Other rooms were far more beautiful because they followed the taste of Henri III—a zodiac room, for instance, and a room of ancient Roman busts of emperors. My favorite was the handsome Commodus, with his beard and curly hair, till I read about him and discovered that he renamed Rome (and the twelve months) after himself, fought in the ring as a gladiator (and charged Rome for the pleasure—and nearly bankrupted it), decapitated ostriches and Roman citizens who were missing feet for one reason or another. He sounded like a bad ruler and I came to despise him, despite his good looks. He thought he was a reincarnation of Hercules and our bust showed him holding a club and wearing an animal skin.

I would commute from Paris to the Var by train, changing from an express to a local in Marseille, and on one trip I saw Helen, the American I'd met at the Red Duke's. She was very friendly and sat beside me; first class was nearly empty.

I noticed she had a large, bluish diamond, which looked distinctly familiar. I was certain it was a ring Addy had given me because he'd based a whole lecture on it, about a diamond's "angle of incidence," its "dispersion," and "pavilion facets," something I'd paid close attention to because I thought his self-esteem was linked to that sort of expertise (when I still cared about propping up his ego). I'd never liked the ring because it was so large and square that I couldn't get a glove over it. I'd stopped wearing it. I'd never noticed it had gone missing.

"What a lovely ring," I said, my heart pounding. The sunlit landscape was streaming past, little farms, antiquated farm equipment, impover-ished French villages with fading signs on blind walls (SUZE with a ten-foot-tall picture of a woman's hand holding a cocktail glass of yellow liquid, the whole advertisement losing color by the instant). When I looked at the poor, sunbaked villages, devoid of people and traffic, the shutters closed against the heat, and in my mind contrasted them with the manicured luxury of Paris, its pale limestone façades and sweeping boulevards, I thought of the capital as a fiery carbuncle growing on the pale, flaccid bum of the nation.

"It looks familiar," I said, "but I know nothing about jewels."

She looked stunned, then laughed suavely and said, "I don't wonder. Addy gave it to me for my birthday last October."

"Yes, he must have showed it to me for a moment before he gave it to you," I lied. I could feel my face burning. "I knew I had seen it somewhere."

In my own jewel box, I thought.

"It's such a delight to see you again." I said. "How was that trip to Marie-Galante?"

"Where? Oh, okay. Henri loves it. Miles of untouched white beaches and palms, but no decent hotels. They're good cooks, though they put Grand Marnier in everything."

"Are you Adhéaume's mistress?"

"*Was.* I was years ago. Then he found out I was the only *poor* American in Paris." She looked me over from alligator shoe tips to frosted curls. "He moved on to bigger and better things." She smiled, remembering some-thing. "When you two took this very train on your honeymoon to go to look at the family château, I was traveling in the car behind yours. Of course, *later*, he became more and more devoted to you."

"Of course," I whispered. "Did you stay with . . . the wedding party?"

"Yes. I stayed in the village hotel at the foot of the château, speaking of indecent. You must have noticed his long nocturnal walks. I wore no scent and even bought the worst unscented soap so you would suspect nothing. What could be worse than having your groom cheat on you?" Her teeth were very shiny.

"Of course now I'm inured."

"Evidently. I would never have dared being so honest otherwise."

"That's my ring," I said.

"What a devil, that Addy. Are you very fond of it? Do you want it back? You could wear it without saying anything; that would shock him, if he bothered to look at your hand." She started to pull the ring off.

"No, no, you must keep it. It looks so well on you. My hand's too little for it," I said, a bit cruelly.

"If you're sure . . . ? It must be wickedly valuable. I insist you take it back."

"All right. You've spared me having to observe Adhéaume's old age."

"You're putting him out to pasture?" she asked. I just smiled a dazzling smile.

It was such fun wearing that ring at breakfast the next day.

He didn't say a word but blushed through several colors.

But he did go through what seemed an entirely unmotivated attack on American mothers and grandmothers. He criticized their loud laughter, their bottomless thirst for being amused, their weird "feminist" way of defying men while at the same time fishing outrageously for compliments from them, their way of dressing too youthfully and having their faces lifted (which he called *hygiène de peau*). "They don't want to fool anyone by being radically *'lifté'*; they just want to look like other face-lifted women, to prove they're rich enough for the surgery. Their happiness is completed with a little dog and a draft."

They belong to no particular milieu and want only their own garish independence. When someone French asked Bobbie Jean her age, she said, "I don't remember." When her interlocutor insisted, she replied, "How do you expect me to remember a number that changes all the time?" That was considered very witty, though Addy thought it was impertinent and "typical." Later he muttered that American women represented "an unknown model," *un modèle inconnu*, and weren't "realistic."

CHAPTER II

It was about then that I took my first lover and started my salon. He was an Italian prince and at first I thought he preferred men. He took me to the theater one evening and after the play to supper at Le Grand Véfour. Over our food he said he liked the play by Anouilh that we'd just seen because it embodied the typical French virtues of "irony, lightness, and speed." I was so impressed and enjoying myself so thoroughly (though he wasn't handsome or young), I asked him to repeat what he'd just said, it was so intelligent, and he did so with some embarrassment (he was afraid of sounding pedantic) and then, after my third glass of Chablis, I blurted out, "*Êtes-vous pédé?* (Are you a fag?) Do you like men or do you like women?" And he said with a sweet smile and in a low voice, "I like flowers."

"No, seriously?"

"Women. I hope that doesn't disappoint you."

"Why should it disappoint me?"

"Some women feel safe only around their capons. And those men are usually more clever than us dull normals all normaling around."

"You're so refined. And mysterious. And such good company. That's the only reason I thought you might be homosexual."

"I'm also Italian."

"So?"

"We're pleasant people. Stendhal said, 'The French are Italians in a bad mood.'"

I laughed, the new tinkling French laugh I'd exchanged for my American gasp-and-roar. "You're an enchanting man," I said.

"Not exactly the virile adjective we were hoping for."

I touched his leg under the table. He smelled wonderful: bergamot, I guessed.

He said, "I'm so afraid of assertive American women that you'll have to take all the initial steps."

"Toward what?"

"Whatever your heart desires."

In the car home (it was raining), I leaned over and kissed him. "How do I know if you like it?"

"Now you know the dilemma we men constantly face. Yes, I like it. Lots."

"I've always dreamed of being the active one. On top. In charge." I looked out after a sudden deluge of rain swamped the window; maybe an over-heavy branch above us just bent. "Do you like to be tied up?"

"I've never tried it. But it's an intriguing idea."

"Are you from Rome?"

"No. A village in the south. Teggiano. I'm not only the prince of Padula but the duke of Teggiano. Our patron saint is San Cono. He's named that after his cone-shaped head, which has something to do with the Trinity. He also used it to deflect cannonballs aimed at the Teggiano castle."

"Saint Conehead? How delicious. And you a prince?"

"Every other person in Italy is a prince. And in southern Italy we use all our titles. 'Prince, would you like something to drink?' 'Thank you, Prince, but I already have some prosecco.' It makes aristocrats from elsewhere laugh at us."

I was familiar enough now with this form of aristocratic self-mockery not to take it too seriously. It was of a piece with titled ladies who claimed that their couture dresses came from a secondhand stall at the market on the Ile de Ré or that they'd found their Hubert Robert painting of the Roman forum in a Brussels bistro covered with grease. I suppose now we would call it humble-bragging; it was intended to defuse envy of everything but their discerning eye, or, in this case, to laugh at their pretensions to an ancient title they had a perfect right to bear. Or to tease them for the ancestral castle they were fortunate enough to inherit.

"I'm so bored. I'm thinking of starting a salon, or is that idea a little *desuète*?"

"What sort of salon?"

"Music. At literary salons you have to listen to writers read. Or, worse, talk."

"A music salon sounds very amusing. I'll help you if I can. Would Adhéaume approve?"

"Who cares? He's too busy restoring his family château or going to auctions or bedding new mistresses."

The prince just arched an eyebrow. "Do you know any composers?"

"No. Are they difficult to find (*dénicher*)?"

"I know a music critic for *Figaro*. I'll ask him for a list. I assume most composers want a free meal. Which will be your day?"

"My day? Oh—Sunday. It's always so gloomy, Sunday."

"We'll invite the *gratin*, the ones who think of themselves as intelligent. Critics, of course. Will your salon be avant-garde? Nothing hummable, squeaks and squawks? Or melodic—Auric, Honneger, that sort of thing?"

"What's chicer?"

"Squeaks and squawks."

"Then it shall be avant-garde."

"You'll have to buy big speakers and a state-of-the-art tape deck. The music is really and truly unbearable."

"Bring it on. Only the philistines will protest. It will be a sort of test."

I felt guilty taking up any hobby that would consume my time when the children were still so little. They didn't need me. They had the wet nurse and soon the new German nanny whom Adhéaume was lining up, and the house servants were always fluttering around them, but people were constantly saying children grew up so quick that I was afraid of missing something irreplaceable. I hadn't had my tubes tied nor was Addy out of commission, but I felt these two children were my legacy, my *patrimoine*, and like Chinese women during the Cultural Revolution I'd be sterilized if I exceeded my limit.

His name was Ercole Moncada. Principe Moncada. I found him very attractive. I kissed him on the lips when we reached my doorway on the Avenue Foch. The usual streetwalker was standing in the doorway. We nodded at each other politely. The prince said, "*À bientôt, j'espère*."

He was wearing a dark blue suit (not as tight as one of Addy's), a white shirt, and a plain dark-blue silk tie. He had a white linen handkerchief, not in stiff little peaks but sumptuously casual in his breast pocket. He wore a gold ring mounting for a black cameo, a Roman emperor, no doubt. He was tall and slender, with a full head of long, straight silver hair pushed back from his face. I wondered if he'd have white chest hair and hair on his shoulders. Men! But I loved his bergamot cologne and I'd felt its aura pulsing around me all evening; irrationally I ascribed it to him, to his body.

I thought about him as I undressed and lay in bed. Maybe I'd never been in love with Addy, but I had nursed the illusion that he loved me, at least as the "little mother" of his heir, Foulques. Some days the only time I'd see him was when he visited the nursery, held his son, and even threw him in the air (which I hated). But Foulques seemed to find it exhilarating and smiled his toothless, senile, slightly mad smile. Adhéaume gave me no credit as a parent, as if I'd been nothing more than a surrogate, a *mère porteuse*, as people say now—as if I'd done nothing more than *carry* the fetus. His coldness to me left me feeling very wounded, as if he'd married this raw-boned, big-toothed Texan for her money alone, which everyone said but I hadn't wanted to believe.

It was insulting, I felt deeply humiliated; he'd raided my womb as he was emptying my coffers, transferring my family wealth into his family château, grafting my babies onto his family tree. He'd won on every front and I felt like—oh, I smelled the faint echo of bergamot on my hand. I thought that probably Ercole was just one more duplicitous European, but I was tempted to believe in him. I felt torn between the modesty that had been drilled into me and my desire for revenge.

Two days later Ercole's chauffeur delivered a little tree of bergamot oranges, clearly labeled with a neatly printed botanical word planted in the soil. The fragrance was bewitching, unforgettable. I looked it up in a multivolume Larousse and found it was called sour orange or sweet lemon, which left me slightly mystified. The oil of its peel was used in the eighteenth century for the first eau de cologne. It was the flavor of Earl Grey tea. The oranges were greenish, larger than lemons but smaller than oranges. The leaves were polished. I found a handwritten note in a crested envelope: "I had this little tree brought by car from southern Italy because you said you liked the scent. I hope it's not overpowering. I have no idea how to care for it; my gardener says to water it once a week and give it lots of sunlight (good luck with that in Paris). Your faithful servant, Ercole."

His closing sentiment excited me. Two days later, when Addy had left for the Var, I sent Ercole a pneu inviting him to stop by for a drink—late, around ten thirty or eleven. I addressed it to "my faithful servant," and signed it just "Y." I felt my breasts twitch, or did I just imagine that? I didn't let myself think too much about what I was doing.

At ten forty-five a servant brought the prince into the smaller salon, where I was sitting by the fire. I rose to greet him. The servant gave him a whiskey and soda and withdrew, closing the double doors behind him. The prince took my extended hand and bent toward it. He was wearing white trousers, a dark blue jacket, a rose-colored polo shirt, and a foulard, as if he were on a yacht. "Sit here, beside me." I'd made that delicate transition to the informal *you*, but he persisted in addressing me as *vous*, as if I were older or more important—or more powerful. It could have been a rejection of intimacy, but I didn't take it that way.

I said in a very firm voice, "I wore boots for you."

He lowered his eyes and said, "Thank you."

"Kiss them."

He slid to his knees beside me and without looking up bent to kiss my boot.

"Good boy," I said.

There are so few moments in life, especially social life, when one is required to be bold. Usually, everything, from which direction to walk to which restaurant to choose, is arrived at through a micro-series of confer-ences and concessions as one coaxes forth reservations or mixed responses or hidden desires. But in this kind of domination sex (or so at least I imagined) the least hesitation or wavering of the will would make the mood evaporate. As I would learn, the great enemies of sadism are laughter and irony because they require perspective and evaluation, a fatal distancing. Just as the facilitating angel (or devil) was determination. What was sexy was one will making another will bend to it.

"You can take your clothes off," I said.

"Thank you, thank you," he muttered. Only now did he look up at me from his kneeling position with supplication in his eyes. He looked twenty years younger. He shrugged off his jacket and pulled his shirt down (for a moment his silk foulard was still tied around his neck and hanging down on his chest, as hairless as a ballet dancer's, a *danseur noble*, I thought inconsequentially). He unknotted it, stood, with his head down, awkwardly stepped out of his moccasins, undid his trousers, and peeled off his underwear. Big penis, small patch of hair, no paunch, large nipples with a history, I thought, which thrilled me. My hunch was right! A hard erection. He must like this sort of thing!

That first time I didn't get much beyond twisting his nipples and whispering insults. When I called him a pig (*cochon*) he had a climax without touching himself. I was very gratified and within seconds I had my orgasm, though I did touch myself. I heard a clicking sound and thought I noticed a flash, but a minute later I dismissed that paranoid notion as just the evidence of a guilty conscience. I smiled and shook my hair out and pulled him up beside me and kissed him; I'd hiked up my skirt but otherwise stayed fully clothed. It was the first time I'd ever enjoyed sex with a man. I was very affectionate to him, still just following my instincts. I wish I'd read a manual or something or Sade.

Ercole and I had lots of fun together and our sex roles didn't inflect our off-stage behavior. We were good pals and laughed a lot. He showed me pictures of his castle, which looked like an anthill with flags; he even showed me Saint Conehead, with his neon halo! Much more impressive was the monastery at Padula, a baroque masterpiece that Napoleon had looted of its paintings but that was overwhelming architecturally with its vast cloisters, its inlaid semiprecious stone altars, its trompe l'oeil octagonal tower.

We found a little shop on the Rue des Archives that sold leather whips and manacles; we were nearly breathless when we got them to his place on the Rue du Bac. We didn't talk at all on the ride back and my hands were shaking as I tore open the overly ingenious French package.

I'll draw a veil over our exploits lest I offend my younger readers but suffice it to say that I spent hours daydreaming about Ercole's next humiliations. I found my thoughts were far more occupied with punishment than music. Though for all that, my thoughts (and deeds) were highly creative—constantly daring myself to go further and further while always advancing a controlled, coherent narrative. In the end it became more verbal than physical, with me barking commands and he whispering compliance. Sometimes I felt a twinge of performance anxiety just before he was due to arrive, but his gratitude (he even wept grateful tears) banished all stage fright and elevated me in my own eyes. I saw myself as beautiful and imperious, and since I was both things our sport didn't require too much playacting.

My husband, who spent hours every day on the phone and gossiping at the Jockey, was soon abreast of my intimacy with Prince Moncada. "I see you've taken up with Ercole. Isn't he a little old for you? Isn't he impotent? How does he like that worn-out pussy of yours?"

"He likes it fine," I said, "since he got past the worn-out part. He has a very large penis."

"How Texan! Texans are always saying Texas is as large as France—but there's nothing *in* Texas! Whereas France is so varied, from the palm trees of the Côte d'Azur to the pines of Burgundy, from the cold Atlantic coast to the hundreds—thousands!—of châteaux, from the Pyrenees full of bears to the Breton coast crowded with oysters. You Texans always care about size rather than quality."

"His penis is of the highest quality. He's a prince and a duke. You sound like a travelogue."

Our first composer was a Greek, Kolonakis, immensely respected and utterly repugnant. His face had been shot and deformed in the Greek civil war against the monarchists (Kolonakis was a Communist). He was due to be executed when he slipped (illegally) into France, where he studied mathematics and architecture (he worked in Le Corbusier's atelier). None of the prominent composers in France (Honegger, Nadia Boulanger) liked his music. When he asked Messiaen if he needed to study harmony and counterpoint, the older, bird-crazed mystic said, "No. You already know mathematical and scientific theory—that should suffice," and Kolonakis turned around and did a composition based on the mathematical expansion (or was it saturation?) of gases, and soon was doing game theory, set theory, and stochastics, whatever that is. *Musique concrète*, electronic music—you name it. If it was avant-garde and intolerable he was for it. He had a silly journalist wife whose trademark was round red glasses, and a whiny daughter.

He was reserved and his conversation was very abstract, or concrete—anyway, impossible to understand. He never looked us in the eye. I think he could see right away that we were rich dilettantes just waiting to be milked for money; that we were foreigners like him made us more attractive. A bit exotic. Naive. Ercole and I had him for dinner and we peppered him with questions, as no real French person could possibly do. We were complicitous in a way I'd never been with Addy; I toyed with the fantasy of being married to him but wondered how divorce would affect the children. Was divorce always a bad thing? What if it cut through unbearable tensions? I think Kolonakis was puzzled how such uninformed people could like his work; it was all about being initiated.

But he liked being humored and having his hopes raised. I showed him our immense reception rooms and said that we wanted to stage a performance of music by him and his friends; it could be on a Sunday evening with champagne a-go-go and hot food. He could invite whoever he liked.

He warned us that we would need to warn the neighbors—it would be deafening. We could also have (via a recording) the Paris premiere of Charles Wuorinen's Third Symphony—the American, won the Pulitzer, you know, he was passing through Paris on his way to Stuttgart (the performance would be in the presence of the composer). There were other Americans who could be had for the price of an airplane ticket and a hotel room—Gordon Mumma, Roger Reynolds, Robert Ashley. "The ultimate, of course, would be Boisrond."

"What about Stockhausen?" Ercole asked (he'd been doing his homework).

"Can you afford twelve musicians?"

"Oh, yes," I said.

"Certainly."

"Or we could have a pianist play some of the *Klavierstück II*," Kolonakis said.

"Great," I murmured, nodding vigorously.

I hoped he wouldn't ask me what was so great. He was the most unsmiling man I'd ever met. I thought how lucky earlier musical *salonnières* had been with their Debussy and Ravel. "But we don't want just these foreigners *en passage*. We want French composers who will come back each week," Ercole said. I added as our ultimate bait, "With your decision we can present the best composers at the Salle Pleyel," naming the most prestigious concert hall.

"My decision?"

"You can name the best."

"I don't think in those terms," Kolonakis said, but I could tell he was pleased in his grudging way.

After he left, Ercole and I fell into each other's arms. It was as if we'd both trod a high wire for the first time and the audience below was roaring its applause. He was passionate yet tender and not at all kinky. Nor was I. We'd performed as a perfect team together. Though we were frivolous and ignorant, we'd hoodwinked one of the most savvy artists around. We felt like sexy teenage con artists, incestuous brother and sister using our pretend wealth and titles to leave a mark on the world. We knew perfectly well that we'd be forgotten in fifty years like all the other Parisian *mondains*, with their couture clothes, their restored châteaux, their Bugattis and Goyas; their white parchment interiors; their *bals masques* on themes (heads, kings, surrealism, impersonations); their black bamboo *fumoirs*; their friends in Bohemia, the Church, the government, the police, the gestapo, the arts; their famous team of chefs, their first editions; their lifeguard lovers; their Thoroughbred horses; their royal houseguests: all forgotten unless their names were perpetuated through the arts. This life is ruled by the rich, the fashionable, the trendy, and the beautiful; the afterlife is ruled by artists and scientists alone.

Although I was in my mid-twenties, had borne two children, had a disappointing marriage, and certainly wasn't innocent, I was inexperienced. I was beginning to learn the codes of this ancient, capricious world I'd joined, but I still didn't understand this inconvenient stranger I was yoked to: myself. I could feel the elephant's immense, delicate ear in the dark but I still knew nothing of its feet, its trunk, its weary, expressive eyes, its mud-spattered hide, its big gleaming tusks, its tucked-away mouth gently chewing grass, its little-girl tail, its matronly, mountainous bulk suddenly lunging and teetering to its full height. I'd felt only the delicate, vein-rich ear. I knew nothing else of this stranger I was living with, pacific but warlike, silent until trumpeting.

Ercole was reassuringly older, the heir to an ancient title, an insider who never flaunted his privilege, rich enough to be indifferent to my wealth, fluent in six or seven languages, related to most of Europe, modest, polite and kind, madly in love with me. He was tall, well dressed without the usual male narcissism, he enjoyed submitting to me in bed but he wasn't passive or cringing or even very servile unless I switched on that particular red spotlight—in which case he instantly assumed the position. I didn't have the will or desire to dominate him except in bed. I visited a sex shop and bought some tit clamps and a big black rubber dildo. I had to keep him interested.

Not that I had to work at it. Everything I did (or just *was*) delighted him. He liked the springiness of my body, my perfume (*Ivoire*), my cunt and its modest curtain of blonde hair; he said I was a *femme fontaine*. I didn't know what that meant. "It's just that you are always . . . wet down there." I thought it was nice to have a feature ascribed to me that I'd never noticed before. When he kissed my breasts and buried his face between them, I pointed at my stomach. "No, here—this is the good part." He held me by the wrists, pinned to the mattress, and with a sad—or maybe just a tender—look, he stared at me and said solemnly, "All your parts are good, my darling."

Soon my Sundays were thriving. At first the musicians clung together in one corner. They seemed overawed with the vastness of our rooms on the Avenue Foch, or maybe they were intimidated by so many titles and such suave manners in our other guests; the members of the *gratin* were polite, though their enthusiasm for electronic music seemed feigned even if their pursuit of the latest cry (*le dernier cri*) and of the true genius of the moment (*le vrai génie du moment*) was spirited enough. Kolonakis told us that in the Left Bank world of artists people were excrutiatingly frank and given to *rosserie* (nastiness), whereas the *gratin* seemed the last civilized beings on earth. We could say cruel things ("She's gone to a better demi-monde"), but in the name of wit.

For my Sunday teas I had mountains of little sandwiches of all colors, pyramids of vanilla or raspberry macaroons, *pains au chocolat* still warm from Boissier, babas, and brioches. If it was a long, demanding composition that lasted over two hours I had something warm like a lamb navarin or a Moroccan couscous, which was still a rarity in those days. The children's German nanny helped translate for some East German composers.

We were determined to snare Eugène Boisrond for our Sundays. He was famously disagreeable, anti-Semitic, but weirdly compassionate toward the poor; he earned his living as a doctor, a general practitioner to the needy. And he lived amid them in a dirty little pavilion in Saint-Ouen. No one had ever met him, though his strange compositions had all the other composers in awe. He was some sort of mystic (but an atheist, of course) and his scores looked like mandalas. It was anyone's guess how to play them, as arbitrary and undefined as Bach's *Art of the Fugue*. The scores were so beautiful they were suitable for framing.

To get up our courage to beard the lion, we were drunk by noon. I had the cook pack a little osier basket with crustless sandwiches (paté, foie gras, cucumber) and splits of vintage champagne and little sweet or savory pies and we went to his address unannounced. The door was opened by a maid missing a few teeth (we later learned she was his much younger English wife) to reveal two nude babies trailing dirty nappies. "*Qui êtes-vous?*" she asked. We introduced ourselves in English and said we'd brought lunch for everyone and we were here to meet the great man. She gave her name as something like Paraffin or Peregrine and said Dr. Boisrond was seeing patients in his clinic downstairs. We said we'd wait and, uninvited, sat down in chairs burdened with dirty clothes. Paraffin left the room (one of her legs was shorter than the other), and went clomping down the stairs while sighing noisily, leaving us alone with the children, the youngest drooling on his sunsuit, the oldest staring at us while reaming her nose with her finger.

At last the doctor came steaming into the room in his white coat, his stethoscope around his thin neck, his face pale with anger. He was bald on top and his white fringe was cut down to the quick. We stood, laughed a bit, and told him in our slurred speech what great admirers we were and that we'd brought lunch. He glared at us and took a moment to respond, never smiling. "You're both drunk. You weren't invited. Take your food. Get out—now! I don't like people like you. I know you're cultivating musicians to show off at your salon but I'm not interested. Get out! Don't ever come back."

Paraffin was wringing her big, unpainted hands and grimacing with a little tic of a smile. I wondered if she might be a man, a transvestite, or just English. We went scrambling for the door, and going down the stairs I fell and felt a terrible pain stabbing me in the knee. The doctor looked out the front window and closed the blinds. Ercole carried me to the waiting car and we had the driver take us to the emergency room at the Hôtel-Dieu. I was weeping and even yelping from the pain, which was so severe I didn't worry for once what sort of impression I was making. I was carried into the *Urgence* and luckily it was empty and I was seen right away. A nurse disinfected and bandaged my knee. I was taken in a wheelchair to a little room about five minutes away and X-rayed. When I was brought back to the waiting room and Ercole, another nurse gave me some strong painkillers. In fifteen minutes I was feeling better and had stopped crying. At last a thin, young, mustached doctor came in, waving an X-ray. He said, "You've had quite the fracture; I'm going to have to set your leg in plaster."

The sedative was so strong that soon I was asleep and woke up only from time to time as the doctor and the nurse embalmed my leg. Then

I was wheeled back to Ercole and he whistled like a schoolboy when he saw my cast.

"Is *monsieur* your husband?" the doctor asked.

"Brother."

"Will you have someone to look after you, Madame—"

Stupidly I said, "*Je suis la baronne de Courcy.*"

"Of course," he said nonsensically, slightly inclining his head as—a reverence? A bow.

They gave me a small paper envelope of twenty more painkillers and an appointment for a week later. Ercole paid them something. A hospital porter wheeled me out to the car and Ercole tipped him and lifted me onto the back seat, making sure my leg was stretched out on the seat. The man guided the wheelchair back into the emergency room. Ercole sat up front with the driver. He looked back, reaching to squeeze my hand reassuringly. He caught my eye and we both burst out laughing. I tried to sober up; I was afraid it was the pill that was making everything so hilarious. But we both had a *fou rire* and soon we were bubbling over, each in turn and then simultaneously.

When Clementine, my maid, in her starched white apron and cap, opened the door her mouth fell open. "*Mais oo-la-la. Qu'est-ce que çela? Mais vous avait eu un incident, Madame. Monsieur le prince, je peux vous aider? Portez madame par là, dans le salon. J'appèlle un medecin, Madame?*"

I assured her everything was all right. The prince carried me up the stairs to my bedroom and stretched me out on the love seat. Clementine was rushing around clucking and approaching me to straighten my skirt and unlace my shoes. I asked her to bring me a glass of water and the prince Scotch *avec des glaçons*. "*Tout de suite, Madame la baronne.*" Through my haze I smiled at Ercole; I probably looked tear-stained, my lipstick mumbled away, my mascara streaked, but I *felt* like one of those dazzling, creamy Hollywood actresses shot through gauze, tiny backlights sparkling in her eyes and defining the glycerine contours of her lips.

We entered into a new phase of our relationship. We still had our Sundays, with the delicious food, horrible, rumbling music, social awkwardness between *gratin* and *canaille*, but we also had our Tuesdays,

Wednesdays, Thursdays, and Fridays alone, driving into the country to see the Château de Vaux-le-Vicomte and eat there in Le Nôtre's garden by candlelight while listening to a scratchy string orchestra play Lully, more soothing but no less dull than the music we were sponsoring. As spring turned to summer I was released from my itchy cast (still pure white, though in Texas my sorority sisters would have scribbled all over it and drawn wobbly hearts). We motored to Deauville and Ercole showed me the spooky *Psycho* Second Empire house, all gables and shutters, his family had rented many summers long ago. We had a wonderful seaside dinner at Trouville and he indicated to me his rather battered-looking small yacht, the *Felice*, in need of a coat of varnish.

We drove out to Chantilly, where he'd somehow arranged to keep two racehorses in the historic stables (they were named Jicky and True Love). He said they were both males and earned him lots of money when he put them out to stud.

Every once in a while we'd break the silence and one of us would just say, "Boisrond," and we'd both burst out laughing. We were like those prisoners who've told all their jokes to one another so often that all they needed was to call out "Number Eleven" or "Number Three" in order to collapse with laughter. "Boisrond," one of us would say, and soon we'd be falling about. If we were in the nursery the children smiled sympathetically but looked puzzled. The prince was a good cook and would rustle us up some pasta, a spicy puttanesca, which he said was what whores would cook late at night for their customers (could that be true?). We spoke English most of the time, French when there were others around. Ercole said in his family they'd always spoken French at the table. Not only did he spend his summers in France but after the age of fourteen he attended Le Rosey, a French-speaking school in Switzerland. He told me his first lover had been another boy at Rosey, an Indian prince; he'd gone back to India with him, to Srinagar, a beautiful city in Kashmir with snow-covered mountains in the distance and brightly painted houseboats on the lake. They were known as "the two princes." The lover was Muslim, which meant he was circumcised—the first circumcision Ercole had ever seen up close. He preferred it to his own abundant foreskin; it was "cleaner." The city was warm in the summer but not hot;

it was filled with mosquitoes, mosques, and temples, Hindu and Jain.
They listened to records of a singer of ghazels, Begum something. Rather
eerie, but he grew to like it. "Maybe that's what prepared me for our odd
musical tastes," he said, laughing. Then he went silent as he often did
when he thought he'd said something banal or vulgar or middle-class.

"Maybe I'll send my children to Rosey," I said.

"They'll meet lots of future monarchs. It's the most expensive school
in the world: one hundred thirty thousand dollars per kid per year. The
winter months are spent at Gstaad skiing. That's the campus in January
and February."

Adhéaume was seldom around. He only raised an eyebrow when he
saw my leg in a cast. "I won't ask you how that happened," he said. "You
must be tired of answering that question."

I shrugged. "How's the house coming?" That's what I called the
château—the house.

"It's so much work. And the children?"

"Fine."

"And Hercule?" Addy preferred that to Ercole because that allowed
him to linger on "cul," "ass," or "sex" in general (ribald stories were called
histoires de cul).

"The prince is fine," I said. He knew I knew that one of his friends at
the Jockey said, "For me humanity begins only with the rank of baron."

The next time I was alone with Ercole I said, "I was so happy you told
me about your boyhood flirtation with the other prince."

"Why?"

"I get crushes on girls. My first experience was with a girl. We were
fourteen."

"That age . . . My theory is that oversexed teens, at least in the past,
always had sex with other kids of the same gender. It's easier, more available, just as exciting and romantic, and sophisticated people don't take it
seriously. Homosexuality isn't dynastic."

"I still find myself attracted to women."

Ercole stroked his chin and said, "Men and boys leave me cold. But
the idea of two women excites me, I suppose as it does most men." He
went silent with embarrassment.

After I poured us more tea I said, "If we ever find a willing victim . . ."

He stood to take his cup, bent down to kiss me, and said, "So much for this famous American puritanism."

"Texans aren't Yankees," I nearly shouted. Then I let out a rebel yell and the governess came out of the nursery looking worried. "Is the *Freiherrin* all right?" It was Addy's idea that the children's first language should be German. ("Since it's so difficult. Anyone can learn English and the romance languages.")

The prince also looked startled, then pleased. He examined me with a new respect, as if he'd just discovered I had infrasonic powers. I suppose I felt a little guilty "cheating" on my fortune-hunting, mistress-collecting husband, but only out of some vestigial Dallas prudery. What the French called our "puritanism," though they had no idea what that word meant.

We had passed to that most intimate of all stages—Ercole and I could read together in companionable silence. Sometimes I would forget where we were and if he made a comment I'd have to pipe myself back into reality, to this study on the Avenue Foch, to the realization that Ghislaine and Foulques were napping in the next room, that the German nanny was humming a Prussian melody to the children.

Ercole decided to paint my portrait—or rather to draw it in pastels. He seemed to know what he was doing. He rolled up his sleeves and took a board onto his lap. I arranged the lights so they were trained on a bergère, which I occupied. I was prepared for the worst—big teeth, a swirl of egg-yolk-colored hair, the full-on frontal grin of a madwoman, clown's patches of red on my cheeks. But of course I hoped, as everyone does, for something insightful, idealizing and charming, an expert vision rather than an incompetent daub.

He squinted at me in that artist's way of studying the angle of your cheekbone or the tilt of your nose, which is suddenly more important than your soul, even your consciousness. They say babies are attracted to human faces because our features maximize light and shadow in a compact space—the slash of a mouth under the rudder of the nose and the liquid, moving eyes under their batting curtains of fringed tissue (I'd noticed my babies were magnetized by my face). Artists are the same, looking at the commotion of light and dark inscribed in the narrow orbit of the face, this oval posed on the flexible column of the neck.

Ercole looked at me with a cold, scientific expression, not registering or reacting to my words (I was silent) or my *moues* (I was motionless). For him I was a still life of fruit and vegetables, *une tête composée*, a code of lights and shadows. The German nanny brought the children in for a minute. Just taking one or the other (usually Foulques) in my arms made me melt. And also feel rather dirty—why was this new mother having an affair?

"Tell me about your life," I said, when they had left in a Teutonic flurry of guttural sounds and tut-tuts.

"At Rosey you had to follow the curriculum in French or in English, so I chose French, of course, though my Indian prince spoke to me in English, a rapid, singsongy English that tripped over certain consonants and darkened certain vowels. I was a good swimmer and equestrian, played an energetic game of tennis and skied well, even liked danger, and at Gstaad had a helicopter fly me to uncharted mountaintops where there were only wolf prints in the snow.

"I played soccer but didn't follow the teams. I thought being a fan, *un tifoso*, was silly or maybe ignoble. After school I went to Brazil, where my father had a huge ranch near Ouro Preto. I loved the old baroque city. I learned Portuguese—well, their kind of Portuguese. I had known some Orléans-Gonzagas at Rosey and they became friends in Brazil. One of them, I think the pretender to the throne, was a nice enough guy, a nature photographer, I forget his name. But we partied a lot. While there I met Isabella from Uruguay, a real beauty who'd studied art history in Paris. At that time I was thinking of becoming a diplomat and she'd be perfect as the wife of a consul or cultural attaché. Beautiful, fluent in three languages, *grande bourgeoisie* who knew how to flatter foreigners and manage a staff and set a table and talk about art to avoid politics. We got married in Montevideo and were together twenty years and had two sons.

"I tried to get into Sciences Po here in Paris, but my grades weren't good enough. Then we moved to Rome, where I became a painter, and we lived in a family palazzo near the Campo de' Fiori. I had a show at the Obelisco Gallery but nothing sold and no one came except relatives. I did abstractions with glossy, gooey brushstrokes like Soulages. I thought of growing raisins—"

"Grapes," I said.

"Grapes on one of our estates near Genoa, but I was allergic to wine (I drink Scotch as you know) and soon gave it up. We went to my village in the cool months and Isabella learned Italian and even my dialect and wrote a Campania cookbook, but she was bored, took up with an archaeologist from a dig near Naples, Dutch guy named Hoob Something or Something Hoob—and everything just frittered away. She left me and I think she and Hoob live now in Asunción, which is the cheapest capital in the world."

"Where is it?"

"Paraguay. They took the children, who are now grown-up. Pedro is an ecologist and Martin is a businessman in Spain, in Valencia—he sells cars, I think. Hoob is digging away, but now prospecting for oil in a region called the Chacos. I find I'm happiest in Paris and Teggiano, my castle. I've never settled on a career, though I've learned to play the guitar and of course I have my horses and the village takes up a lot of time, what with the celebrations around Saint Conehead and some sort of Renaissance marriage with a princess from Urbino that gets celebrated every year in late summer when everyone wears Renaissance costumes and there's lots of loud drum-beating."

"And mistresses?"

Ercole just smiled in that maddening way Southern Europeans have of not answering an indiscreet question. If the question is repeated they just smile more.

"But what was your life like with Isabella?" I asked. Of course, between lovers such questions are never innocent; the interrogator wants to know what lies in store for her and the responder is carefully shaping his response to indicate likes and dislikes and to make himself appear in a favorable light.

"She was neurotic? *Caractérielle?*" he said, looking for the word in either language. "In front of other people (not our sons) she would play the *principessa*, even mention my modest accomplishments, but when we were alone she would go on weeklong fasts of silence, treat my goals as trivial, my lineage as probably fake, make a loud, hissing sound like a goose if I touched her. She turned our boys against me and taught them the English word 'malingerer' to describe me, as if I were lazy or hyperchondriacal by nature. Pedro invented a new last name for himself, joined the Communist Party in Italy, and refers to me as 'comrade.' He'd sooner die than admit he's a prince. He says he's an ecologist, whatever that is if you're not a professor, but he lives off family money as we all do. Martin married a Catalan girl and has taken over her father's Mercedes dealership. He works very hard, speaks perfect Spanish, which of course he learned as a kid from his mother—pretends he *is* Spanish but from La Mancha—makes a good living, has no interest in us.

"I don't think Isabella really approved of me, once she saw that I had no direction in life. Here I was, in my fifties, still seeing a psychiatrist, trying to find myself, as they say. Then one day I was sitting in my Rome palazzo and listening to Schubert's *The Trout* in the rain. It was sunny outside and the rain looked like silver streaming through the sunlight. I was drinking a Cinzano with the most fragrant lemon peel you can imagine—cedro, those huge lemons from Sicily or Procida, too bitter to eat but good for perfume. I thought, I have found myself—and I'm here, comfortable, the music is complex enough to keep me awake but also melodic enough to delight me, wondrous in the way the piano enters, really like water pouring over white stones. Why should I be looking for a job? Jobs are always annoying. You can't travel when you want to. You can't sleep in when you're hungover. You can't read till dawn. And why take a job away from someone who needs it?

"If a couple has money they can each live apart, separate bedrooms, different friends. Two of my Italian friends here in Paris—he likes gardening in the South of France, he's famous for his gardens, she likes *une vie mondaine* in Paris and has people to dinner five nights a week, which he can't tolerate. They phone each other every day and are very kind to each other. When she's in the Midi she drives. He hates her driving and lies down in the back seat. He says he doesn't mind dying but doesn't want to see it happening. They get along perfectly. But they have the same *tempi.* They're both always busy, whereas Isabella is *presto* and I'm *lento* and that was the problem."

"It sounds as if she's not very kind, either," I said, but then he showed me his sketch of me, which many people would be satisfied with but which I thought looked too "commercial," as if he'd studied at a school for illustration advertised on the back of a matchbook, everything from the swoop of hair to the star in my eye, the stylized nose of two lines and two dots for nostrils, the long lashes, the unified teeth as if I were wearing a boxer's mouth guard.

"Hmmm . . . ," I said in a noncommittal British way. I was disappointed, not by a lack of skill (which I'd anticipated) but by a failure to look, really to look at me; his commercial conventions had occluded his actual powers of observation.

And yet he was very attentive in all the ways that counted. He knew what I liked to eat, that (unlike the French) I liked an open window and a breeze, that I needed to spend an hour alone with the children every afternoon, that I liked riding in the car beside him with no goal and with only occasional chatter, that I liked to go to the Louvre with him and just take in one room or two (he liked medieval armor, I preferred ancient Greek sculpture). My afternoon hour with the children was ransom paid to my conscience. I loved them, I knew they were too young to remember anything, but I worried that my seeming indifference, my truancy, would damage them for life. Sometimes Ercole and I would drive to the country, maybe south toward Vendôme, and leave the car behind and walk through the countryside, which was absolutely without interest except fascinating, just the smell of wet foliage, the occasional stand of trees, the less occasional passing tractor, the fenced-in cows who'd come as near as possible to us in their placid way, the huge heavens full of moving gray clouds, the low-eaved houses that looked deserted except for the few pieces of laundry drying on the line and flapping in the gathering wind, the fields of chrome-yellow *colza* (which in English is called rapeseed), brilliant patches of color in this landscape of dull, muted tones, the village where Ronsard was born. I was privately exhilarated that here I was, a big dumb Texas bottle blonde, living in France, not the tourist's France of châteaux and cathedrals but this solemn, everyday France of fields and cows and clouds, "everyday" except that, over there, was where Ronsard was born. I'd escaped Dallas. Sometimes I had to look up words in French in the bilingual dictionary to remember what they were in English. What did *voire* mean, something like "more precisely"?

I assumed that Addy was staying informed about our dalliance, but I didn't really care. Or rather, quite irrationally, I thought he might learn something from it—to be more considerate, less greedy, more solicitous—oh, it didn't make sense, but I wasn't about to let either Ercole or Addy go and my only hope was that this affair would be somehow "educational" for my husband, a learning experience.

I suppose I wanted at least the semblance of stability in my life for the children's sake. Our father had been so cruel to Yvette; it seemed very important to avoid comparable mistakes with my twins. Sometimes I felt detached from them, but wasn't that what a shrink would call a defense against feeling too much? I was still technically what people call young, therefore forgivable, but I felt terminally weary—and afraid of loving anyone too much. I was prepared for any rejection from anyone. Other people might think I was frivolous and spoiled, but my heart was cold, ever alert to the first sign of catastrophe. I looked like a *femme du monde* but in truth I was a seasoned soldier.

One day in Paris we spotted Helen at a café and asked if we could join her; that was easier to do because she and I were both American. I wondered if she was growing into her face-lift—it looked more natural, not so wounded, the planes molded out of terra-cotta, not struck from marble. She and Ercole got on famously; they'd both just seen an arty movie and discussed it endlessly and enthusiastically. I kept smiling as when friends exclaim over Corfu, where you've never been. I could see Helen was charmed by Ercole; when he got up to buy cigarettes, she whispered, "He's cute!"

"So are you," I said, which startled her, then made her lower her eyes coquettishly.

"I've never been with a woman," she said.

"Believe me, it's wonderful."

"I believe you," she said, looking into my eyes. She was dressed in a white middy blouse with a sailor's collar and a dark blue foulard. I leaned in to pour the rest of the coffee in the little pot into her cup. The day was warm enough that we were sitting on the terrace at Les Deux Magots, looking out at the church. It was before the full tourist season, so we kept studying the passing faces, thinking we might know someone. We spotted an ageless American man, Howard, with his lover-companion, who'd been his tennis coach in boarding school. Howard's grandfather had invented the airplane or something; he lived on the Rue du Bac in an apartment full of the latest gadgets and with an immense terrace. Helen said, "Hello, Howard."

He stared at her and said, "I'm sorry, who are you?"

"I'm Helen. We had dinner together last night."

He slapped his head theatrically and said, "Of course!" He kissed her on each cheek and hurried off to his table inside, where his coach-companion was already seated.

Helen said, "Poor thing. But if I were a dishy boy he'd remember me. He drinks so much but never ages."

I said, "They say his secret is sleep. He sleeps twelve hours a night. And he has a full facial at Carita every day. One of the girls there told me that. He likes the boys very young, dangerously young."

"I hope he knows officers in the police *mondaine*."

"His companion handles all that," she said. "But tell me, where did you meet Ercole?"

"We both like serious contemporary music. You must come to one of our Sundays."

"Yes, come," Ercole said, rejoining us. "This Sunday we have a very interesting middle-aged French composer named Boulez, very engaging and cerebral. The week after we have a Mormon, La Monte Young, a minimalist. It seems he has a soloist come out onstage in tails and with a score that he props up on a *pupitre* and then he beats a frying pan twenty-two times with a spoon while frowning at the score. I think it's called *Twenty-Two*."

Helen said, "This ridiculous twentieth century." Ercole added, "He has another piece where he just builds a fire onstage."

"Not exactly 'The Blue Danube,' but it sounds fun."

We girls swapped phone numbers.

Ercole confirmed that he found Helen attractive and the next day I phoned her around eleven. She was awake but still in bed. "I saw no reason to wait till Sunday," I said.

"No reason at all," she said boldly.

"There's a particular high-wire transvestite from Texas we want to see Thursday. He's at the Cirque d'Hiver Bouglione but we can just go see him or her at ten and then come back here for a late supper, just the three of us. Do you like oysters?"

"Sounds like a plan—love oysters. Aren't they supposed to be an aphrodisiac?"

"One can only hope. We'll swing by and pick you up. It's at the Cirque du Nord."

The funambulist was minuscule and spectral in a purple tutu, a dwarfing cyclamen wig, and lots of makeup. She pranced up and down the high wire in blue capezios, holding a horizontal balancing bar in her hands that she got rid of in order to do some backflips. Thunderous applause. She pulled off her wig and suddenly was a man and bowed from the secure crow's nest. We rushed backstage to congratulate her and were at last led down fecal-smelling corridors in a neighboring tent and finally into a dressing room, more closet than *loge*. She was eating animal crackers like a child and was wearing a red silk robe and towel turban and methodically cold-creaming her face clean. Under all that she was a little balding man with bad skin and an overbite; her body was terminally thin, a baby's formless body, hairless, like a fetus in a jar of formaldehyde. We talked for a moment, established that I was a Texan, too, learned that she hailed from Waco and was named Earl. Ercole said, "You're an earl?"

The performer said, "No, my name is Earl."

He/she seemed so shy and joyless, eager to scurry off to some anonymous *banlieu*, no doubt; meeting her was a real "buzzkill," as kids say now. We hurried away after congratulating her again and my saying she was "doing the Lone Star State proud." I imagine she was one of those Americans who feel contaminated speaking in English; she immediately barked something to a friend in French.

At home we had a big platter of oysters then *fruits de mer* that the cook had brought from a bistro nearby—there must have been a hundred creatures on the iced nickel tray, everything from tiny periwinkles we had to eat with a straight pin to big baroque oysters smelling of lemon and the sea, giant crab legs and clams and mussels ("I'm afraid of eating raw mussels," Helen said). After we cleared away the tray and all the apparatus and empty shells, the servant brought in warm finger bowls and a fricassee of three different kinds of mushrooms. For dessert we had orange ice with candied orange peel and candied mint leaves. We drank two bottles of a nice Vouvray.

I knew I was doing something irrevocable, a real injury to my marriage, but I said, "Let's go into my bedroom. I have a TV in there and there's something I'm dying to see." They followed me but when we were all sprawled on the bed I dimmed the lights and began to kiss Helen and to stroke her lovely delicate neck. I didn't much like the taste and feel of her lipstick, but I exulted in her girliness, the warmth and softness of her pliant body pressed to mine. I was propped up on one elbow and bending over her. She was lying on her back with one leg slightly bent. On her other side Ercole was lying on his side, kissing Helen's ear just above the diamond clip. He was rubbing his body against hers. I reached over and felt his erection through his trousers. I took Helen's hand in mine and pressed it against his penis. Again I heard a strange click—was I fated to hear it every time I slept with Ercole?

I'm not of the generation to go into detail about all this, but soon Ercole and I had undressed Helen. She lifted her buttocks as we slid off her very frilly panties. She sat up and kissed me while Ercole undid her brassiere, which released its delicate, full weight into my grateful hands (and eventually my mouth). Since Ercole was an experienced lover and since I *am* a woman, we both knew to go slowly and gently.

Helen touched me between the legs and whispered, "Oh my, you *are* wet . . ." That seemed to excite her. Soon we were all out of our clothes. First Ercole stood and undressed and untied his shoes, then he took over with Helen and I disrobed. Three-ways are first and foremost a problem of etiquette—no one should feel left out.

I caressed her as an ideal version of myself. I smelled the perfume on her neck and wrists, I sifted her hair from hand to hand as if it were gold dust to a miser, I felt the contours of her sumptuous body, not in a spirit of rivalry but of astonished veneration. I touched her superstitiously, as if she contained some wonder-working mystery, some essence that couldn't be inhaled or seen but somehow *felt*. She was *une idole*, if that means she was at once emblematic and real, a breathing woman whose hands were surprisingly warm, as if her hot blood were irrigating them, and her skin was so subtle her touch was surprising. Once I'd met Hélène Rochas at a party; she was the least pretentious and most captivating woman I'd ever encountered. When I'd mentioned to the worldly, gay man who'd introduced us how impressed I was, he shrugged and said matter-of-factly, "Yes, but she's a famous *idole*," and I'd been struck by the designation and what was apparently the common acceptance of her status. That was how I felt about Helen. She was affable enough but her conversation had a sovereign's deliberate banality; her mystery was not to be located in her manner but in something strong though intangible seeping out of her pores.

I could tell by her contractions around my hand that I excited her, but she was drawn to Ercole as to something familiar and soon he'd slipped into her and was riding her, which gave me a pang of jealousy. I was kissing her and playing with her breast, like Gabrielle d'Estrées tweaking the nipple of the duchess of Villars. Suddenly Helen surged up, lifting her arm and saying in a shockingly normal speaking voice (and in English), "I feel so alive." I think that triggered something in both Ercole and me; we began feasting on her lovely pale body with a new intensity. Her hips bucked with one orgasm, no two! Three! I looked at her tear-stained face, all her lipstick rubbed away to leave white lips, as if something studied and feminine had given way to something primitive and female.

All three of us subsided into a wordless, moaning conclave; we needed to console one another for having weathered such pleasure. My only fear was that we'd never feel this good again. Would Helen think we could reproduce this passion every day?

I heard one of the twins crying; I pulled on my robe and rushed into the nursery, guarding against the primal scene of maternal nudity and the odors of sex. When I had finally rocked Foulques (wasn't a *foulque* a coot or some sort of small game bird?) back to sleep I laid him carefully in his crib. I rejoined both my guests, who had fallen asleep. Had I broken a taboo? Would the moment of maternal coitus "imprint" the baby duck?

CHAPTER 12

A lthough I had intended to use the dildo on Ercole, I ended up employing it on Helen. I became slightly jealous that each time we all three got together, Ercole devoted himself mainly to Helen and began to treat me as if I were another man and we were both busy (as they say in old-fashioned porn) "pleasuring" her. He would kiss my neck and pat my ass when I bent over her and blocked his access. I wasn't sure who I was really jealous of—him for ignoring me or her for moaning louder when he penetrated her. Was she such a conventional woman that she had been raised to prefer men, even though I was the one who knew how to stimulate her clitoris with my finger? (I'd cut my nails short and stopped varnishing them.) I held the secret to her orgasms but as she climaxed she wrapped her arms around his neck, not mine.

After a few weeks of that I thought of arranging to see her one-on-one when I discovered that they were already seeing each other privately, and I was livid. I had pickpocketed Ercole's agenda and found a date and time and Helen's name. I confronted him and he shrugged and said, "I thought we were all evolved."

"Evolved? What does that mean? Walking on hind legs?" I asked.

"Sophisticated. Free. After all, you're a married woman. Your husband could be the indignant one." I must have looked close to tears; Ercole, who was kind, said, "It was only the one time. I was just curious. And randy."

"Was she the one who made the date, or was it you?"

He just smiled mysteriously.

"Answer me," I insisted, though I knew in our world—*their* world—insistence was a breach of etiquette.

"I honestly don't remember," he said in a quiet voice. I had to lean in to hear him. I realized I'd raised my voice and his soft tone was a rebuke.

I started discussing our musical salon. I hated being the jealous one, the angry one, the slighted one. In high school and college I'd always been careful to be pursued, never to pursue, to leave and not be left. Easier to stay in control when you're self-centered, as I was in school; I was genuinely indifferent to everything back then—rich, beautiful, a debutante, careless about the hearts I broke, about the bad grades I earned, about the friends I neglected and the friendships that lapsed. I could always retreat back into the fiction of childhood, the age that avoids all consequences. At the beginning with Ercole I'd been a mystery, partly because I was a foreigner given to strange gaffes, partly because I'd played the dominatrix, partly because I'd expected nothing of him except to playact at obedience.

I recovered, or at least I convinced him, I think, that all was forgiven and I'd probably forgotten the whole incident. I thought that to be successful in love requires a certain courage, an acting *as if* one is sane, self-respecting, autonomous, an ability to fake it till you make it. Jane Beth used to talk about being "cool," which I think was a word out of the jazz milieu, something that black men on heroin could impersonate, whereas in reality they were spooked by the possibility of being busted for drugs, they had stagefright like all performers, they wanted the respect of silent attentiveness from this drunk, noisy, giggling audience of white people rattling forks on plates and talking—oh, they had to be *cool* as they improvised on their instruments, skirting audaciously around the melody, observing the chord progressions while squeaking and spluttering ever more wildly—the coolness of carved ebony gods stiff in their hieratic elegance, their unreadable faces, fluid in their improvisations.

I wiped my hand over my face and refocused. I had to be casual, insouciant, self-respecting, but in fact I was very hurt. Maybe because I'd failed with Addy, or rather he'd failed me. From time to time—as in *now*—I panicked when I realized I was far from Dallas, cut off from my language, incapable of assuming any word or gesture, of even finding the switch on a light or the ground floor on an elevator. What if I became gravely ill or paralyzed? Who would take care of me? Or if I had a stroke and could no longer speak or understand French? I knew for sure that I didn't want to die abroad.

About a week later I took my French tutor, Berenice, a nice, extremely thin woman from Amiens who overarticulated in an upwardly mobile way, to dinner at Le Voltaire. The owner and his wife seemed embarrassed and wanted to seat us for some reason in the secondary room, not the one looking out on the Seine but the one at the end of the corridor on the right. "But we'll sit at my usual table," I said, irritated that they would try to shunt me off. Was it because we were two unaccompanied women? As soon as they led us in, I saw a friend, the Trieste composer Raffaello de Banfield, who was eating alone and kissed me on both cheeks; he was very rich and was partially subsidizing my musical evenings, even though his one-act opera (I'd heard a recording), *Lord Byron's Love Letter*, was sub-Puccini and infinitely easier on the ears than my lot's music. His opera had been performed (with Raffaello conducting) because the libretto was by Tennessee Williams.

Then I saw Ercole in the back booth with Helen, where now the Baron Redé sits with Charlotte Aillaud, Juliette Greco's sister. But Ercole and Helen were just as cozy, kissing each other like lovebirds. I signaled the waiter and said we'd like to be in the other room after all. My guest felt there was a draft in here. Luckily Berenice was hyper-discreet and didn't question me or object. We made it out without being spotted.

CHAPTER 13

Dear Yvonne,

I thought I'd write you on our birthday, August 8, though who knows how long it will take for this letter to reach you. I don't believe in astrology but I guess we're Leos, which should be a warning for me, a lesson in humility. People say Leo women like to be in charge, in control, and are very susceptible to flattery. Maybe that's why I work so hard to obey, to follow, to be humble, since I must fight my natural inclinations. Do you like to be in control? You write that Adhéaume is spending all your money and has moved his parents into the restored castle. You mention being unhappy in love. Do you mean with Adhéaume or with someone else? (Forgive me if I'm infringing on your privacy—I'm not accusing you of adultery!) I'm glad to hear you're tending a music salon; Saint Cecilia is one of my favorite saints and the music of Bach and Palestrina seems to me God's speech. It must be so delicious to live in that ethereal realm of endless melody, the most universal of all the arts (though no two people can agree on what a piece of music "means").

Here I am in Jericó and I'm reminded of the passage (Luke 19: 1–10) wherein Our Lord was wandering through that town, the Jericho in the Bible, and a rich man, the tax collector, Zacchaeus, who's very short, climbs up a tree in order to see Him. Jesus, spying him, says, "Zacchaeus, come down, for I want to go to your house. I want to stay at your house." And Zacchaeus does come down and leads Jesus to his house. But the people are grumbling that Jesus should stay with such an evil man. Before long they overhear him declaring to Jesus, "I am going to give half my property to the poor, and if I have cheated anybody I will pay him back four times the amount." And Jesus says, "Zacchaeus, today happiness has come to your house."

When I asked my bishop what was the meaning of this passage, he said that the true meaning of a genuine conversion must be expressed in deeds. And I wondered what deeds of mine grew out of my conversion. And I thought I would follow Zacchaeus's example and distribute alms to all the poor of the village, but it caused the most awful stampede of greed and grasping and beggars flooding the town crying and begging, so then I decided to dedicate a richly gilt and painted and stuccoed (they do the most marvelous stuccos here in the Portuguese style) chapel to Saint Catherine of Siena. Our missionary order, as you know, is dedicated to Saint Catherine. Concealing my own identity and working through the bishop, we assembled the most wonderful team of artisans, who illustrated the miracles of Saint Catherine. I was most affected by the one in which Saint Catherine exchanged hearts with God. Afterward she ate nothing but holy sacraments, the body and blood of Our Lord, which she feasted on daily. The local artisan portrayed Catherine as a brown-skinned indigenous woman in her white wimple and God as a cloud-borne deity, brown-skinned and slightly chubby. They held out bleeding hearts to each other, which looked like hunks of venison. After God implanted his heart in her body he sealed it and the scar could be seen ever after. Catherine is the patron saint of journalists because she wrote hundreds of letters. In one panel the artist depicts a journalist with a cigarette in his mouth banging away on his typewriter. It's all delightfully fresh and naive and infused with God's grace. One side panel renders the Crucifixion with the Blessed Virgin kneeling at the foot of the Cross. The other side panel is of our local religious, Blessed Laura Montoya, healing a few indigenous people, who look like exposed tree roots.

We had a solemn Mass to celebrate the unveiling of "my" altar; Bishop Oscar officiated. His sermon was all about Saint Catherine, who may have been an obedient nun but was a headstrong daughter. She defied her father's wish for her to marry her dead sister's widower. Instead she wedded Christ in a mystical marriage; her rather unusual wedding ring was Jesus's foreskin—which is the only part of him he left on earth since he ascended bodily to Heaven. You may think of the saints and the Trinity as vague and ethereal, but as you can see their faith and deeds were often daring, even scandalous.

I was unable to get the image of Jesus's foreskin slipping over Catherine's emaciated finger out of my mind. I confessed this unseemly thought to Bishop Oscar and he told me that I should regard it not as a temptation from the Devil but as a great blessing from God. Once he gave me permission to entertain this shocking thought, it was as if in my dreams and daydreams I was now free to lie down with my Lord, with his broken, livid, painfully thin body, which I'd contemplated so often suffering on the Cross. I knew his body better than my own; when I bathe, like all the nuns, I wear a simple loose-fitting smock into the tub, disguising all my shameful parts, and I wash myself sight unseen. I've mentioned before the spell cast on me by the odor of Oscar's perspiration. In my mystical embrace of Jesus's body this odor was combined with the sweet perfume of incense rising from the priest's swinging thurible.

In her *Dialogue* Saint Catherine hears from God himself that the meaning of the verse, "Whenever two or three will gather in my name . . ." is that the solitary individual cannot worship alone but must be joined by at least one other person, the Friend. I asked Bishop Oscar how he interpreted this passage and he said, "It's obvious. God cannot hear the hermit. He or she must join in prayer and adoration with at least one other person. 'If there be two or three or more gathered together in My name, I will be in the midst of them.'" I waited for Oscar to draw the parallel with us. I looked at him hungrily. (Saint Catherine thinks the pious must be hungry for God's grace.) Oscar blushed and looked away and said, "We are Friends in Jesus. Together we contemplate him hanging by his arms from the wood of his Sacred Cross, suffering for our redemption. He is God and man rolled into one; God is like the yeast that makes the bread rise."

I was so moved Oscar thought of me as a friend that I smiled. In that moment I was guilty of self-love. I think, sensing my sinful feelings, Bishop Oscar told me, "When Christ was crucified, his body became disgusting. He suffered more than anyone ever suffered. Blood and tears and saliva and pain poured forth from him. He was horrifying and his death shameful. He died between two thieves. He was like a worm in the dust. You must contemplate him with repugnance. If you want to measure the gravity of your sins you must look at his twisted, bleeding, repugnant body and say to yourself, 'I have left him like this. I killed him. To clean me of my filth he became filth.' Never forget that in order to redeem us God kneaded the human into the divine—and it was as a human he suffered for us and redeemed Adam's sin."

I had rarely heard the bishop speak with such urgency. He really did want us to see that Jesus was human and that his suffering was unbearable, that he wasn't some sort of impervious divinity, that the nails drove into his flesh and that the spear gored his side, that he suffered from the soldiers' mockery, that he felt abandoned just as we would.

How are the children? It must be odd to have fraternal not identical twins, to see the differences between male and female. Of course, you and I may be identical in body but maybe not in spirit—or maybe yes, that your spirit is as virginal as mine, as fierce and militant, though I strive to be humble and meek. And maybe I am as sensual as you, though I want so desperately to be pure. The least pure thing about me is that when I think of my marriage to Jesus, to surrendering to his sweet embrace, or when I think of Saint Catherine's wedding ring, I feel waves of heat crawl up my torso to turn my neck and face red in strange blotches of fever blossom and (I would confide this only to you) my vagina becomes extremely wet. We sprang from the same zygote—do you have these symptoms of desire and ecstasy? For me they are painful proof of the Old Man, the unredeemed part of me; they are my stigmata, as in stigma.

Did you know Saint Catherine had a twin sister who died at birth?

You must think I've gone crazy with piety. And yet I love my students, and my little future priest, my postulant, has become very good at Greek.

I think the diocese will try to send him to Rome to study the classics and theology. He's a tiny thing; I think his body was stunted from hunger. But not his mind! He is curious about everything and often he asks me questions about the scientific nature of the world I am unable to answer.

Oscar's best male friend, a very outspoken priest from El Salvador named Father José, has been assassinated, mowed down in the street by gangsters in a passing Chevrolet. His parish was in Chocó, a nearby coastal town, where he would preach against the authorities and the landowners. The cardinal tried to silence him, but he kept denouncing the enemies of the people and reminding them that God did not want anyone to be landless or hungry. He saw how the landowners held their campesinos in virtual slavery. I'm reminded of the Roman centurion who asked Jesus to cure his ailing slave. Jesus said, "Bring him to me," and the centurion said, "If you say a prayer he will be cured no matter where he is." Jesus was astonished and said, "I have never seen such faith, not even in Israel," and the slave was healed. For me the centurion's concern for his slave is the remarkable part of the story. In the eyes of God no man is a slave. We must love one another, even if they dislike us. We must love the murderers.

Bishop Oscar was so saddened by this event, the death of Father José, that he said, "This will be my fate, too."

"Oh, don't be foolish."

He thought for a moment and said, "Our faith—yours and mine—is folly. Our God is a fool; he's mad with love for us."

"But you do such good works. You must live for the sake of others."

Bishop Oscar said, "God will continue His work. He has other soldiers. I am happy to die for the Church Triumphant."

This is preposterous, I thought, and wondered if there really was a God and if Jesus had been just some desert charlatan and I'd been worked for my money.

I could smell the sulfur in the air and knew the Devil had visited me. In bed that night I said a hundred Hail Marys and two hundred Our Fathers. God forgave me and shed his grace on me.

I was the only attractive, educated, sophisticated woman among the religious. The others were squat, simpering, childish, simple; they were also all Colombian, undoubtedly the homely, unmarriageable younger sisters, and one childish Filipino.

There! I've said it and will never have to say it again.

You've never seen anything more absurd than all these buxom women playing catch during recreation, bobbing up and down in their long black dresses and white wimples. Or the way they were all giggling inanely when we took our first vows, glancing at one another slyly or at least with complicity, and smiling with foolish radiance when the Mother Superior called out their names and they went up to the altar to receive the priest's blessing and a prayer card with a silly rhyme in Spanish and a poorly printed color picture of the Blessed Laura. They all got encouraging nods and smiles and giggles from the other postulants when their name was spoken through the loud speakers; they knelt among the Easter lilies they themselves had placed around the altar only an hour before. In the audience were their tall, skinny brothers in shoes and no socks, their shiny black hair parted on the side (the girls' hair was parted down the middle), here and there holding aloft a child the better to see, the child sucking a dirty thumb, her pink bow coming undone or his eyes falling shut in the spring heat. Here were the wide mothers dressed in black, smiling toothlessly, or the wizened grandfather with his hollow cheeks and four days' unshaved white stubble.

Just to prove to you I'm not entirely negative, there is one person here I adore—Mercedes, a chatty, smiley Filipino woman. Maybe it's because she's physically attractive. Funny. Reasonably good English. Big heart.

I think we may accompany my student to Rome together. And, of course, I respect our Mother Superior. And don't get me wrong. I love the atmosphere of our convent and its wonderful alternation between silent contemplation and cheerful industry. We make candles by filling long, slender upside-down molds with pure white wax. We bake tasteless tortillas and then stamp out piles and piles of the hosts, all the while saying prayers. We tailor and sew holy vestments, altar clothes, banners. We grow our own food. We run an infirmary. We're always providing supplies and sleeping bags for missionary nuns (that's our main purpose) to travel into the jungle to clothe, convert, and feed the indigenous people. Unwanted babies (mostly girls) are "exposed" on our doorstep and we take them in and raise them in our orphanage. We give them names, change their diapers, teach them to sing, encourage them in school, patrol their dorms after lights-out, try to keep the teens (with varying results) from smoking, drinking, and getting pregnant. I like to sit in on chemistry and biology classes—subjects that never interested me in the past, as you well know. Because of my tutoring I've kept up my Latin and Greek and I've even tried my hand at translating Book IV of *The Aeneid* into English (and Spanish) verse. I read Spanish poets (Quevedo is my favorite). I also like the dramatist Valle-Inclán because he's funny (but *so* satirical; he may be on the Index, I'll have to check).

When I took my vows of chastity, poverty, and obedience I had to hand over all the money I possessed, but as you know when we turn thirty we'll come into our full inheritance and then when Daddy dies we'll probably inherit more. Most of the time I like or want to like being poor and am pleased I brought an important dowry to the convent, but at other times (like now) I'm frustrated I can't hire armed guards to protect my beloved Bishop Oscar. But he argues that if Our Lord could sacrifice Himself for our redemption ("The Scandal of Redemption," as he puts it in his memorable way), then His priests must be willing to follow His lead. I don't know what good armed guards would really do against the rich and powerful if they're determined to murder their enemies, but I hate not being able to defend those I love.

A good Christian wouldn't have those she loves more or less, but if I'm honest I'd have to say I love Oscar and Mercedes more than everyone else, even you, my beloved twin. It's so odd thinking we're identical genetically but so different in temperament—or are we? I suspect I'm much more calculating then I admit and you're much more ardent than you think.

Do you think we'll die at the same moment on the same day?

Let me tell you about Mercedes. She's always smiling, and you'd think she had a childhood as privileged as ours. In fact, however, she was so poor in the Philippines that her family couldn't afford rice and to this day she beams with pleasure over a bowl of white rice. I keep telling her that brown rice is more nourishing and healthier but her mind is made up;

she doesn't notice all the privations of convent life as long as she can have her bowl of white rice from time to time. You may be a baronne but Mercedes believes she's a princess with her gold-tipped black lacquer chopsticks digging into a clump of sticky rice. When she was a little girl she'd spend a dime filling up her bicycle basket with ice, head down to the port, and buy thirty or forty good-sized fish from a fisherman. Then for the next four hours she'd go from door to door selling her fish at a slight markup. The profits she'd hand over to her drunk, violent father. Her mother had an arm her father had broken so often she had it in a sling as far back as Mercy could remember. Her brother, Enrique, just two years older, died last year (they are in their forties) and for months Mercy had red eyes rather than her usual smile. He had a heart attack, and at such an early age! It seems in dealing with their sadistic father and meek mother Enrique was Mercy's ally, if only in helping with the fish or laughing at their parents once they were out of earshot.

She's a bit of a racist and has nothing good to say about Filipinos, who she thinks are ugly. She's actually lovely with her honey-brown skin, her richly undulating black hair, her high, firm breasts, her perfect white teeth, her merry, dark eyes. Yes, she may be short but that only adds to her childlike vulnerability. I feel like grabbing her and waltzing her around the room. She has a horrible sense of humor and no matter how remote the allusion she's always spotting a sexual double entendre and pointlessly laughing at her wickedness. She knows how her ribaldry irritates me and she's constantly teasing me for my American puritanism.

Are we really puritan? How do you like off-color jokes?

She looks up to me as a higher order of being, as if I were an angel. Her adulation or respect embarrasses me. I'm constantly listing my shortcomings and sins but she takes that as only one more proof of my superiority. I'm afraid she admires me partly for my coloring, my thinness, my being soft-spoken, all of which are involuntary "virtues," just as much a product of our upbringing as is her horrible unfunny ribaldry. She's incapable of walking past a bowl of fruit without rearranging a banana protruding from two nested apples—and then leering and giggling.

We always eat our meals together. Though we have to eat in silence, thinking about Christ's Passion, it's a comfort to know she's beside me; I can almost feel the heat coming off her smooth, chubby body or the warmth of her misplaced admiration for my worthless self. I confess every Saturday to Bishop Oscar so I can receive Communion on Sunday. At the end of one confession he said, "My daughter, may your spiritual father make one remark?"

"Of course."

Through the grill the bishop said, "Perhaps you and Mercedes are becoming too close, intertwined. At first I thought it wasn't my business, but your welfare *is* my business. Friendship, of course, is commendable, but friendship for *all* humanity. You must not make an idol of one individual. For instance, for a while I found myself thinking about you, your radiance, your shining face, your soft voice, your fleet, graceful way of walking. But then I recognized that I was singling you out in my thoughts and prayers, and with unremitting self-discipline I diverted my attention away from you." (Oscar's English is pretty literary since he reads G. K. Chesterton almost exclusively.)

I smiled. I exulted. He loves me, I thought.

"Yes, Father," I said meekly. "I will sit with a different religious at every meal."

"That is a good beginning. And say a decade of the rosary every time you begin to think exclusively of Sister Mercedes."

"I will obey you in all things, Father." I tried not to sound satirical.

How strange, I thought, smiling. Poor man—he's jealous!

When I began to avoid Mercedes I could see she was deeply hurt—proof, if that was needed, that Bishop Oscar's observation about our being too dependent on each other was true. Mercy's face went as white as her wimple. She rushed up to me with her usual conspiratorial smile but I brushed past her, emitting an ice-cold, unfocused smile as only we white people know how to do. She was like a trusting, tail-wagging puppy who is struck rather than stroked. I sailed past her over to a table far from our usual one, indicated I wanted to squeeze in on the refectory bench next to Sister Maria Luisa, smiled and nodded to my new neighbors without a glance back at Mercedes, though I could feel the storm cloud of anger and pain hanging over her head. It was that powerful, her dark thought transmission.

The next day I sat with other religious as a way of calming Mercy's jealousy. I didn't want her to think I'd abandoned her for another particular woman, but that strategy only made her wound sharper, more painful; she burst out in tears and had to leave the refectory. When I passed her in the hall later that day on the way to vespers, I grabbed her arm and whispered, "People have been disapproving of us for being such close friends. I'm pretending to be distant so that we can go to Rome together." Her face, paralyzed with pain and disgust, quickly melted into smiles. Her eyes were red from crying and her face looked swollen, but now the sun was emerging from the storm clouds.

She isn't subtle. Whenever she'd catch sight of me after that she'd smile and even wink, though she didn't really know how to wink and for an instant would close both eyes. One day I was kneeling and praying to Saint Catherine at "my" altar when Mercedes was suddenly kneeling beside me, her lips frantically whispering prayers but her tiny, hot hand sliding into mine.

At that very moment I was reading and meditating on Saint Catherine's *Treatise of Discretion*: "The soul cannot live without love, but always wants to love something, because she is made of love, and, by love, I created her . . . I will love, because the food on which I feed is love. If you will love, I will give you that which you can love."

Instead of withdrawing my hand, which had been my first (and sinful) response, I squeezed her hand hard. Saint Catherine had given me that which I could love. I thought it was a sin to reject love in whatever form it was offered. We aren't loved that many times in life and it may not be in the form we desire. But each time it is given it is a token of God's love. God is a madman because he loves us so much that he sent his only son to us to save us from Adam's sin. God is invisible but he veiled himself in flesh that you might see him. He was irrefutably human, and on the wood of the Holy Cross he was in grief and torment. Yes, he was blessed even in his torment, because his nature is also divine. In Saint Catherine's words,

God created you out of love and the only way you can thank me is by loving not me but your neighbor, even if he hates you. Jesus is a bridge that begins on earth and ends in Heaven; he is a bridge of pure love.

With these passages in mind, I gripped Mercy's little hand and stroked it with my thumb. I felt waves of reciprocated love (God's love) ripple through me. I thought, I'll never repulse love again—not sensual love but spiritual love.

CHAPTER 14

I set out for the Var in my little powder-blue sports car with the two children bickering then sleeping for long stretches in the back seat. I drove as fast as legally possible through that cold, rainy October day. The fields had already been harvested and were gray with overturned soil. Big white clouds lined in lead, like tumbling acrobats in dirty chiffon, pursued one another across the lowering sky. I had the radio on to keep me company.

The twins got grouchy and restless. I couldn't blame them. With some difficulty I found La Pyramide, where we had a hotel reservation. At the time it had a reputation as the best restaurant in France, but I wouldn't subject the children to all the endless rituals of a three-star restaurant. From room service I ordered chicken breasts and peas for them, hold the fancy sauces and the mint sprigs in the peas—and flan for dessert. For myself I ordered short ribs and cabbage braised in champagne and a split of champagne and half a carafe of Bordeaux (yes, Saint-Émilion). I propped the sleepy children up in their double bed and found a children's program on the TV. They spoke only three-word sentences, but in French, English, and German. They were sound asleep by the time the food arrived. I tucked them in and watched a movie while I ate my dinner, then collapsed the wings of the table and pushed it into the hallway. The country was so quiet only a few giggling diners broke the silence, followed by their slamming doors and the roar of an expensive motor and the racket of flying gravel.

When I opened my eyes next there was daylight and the twins were wide awake and looking at me apprehensively. They were reassured when I sat up and smiled but Ghislaine pointed to my face and started to cry. I went to the mirror and saw a big black circle on my right cheek. Oh, I'd fallen asleep on the chocolate mint they'd placed on my pillow. I washed it off and turned and said, "See, Mommy is all right." I hated that moronic way of referring to myself in the third person. By this time the twins were jumping on their bed. I ordered some poached eggs and cereal and toast for the room. The children were so overexcited that I had trouble getting them dressed. Foulques's little white shoe refused to go on. I'd broken out in a sweat and was still in the terry-cloth robe I'd found in the closet.

At last we were back on the road. The children were in the back seat. They each wanted to pee but I had no idea where to take them. They were whining, close to crying, and so was I. Then I saw a big filling station across the highway. It was clean inside and I brought Foulques with Ghislaine and me into the ladies' room and found an empty stall. I had to hold Foulques up under the arms since he was so little. Endless whimpering and irritation. I filled the gas tank. I would never travel alone with the children again.

Luckily, bladders empty, stomachs full, they fell asleep. Three hours later we were crossing Provence and into the Var. After another two hours they were sniffling with hunger again and muttering, "Potty." "We're almost there," I said bravely, though I'd gotten lost and we were in ghastly Draguignan.

Finally we pulled into Tourtour, so named for its two towers (one belonging to the Grimaldi family). It's a small village with a large, sloping town square, surrounded by several art galleries showing impastoed horrors of olive trees and lavender and hosting three spawling bistros complete with Japanese lanterns and wobbly metal chairs teetering on cobblestones.

We drove past the town walls, down a one-lane road with several twists and turns under a dark canopy of leaves, and finally through the open gates to the estate. The herbaceous borders were outlined in tiny white Christmas lights. An odd lapse in taste, I thought, though pretty.

The château, Quercy, with its dark towers, loomed up before us. "We're here," I said, and looked through the rearview mirror at the twins' sullen, suspicious faces.

The children seemed exhausted. *I* was exhausted. And a little apprehensive. My in-laws, who were sweet but forbidding, would be at the castle, and Addy, whom I hadn't seen in three months—would he expect us to make love?—I didn't think I could bear it. I was still feeling betrayed by Helen and Ercole, though I had to admit that with them I'd discovered how wonderful sex could be. The idea of returning to my *marital duties* seemed even more unpleasant. And sex of any sort struck me as merely annoying now.

Where was everyone? It was late in the afternoon—in fact the dull, soft-voiced, leaden chapel bell was ringing four—but after I crossed the absurd drawbridge on its prerusted chains that Addy had devised and entered the great reception room (which was so cold I shivered) with both children in tow until Ghislaine demanded maddeningly to be carried, I found no one. Had they gone off to see the sights? Where were the servants? I was so longing to hand the children over to someone, but now it seemed I would have no rest.

I could hear voices in the kitchens. I called out, and the voices abruptly ceased. Then I could hear rapid steps and the fat cook with the sweet face, whose Provençal accent I could barely understand, came running through the mammoth stone doors, her forearms white with flour. "*Oh, Madame la baronne!* We were expecting you this morning. The family has gone sightseeing. They will be back soon." Then she shouted down the hallway, "*Philippe, venez vite!*" And suddenly a nice lanky young man in livery but with his sleeves rolled up to reveal his strong, thin, unpleasantly hairy forearms was swooping down to pick up Foulques. "*Mathilde, venez vite!*" he called out. Another servant, a young woman in a long apron, as long as her hemline, came trotting out and with just a shy, murmured greeting took the wriggling, impossible Ghislaine out of my arms. The children looked bewildered by all these new people and the unexpected activity. Ghislaine for once didn't cry but stretched her arms out toward me. I said to her, kissing her, "This is Mathilde. She's a friend."

Mathilde frowned and said, "Oh, you speak to her in English," as if that represented a real problem.

"We speak to them in both languages," I said in my accented French. "They're twenty-two months old now and can say two- or three-word sentences in French and English. And in German."

"I don't know English."

"All you need to know," I said with a smile, "is that 'uppy' means she wants to be carried."

"I must remember that: 'uppy.'"

"She'll make it clear enough. I think they both need a diaper change."

Whispering "uppy" to herself, Mathilde hurried off up the very grand marble staircase, followed by Foulques and Philippe. Another servant, her hair all matted on one side from an afternoon nap, rushed in to nod her head at me in acknowledgment of my exalted status. She led me to my room, showed me the toilet, the cunningly concealed closet, and a second later a teenage boy had retrieved my luggage from the boot and rested it on a portable rack. He murmured something about "baroness" as well.

In an instant they were gone, after the young woman had showed me the velvet rope to pull for service. I couldn't wait to be alone. I kicked off my shoes and lay on my great canopied double bed with the green velvet bedspread, *mon lit d'apparat*. It smelled like glue (cow's bones?), probably from the velvet appliqués. The cook, now free of flour but panting from the stairs, let herself in with a silver tray and a pot of tea and two plain cookies dusted in powdered sugar. I touched them—they were still warm. I smiled my thanks—I felt so feeble. The cook, with her big, comic features like a clown's, puckered her huge lips and held her fore-finger to them and tiptoed out in an exaggerated way.

I ate the cookies (almond) and drank half a cup of the Lapsang tea. When I woke up again, there was Addy with a stranger, a tall, fat woman who was so white that the tiny moles sprayed across her neck looked as if they'd been inked in. He said, as I oriented myself as to where I was, "Sleeping in the daytime?" I wondered why he was speaking English, which he usually avoided; it must have had something to do with the big woman, who was wrapped in a dress of white gauze. Even he must have thought that sounded like a strangely cold greeting, so he added, "Welcome home, darling."

"The driving really took it out of me. In fact, I dreamed I was still driving." I smiled at the pale lady, who smiled back. She had unusually small bad teeth.

"This is Foxy Mecklenburg, my cousin from Bavaria, a very distinguished music critic and academic. She arrived just after you. My wife, Von Courcy."

Von, I thought! I knew Addy thought Yvonne was common. Did he think "Von" sounded aristocratic? German? Was Von a polite *hommage* to the French particule?

"I told you you shouldn't drive all the way," Addy added. "Remember France is as big as Texas."

Foxy laughed, revealing her small bad teeth again. "Texas? Have you ever been to Texas?"

"No. You?"

"I went to Dallas to hear Lauritz Melchior."

"And how was it?"

"I loved it. Yippee-ay-oh," she sang out in a high, quavering voice. "Texas, not Melchior," she clarified.

"Let me show you how I've restored things. Foxy spent summers here as a child. Maybe, Von, you'll join us."

"Gladly," I said, "if we can stop off and see the children."

"Yes, I'm sure they'll like the nursery. It's been beautifully restored."

"Children don't register beauty."

"*Mine* will, surely."

Foxy patted him on the hand, somewhat condescendingly, I thought, as if to soothe a wounded vanity.

Addy led us through the huge castle, all four floors of it. There are only so many ways of saying "ooh" and "ah" and "*très beau*," especially if you're not encouraged to ask questions or make comments, least of all to relate all this beauty to your own inferior, miserable experience. Being just a rubber stamp of approval is tiring, even humiliating, but I remembered that Addy's main point of pride was his taste and his greatest talent, the knack for "arranging things." We mere mortals (or, worse, Texans) could buy beautiful things if properly guided, but the one task we couldn't do, it seems, is gracefully compose them or idiomatically arrange them. Barbarous as we were, we just didn't know what to do with our baubles and gewgaws once we owned them.

Suddenly I could hear the children's laughter and voices. "Oh, are we near the nursery?" My life, my love, all my happiness . . .

"Yes," Addy said, irritated that his tour had been interrupted, "I forgot to indicate it. Here we are," and he led the way through a heavy, carved ogival door. The children looked up, startled. They had been freshly bathed and dressed in their best white clothes and their nanny was reading a week-old newspaper in German. Ghislaine looked really lovely, like a Romanov princess, with her beautifully braided spun-gold hair, her nearly transparent skin, her tiny, precise features like those on a newly minted silver coin before anyone touches it.

"Papa, Papa!" Foulques cried, running toward his father and hugging his leg. I'd never witnessed the child make such a display over his father, whom he usually shied away from and whom he hadn't seen in a while. Ah, I understand, he's almost two now. I think I read something in Dr. Spock about boys shifting their affections from their mother to their father at that age.

Adhéaume seemed terribly pleased as he glanced at his cousin to see what impression this domestic scene had made on her. She just smiled, exposing her tarnished teeth. I thought aristocrats always had perfect teeth—maybe not in postwar Germany.

"Foulques, this is your aunt Foxy, Princess Mecklenburg." The child hid behind his father's leg.

"Fuck?" Foxy asked. "What an extraordinary name."

"It's Foulques," Addy said, frowning, "after one of our ancestors, a crusader."

"Oh, you poor child, what a horrible name," Foxy said, bending down and looking him in the eye; Foulques ducked back again behind his father.

"It's a very noble name," Addy said, vexed. "I'm not sure anyone called Foxy should complain about a name."

"My real name is Maria Frederica," she said simply.

"Give me a second to freshen up," I said. We went back to my room, Foxy and I.

I brushed my teeth and hair, put on lipstick, changed my dress, all in minutes.

She came over to me and laced her arm around my waist. "Come, my dear, we'll go through the galerie d'Hercule and descend the grand staircase and you can greet your mother and father-in-law in the Zodiac Room." She emphasized each of these names in gentle mockery; she might be a princess, I thought, but not a pompous one.

On the way down, I said, "So you're a music critic."

"Only one of three on the *Süddeutche Zeitung*. My 'beat,' as you say in America, is baroque music—Bach, Buxtehude, like that."

"Your English is excellent."

"I went to school in New Hampshire, but I can't speak a word of French."

"Nor I of German," I said, smiling.

Since the children's nanny was Frau Dichter, Foxy talked in German with her, though Foxy reported she had a low, childish, Saxon way of speaking and referred to her cat Mozart familiarly as "Mözi."

I liked Foxy instantly, and though no one could say she was beautiful, I found her sexy—to the touch. It was most extraordinary, holding her by the waist, I felt a *womanliness*, a firmness, even a slight physical heat emanating from her. Our bodies liked each other. I didn't want to gross her out by seeming overly affectionate, by stroking or squeezing her, but there was nothing offensive in just holding her by the waist, surely, something she'd initiated, a sisterly gesture, not an amorous one.

Everything was very Mer-Mer, if that meant chic-Medieval, but a Vegas version of it—all polished and gleaming and on a scale that was slightly wrong. To be fair, it was all new, and no one had ever seen a brand-new castle before, just as no one living had ever seen Notre-Dame de Paris stuffed with silk banners, but that was how it originally looked. Before the flying buttresses and the spire were added.

"German is very very difficult," Foxy said, "but I think you're smart enough to learn it." She smiled. "Especially with the right frau professor."

"I'd offer to teach you French if you wanted to speak it brokenly and with an East Texas twang."

We entered the Zodiac Room, which was as high as it was wide, but I had nothing but an initial impression of scales and a goat in bright colors and there a crab and a sun because my parents-in-law were sitting in matching, armless slipper chairs upholstered in bright green plush, a lustrous velvet, the green of a meadow in sunlight after a rain. They both looked very tiny in this tall room and on their chairs, which somehow upstaged them, dressed as they were like people from the last century, he in a wing-tip collar, which I'd never seen before, and a silk cravat and a gold stick pin with eyes, she in a capacious dress that looked like bed ticking, striped horizontally in blue and white, her straw hat tossed on the gueridon. "*Ma bru*," she said, using the French word for "daughter-in-law" that was correct but sounded rude, like "Jew," as she rose to kiss both my cheeks but keeping her body at some distance. "*Ma cousine*," she said as softly as a sigh.

"So wonderful to see you again," Foxy murmured in English.

Adhéume's father, Eudes, kissed my hand and Foxy's. He asked me, "Did Adhéaume show you the tablet listing the family saints?"

"That will have to be for another day," I said. In French I begged them to be seated.

Adhéaume arrived with a very happy Foulques and a whiny Ghislaine. Eudes held out his arms to Foulques, who glanced nervously at his father. Addy was nodding and smiling encouragingly. "*Je suis ton grand-père*," Eudes said gently. "*Tu ne me souviens pas?*" I'd never heard before any French speaker pronounce the *ne* in conversation.

They were extremely nice, mild people and it was hard to imagine they'd produced someone as rude as Addy. Maybe he saw them as genteel antiques not to be emulated if one wanted to be up-to-date and a winner. He respected them, as he'd often told me, but primarily because they were family and his progenitors and aristocrats like him and now his son. His values were so strange, like those Catholics who say they respect the papal office but don't like this particular pope. Was his respect for them completely formal, titular, just as his faith was active only on Christmas and Easter and during baptisms or last rites?

The father was reputed to have had an affair with Rita Hayworth but it was difficult to imagine this dry, tidy little man with the tweezered white mustache and the wing-tip collar who pronounced his *ne*'s in the arms of the Mexican redhead. But he'd been quite the lady's man, it seemed, and a sportsman who'd owned the Thoroughbred Victor Emmanuel, winner at Longchamp, a playboy who was now going deaf and lost the family fortune speculating on Bolivian copper and seducing both respectable women and cocottes, a favorite of the scandal sheets. His wife was broad in the beam with a sweet face—almost as sweet as her perfume, lily of the valley. She must have been the most inoffensive woman in the world, every word stuttered, then retracted, her eyes closed as she spoke and opening only at the end of a sentence. I felt that they'd been sitting for some time in their green plush chairs, speechless. Isn't that what "infant" meant, without speech? They seemed like old infants.

His mother was born Victorine Lambeth (was that why their horse was named Victor?) and her father had been the son of Lord D'Amour, though English had been lost along the way, if not her fierce blue eyes and pugnacious chin.

We were all at a linguistic loss and I felt it was incumbent on me, the Texan, to translate. "Foxy says she spent summers here as a girl," I said in French first, then English.

"Then. Very dirty," Victorine hazarded in English with a triumphant smile.

"Yes," Foxy said, "it was a pit. Addy's restored it—or rather *invented* it—brilliantly."

Victorine's triumph was short-lived with this onslaught of unfamiliar words.

Addy said in English (which I translated for his parents), "For this room I had nothing but the name to go on, those filthy revolutionaries, led by our own bailiff, I might add, x'd out the original paintings with charcoal."

"Addy," I asked, "how do you say 'bailiff' and 'charcoal'?"

"*Huissier. Charbon.*"

I translated but Victorine seemed slightly put out, as if I were insultingly offering help where none was needed. I thought I'd let her flounder about on her own for a while.

Like most family members at a social impasse we turned our attention to the children, who by now were wild things, chasing each other around and screaming—in English, which seemed to make it worse. Their grandmother, though resolutely polite and sweet, still managed to radiate disapproval, which she expressed by looking pained. Which only intensified when Ghislaine fell and started to sob. Victorine rushed over to comfort the child, but a vexed Ghislaine wriggled off her lap and ran to me, and the grandmother darted a searing glance at me, as if what else could you expect from a Texas outlaw who'd turned the child *sauvage* and prejudiced her against her own grandmother. She never said anything and Eudes I suspected was usually checked out, like some Petainist dignitary who'd outlived his moment. I always thought they imagined I'd somehow sullied their bloodlines, a pollution they'd accepted in exchange for lucre. They were thinking of their generations to come as did the French who built the Gothic cathedrals, knowing they wouldn't be finished for 150 years. This old man with the tweezered mustache and the rigid spine had "ruined" the family but Addy had "saved" it by marrying a bartered bride. Except the bride wasn't happy, the groom was a foolish, odious spendthrift, and his parents were the purest expression of French bigotry and tunnel-digging weasel determination, though with beautiful manners.

The governess came in to scoop up the children, speaking in German baby talk, I suppose.

To irritate me Addy was complaining to his parents about Ercole: "He's the sort of man who wears a wristwatch with a white tie."

They both made disapproving sounds. Victorine, the dingbat, closed her eyes and said, "Who is he again, dear?"

Addy said, "A new friend of Von's."

Apparently they both recognized my new nickname, because they looked at me, albeit noncommitally. Maybe they'd chosen "Von" at a family conference.

I said, "My father also disapproves of wristwatches—he thinks they're effeminate." That puzzled everyone.

As we struggled for a topic, Adhéaume started to explain to his parents that in the Middle Ages the signs of the zodiac were associated with body parts—Cancer the crab with the lungs, Virgo with the waist, Aquarius with the knee, Taurus with the shoulder, and I forget the others. I started to translate for Foxy, who was sitting next to me, but she whispered, "Forget it. I don't want to clutter my mind with the medieval zodiac."

Victorine asked me if I would translate her fond greetings to Foxy's mother and to ask her how she was doing.

In reply, Foxy said, "My mum is such a character. In the village she saw a tradesman with a cart and two horses. One of the horses was so adorable that she unhitched it and rode away bareback," which I translated as, "She has such fond memories of you both and sends you all her love."

Victorine smiled her smug little smile.

After a painful dinner (Addy pointed out that the painting by Mignard on the wall was of this very room, a comment that I didn't translate) Foxy spoke of the deplorable backward state of serious music in France, which I did translate, since it was disagreeable. I said in both languages, "But what about Xenakis? Boulez?"

"Xenakis is Greek and very uneven. Boulez is interesting but doesn't produce much. But how do you know of them? I'm impressed."

"Music is Von's forte," Addy said. "She and her Italian friend—the Hercule of the notorious wristwatch—have a music salon."

"I love music," Victorine said. Her eyes fluttered open for an instant then closed. "So soothing."

"I like music, too," Eudes said, "as long as it's Offenbach."

"You like Bach?" Foxy asked, not understanding. "You can never go wrong with Bach."

"Offenbach."

"Oh."

"*Le can-can.*"

"*Vraiment*, Eudes," his wife said, smiling, in mock shock and disapproval. "*Tu exagères.*" Then she brought out an English word from the nursery: "Naughty."

After dinner Addy asked me to take a walk with him to see the folly he'd rebuilt, a preruined Greek temple. It was still light out at ten P.M. The temple was beside a promontory, which gave me ideas. I looked down at the olive trees far below that the farmer must have stopped cultivating. They'd gone wild and were shaggy and overgrown. I said, "This is so beautiful, Adhéaume."

"Yes," he agreed. "You must admit I have a talent for *arranging* things. And for *scénographie*."

I double-locked my door that night, but I didn't need to. I realized Addy was no longer attracted to me—thank heavens! I wondered who his new mistress was and where he'd stored her.

I loved our boring days, with nothing to do but dress, stroll, daydream over a book, wash, change clothes, eat, undress. Since the children were so unruly it was decided that I would eat with them in the nursery, which suited me fine. No more translating. I let Addy do that for Foxy. I would take long walks with Foxy. One day we ran into Addy and I said, "Your chrysanthemums are lovely. I never thought you were a gardener."

"But I have a friend (*une amie*) who lives nearby and she helps me." Addy often began a sentence with "But . . ." as if he couldn't imagine an utterance that wasn't in opposition to something I'd said, as if he were asserting something contested.

"Ah! *Une amie*—quick work."

"She's just a little countess from Entrecasteaux, famous for its sundials."

"Well, she has a green thumb," I said (we were speaking English for Foxy's sake), "but I imagine the rest of her is the color of a veal daube. The way you like them."

"You must be very bored with us," Addy said to Foxy.

"I command you not to say that!" I said, laughing. "You didn't hear that, Foxy." I waved my hands in front of her eyes and chanted, as if hypnotizing her, "You love it here and will never leave." They both laughed.

On rainy days we wandered around the château. The massive dining hall in the Charles X style led to the guards' hall, where we'd play cards in the window nooks. Or we played billiards on the massive, if slanting, green baize table, while the gold-lettered inscriptions on the wall clamored, *VIVE LE ROI! VIVE LE ROI! C'EST MON PLAISIR*, in honor of Henri III, who once spent the night here on his return from Poland, where he'd also been king.

The château library contained nothing that interested me except some ancient numbers of the *Edinburgh Review.* In the Flower Bedroom blue nigellas, red tulips, and white lilies (the tricolor) were painted on the walls, shutters, and coffered ceilings. Who had been the Republican? I wondered. Everything was in order and ready to go. There was soap in the soap dishes, quills in the *plumier,* eau de cologne in the water closet.

I knew that Addy was related to everyone and could summon hundreds of rich or titled people to a masked ball, but he had few friends. No one dropped in on us. His parents, apparently, were installed in the château for good. I often overheard Addy quarreling with them, jeering, hissing, or murmuring that ultimate French expression of disbelief or mild outrage, "*Quand même!*" I was glad he had them to convince him that he was leading a life, that their grudges, delights, abbreviated references to distant events or nicknames for relatives—that all this hubbub and buzzing could animate their loneliness. I had always been amazed that great-aunts and sorority sisters or old aristocrats could fill up their days with chatter. This ongoing process of knowing names, keeping schedules, assigning duties, writing letters, evaluating new acquaintances, at once familial and competitive, could stave off the grand silence awaiting us all. Was this marriage proposal suitable or a mésalliance? Was his title mediatized under the Holy Roman Empire ("neither holy, Roman, nor imperial")? How were the Courcys related to the Gramonts? Was she the first woman of the *gratin* to utter the *mot de Cambronne* ("shit")? The frowns, smiles, whispers, the stains and how to get rid of them ("white wine to dilute red wine"), the schemes ("But how to introduce them when she won't answer the phone?"), *les bonnes adresses* and the precious contacts, the plans for trips, charities, and *goutés ouvroirs* (working teas where aristocratic ladies knitted for the poor), the dull, passed-along *mots,* the semiprecious stones of conversation ("She said that when she was young she was a dream, though as an old woman she's become a nightmare"). I thought they'd spent their lifetimes reading *Paris Match* and *Allo!,* debriefing friends on the phone for hours, relaying tepid scandals, quizzing members of the government or the Goncourt Prize committee over dinner, courting today's genius, lowering their social standards by frequenting mere journalists ("She's common but amusing—and so up on things!"), criticizing one another's clothes ("Forgive me, but that color gives you a dirty complexion" [*une sale gueule*]), comparing prices, debunking genealogies, relishing rumors of divorce, bankruptcy, corruption. Although he claimed to be so sure of his taste, Addy tested out each new wineglass or fork against his mother's approval ("You know," he said, "Henri first introduced forks from Poland, where they invented them"). Addy would casually refer to Henri III by name, but his mother would say, "Yes, I know his majesty the king did us the honor of once accepting our hospitality."

Addy not only had spent a fortune on the château, he was also redecorating all twelve rooms of the Avenue Foch apartment. He wanted to celebrate its completion in a year with a masked ball. I heard him saying to his mother, "We could have surrealism as our theme; you could come as a sugar cube soaked in absinthe with a tiny spoon as your hat."

"I know!" she said. "We could have a Proust ball and everyone would come as the character they were related to."

"I'd like to be Odette with lots of orchids—like a prom queen," Addy said. Occasionally, he could be very camp. "But seriously, it would be easier on everyone if we had a peasant ball. Pater"—that's what he called his father—"could come with three pigs and a scythe."

"And me?" Victorine asked.

"As a baker woman, like the one who stormed Versailles and dragged Marie-Antoinette off to Paris and prison and eventually her beheading."

Victorine held up her crossed forefingers as if to ward off the Devil. For her, all of the Bourbons, no matter how remote, were sacred and present and never the source of humor.

Foxy was restless and constantly in motion ("*Elle a la bougeotte*," Eudes said). She liked to walk through the grounds and could spend hours in the vegetable garden, which was immense. She was always propping up a vine or lifting and replacing at a different angle one of the huge gourds or swollen melons. She liked to roll a few sticky leaves of rosemary between her fingers and let me smell their piney odor. We would pass the eight symmetrical bowers radiating out from an old fountain of a cherub holding a drooling fish upside down in his chubby arms. We'd take our tea in a stone pagoda decorated with chinoiseries. The princess's room had eighteenth-century wall paintings illustrating La Fontaine's fables. Her bed was an ottoman and the embroidered Courance sheets a hundred years old. We would sit by a fountain of the nymph Arethusa, the one who became an underground stream rather than submit to the embraces of a river god, Alpheus. In Shelley's poem they reconciled but I'd rather think she remained a militant virgin.

"Are you happily married?" Foxy asked out of nowhere one day.

"What do you think?" I said with a bitter laugh. "Adhéaume is impossible."

"I agree. Selfish. Silly. Superficial. Snobbish."

"The four S's," I said. "What are they again?"

She repeated them and I laughed. I said, "It took me a while to understand how awful he is since he's a French baron and I'm a cowgirl. But now I can predict to the word, to the second, what he's going to say. Was he always so dull? And hateful?"

"Dull and predictable, even as a child. I think he took refuge in conventionality, in doing and saying everything *comme il faut*. He was ashamed of his poverty, of his silly playboy father, of his tediously pious mother. So dull from the start. What they call a young fart. But he's grown into his hatefulness. When he was poor he was cringing but now that you've made him rich he's become his true self: arrogant. Intolerable."

"So it's my fault?"

A sudden gust of wind blew the water from the fountain of Arethusa over us and we leaped up and laughed and headed back to the château.

"Your fault?" Foxy said. "Oh, my dear, not your fault at all. Think how some men, superior men, might have reacted to sudden wealth. My great-great-uncle Prince Albert became a better man after he married Victoria; he combatted slavery worldwide, built model homes for the poor, extended university education to include science, I think—and wore genital jewelry!"

"He *what*?"

"You've never heard of a Prince Albert? Men in those days wore very tight pants and he didn't want to show his large member so he had a metal ring put into his foreskin so he could tie his penis back and attach it to his belt loop. But it turned out the queen, when they were naked at

Balmoral, loved the ring, which knocked against her clitoris. They had nine children and she wanted more! No wonder when he died she went into mourning for forty years—what woman wouldn't?"

"You just made all that up, naughty girl."

"No, I swear it's true. It's a bona fide piece of family lore."

I rather liked thinking about a man's organ, now small and slippery as a fish, then big and red and rigid, imposing, claiming innate prerogatives, both hard and plush like a brass trumpet lifted out of its velvet case, something constantly changing size, now primitive and vascular, now filling out, rising up, hard as bone, smelly and corkscrewing and hairy, an amateurish pipe bomb, something through which we express the soul and pump out hot love but that is bestial, a beast that never must be entirely trusted nor released from his chains. The Frankenstein's monster of the body, the King Kong of the soul.

I told Foxy that I so loved our children that to my mind they almost justified my bad marriage.

I got to like the Var, our slimy, smelly moat with waves of mosquitos floating above it, the sound of faraway dogs barking, the look of the stunned cows, still as sculpture in the evening light, the white quarry scars, the exciting jeep ride into Tourtour for dinner alfresco, the surrounding mixture of Dutch and English at neighboring tables, the spotlit ancient walls, the average food, the copious wine, the joyful, nearly hysterical way the children ran around the square with other bored tourist children. I was fascinated to see my kids interacting with others. At their age they were almost psychotically self-centered; it didn't really matter that they spoke mutually incomprehensible languages. They were addicted to the running and yelling, that was all.

What I liked the most was the tedium and the paralyzing heat, the way I had nothing to do at the château, nothing at all except to daydream or fall asleep in a cushioned deep window embrasure against the always cold stone merlon. I read Hugo's epic poem *La Légende des siècles*, which excited me because I could understand it and bored me because I could understand it.

Foxy left and I no longer felt pleasantly tired but anguished with ennui. I continued to take my meals with the children, but soon I fell into a somber reverie. It was so hot I'd pray for rain. As soon as the sun would go down the crickets would stop their tedious, frantic sawing and the tree peepers would take over. Every room was filled with the smoke of green burning mosquito-repellent spirals. I thought that in the Middle Ages I would have been obliged to attend Mass daily, I would have feared rodents in the granary, the slightest cut that could turn gangrenous, a raid from the next castle over, the Black Death, the next gathering of drunken, smelly, lecherous crusaders, their hands greasy with grilled pork—never a dull moment, if you throw in the odd mystery play, joust, or failed attempt to turn lead into gold. Much better than all this anxious peace, this attentive solitude.

Whenever I would go past the Zodiac Room I'd hear Addy, Victorine, and Eudes all talking at once in some whispered *conciliabule*; what could they find so gripping? I knew that the family could spend hours arguing the merits of one brand of candle over another or dissecting some slight, real or imagined, that had been visited on them. They could fuss over Addy's sick stomach at great length, Victorine holding out for carrots boiled in Vichy water and plain, butterless rice, Eudes promoting the regimen of three whole days without wine and of vigorous morning walks. If they saw me scuttling past they'd go silent. One day Addy came into the nursery to say that Mater and Pater wanted to have a word with me.

"With me?"

"Yes, with you."

"When?"

"Now."

I found them in the Zodiac Room, she crocheting pot holders, he playing patience, slapping the cards down impatiently. "Come in, dear," Victorine said, closing her eyes. I sat precariously on the edge of a chair as if I might fly away at any second. Eudes cast his cards aside, wished me good evening, and turned his chair toward me; Victorine put her knitting down.

"Did you have a good day, dear?" Victorine asked. "Those children must wear you out. I see you flying by like the Dutchman." She opened her eyes; that's how I knew she'd reached the end of a sentence. We had polite chat for about ten minutes. Then she touched her crocheting nervously without lifting it. "Dear," she said, "Eudes and I are so grateful that you're such a patient, attentive mother. In my day parents saw their children for only a few minutes for a good-night kiss. This modern way is so much kinder, warmer, more Christian."

Had she really said "more Christian"? I knew she was very pious, but I'd never before heard her make a direct reference to her faith.

"But there's one tiny thing."

"Yes?"

"We all wish you wouldn't speak to the children in English."

"Why? Don't you want them to be bilingual? They hear French all day long."

"Why should they be bilingual?"

"In case you didn't notice, English has become the international language."

Eudes, who'd been nodding like a Chinese doll, now said, "English. Perhaps. But don't you speak a . . . dialect?"

Victorine picked up her knitting, said, "Really, Eudes," and put it down again.

"I speak English with an American accent. With a Texas accent. People says it's substandard but everyone can understand it."

"The Princess 'Tiny' fur und zu Hohenlicht had trouble with it," Eudes said.

"Tiny Fur is deaf," I pointed out.

"That must explain it," Victorine murmured, unconvinced.

Of course this conversation was ridiculous but it made me very, very angry. I thought, How dare they? Here they were living in my château, ordering around my servants, eating at my table! . . . But that wasn't really it. What I resented is that they would thwart my communication with my children. They wouldn't like the children speaking broken French with a Texas accent; that's why I left French to the native speakers and it was no accident that ours spoke the best French of all, supposedly, the French of Touraine. They were really trilingual—what with their German. If they wanted them to acquire an Oxford accent, they should hire a poor, upper-middle-class English tutor. Meanwhile I'd make them sound like regular Americans, the most reassuring and democratic accent in the world, the language of movies and pop songs, the language of business, newscasts, international colloquia, airports.

But that was all the rational argument. For me it was intensely emotional. I felt I was being stifled. I was outraged. They'd used my big blonde body and my fortune, but now the broodmare could be put out to pasture. In my loneliness my children were my friends, my treasure, my creation! I loved them, maybe inordinately, but I had no one else to love.

Suddenly I was terribly homesick. I thought, I don't want to die in France. I wasn't even sure I wanted to live there.

I said, "It's really none of your business how I speak to my own children. I don't see them as Courcys but as mine. Mine. You may have dynastic ambitions for them. You believe in the *patrimoine* that you're going to hand down to them. But I don't see them as little aristocrats who must be polished so they'll marry well and reflect well on the family name. Perpetuate the family name. Wear your seal on their signet rings. Attend *les bals blancs* for debutantes. I see them as my children. If you don't watch out, I may change their foolish Christian names and take them back to Texas."

When Addy came into my room that night his face was white, a new ugly muscle had surfaced in his jaw, his lips were bloodless, and his nose had grown. "How dare you speak to my parents like that! Mater is still shaking like a leaf. You know she has a bad heart. I never saw such ruthlessness."

"Your mother is tough as nails. I had to draw a line in the sand."

"Oh, you Anglo-Saxons, always speaking in metaphors!"

"Let me put it in plain French. I'll speak to my own children in whatever way I choose. They're as much Crawford as Courcy."

"Alas."

"You and your parents haven't taken out a copyright on my children."

A new, sly thought dawned on his face. "Don't imagine you can cut me off without a penny," Addy said. I could see he'd had this talk many times in his head (or with his parents).

"That's never entered my mind."

"Or that you'll get custody of the children."

"Of course I will. The mother always wins."

"Not when she's immoral. I managed to take photos of you and Hercule and Helen naked in bed, performing unnatural acts."

"You're bluffing," I said, but I remembered those odd clicks.

"They're in a safe at my bank in Paris."

"What would you do with the children? You scarcely speak to them as it is, though Foulques is desperate for your attention."

"I would make their lives miserable, just to spite you. I can't hurt you but I can hurt you through them."

"Say that again: You'd make their lives miserable? Why would you do that to your own children?"

"Yes. If I got custody—and I would from the judge in Paris at the Cours de Cassation, he's my mother's cousin, and given my proof of your adultery *and* perversion, and the fact I'm from an old French family and you're an American nobody—if I had custody I'd send them off to an inferior, very strict provincial Catholic boarding school where they'd be punished frequently, would always go hungry, so hungry they'd suck the starch out of their sheets. If they stole food they'd have to kneel with their bare knees on hard chickpeas and say the rosary for hours till their legs bled. They'd be allowed to bathe only once a week in water their classmates had already dirtied, and they'd learn nothing but Latin."

I could see he'd already dwelled on this . . . revenge in detail. "But why on earth would you do that?"

He wasn't to be deterred in his presentation of the revenge he'd elaborated. "You wouldn't be permitted to see them more than twice a year, and when you did they'd have forgotten their English, forgotten *you*, become dirty, cigarette-smoking louts, ignorant and resentful—and they'd know it was your fault, if they thought of you at all."

"You're unspeakable, intolerable."

"I can't love them since I know you gave birth to them through that filthy cunt of yours."

I burst into tears and raised my hand as if to ward off his blows. I felt his horrible words to be slaps on the face. When I composed myself I was angry I'd given him the pleasure of seeing me cry. I asked him to leave my room.

Once I was alone I put on my robe and headed out into the airless hot night. There was no moon. When I was sure I was out of earshot, I let myself sob. I didn't even recognize my pained sounds. I guess I'd never made them before. It was as if I were discovering a wounded, frightened girl within me, someone I hadn't even known was in there. Or if not a girl then an animal.

I couldn't see anything, it was so dark. I was walking over the dry, fragrant grass of the Midi. I could hear the fountain of Arethusa plashing somewhere up ahead but I couldn't see even its faint outlines. I was apparently walking down one of the eight bowers that led to the fountain. I could hear a dog barking antiphonally to another dog—both chained, no doubt, or caged. The peasants bred expensive dogs and kept them in cruelly narrow cages until they sold them.

It crossed my mind that my sobs might be heard after all, that someone would rush to my side to comfort me. But who? The servants wouldn't. They were asleep after a grueling day of work. Besides, they wouldn't know how to offer a hug or a handkerchief to the baroness. Addy and his parents hated me, I'd discovered.

I felt so alone, in this wretched country where no one shared my sense of humor, where I'd met a bunch of shabby, egotistical composers, where my only American friend, Helen, had betrayed me with Ercole, where my husband (what a fool I'd been to marry him!) despised me and plotted ways to turn our lovely son and daughter into hungry, squalid ruffians.

I walked and walked in the darkness, the airless night humming all around me like a sarcophagus. I even laughed for a second at the grotesque image; why not laugh? I had no audience for whom I had to play anguish. I *was* anguished, but I didn't have to represent it.

Why had Addy become so vile? Because I'd stood up to his sacred parents? Or had Foxy told him that I was bored, resentful, and restless? Up till now he'd always been polite in his icy way. He prided himself on his politeness. Had Foxy warned him I might bolt? Get a civil divorce, which would leave him in a bind, since the only valid divorce in his world would be a Vatican annulment, hard to obtain? He knew Daddy's lawyers had insisted on a pre-nuptial *séparation de biens* and that he would be penniless and crippled with debts if I left him. He'd hoped to have access to my full fortune but he (and his creditors) had learned I'd come into all that money only when I turned thirty. I'd always resented Daddy's strictures before, but now I saw the wisdom in them.

If I divorced and went back to Dallas, would I still be a baroness? Probably, until I remarried, if and when. I was sure Bobbie Jean was counting on my being a permanent baroness. She'd love to introduce me to her Texas friends as gin-you-whine European nobility.

I felt frightened. By the night and the sound of frogs in the moat. By a sudden rustle in a nearby bush. By my utter lack of allies. By the look of scorn and hatred on my husband's face.

Had he been drinking? Would he apologize tomorrow? Would he even remember what he said? *In vino veritas?* Or did alcohol cloud your judgment and let you say things you didn't mean? Had he been harboring this hatred for a long time? From the beginning? Did he hate me for not being French? Helen had told me once that Addy felt certain he could manipulate foreigners, especially stupid, babyish Americans, that he believed no one was as cunning as a Frenchman or so perfectly retrofitted for survival as a French aristocrat. Maybe when he preened himself over his ability to *arrange* things, he not only meant the knack of combining and staging bibelots and furniture but also his skills for maneuvering in the world and bending others to his will.

I guess I was shocked by what had happened to our marriage. From the beginning I'd suspected the terms of our deal—his title for my money—but I'd assumed that we'd always maintain terms of respect and cordiality. I knew wives in Texas and France whose husbands beat them. We hadn't gone that far, maybe because Addy knew I was stronger and fitter than he and because he'd witnessed my turn at dominating Ercole.

By now in my sightless nocturnal wanderings I'd arrived at the promontory overlooking the olive trees gone wild. Was it my imagination or could I really hear the distant surf near Cassis? Or was it just the sudden pandemonium of the wind in the aspens (which, more poetically, were called *trembles* in French)? I was careful to watch my step. I could easily plunge to my death from the promontory. Which didn't sound like such a bad idea just now.

~

We returned to Paris. Victorine and Eudes remained at the château for another month before being driven to their minuscule apartment at a good address in the sixteenth arrondissement near Mme de Castiglione on the Avenue Mozart. One of the servants drove my little car back to the Avenue Foch. I traveled with the German nanny and my own maid and the children in a compartment of the train from Marseilles. Addy sat by himself in the next compartment over.

Since our horrible argument we barely spoke. In front of other people he always referred to me as *Mme la baronne*. The few times he spoke directly to me he addressed me formally as *vous*. Usually he communicated with me through little notes he had his valet deliver to me.

I came back to life in Paris after the torpor of the Var. Just walking down the Rue Saint Honoré, for instance, past the shops and bookstores and cafés on one side and the Louvre on the other, revived me, piqued my curiosity. I wanted to see what women were wearing, what everyone was reading, what curiosities I could find in the antique stores; I wanted to stop in my favorite café for a Mont-Blanc of squiggles of *marrons glacés* built up into a sweet hillock.

I liked the way well-dressed men looked me over and smiled appreciatively. I existed in someone's eyes, in my white Courrèges go-go boots and my very short skirt. The calfskin running up my calves felt like glove leather, snug and warm. Rain was threatening and I was walking with my furled green silk umbrella (the one with the duck head handle) as a cane, and I felt as if I were in a Fred Astaire–Ginger Rogers musical. In Dallas, middle-class men didn't dare to check me out on the street (nowhere in America except New York); they'd move in on you only when you were seated (in a hotel lobby, on a train, in a bar). But in Paris they looked you over from head to toe, even the women, maybe just to check out your boots. The men seldom said anything, though policemen and African garbagemen smiled, as did construction workers. I felt safe but noticed, which I liked. At the castle the servants knew not to gawk at the baroness, Addy was indifferent or hostile, Eudes was entering dementia, and for the townspeople I was a tourist or a summer person: a member of a different tribe.

Although I wasn't much for reading, certainly not in French, I enjoyed strolling past the *bouquinistes*, especially on the Left Bank, all the way from the Tour d'Argent to the Louvre. I picked up books at random, looked through the prints, seldom bought anything, then jumped in a cab and went to Carita to have my hair and nails done (I used a very faint pink pearlescent polish). My hair had gone from blonde to blonde streaks (I think they called it "mesh," or *mèche*, since they put a skullcap on your head and used steel needles to pull strands of hair out through wide-woven holes and dyed only those strands). I liked chatting with "my" girl, Caroline from Toulouse, though she'd acquired a snooty Parisian accent, dropping syllables, rattling along, using lots of foul language, argot, and even *verlan*. She was the definition of chic, so I assumed her way of speaking was the current mode, just as her great straight wave of black hair falling over her face must be *le dernier cri*. From there I went to Givenchy to see the spring collection. Audrey Hepburn was seated on the couch beside me and we chatted in English a little bit, though we were both very serious about writing down our orders. She was so slender, her cheekbones so high, that I felt a bit of a cow beside her. Givenchy himself came out and sat in a chair beside us. He looked like the aristocrat he was with his great height, beaked nose, startlingly blue eyes, and full head of white hair. Once the *défilé* began he disappeared.

The children were now speaking French better than I and would look puzzled when I made a mistake in gender. I assumed that because the word for "cloud," *nuage*, ended in *e* it must be feminine but the children looked bewildered when I said "*la nuage*." They glanced uneasily at their French nanny and Ghislaine said, "Isn't it *le nuage*?" and the nanny said, "It's impolite to correct *Madame la baronne*." I laughed and said, "Not when she's wrong." I was so proud of my educated little children.

Ercole sent me a friendly note asking if I wanted to start giving our musical salons again. I wrote back and said why not and invited him for tea in two days' time. I thought it was best to stay on his good side in case he was called in during future divorce proceedings.

When he came by on that Wednesday afternoon he kissed me on both cheeks in a perfunctory way and excitedly launched into praise of a new young composer. "He's called Jean Barraqué and André Hodeir—you remember the critic André?—claims his is the finest piano sonata since Beethoven, though no one's heard it. Jean is the lover of both Michel Foucault and of Boulez, and it seems they're all big, big drinkers. But Jean is the real thing. If we can get him it will be a *scoop*." He said "scoop" in English, which I thought was endearing.

Being a woman, I couldn't resist asking him how Helen was.

"She's eager to see you," Ercole said. "She misses you and says it was all just a misunderstanding."

"What kind of misunderstanding?" I asked implacably.

"She certainly wasn't rejecting you."

"Are you still sleeping with her?"

"We're getting married."

CHAPTER 15

Dearest Yvonne,

I'm here in Rome with my beloved Mercedes and our student Pablo. We're so excited to be in the city of so many relics of Saint Catherine of Siena. Her body (or most of it) is under the altar of Santa Maria sopra Minerva, a church built over an ancient temple to Minerva. You might remember it as the one that has a Bernini elephant supporting an obelisk out front. We're staying, Mercedes and I, in a Roman convent that owns Saint Catherine's left hand, Monastero della Madonna del Rosario at Monte Mario. Her head is in Siena, which is rather far away, and we probably won't get there to see it. We have been to a church where she is supposed to have died or made her "transit."

Of course, the whole city is filled with sacred sites—the Holy Stairs, which Christ ascended the day he died and which we climbed on our knees, all twenty-eight marble steps, earning ourselves a plenary indulgence. The Vatican, where the Holy Father lives; Saint Peter's Basilica, where Saint Peter himself is buried; Santa Maria Maggiore, where miraculous snow fell—and so on. I could mention the prison on the Capitoline Hill where Peter was held before he was crucified upside down, or the Basilica that commemorates Saint Lawrence's martyrdom when he was roasted on a grill, or Sant'Agnese in Agone, which displays the skull of Saint Agnes (Iñez in Spanish), a twelve-year-old girl who was martyred in the third century A.D. for refusing to marry. She is the patron saint of virgins and gardeners and was beheaded.

But everything in Rome reminds one of our Catholic past or the ancient pagan past. In normal streets with stoplights and shop windows suddenly the founding church of the Jesuits rears up or the Pantheon, like dinosaurs in Japanese movies invading slick, modern Tokyo. All of Rome smells like wet clay—remember when we would leave globs of wet gray clay we were modeling under moist cloths in shop and the whole room would smell like a flooded riverbank?

We're guests in a cloistered order but we get out and about, as busy as Saint Teresa of Ávila. Don't imagine we're just visiting morbid holy relics; we walked up all those steps today to visit the Capitoline Museum and saw *The Dying Gaul* and *Antinous* and huge marble feet from ancient Roman statues and the shocking "religious" paintings of Caravaggio, which I treasure because they show the average, poor people of his epoch, not just the gentry. Tomorrow we'll be visiting the ancient forum and the Colosseum (of course, for a Christian the Colosseum is also a church where so many early believers became martyrs and died). Almost every church attracts us. Our favorite so far is Santi Quattro Coronati, where the nuns belong to a silent order and educate the deaf.

Mercedes is the most wonderful companion. Everything makes us laugh and I feel like a teenager all over again. I suppose we're not very decorous, bobbing around town like penguins in our black-and-white habits, usually doubled over with laughter. We laugh at each other's silly wisecracks; I hope people don't think we're laughing at them! Of course, we try to keep our eyes lowered ("custody of the gaze"), but when we do look up we're always awed by how elegantly dressed the men and women are. Everyone here is beautiful! Even the waiter in a simple trattoria will look like a god. What's especially reassuring is that Rome is filled with religious—nuns and priests of every country, size, age, color, and order.

Mercedes is always in a good mood, which makes me feel churlish at times. I don't think she's ever been on vacation before. She's so grateful, so appreciative! Poor thing, she's always worked so hard, and even in the convent they think it's normal to ask her to clean out the toilets, whereas I'm given more ladylike chores, like planning out the menus. At first she treated me like a lady of a race apart, but now she teases me all the time, usually with raunchy jokes. You ask how a Filipina ended up in Colombia? I think she was living in Medellin already as a housekeeper when she joined holy orders. They have so few jobs in their own country. We're very close. It's strange—we have nothing in common. Class, education, family background, life experiences, language. Everything is different. It's a tribute to her sweetness and her deep humanity that we've become such friends! Of course, we have our belief in Jesus Christ in common. And in love!

As Saint Catherine said, "I wish for no other thing than love, for in the love of Me is fulfilled and completed the love of the neighbor." Just as I love Our Lord and weep constantly contemplating his sufferings on the Cross, in the same way I love Mercedes for her purity, her kindness, her compassion, her generous nature. Although she and I have "nothing" in common, we share the greatest thing: love.

Tomorrow we will have an audience with the Holy Father (along with fifty other nuns), and we are so excited I doubt we will sleep a wink tonight. The pope is a very kindly and humble man who has given his papal tiara, diamond ring, and cross to charity; he has abandoned all ecclesiastical pomp. Apparently he knows a lot about Vatican politics, which can be thorny, since he worked in the Curia for fifteen years. Like all the recent popes (except John XXIII) Pope Paul VI is an aristocrat. He has traveled to five continents—he's called the Pilgrim Pope. Paolo Sesto always looks melancholy—they call him Paolo Mesto ("sad"). Some awful Frenchman, Roger Peyrefitte, claims that the pope is homosexual and that his lover is a handsome actor. Of course, that's a sacrilegious calumny, since every priest is celibate, but I must admit that even if it were true, it wouldn't shock me. The poor pontiff is in such bad health, he is so old and solitary in his august position, how can we begrudge him a little pleasure? Many times he has threatened to retire, but as he says, "Kings abdicate but popes never do." Loving Mercedes has made me more tolerant of every form of love—Saint Catherine understood: I will love, because the food I feed on is love.

We've checked on little Pablo, who seems very happy with his new Franciscan "uncles." They all speak Spanish to him and those who can't converse with him in Latin (Pablo is a star Latin student and can even translate right off a Spanish newspaper into Latin). The monks seem very happy to have recruited him, such a pretty, intelligent, *pliable* boy.

We stood in front of the Fountain of Trevi for ten minutes. Even in that canyon of buildings there was quite a breeze and we were soon soaked, the cold spray in our faces.

As you know, Mercedes and I are coming to Paris next Saturday for a week before returning to Bogotá and eventually Jericó. We will be staying with the nuns at Sacré-Coeur; let's say we'll meet in front of the church (in Montmartre, right?) exactly at noon on Monday. I will try to phone you Sunday afternoon to see if that plan will work for you. Of course, we don't want to be any bother. But I'm dying to meet my niece and nephew. And I'm sure you will like Mercedes. She's adorable and even speaks a few words of English.

I have to warn you. Daddy and Bobbie Jean are coming, too. They'll be staying at the Ritz but I'm sure they'll want to see us constantly. They'll never come to Colombia, which they've decided is too dangerous. Daddy says he wants to discuss something serious with us. Wonder what it could be.

CHAPTER 16

I can remember when I first saw Yvette in Paris. There she was standing with another nun in front of Sacré-Coeur. Her face looked so small and pale inside her black robes. And lined—I wondered if I had aged in the same way. But she broke out in a big smile and she was waving as I climbed the last steps to meet her. The other nun—small and brown with a punched-in nose—was also waving and giggling and jumping up and down with glee. I'd noticed before that nuns were either cruel and whiskered or moon-faced and childish, as if their "vocation" made them either mean eunuchs or gleeful infants. I guess I preferred the infant kind. Yvette and I embraced and squealed like sorority girls, which seemed to startle the other nun; I kept holding Yvette out at arm's length: "Let me just look at you! You look wonderful, honey," I lied. I'm not sure I would have recognized her in a crowd.

I'd never been this close to Sacré-Coeur. I didn't like it, with all these creepy Arab thieves wandering around, smoking reefers, staring at women and men alike, frightening the Christians. And the church itself was appalling, with its pseudo-Oriental domes, its cold slabs of stones, the whole thing built to express France's penance and loss of self-esteem after its defeat in the Franco-Prussian War of 1870 and the horrors of the Commune, a starving population under siege eating the animals in the zoo, the first real Communist experiment. The whole country felt abandoned by God and put up this tasteless monstrosity to win back God's favor, as if he were a cigar-smoking, philistine bounder of the period. Of course, the French had been defeated under Napoleon, too, but at least it was a glorious defeat, whereas Napoleon III was a coward incapable of making a decision and the Second Empire was the over-confident low point in French culture, with the can-can and whores a-go-go.

I'd dressed very soberly for the occasion in a gray, pleated skirt and a tailored blue wool suit jacket with power shoulder pads and braided frogs up the front, no jewelry, a simple cloche with a gray feather, just one. Polished black spool heel shoes, dark bazille stockings, a simple handbag of sumptuous black glove leather with a gold fastener (I hoped it wouldn't attract the thieves). I didn't mind looking rich but I was trying for the rich matron look, nothing flashy.

My sister the nun.

"Let's walk down the hill to the Abbesses metro stop where I left the car." I suddenly feared an impropriety and I said, "You're allowed to walk, aren't you? You can spend the day with me, can't you? Yvette, Mercedes . . . Do you have new nun names now?"

"Yes, as long as we're back here for vespers," Yvette said. "In the early evening," she explained. "Yes, I have a new name, Mary Catherine. Mary because all the nuns in my order are called Maria Something. Catherine after Saint Catherine of Siena. Mercedes is Maria Immacolada. But call us by our baptismal names. I think the conference of bishops going on now is going to rule that all the new nuns should keep their baptismal names."

"How interesting. I've heard that they're saying Mass now in the country's language, Spanish, French . . ." I tried to make it sound jaunty in case I was saying something controversial.

We were going through a little square where Japanese tourists were all dutifully eating their onion soup. Some of them were fearfully approaching the artists' easels propped up here and there displaying paint-ings of the Moulin Rouge windmill or of the bulbous towers of Sacré-Coeur; all the paintings looked mass-produced by palette knives slapping down gooey impasto strokes. The painters themselves had berets and pencil-thin mustaches and blue smocks and were holding palettes and brushes; most of them were smoking. But I thought, I'm no one to laugh, walking with my nun-freaks.

It was getting cold and the wind was swirling through the nuns' habits. I wondered what they wore underneath, a thought that made me tremble. I could picture only horrible wool panties, gray, heavily wired, and white ankle socks and industrial bras, cruelly wired as well. And yet they were almost giddy with happiness. They seemed startled to discover my "car" was a limousine with a driver. My guests settled in with their voluminous skirts and I dashed around to the other side to get in; I felt as if I were out with my great-aunts. Jean-Pierre, our driver, looked suitably impressed. He wasn't his usual wry, jokey self.

I sat next to Yvette and lifted the cross around her waist for a second; it was very heavy. I couldn't imagine lugging that around all day. As we drove through the city I tried to point out all the sights—the Louvre, the American embassy, the Champs-Élysées, the Arc de Triomphe—and then we were gliding down the Avenue Foch and Jean-Pierre was holding the door open. There was my favorite prostitute, Cybille, standing in my doorway out of the cold, wearing a very short gold lamé skirt and a monkey-fur chubby. Rather ostentatiously (considering my companions) I said hello to her and wished her happy hunting. She thanked me and bowed her head to the religious and even sketched in the sign of the cross, which looked absurd given the amount of makeup blazoned across her face. My nuns whispered, "*Hola!*"

I asked the butler to light the fire in the small sitting room and bring us a copious tray of varied crustless sandwiches. And tell the *fraulein* to bring in the children. We settled in on the little blue love seats next to the fire in the small salon and were soon given hot cups of fragrant black tea. Mercedes took three sugars, Yvette and I none. I asked Mercedes how she liked Rome. Yvette translated and Mercedes clapped and bounced in place as a response. I thought how ill-favored she was, though obviously Yvette was smitten with her. Maybe she was a cute little package under all that mournful wrapping.

"We loved our audience with the Holy Father," Yvette said. I checked her expression to see if she was being ironic but it seemed all irony had been bleached out of her. Did you have to be an idiot in order to be holy? I felt like weeping over my lost Yvette, but then I reminded myself she'd always been unbelievably kind. What was new was her sweetness, but maybe that was caused by the proximity of her love, her Mercedes.

The children were brought in. They could say words in German, French, and English, but French was their go-to language if they really wanted something. I was afraid Yvette would swoop down on them like a giant black crow and frighten them, but she held herself back, and said, "They're adorable." She pronounced Foulques's name as if it were two syllables in Spanish; I realized she'd never heard it said out loud. The children were curious but a bit bewildered; they were at that age when you think if you close your eyes you vanish. They closed their eyes for five seconds at a time.

I said in English, "This is Mommy's sister, Yvette. We're twins also— like you two." Ghislaine seemed to understand and looked back and forth from Yvette's face to mine. She was utterly still, and then in frustration she rubbed her fists in her eyes, scrunched up, and started acting silly. That was the way she'd react when people talked about her for too long. She and Foulques started hitting each other playfully and giggling, sticking out their tongues and saying, "*Un deux trois, je vais dans le bois, quatre cinq six, cueiller des cerises, sept huit neuf, dans mon panier neuf, dix onze douze. Elles sont TOUTES ROUGES,*" and they fell about laughing, twisting and turning, Ghislaine showing her lace-trimmed panties. I could see Yvette was hypnotized. Was she thinking these could be her children? She kept looking at Mercedes with a little smile on her face, as if to guage her reaction, hoping they were sharing this moment. Did they want children, their own children? The butler brought in the sandwiches, then came back with an urn to refill our teacups.

"And who is this gentleman?" Yvette asked, smiling at the butler.

"Georges-Thomas," I said. And Yvette shook his hand. The poor guy looked completely flustered. It took me back to the time years ago when Yvette set out to go shopping with Pinky. This misplaced egalitarianism always ended up injuring or confusing the servants. And yet Yvette persisted: "*Je suis Yvette.*"

Poor Georges-Thomas murmured, "*Enchanté.*"

Yvette gestured toward her friend and said, "Mademoiselle Mercedes." She even stressed the last syllable of her name as when the French refer to the automobile. Georges-Thomas clicked his heels together and bowed his head: "*À votre service.*"

As if things hadn't become awkward enough, this was the moment Adhéaume chose to come into the little salon. I heard him say to Georges-Thomas, "*Un whiskey. Pas de glace.*" (One never thanked the servants or said "Please.")

I wondered how Adhéaume would treat my sister. Since he despised me, would he make her feel miserable and unwelcome?

Not at all. He became utterly charming, as only he knew how. He could play the charm card so suavely because he had been trained since childhood to be polite and accommodating, especially to women, even if they happened to be nuns. His parents were very pious and never lost a chance to produce a list of the family saints. His mother was fundamentally egotistical, gossipy, and small-minded, but she was off to Mass every morning. And her good works (knitting for the poor) would have earned her more indulgences if she knew how to do anything else. Eudes was the sort who stood in front of the church smoking with the other men except on Christmas, Easter, and All Saints, when he knelt and took Communion with a sour, reluctant look on his face. Adhéaume had gone to Catholic boarding school, where the nuns must have been cruel, though he was at ease around them; they were part of his Frenchness.

He spoke to Yvette in English and even managed to maneuver his way through a few words of Spanish. "I didn't know you could speak Spanish!" I exclaimed with a smile.

"I used to hunt with the prince of Asturias," he said. "And he was monolingual. I still have a few surprises for you up my sleeve."

Foulques was annoying his father by clinging to his leg and saying, "Uppy, uppy."

"*Fraulein*, the children have amused us enough," Addy said and she picked them both up and swept them away. They looked so startled they didn't make a sound, though a moment later I could hear them mewling in the hallway. I hated to see them whisked away. No wonder children hated adults and identified with the dog.

Yvette said, "That was my first time to see them. They're both angelic."

"Terribly spoiled, you meant to say, but I'm content they pleased you. At least they're not ugly," I said, "though don't be fooled by Ghislaine's beauty. She's a little devil."

Yvette frowned for a second upon hearing this coldhearted assertion. I was pleased I could still read her thoughts after all these years and despite her piety. It seemed she could read mine as well, because she reached across suddenly to squeeze my hand, a gesture Addy clocked and was undoubtedly trying to decipher. Sisterly solidarity, presumably, but solidarity against what? I could tell he was running through his words; he must have understood because he said, "I adore those children. They're so sweet and intelligent. Angelic, as you say." I had to admire Addy's perspicacity. There was no one on earth who wouldn't find him agreeable on first meeting. I could imagine Yvette's suspicion that my marital complaints must be all invented.

"Here's a telegram for you I found in the entry hall." Addy handed me the envelope.

"Oh," I said. "It's from Daddy."

I looked at Yvette. She had pulled out her rosary and was saying it, but slowly, in a distracted manner. Mercedes stood and said something. Addy bowed his head and led her away, smiling. Over his shoulder he said, "She wants to nap, but I'm sure she's saying that only out of discretion."

"Isn't she adorable?"

"Yes," I said. "I can see you're completely smitten."

Sister Maria Caterina must not have liked the pagan sound of that because she said, "She's a very good Christian. She's as playful as Saint Thérèse de Lisieux, wanting to be the Christ child's toy."

"Or yours," I added.

"Strangely, my English has deteriorated. I never speak it except with Bishop Oscar."

"How is he?" I asked, suitably warned for my frivolity.

"I miss him so much! I know we religious are not supposed to single out particular friendships, but he and Sister Maria Immacolada are dearest to my heart, I must admit."

"Addy will want to give a grand dinner for Daddy."

"I hope it will be lunch, since I must be back to the convent in the early evening."

"Of course. Addy will understand."

Yvette sat beside me on the blue velvet love seat. "Your children are enchanting. So full of animal spirits—and, I'd say, of supernatural spirit, too."

"How do you feel about seeing Daddy?"

"He and Bobbie Jean are both God's creatures."

I raised an eyebrow and said, "I wonder."

Yvette caught my eye and started laughing, which she immediately suppressed. It was my first glimpse of the old Yvette.

When Addy came back in he said, "The holy sister is resting nicely in the guest room. So! Your father and his wife?"

"Bobbie Jean?"

"Such a mysterious name to a French. She might as well be called Genghis Khan. So we will have a big dinner in their honor—and Yvette's and the charming Mercedes's."

"The nuns must be back at the convent by vespers, darling. Lunch?"

"Oh, of course. Do you think tomorrow is too soon?"

"It's perfect," said Yvette.

Addy added: "How careless of me to forget the rules."

I could see how impressed Yvette was by Addy's kindness. I wanted to whisper to her, "Don't be fooled by it!"

"You can eat meat?"

"Rarely. But that would be a real treat."

"And white rice!" I remembered that was Mercedes's favorite.

"Then it's settled. Just among us. One o'clock? Maybe I'll ask my parents to come by for dessert?"

"That would be grand," Yvette said. "Such a pleasure and honor to meet them."

"They're the ones who will be honored. They're very pious." That didn't sound quite right. "And they're very devoted to Yvonne and her family."

"Why don't you invite them for lunch?" Yvette asked.

"They don't really speak English, alas. It will already be like the United Nations here with Mercedes."

"Don't worry," Yvette said. "I'll translate for her."

"Just think," Addy said. "Two Texas girls, one excellent in French and the other in Spanish."

"Well," Yvette said, "many Texans can speak Spanish. It's really the second language. The big stores require all workers to speak both."

"Any allergies? Food dislikes?"

"Daddy doesn't like fish," I said. "Bobbie Jean eats everything."

"I gathered," Addy drawled. "Well, leave it all to me. It will be perfect. I'll serve it on the dishes from the Compagnie des Indes with my Venetian glasses and my vermeil silverware."

"I'm afraid Daddy will scarcely notice."

"He can always learn! In any event I like a pretty table—the round pearwood table in the library. Could you phone them, darling?"

They came the next day at one and they seemed wowed by the Avenue Foch apartment, which was larger than their house. I think Bobbie Jean felt sorry for me that so much of the furniture was old, but she could appreciate a bit of the grandeur.

The lunch conversation was torture. Daddy insisted on being seated next to Yvette, which threw off Addy's *placement*. Four women and only two men . . . Then their East Texas drawls were nearly incomprehensible. When Addy, for a loss of a topic, began to explain his additions and restorations to the family castle, Daddy cut him off and said, "I don't know what a fleur-de-lys is but I'm sure it's costing my Yvonne a pretty penny." Addy had been explaining how he was designing a giant fleur-de-lys of flowers on the château wall right next to the drawbridge.

"Yes," Addy said, "it will be very pretty."

"No," Daddy persisted, "it will cost a lot of money. Young man, I've been reviewing your expenses and this has gone way out of bounds. Your pockets have holes in them."

"Yes," Addy said gaily, "I'm very *dépensier*, but they're all solid investments—and beautiful! You appreciate beautiful things, don't you, Mr. Cravfjord?"

"It's Crawford to you and no, I don't"—he pulled out an invoice and unfolded it—"I don't appreciate fifteen thousand dollars spent on a lewis ex vee commode. Why the hell can't you buy a new porcelain toilet like everybody else for fifty bucks? I have bills and bills from you for all this broken-down furniture of yours. You could get this old stuff for almost nothing from the Salvation Army."

"Are you serious? *L'Armée du salut?*"

"If you like old things. Me, I prefer what's up-to-date."

"Oh, P.M.," Bobbie Jean wailed.

"You don't know what you're saying," Addy said angrily, flushing red. "The *soi-disant* old things I've bought are all the rarest, choicest antiques, which will increase in value immeasurably. I am building up your daughter's fortune—tripling it, four times."

Now it was Daddy's turn to go into a rage. And I knew he was even worse at controlling his temper than Adhéaume. I tried to change the subject or at least the setting. "Shall we go into the next room for our coffee?" I rose but no one else joined me as I sailed into the little salon.

I could hear Daddy rumbling, "Now, look here, young man, my Dallas banker has told me that at this rate you'll ruin my precious Yvette." (He had confused my name with my sister's.)

Addy said, "I have nothing to do with Yvette's fortune."

Daddy wiped his hand over his face. He'd sooner die than admit he'd made a mistake. "My Dallas banker, Jack Teddlie, tells me the only way to protect my daughter's money is for her to divorce you."

"Oh, P.M., you don't know what you're saying. You promised me."

"Let's join Yvonne," my sister said calmly.

"Y'all go on in. Yvette, stay here. We've got something to discuss. That's right, get along." I could hear Addy inviting Mercedes in Spanish to join him. She said, "*Gracias*," but she reminded him they had to be back at the convent before long.

"Close the door," Daddy shouted. I leaped up and did so.

A full-stop silence installed itself in our room. At last I asked Bobbie Jean, "Have you ever seen Versailles? The real Ver-sales?"

"What's that, dear?"

"Ver-sales. It's a royal palace forty-five minutes out of town."

"I know perfectly well what Ver-sales is. I studied up on it—yesterday."

"That might be a nice day trip for you and Daddy. I could go with you in our car. I'm not an expert but I could show you the highlights."

"I think P.M. wants to fly home tomorrow. He doesn't much like Paris, you know. He says he'd rather visit Houston. It has everything—fine gentlemen's shirts, the Antiquarium, dresses from vintage to top-end designers, the best steak houses . . ." She was running out of steam. "Everything . . . They're building a galleria shopping center like the one in Milan, Italy, only better. Soon they'll have a butterfly exhibit where you can watch these lovely insects sipping nectar or one might land on the lucky visitor."

"How ghastly!" Adhéaume said.

I leaped up, rushed to the closed door, and threw it open. There I could see Daddy seated but sticking his hand up Yvette's habit. She was crying. He looked crazy, his mouth working soundlessly. He was drunk.

She was standing there, allowing this terrible thing to happen to her, her oldest fear, the end of her vows of chastity, the ultimate defilement. In our family the worst things imaginable happened so fast they couldn't be understood. The horrors weren't unprecedented but were instantaneous. I could hear Addy chuckling.

Just then the butler announced Adheaúme's parents.

I had the strongest desire to brush past them and to run into the street. I could hear the waiter joking with the cook down the corridor and I wished with all my might that I could change places with them. My eye was suddenly taken by a big framed black-and-white etching of Palladio's Villa La Rotonda. I wondered how many Palladian villas there were in the Veneto.

Victorine looked around her slowly and saw, in the other room, a white-faced, sobbing nun being felt up by a seated old man, then in the small salon her own son sneering, a badly dressed old woman saying, "Oh, P.M.," and a brown-faced miniature nun shrieking, "¡Ay! ¡ay! ¡ay!"

Victorine said, in a slow, awed voice, a complex French sentence: "*Curieuse réunion où je ne suis peut-etre pas tout à fait à ma place*" ("Strange meeting in which I'm perhaps not completely where I belong").

~

In his confusion (had he suffered a stroke?) Daddy made little sense. Addy had accompanied the holy sisters back to their convent. Bobbie Jean commanded me to order her a taxi, which I did gladly. Victorine and Eudes had gone up to the nursery after I'd assured them that the children had seen nothing and that when they came down my "guests" would be gone. When they found me to say goodbye Victorine's lace-trimmed dress was wet; she'd been splashed, she said with an indulgent smile, by the twins, who'd been in their bath. Adhéaume wanted them to take a cold bath every day but the French maid, because of their protests, filled the tub with warm water; when their father would be heard on the creaking staircase coming up to check, the German nanny would pour in a pitcher of ice water.

Victorine asked me why that nun had been weeping. "That nun was my sister, Yvette. The little nun is her companion," I said. "I'm sorry we were having a family contretemps and I was unable to introduce you."

Victorine said, "And that other sunburned older woman made up like a *louesse de chaises*" (a woman who rents out metal chairs in the Luxembourg Gardens for a franc)?

"My father's wife."

"Ah, of course."

Adhéaume's mother cherished these savory bits of gossip like a rodent squirreling away nuts for the long winter. I could see she was hoping for one more nut to add to her cheek pouch but didn't dare seek it out. She and Eudes subsided and headed for the nearest taxi rank. No doubt she was congratulating herself on her "discretion."

Later, at the cocktail hour, Addy came into my little boudoir with a glass of iced vermouth and a lemon peel. I thanked him as I screwed my new ruby earrings in place.

"Your family really is mad," he said, as if he were simply making an observation.

"Do you find a lesbian nun and her incestuous father eccentric?" I asked.

"And your *pater* was so rude to me."

"He thinks I must divorce you. That's the only way to protect my fortune."

"In my family," Adhéaume said, "adultery is preferable to divorce. Adultery is normal, expected, whereas divorce is against the laws of the Church and a social scandal." I didn't say anything. After a moment

Adhéaume erupted with, "That's so American! To worry about the money. I don't beat my wife, I gave him two lovely grandchildren, neither retarded nor criminal, no one in Paris *frivole* talks of anything else except the Courcys, I'm accumulating treasures that will quadruple in value, I've already been contacted by the Metropolitan Museum of Art and a scout for the Rockefellers. Did I tell you that the furniture at Versailles under Louis the Fourteenth was sheathed in silver until the king had it stripped to pay for one of his wars? And that the only silver replicas exist in Denmark—and that now I've bought them? Of course, the chairs and bergères and the *duchesses brisées* are unrivaled in the history of furniture."

"Daddy is far from convinced."

"*Daddy* is an uncouth simpleton. Besides, you can't divorce me. Remember, with the evidence I have of your depravity I'd get custody of the children and I'd make them miserable as retribution against you."

"You love them. You wouldn't do that to them."

"And they've been so spoiled till now that a Spartan convent school would seem all the more painful. What does my mother call Ghislaine? Her majesty? Soon she'd be a miserable, devious little wretch, dirty and smelly, ignorant and superstitious, her brother a stunted, malnourished ragamuffin. Something right out of *Les Mystères de Paris.*"

Which I'd never read and Adhéaume, I was confident, knew only by reputation or a high school précis. Frenchmen of his generation knew nothing and had heard of everything.

I was wretched. I recognized Daddy was determined to stop paying Adhéaume an allowance and to change the terms of his will, making my eventual inheritance dependent on our divorce. He would have insisted on these terms even if Addy and I had a love marriage, since Daddy felt the only important thing, in the end, was money. Love would come and go, happiness was fleeting, but depression on a feather bed was better than depression on a board. I didn't dare tell my father that Addy had compromising photos of me and that almost certainly he would get custody of the children, whom he would pauperize and victimize in order to punish me.

I hated Adhéaume and his boring, conceited, worthless parents. When Victorine phoned to see if I would go with her to Puiforcat to select flatware for the château, I told her that she must make the choice on her own, that only she had the exquisite taste necessary. I could tell she didn't know whether to be annoyed or flattered. "Oh," I said, "and be sure to order the toucan pattern of plates from Hermès."

"The what, dear?"

"Toucan. Hermès."

"Hermès makes dishes now?"

"Yes, the most beautiful. Perfect with your Puiforcat."

I didn't mention a casserole dish cost a thousand dollars. My reasoning was that Daddy would see red when he received the bill. And then what?

I was frozen. I couldn't do anything. I was trapped. I thought it was so unfair that Addy had his wife-swappers, and I'd lose my children due to a not-very-exciting three-way with partners who'd betrayed me and married each other.

I should never have married Adhéaume! I could see now how Spanky had led me to slaughter. I was going to fill the empty family coffers, a classic American plot. The bartered bride. I would be forced to face my own children being brutalized by their father.

I'd always felt too entitled to harbor resentments, but now I found myself daydreaming about Addy's death and destruction. Although I still appeared the soul of Southern graciousness with an admixture of French aristocratic ostentatious politeness, I secretly imagined violent revenge and sadistic scenarios. At that time I went to the very kitsch Pagode movie theater to see a revival of Melville's *Bob le flambeur*, a crime film—which only fed my violent fantasies. Or could I hack him to pieces and burn the body fragments like Landru, who'd inspired Chaplin's *Monsieur Verdoux*? It was an antiwar film. Just before Verdoux is guillotined he says, "If you kill one person you're a criminal; kill a million and you're a hero." But I couldn't imagine overpowering Addy on my own, and drugging his drink seemed inelegant.

I still had my avant-garde music evenings. One evening was devoted to Ligeti, the Hungarian composer. He was impossibly ugly with thick lips, gray teeth, and no brow, and I wasn't surprised he was born in Transylvania.

Until he escaped from Hungary he'd been obliged to write conventional easy-on-the-ears music but as soon as he came to the West he made a beeline for Germany and Stockhausen, turned out electronic and near-electronic music, and soon became a "serial killer" in the Schoenberg manner. Helen came to our events with Ercole. Sometimes she brought other *femmes du monde*. She made a big point of saying she found the conversation of the *gratin* impossibly dull, with its endless marriages and baptisms, its "schedule" of chic watering places, its chirpy gossip camouflaged as "news of the Rialto" (scandal-mongering that was too obvious was dismissed and stigmatized as "worthy of a nosy concierge"). She claimed that she could abide only the talk of creative geniuses, though frankly I found my geniuses to be petty, covetous, and competitive.

Helen would always sit next to me and hold my hand, drawing arabesques with her finger across my palm. I suppose once I would have found that seductive, but now I was just irritated. Was she trying to see if she had the same power over me? I don't think she was that devious; rather, she never wanted to admit to herself that a freedom or opportunity was in the past, that she had chosen at a fork in the road one path over another. She lived in a permanent state of nostalgia and ruled over the empire of missed chances, which I found morbid, confusing, and pointless. It was as if she couldn't fully authorize the choice she had actually made and wanted every affinity to remain elective.

Ercole, on the contrary, was happy to live out the consequences of his decisions. He didn't like choosing, but at least he had the courage of his choices. He told me, just to make me laugh, that his first wife, Isabella, was such a frightened virgin that on their wedding night she'd crouched for hours on top of the armoire until he could coax her down. They slept chastely like brother and sister that first night. Later, she'd become quite the tiger and poor Dutch Hoob complained she was always in heat and pestering him.

I laughed but I instantly felt guilty as I thought of the miseries my children faced. Daddy was evil, but so was Mommy.

CHAPTER 17

My dear Sister,

Here I am safely back in Jericó with Mercy. We're completely turned around, yawning at vespers, staggering at compline, impossible to arouse at lauds. We're like zombies as we move through our daily rituals, which peeves the other religious, as if we're shirking our work and are guilty of acedia, the sin of boredom that leads to sloth, as if our trip to Rome has made us feel superior to the other women. In fact, we are grateful that the convent allowed us to accompany Pablo to Rome. I may have paid for our travels, but the all-important permission to go there was granted by Mother Superior.

Of course, like any returning traveler who has witnessed life-changing sights, I'm eager to talk about things seen and done, but I bite my tongue lest I awaken some invidia. After all, I've seen St. Peter's and the Sistine Chapel and the Colosseum and the Rotonda church dedicated to San Lorenzo. After all, I've been blessed by the pope himself. I've climbed on my knees up the Holy Stairs Jesus Christ climbed. In Paris at the Sainte-Chapelle I saw a splinter of the True Cross.

You may wonder why I just stood there when Daddy put his hand up my skirt. I think it was Saint Elizabeth of Hungary who believed that wherever she went an invisible cell glided around her and protected her. Moreover, since she was forbidden to quit her throne and join holy orders, she wore her state gowns but over a painful hair shirt that martyr-ized her flesh. I thought of her at the time only because I had the strong conviction that God was protecting me. As you no doubt know, Daddy violated me when I was in my early teens and repeatedly assaulted me until I was sixteen and had grown enough pubic hair to repulse him. I even became pregnant but in the second month fortunately I had a miscarriage. No one ever suspected. I went through the whole ordeal alone. Many times I thought of confiding in you, but I wasn't sure you could keep a secret. Day and night I told myself, "You mustn't tell anyone." I said it like the Jesus Prayer. "You mustn't tell anyone." My grades slipped for a while; I couldn't concentrate on anything or even understand a question the teacher would address to me. "You mustn't tell anyone." I didn't want to betray Daddy, who obviously had titanic needs. Poor man, I told myself, he's a good person and if he behaves so wickedly it must be because lust has overwhelmed him. He must feel so ashamed of himself. Though he frightened me, I pitied him. I certainly didn't want to add to his travails.

I also thought there must be something foul in me to awaken those desires in him. I became convinced that I smelled bad and that if someone at the movies took a different seat it was because they couldn't bear my stench. I knew it was sinful to touch or even look at my private parts, but I kept running my hand over my pubis and sniffing it. Although I couldn't detect a foul odor, I knew I must be radiating it; the rot was infecting me everywhere. I tried to keep my legs crossed in public in order to lock down the smell. I sprayed myself before going to school and eventually carried a bottle of toilet water with me, with which I'd douse myself every time I went to the bathroom. Soon kids sitting near me in class began to complain of the sweet, floral smell of my perfume. It was no longer masking my inner corruption but had paradoxically become the nuisance itself.

I thought I was losing my mind. I broke out in a rash down there, probably because the alcohol had burned my tender flesh. I thought of confessing my anxiety to a priest, but the idea of confiding in a man horrified me. I wondered why nuns couldn't hear confession, at least of young women, but soon I learned it's not for the faithful to question the ways of the priesthood. When I was really in pain, despite applications of the soothing cream I stole from Bobbie Jean's bathroom and after another girl had remarked, "Ooh-ee! You smell like a lady of the night, I declare." I decided to muster my courage and confess my worries next Saturday.

When I entered church and saw the red light over the confessional box, indicating that a priest was in attendance and not listening to a penitent, I boldly entered—and became speechless! The priest, in a kindly, soft voice that I recognized, murmured that he was listening. "Father, I have sinned. It's been a week since I last confessed. I had sexual intercourse with my father."

"Willingly or against your will?"

"Unwillingly."

"Did you derive any pleasure from the act?"

"No. It was painful."

"Did your father show you pornography to excite you? These are all leading questions, which the Vatican forbids, *crimen sollicitationis*, but I think you may need them."

"Thank you. No, no pornography."

"Were you excited?"

"No."

"Did he give you money or gifts as a reward for the act?"

"No."

"Do you hate your father and wish him dead?"

"Oh, no."

"Are you guilty of scrupulosity?"

"What is that?"

"Imagining a sin where none exists."

"No."

"Then where is the sin? How have you sinned? Have you slandered your father?"

"No."

"Have you had an abortion?"

"No."

"Did you provoke him to sin through lascivious words or bodily movements?"

"No."

"What are you failing to tell me? Would you say you were raped?"

"How do you define that?"

"Were you a willing partner or did your father force you to lie down with him?"

"I tried to stop him. I cried and begged him to stop."

"Then you are without sin, my child."

"But Father . . ."

"Yes?"

"Aren't there some acts that are such an abomination in the eyes of God that they must count as sins?"

"A mortal sin is a grave act, such as murder that must be committed with forethought and intention. A venial sin is a smaller sin, like theft, that will not result in eternal damnation. Both kinds of sin can be absolved through confession and contrition. But both kinds require the sinner to plan, to will, to envision the sin; nothing accidental is a sin and nothing merely undergone. It's rather a martyrdom in your case and is sanctifying." Of course, I'd been catechized and knew everything he was saying by heart. But he must have thought I needed reminding (and I did).

I confessed a handful of venial sins and he told me to say ten Hail Marys and to pray sincerely and to meditate on my sins before leaving the church.

I went to the altar rail, and as I was praying and then saying my Hail Marys I felt such an enormous relief. I kept going over what I'd told the priest to make sure it was completely true; I worried most that I'd somehow tempted my father. But then I realized I was guilty of scrupulosity. Sin didn't work in hidden, unconscious ways. It was willed in the full daylight of intention. I was free! I had no need to be absolved!

I don't know why I bring up such morbid memories. I've read enough psychology to know what I'm calling an "invisible cell" would normally be referred to as "depersonalization" (the feeling that everything is happening in a movie) or "derealization" (the feeling that nothing is actually happening). These symptoms are mostly experienced by women between the ages of sixteen and twenty and are brought on by trauma or abuse. Of course, now I know that Daddy himself was abused as a boy, poor man. And I know I was guiltless and that my mania about smelling bad was unfounded. To be perfectly honest, I think my aversion to sex and my vows of chastity are probably not unrelated to that abuse. Also, to be frank, I'm more attracted to women now then men. Since we're identical biologically if not in our life histories, I wonder if you feel the same velleity. Of course, I wouldn't act on that desire—well, I *did* act on it once in Rome. We were staying in a convent behind the Janiculum, twin beds in a simple, whitewashed cell, a very high coffered wood ceiling, a rugged iron cross, immense windows looking out on a garden of lemon trees. It was night, the window was open, and this wonderful cool maritime breeze was blowing, what the Romans call the *ponentino*, and I felt restless and exalted and in need of human contact. I sat on the edge of Mercedes's bed for maybe an hour, just staring at her beloved face, so peaceful. She was snoring lightly, like the sound of a finger rubbing corduroy. It was stronger than I was, this urge to touch her. And in the most intimate parts. "Better murder an infant in its cradle than nurse an unacted desire," William Blake wrote. Was he just a mouthpiece for the Devil or was his a superior wisdom? I read that verse by him when I was an adolescent and I've never forgotten it. Of course, I was at the age when you'll believe anything if it's said with enough conviction and eloquence; you'll even believe contradictory utterances pronounced with equal verve.

Ever so gently I brushed my lips against Mercy's, and, still asleep, she rubbed her mouth with the back of her tiny, pudgy hand as if I'd been a mosquito. She smelled of vegetable ravioli, which we'd eaten for dinner, and I was intoxicated by the odor siphoning through her parted lips. She must have felt my breath. She frowned and her eyes clicked open. She stared at me, wordless, for a full minute. Finally she started to whisper but had a frog in her throat. She swallowed and said, "Hello." She paused, then said slightly louder, "You can touch me if you please. I'm not drawn to other women, but I will never refuse my body to you. I know you want me. I may sleep through it, but do anything you want with me. I could never say no to you. I don't want to commit the sin of concupiscence"—she tripped on the word and smiled as she repeated it deliberately—"nor do I want to deny you anything. I love you."

After those sweet words I stood and went back to my bed. She had cured me of my blind passion and I slept peacefully until the birds outside our open window started their dawn racket. I hope I haven't alarmed you with this confession.

Did you feel even the slightest stirring of lust looking at Mercedes? I suppose she's not conventionally beautiful—dark, chubby, short—but to me she's irresistible. Everything she said to me was perfection. That she loved me but was not attracted to women. That she would deny me nothing, though she refused to sin. That she would *suffer* my love. That she respected my desperation. Because I am desperate I find it difficult to condemn Daddy. The passions are cruelly real; they whip and spur us into a frenzy, to the point of no turning back. When you are under the lash, you can't reason with yourself. Passion is like grief; people say those feelings will weaken with time, which is demonstrably true, but for the lover or the mourner there is no past nor future. Only the scalding present. No words or thoughts or actions are comforting. Distractions feel sacrilegious. Worse than this present pain is the notion you will grow into some future indifference. That feels like the ultimate profanation, a descent from the quickness of pain into the numbness of everyday life, the shift from tragedy to banality. A betrayal.

And then when Daddy was abused by *his* father? I assume there is an infinite regress of vice and pain.

What do I find so attractive about Mercedes? Maybe because you and I are big and solid, I feel tenderly toward her smallness, her tubbiness, her dark skin, which seems to me not only tanned but infused with heat by the sun. Her guilessness, her stupid playfulness (like her tasteless off-color jokes) make me smile. Her courage and absence of resentment against the society that has been so harsh with her. She likes the other religious, even the sourest nuns. I picture her like a dark version of Botticelli's *Primavera*, scattering her flowers over everyone she encounters, her face always fully visible so we can see the total glory of her smile.

I loved your children, my niece and nephew, though you seemed strangely strict with Ghislaine. I'm so used to the nearly wild but always merry children in Jericó, running free, loud most of the time—holy terrors! Sometimes I listen to them playing outside my window, though I can't see them. They whip one another into ecstasies of excitement and their voices climb and climb perilously high. If you could hold them in your hand it would be like holding a small live bird, its body throbbing, its hot, trapped wings wanting to flutter, its heart bursting with fear or joy.

Ghislaine, in her layers of bleached and starched white skirts, her fixed smiles, her polished pale face like an old-fashioned doll's minutely painted features, her silence betrayed by her tremor—she seems like a member of a different species. The way you made her curtsy to me broke my heart. I can't say why. But I thought of a trained pony taught to kneel in the circus sawdust. You had had to reproach her for forgetting to curtsy; then she dropped her curtsy perfectly and if she was being resentful or ironic she concealed her mood behind her antique bisque face. I wish you could be kinder, softer with her; it must be obvious to her how you prefer her brother.

I could see how proud you were of them—perfectly understandable since I as a mere aunt was bursting with pride. They are so beautiful, dipped in silver, they smell so good, of clean clothes and fresh bread, they are anything but spoiled (though you say the contrary); strangely enough, I found something in them oddly *beseeching*.

I must consider your husband to be a monster because you say he's one, but *prima facie* he seems courtly, attentive, even sweet, but that probably shows how naive I am, how easily impressed. Of course, we grew up among some good guys, but you have to admit the typical Texas man is tough going—egotistical, full of more appetite than courtesy, more macho than manly. Of course, I'm speaking of the natural as opposed to the supernatural man. And it's my job as a Christian to find what's salvageable in every person; when chatting with you I go back in time to our Ranger girlhood when I sneered at most boys, perhaps as a way of ignoring how they preferred you. Or perhaps I was just frightened by them, since Daddy had shown me how much harm a male could do.

We're both lucky to live surrounded by so much beauty—I in my cool, quiet, tile-lined, scrupulously clean and orderly convent, the only rupture in its austerity the swirling gold confections of the chapel, the

excesses of the Churrigueresque style, the shiny pastry-tubed extrava-
gances of intricately carved and gilt cedar, framing painted life-size statues
of royal saints (Saint Louis of France, Elizabeth of Hungary, Hermenegild,
whose own father ordered him beheaded when he abandoned Arianism
and became a Chalcedonian Christian). I live in a world measured by
bells, prayers, meals, duties. You live in an almost equally peaceful world,
one of soft voices, of prevailing fashions, radiating streets, exquisite food,
frivolous pursuits, burnished surfaces, works of art in a city where traffic
sounds are muted, honking illegal, a place misted by rain, where the
height of buildings is regulated, where all items of street furniture
(benches, grills around the base of trees, overhead lights, subway entrances,
newspaper kiosks, public conveniences, and fountains) are uniform and
identical, where billboards are outlawed, where a bulb is replaced as soon
as it's burned out, where the entire cityscape was designed by one man,
empowered by one emperor, where everything is ruled by taste, where
six different train stations serve the rather small population, a city that has
more bookstores than all of America, including two that sell nothing but
antique editions of Jules Verne. In my convent we all dress alike, discipline our thoughts and words, eat the same food at the same hours,
prostrate ourselves before the same God; in your city, everyone cultivates
his or her uniqueness, thinks his or her own thoughts, expresses different
feelings, listens to different music, eats or fails to eat on his own schedule,
bathes or neglects his hygiene, bursts with pride or shrivels with self-
contempt, speaks in a hundred languages, falls in and out of love, skis in
January, travels to the sea in August, invests in property, clothes, jewelry,
lessons, trips. Is the goal to feel pleasure or achieve individuality? If Jericó
for me is where personal desires die, Paris is the place where they thrive.
It is the world capital of the ego, and, as Paul Valéry writes, Can you imagine
the incomparable disorder that can be maintained by ten thousand essen-
tially singular beings? Just imagine the *temperature* that can be produced
in this one place by such a great number of *prides*, all comparing themselves. Paris contains and combines, and consummates or consumes most
of the brilliant failures summoned by destiny to the *delirious professions* . . .
This is the name I give to all those trades whose main tool is one's
opinion of oneself, and whose raw material is the opinion others have of

you. He goes on to say these "unique people" want to do what no one has ever done and never will do. They are striving for the illusion that they alone exist, for superiority is "a solitude located at the current frontiers of the species." I've been rereading Valéry, though his poems and prose are edifying if not pious.

Were you embarrassed by Mercy and me, the big black stork and the small round penguin? Did you hope none of your real friends would come by and be astonished by this freak, your sister? Your twin sister?

But we are twins, which permits me to wonder what your inner life must be like. Do you find solace in friends, your children, reading, your musical soirées? If there were ever a place calculated to seem an earthly paradise, it must be Paris—or at least the Paris of the rich. I suppose the Church counts on miserable multitudes, all those too poor or too ill or too ugly or too old or too stupid to find happiness in this world; but for the happy few of Paris, the present must seem worth giving up paradise for.

Bishop Oscar did not seem happy to see us back in Jericó. Possibly he is feeling the anxiety around us; the local landlords and gentry don't like his weekly radio broadcasts in which he argues that the earth belongs to all of us and must be shared. Last week he said, "It is not God's will for some to have everything and others to have nothing. That cannot be of God. God's will is that all his children be happy." In his closing prayer he said, "Let us not be afraid, brothers and sisters. We are living through difficult and uncertain days. We do not know if this very evening we will be prisoners or murder victims. We do not know what the forces of evil will do with us. But one thing I do know: even those who have disappeared after arrest, even those who are mourned in the mystery of an abduction, are known and loved by God. This is the true treasure of God's reign."

The life of a convent is as regimented as that of an army barracks and I've only run into the bishop once since our return. I started to compliment him on his bravery and eloquence but he just sailed past me; maybe I'm being paranoid, perhaps he is preoccupied or didn't hear me.

I know, all I do is quote other people and you might wonder if I have thoughts of my own. I do, but most of them are generated by my

Mercy-obsessions. During the day I wonder where she is, and I'm constantly taking new routes to my room, to the chapel or the refectory, hoping to bump into her. Yesterday I cornered her at lunch and we agreed to take a walk together through the kitchen garden but then we spotted the bishop staring at us *balefully*; I noticed the dark patches under his eyes, the lines of tension in his face, his pallor. He looked as if he'd passed many sleepless nights. Of course, he must be worried about an assassination. Mercy and I decided against a walk together; I didn't even need to explain this change of plans—she must have had the same thought at the same time. Did we feel Oscar was reproaching us for our happiness?

Oh, yes, the quotation. I'm reading Dorothy Day, whose writings speak to me as a Christian defending the poor and as an American. Citing Henry James she says that we English-speakers need once again to sing the praises of poverty. "We have lost the power even of imagining what the ancient realization of poverty could have meant; the liberation from material attachments, the unbridled soul, the manlier indifference, the paying our way by what we are and not by what we have, the right to fling away our life at any moment irresponsibly—the more athletic trim, in short, the fighting shape." Do you think she'll be made a saint? There is a kind of romantic extravagance in the Christian transformation, a kind of wild abandon, isn't there?

My current job is fabricating candles, tall church tapers, made from beeswax that we heat and pour into inverted brass molds, the desired slender shape. Bundles of ten attached molds are positioned at waist height. There are additives that determine the scent, what's called the scent throw (the range of the perfume), the burning point, the floral odor itself. And of course the prewaxed cotton wick of the right length, which has to be suspended at the exact center of the candle length (there's a perforated tin disk that holds the wick in place). The trick is to pour exactly the right amount of wax for each candle—it's all in the wrist, as they say. We usually work in the morning, when it's cooler.

I like the smell of our candles so much more than the odor of the carbolic soap we make, which is medicinal, even antiseptic, the smell of burnt iodine or something, maybe coal. It's supposed to kill bacteria, but to me it has the sad smell of public schools on a winter evening, of . . . well, frustrated sex, strange to say, not that I'd know one kind of sex from another.

Our bishop posts the times for our confession to him. I saw that Mercy would be confessing a whole day before I would. An hour before her scheduled time I touched her shoulder as we were perambulating in opposite directions around the columned cloisters (chalky white against the deep shadows under the roof and against the brilliant green of our courtyard, rich with big sawtooth agave cactuses). She avoided my glance and shrugged off my hand. We were supposed to keep rotating and to remain silent, but I was tempted to break ranks and run up to her and demand what was wrong.

I was so in love with her—her tender body, her plump lips, her beautiful bouncy buttocks, her generous soul, her smooth, small breasts, the way she gave herself to me so entirely, pretending to be asleep but groaning with pleasure. If the price to pay for having her exclusive love was never to sleep with her again, I'd gladly pay it. If the price to pay for having her body in love was sharing her with another man or woman, I'd never pay it. I wanted her to love no one else but I would accept any conditions to possess her for myself alone. I knew that I was risking my immortal soul by loving her so intensely, but I was already burning in an eternal fire with love's pangs—hell would be nothing new for me.

An hour later she would be confessing to Bishop Oscar. Had she rejected me because she already feared his ire once she told him of our nights together, even though she was blameless—or was she, in the eyes of the Church? She had given me permission to touch her ("I will never refuse my body to you") and sin begins in complicity. If she was cold to me now, how would she be at vespers or dinner?

I was intensely aware of the time and as Mercy's confession approached I couldn't stop pacing and muttering to myself. I felt that the hands of the clock were Satan's wings, unfolding, meeting, then drawing apart. Would Oscar berate her for our intimacy? For her tolerating my sinful molesting? Would he (Lord help us) be jealous of us? Resent the way she'd replaced him in my affections?

I lurked around the chapel, where the austere dark wood confession boxes were. If I drew near I could convince myself I could hear Mercy's childlike voice. Of course, I could see her tiny shoes as she knelt. And then, here she was, plunging forth and almost running to the prayer rail facing the solid gold altar, its brilliant gilded curves and pointed details generating light, a honeycomb of light. I knelt beside her—she must have glimpsed me. She turned her face away from me.

Had Bishop Oscar instructed her to avoid me?

Tears began to leak out of my eyes. I didn't sob, I didn't pity myself, I wasn't trying to attract her attention and force her to say something consoling. My tears weren't a statement much less a plea. No, they were just a matter of *leakage*. I didn't have a handkerchief. I just let the tears glaze my face, incontestable evidence of my pain.

She must have seen my tear-shiny face but (the little darling) she decided to stay resolute. That was what her bishop had told her to do. A tropical rain collapsed on the buildings around us, sudden and heavy and falling straight down for no more than three minutes, everything was abruptly cooler and sweeter smelling.

To sober myself I tried to think of Mercy as a robot, as a machine without a face or body, as stripped scaffolding, as nothing but hinges and plugs and wiring—would she still have the same appeal without her rubbery body and placid face? Without her full lips and ridiculously cute "inny," her inward-twirling navel? Without her soft voice and corny jokes? Was I in love with the packaging alone? If I had to weigh her heart against another, would hers come up lighter? Was hers the beautiful soul I imagined?

Absurd exercise! Her sweetness was so intimately related to her looks, her face and body were such perfect expressions of her spirit, one might as well argue against Christ's double nature as man and God uniquely melded.

I couldn't live without Mercy's love. At first, months ago, I'd talked myself into being in love with her as if to prove to myself I still had merely human appetites or maybe as just an alibi for my yearning (it being easier to accept the involuntary as something *willed*), but at some invisible point I'd really and truly been transformed into someone obsessed—and now it was too late to turn back. I was hopelessly in love except love of this sort was nothing but hope—for a future that would never be permitted, that I would never let myself envision, that I could hope for only as long as it remained unrealized, even unimagined.

The thought of awakening each morning at matins without the possibility of holding her little hand and looking into her playful eyes—oh, that I couldn't endure! How did my love of God shade into the love of this unremarkable woman? Why would I give up my chances to life eternal contemplating God for a fleeting touch or glance from a silly girl who was doing her best to observe her vows? Why would she obey the arbitrary commands of a dusty desert deity instead of surrendering to a taller, richer woman?

Fine words, but I felt my life was ending, that I couldn't breathe, that I hadn't asked for much, that I hadn't even dared to long for mutual love, that I could accept any conditions whatsoever as long as Mercy might give me her little smile, in which the petulance disguised the innocence—or one of her childish "naughty" winks (in which she inexpertly closed both eyes).

She didn't sit at her usual place at dinner and she kept emitting her loud, high, nearly hysterical laugh, a new sort of horrible neighing that I was sure would be reprimanded by Mother Superior, but the older woman seemed imperturbable at the high table, raised on its dark green tile dais, and she was smiling calmly in her reassuring way. Could it be she didn't hear her rogue nun neighing?

I went back to my cell feeling as if I was holding a leaking cistern, my heart, and my task was to return to privacy before all the liquid ran out. It was as if a storm cloud were gathering in my head, smothering my sinuses, drowning my lungs. I didn't want to bring attention to myself but somehow at the same time I wanted someone to intervene and save my sanity, my life . . . Simultaneously I wanted to attract and escape notice.

That night I slept fitfully, threw off my covers then was cold, kept turning my pillow to the cool side, resented all the deprivations of convent life, longed for Parisian luxuries (why not suffer in luxury like you, dear Yvonne?). It occurred to me that the religious life was all hocus-pocus—designed to protect the rich, harbor lazy, gluttonous nuns and monks, supply fresh-faced boys for priests to groom and sodomize, drug the living and tranquilize the dying, provide structure for the mad and merely eccentric, lend meaning to purposeless lives, give old widows in black something to do such as arrange altar flowers or iron surplices or suffer supplices.

Did I love Mercy more than God? Did I want a year with her more than eternity in heaven? Why did the very words "Heaven" and "Hell" sound like something out of a comic book in which the bright colors weren't stamped properly and were bleeding into one another? My mind had become a palestra where the Devil exercised, where he was growing stronger day by day.

I spent the morning packing long white fragrant candles in boxes of twenty, which the local candymaker had manufactured for us stamped with the convent coat of arms—things we could sell along with sweets made of coconut shreds, jars of honey, the soap, eau de toilette—everything sold in our shop at the front gate. Tourists bought our products, other churches, the pious, and the well-to-do.

At last it was my time to confess. At first I didn't say anything. I could hear Oscar's heavy breathing and smell his distinctive male odor. After a moment he said, "I'm listening," and I said routinely, "Forgive me, Father, for I have sinned." Then I told him how long it had been since I'd last confessed and I fell into a painful silence again. Somewhere nearby I could smell tortillas being made—it must be the deacon's wife who lived in a room adjoining the church. The idea that a woman was wisely cooking tortillas reminded me that not everything was tuned to the high drama of the convent.

I could hear Oscar shifting about in his pen like a bronco before it's released in a rodeo. He sounded dangerous or frightened or both—but was I just imagining that? Bored, maybe, impatient at my silence. I was so hesitant because I didn't want to provoke him into saying something we'd both regret. I started to speak in English, as we usually did, but he asked that I speak in Spanish. Automatically I felt less sincere, since I was shaping what I said according to what I could say. And almost every phrase recalled where and when I'd learned it—a second language isn't history-neutral but drags a huge tail of circumstance behind it.

I told him that I'd sinned by worshipping an idol—another nun rather than God. He asked me to name her. I said that was irrelevant.

"Name her!" he nearly shouted. An echo of his voice reverberated through the church.

"Sister Maria Immacolada," I whispered.

He didn't make a sound. I knew that Saint Charles Borromeo had designed the confessional box so that priests couldn't assault nuns sexually, but that precaution now seemed cruelly irrelevant to me. Why couldn't I see his face and how he'd reacted?

"Is your love for her very great?" he asked and now I felt we were no longer staying within the rules. I could hear the anguish in his question.

"Yes. Very great."

He asked me if I'd ever loved anyone with the same degree of passion. I told him that I'd thought I'd loved Our Lord like that and when I'd read of Saint Catherine exchanging hearts with Jesus, the book had trembled in my hand and I'd felt a wound in my side. But that was a feeling I'd worked to prolong, whereas this passion for Mercy was something that awakened in me as soon as I woke up and that absorbed all my thoughts throughout the day, an involuntary anguish to the neglect of my prayers.

He asked me what I found so extraordinary about her and I said I didn't know, perhaps it was her very ordinariness, her simplicity, her innocence—the way she was interchangeable with most of humanity. Yes, that was it. She was human. *Ecce homo.*

That's impious, he said, to speak of a girl in the language drawn from the life of Our Lord. I admitted how grave my sin was. Or my impropriety.

"It's a sin," he said.

He asked me if my feelings were growing stronger or whether I was learning to subdue them.

Stronger, I said.

"You belong in a hermitage," he said. "Where you see no one, where you are fed by religious in a remote place, where you rise before dawn and begin to pray, kneeling on stone, where your thoughts are trained on each nail, each thorn, on the lance in the side and the sponge soaked in vinegar, on the blood slowly dripping from Him like sap from a scarred tree." We were speaking English for some reason now and for a moment I thought he'd said "sacred" instead of "scarred." "It's your only chance to be saved," he said. "You are nearly lost."

"But you and Mercy are the dearest people in the world to me. I don't want to be a hermit. And you said we can only worship in twos or threes."

The bishop told me he was thinking only of my salvation. He said that Mercy had confessed that she and I had made love.

I protested that he was breaking the laws of the confessional, that the priest may not mention—

"I know, I know," he said irritably. "But there are moments—such as a threat to national security or a murder plot—when the seal of secrecy must be broken."

I let a full twenty seconds go by until I asked wearily if he thought my love for Mercy was comparable to a murder.

"To a suicide! Homosexuality has no place in a religious house, a convent. Even among the laity only married heterosexuals are allowed to have sex; they alone are not sinning and they must have sex strictly for procreation. You are a sinner."

I told him that Jesus never once mentioned same-sex love in the Bible. Oscar pointed out that He also said that where He had not set up a prohibition then those of the Old Testament were still in force.

"Then no bacon or shrimp," I said.

"Dietary restrictions are not as serious as a fundamental violation of nature."

"Then male dogs mustn't hump each other?" I hated the sound of trivial discontent in my voice. At last I sighed and said, "I cannot become a hermit. Anyway, she was asleep when I touched her."

He thought for a while and said, "I am not only your confessor, my child, but also your spiritual guide. If you are too weak to live as a solitary penitent, then you must become a missionary."

"Yes, Your Excellency, that sounds like a good solution." I said that maybe only because he'd called me "my child" and something in me was pacified. Or maybe just because I'd called him "Your Excellency" and I felt I must comply. Bishop Oscar had brought God's grace to me. I liked the grown-up but noncommittal sound of "good solution."

Oscar told me that he would reflect on where I could be of use. He told me that in the indigenous community of Karmata Rua Cristiania, only about two hours away by bus, in the Andes, the Embera-Chami live and speak their own language and are known for their painted faces, their way of dancing, their embroidered caps and sleeves, their rather primitive clay bowls and sculptures. They grow coffee, plantains, yucca, and avocados. The name of their region means "land of nettles" in Spanish. They are unsmiling but pleasant, remarkably outspoken, heavily intermarried with Christians. Most of them are themselves Christians, though they respect their traditional gods as well. They practice their traditional medicine.

They live in rather grim buildings of several stories constructed for them by the government, though quite a few families have tin shacks. There are frequent landslides on the hilly roads but people just drive around the fallen rocks. The food sounds repulsive and involves "big-butted" deep-fried flies and goat meat wrapped in goat viscera; they also eat cow viscera, which they call *mule*.

I met a nun who was a tribeswoman of the Embera-Chami. She had a cool, anthropological approach to her past, which she clearly wanted to disown. It was evident that she'd just as soon forget it (she looked no different than the other Colombian sisters), but since she couldn't, she'd sequestered her past into a small field of study. She said that the Andes were heartbreakingly beautiful with their morning mists and rolling green hills, their dangerously steep roads only one lane wide, requiring one of the two facing cars to back down sometimes as much as a mile to a tiny turn-off in order to let the other oncoming vehicle pass, with their sudden midday deluges of rain, their wild orchids and little parrots, their giant cactuses and dripping trees, their truckloads of singing campesinos.

"But why would they want you, the indigenous people? Do you have medical skills? Have you studied agronomy? The native language?"

I confessed that I knew how to teach English, maths, Spanish, Latin, Greek . . .

"No need of dead languages," she said with a slightly offended stare. "These people are just barely hanging on. It will be a real burden just to feed you. There are only about four hundred families. I suppose you could invent some native dances for them, design them some native costumes, help them with their beadwork—tourism is their biggest industry, that and growing coffee. They have nothing to attract tourists for longer than an hour, nothing to sell them but ten-dollar bags of coffee beans and beautiful blue, red, and yellow beadwork on hats and sleeves and beaded bracelets and necklaces with wonderful sun signs and mountain signs. There's a Catholic priest living there but he doesn't seem to do much—just a single mass a week for about five people. No classes. No confessions. Lots of whiskey. I suppose some tourist crackpots would want to buy native herbal medicines, though they're worthless. Oh, everyone is sick with dengue fever. It could annihilate someone as fragile as you."

I saw Mercy working in the vegetable garden. She had hiked up her skirts out of the dust and was wearing a big bonnet; she looked like someone in a Vermeer. Or rather she seemed inaccessible, like people in history. She had tied an apron around her waist, of the same cereal-colored unbleached cloth as her bonnet.

I put my hands in my sleeves to indicate I wouldn't try to touch her. Even so, she looked frightened when she saw me. "We're not supposed to speak to each other for a month."

"A month? Is that what he said? He's very inventive and precise, isn't he? Well, you'll be glad to know I'm being sent far away as a missionary among the indigenous people of Karmata Rua Cristiania."

Mercy's hand wrestled my hand out of my sleeve and kissed it. I could see the tears gathering in her dark eyes, so precious to me. "It's all my fault," she said. "I should have never confessed that. Reservatio in petto—isn't that our right?"

"No, it's best to make a clean breast of it, speaking of petto."

"How long will you be gone?"

"A month? Two? We didn't discuss it."

"When do you leave?" The noon sun was filtering a soft light through her bonnet and tracing the seam above her upper lip with gloss. Drops of sweat were rolling down her cheeks—sweat, not tears.

"He hasn't told me."

"Is he in love with you? Is he jealous of us?"

"Yes," I said. "Yes."

Then I entered the silent period of my love. I no longer spoke to Mercy nor did she speak to me; we were forbidden to communicate. But it calmed me to know that she was faithful to her vows of chastity and that she was unlikely to develop a crush on another woman, religious or secular. I suppose it sounds crazy to you, worldly and "realistic" as you've become, to be like me in love with a woman who doesn't fancy women but who "likes" me. Crazy to be content as long as she doesn't love anyone else and we're able to exchange innocent smiles at least once a day. Of course, I'd rather hold her in my arms and feel her warm cinnamon skin and her wet body writhing and bucking under my intrusive hand, but we have taken vows to forsake the elusive pleasures of this world for the timeless joys of the next. If they exist.

We have tiny, harmless lizards in the courtyard and Mercy likes to catch them, hold them for a moment in her hand, and speak to them. They are warm and wriggling like her. Poor girl, she must be lonely. How ever did such a life-loving girl become a nun? Maybe she was hungry and it was the only alternative to laboring and starving. Sometimes she will sing a little song to her lizard—in Tagalog, I like to think.

The next time I went to confession, a week later, Bishop Oscar asked me right away if I was still guilty of the sin of concupiscence in thought or in deed.

"Perhaps in thought," I said coolly. I felt sorry for him; he was obviously suffering more than I was.

"Give me some details."

I told him that whenever I saw her my heart thudded; I was afraid it would knock through my rib cage and splatter on the floor. But I assured him we didn't exchange a word.

"I know how difficult that silence must be for you," Oscar said.

"Not really. As long as I know she's somewhere near. This may not be a permissible question: Why did Mercy become a nun?"

"I don't know why and if I did I wouldn't tell you. You don't think she has a true vocation?"

I was startled that he would interrogate me about such a crucial aspect of her character. I stuttered and said, "I never asked her. But she seems very p–p–pious and obedient."

"What a hateful word: 'obedient.' I can see you're smouldering with resentment."

I paused and then said, "Yes, I am."

"Do you believe that the state of your soul is my only concern?"

"No."

He sank into silence, sighed painfully, and finally said in a near whisper, "You should say ten Hail Marys and ten Our Fathers and pray for guidance and light."

I slipped out of the confessional and went to the altar rail to pray. A moment later I glimpsed Oscar leaving his booth, his hands joined behind his back and his head bent very low. He seemed to be muttering to himself.

I was about to send this letter to you, when I got a telegram from Bobbie Jean. I'm sure she sent you one, too. Daddy died. Heart attack. Apparently they were going to watch TV together and Daddy was about to sit down when he said, "Why, Bobbie Jean, I can't feel anything in my feet, now my legs. They're moving up, it feels like butterflies . . ." And Bobbie Jean said, "P.M., why don't you sit down," and he did and he died, just like that. Of course, they couldn't hold up the funeral for us. She wants to bury him upstate near the farm where she grew up outside Denton. She must feel rather lost. You know how she led her own life apart from him, with her own women's clubs and charities, but even so she must feel rather lost. Impossible as he could be, he was her husband for years. And he could be a handful. She devoted at least half her energy to him.

How do you feel about his death?

I feel as if there's unfinished business between us. I wanted him to visit me in Colombia and see how beautiful the convent is, how peaceful. Maybe I'm not at peace right now due to my infatuation, but ordinarily I feel secure, knowing where I am to be when, feeling that my life *matters* to those around me and that it is being closely *observed*. Some people might find that kind of scrutiny oppressive or food for vanity but it makes me feel substantial, makes me feel *real*. Back in Dallas I always felt in danger of falling off the edge of the world. Those long afternoons after school and before dinner. Sometimes I was at Christ the King but three or four days out of the week I was alone in the White House. Homework would take me an hour at my desk. Then I would read for an hour, but after a while even that began to feel stale. Maybe because I had no one to talk books with. I've *never* in my life had a real reading pal. I can't even imagine what that would feel like.

Of course, I also felt less afraid. Daddy had me again and again. He was always a potential threat, even in my nun's cell, even in Jericó, as if he could circle the city seven times, blow on his ram's horns, and make the walls fall down. In my frightened little girl's mind he was that powerful; he even had a special covenant with God allowing him to destroy me.

You must feel *sewn* into history in your medieval château, as I do in this very old convent. Poor us in windblown dusty Texas, where the oldest thing is the Alamo (about 1800, as I recall from our Texas history class). We had no roots—everything was a simulacrum (White House, Ver-Sales, Alhambra). The "old" families were cattle people, homesteaders, and eventually oil men, but Texas had only a few thousand citizens when the Texas Republic was annexed in 1845 by the United States. It was a rough, tough state at war with the elements and the Comanche.

Daddy was from such a poor family in the Hill Country outside Austin. He never did believe fully in his oil millions and though he diversified his portfolio by buying Dallas real estate and lived as frugally as Bobbie Jean would let him, nevertheless he treated all of us regally. He sent both of us to college, and before that to Hockaday. He bought you a pony and had it trained and stabled. He rented us an apartment in Austin. He paid for an elaborate debut for you and then a big Paris wedding. He gave the convent a handsome dowry for me. He bought Namaw an assisted-living apartment in downtown Dallas. He gave Pinky a comfortable retirement fund. Of course, he could be impossible, but I don't think Namaw ever wasted the least bit of love on him—till he became rich. Our mother loved him in her haggard, dutiful, unquestioning way; Bobbie Jean never loved him, I'm convinced, but her father was that awful, boring, self-centered racist math professor, poor sinner, who thought he was so funny with his racist jokes. People can summon up only the love that was bequeathed them.

We moved as far away from Daddy as we could get—to Colombia in my case, to Paris in yours. Neither of us lives in our native language. I'm called Sister and you're called Baroness. We never returned to Texas. Of course, he abused me and got me pregnant when I was still virtually a child, but he was so starved for love, such a social misfit, so incompletely socialized, that he had no idea what was off-limits. Most people are subject to checks and balances throughout their lives, which inhibit or extinguish their criminal urges, but Daddy grew up in that village under the roof of a tyrannical father for whom he had no respect and who abused him and had no sense in the first place. They were all hungry, uneducated, dressed in rags, and Daddy had to fight off the schoolboys who taunted him every day for being poor and scrawny. Remember the story of the kid who snitched on the other boys and they paid him back by sawing his right leg off? That's the world he grew up in. Only a generation back his grandparents had fought almost constantly with the Comanche and Daddy's great-aunt Bea was raped and scalped by Indians. It was a lawless world. Later, after he became rich, he had no friends who were his equals. He associated only with his employees; for them the boss was always right. How could he ever learn from the help what was considered unacceptable? Of course, Pinky and the others were good, moral people, but they weren't going to criticize Mr. Crawford and lose their jobs. At first he was isolated by his poverty and then by his wealth. He never had peers who could ride herd on him. To the degree he understood morality he tried to do right by folks. But he was both the pauper and the prince and isolated at both periods of his life. Bobbie Jean was hopeless; she just wanted to rise in that squalid little world of Dallas "society." Our real mother, Margie Ann, was a deeply moral person but afraid of her own husband. He expected her to wait on him at the dinner table. When Daddy read her diary and had to recognize how he had tortured our poor mother, whose death was partly brought on by her physical exhaustion, for the first (and maybe only) time he had to repent of his past cruelty. I'm convinced that was why he was so eager to grant

Bobbie Jean's smallest desire; he didn't want to worry another woman into an early grave. He wanted to be good.

But he wasn't good. He was a monster. He had been brutalized by his impoverished childhood, and, given his exceptionally strong pride, he was deeply wounded by his family's low (nonexistent) status in their village. He was a physical coward, too skinny and out of shape to fight. In Texas, physical violence is just under the surface and the simplest disagreement can end in a hospital. Men don't have to be handsome or intelligent. They must be rich and angry. Daddy was inclined to be a sissy; he never felt comfortable except among his dependents; he knew every day of his adult life that as a boy he'd been sodomized by his daddy. But to the world he put on a belligerent, frozen-faced, slow-talking demeanor. His favorite actor was John Wayne.

I pray for his salvation. As you know, I don't believe in Hell, but I do think there's a cold, empty place where the unsaved go, a sub-zero desert, a floating, eventless emptiness, the very aridity that nonbelievers picture as the afterlife, not the lively homecoming parade that we Christians believe in with its clangorous, brightly lit floats.

He loved us both, but me he loved in an unhealthy, tormented way. Why? Maybe because I was the weird one, the nerdish one, and he felt I was more vulnerable. Maybe because I reminded him of himself. Or his mother. I really hated him; I think most abused children hate the men who abused them. And yet, now that he's dead, I feel I want to sit down with him, on eternity's curb, and hash it all out. Of course, there's no getting to the bottom of what he did to me.

I never told you this, but once when we were living in Austin Daddy was hospitalized with pneumonia and Bobbie Jean called me and said that if I wanted to see my father alive I must come immediately.

I didn't think about it twice. I don't know where you were—maybe in Houston. Yes, you were in Houston with a sorority sister. I rushed to the hospital. He was allowed only one visitor at a time. When Bobbie Jean came out, I went in. There he was, hooked up to tubes and monitors. I thought he was asleep. I said, "Daddy, it's me. Yvette." And he woke up, grinned with his awful little brown teeth. He threw back his sheet and he was completely nude. He said, "Powder me."

I ran out of the room; Bobbie Jean could see I was sobbing. Maybe she thought I was afraid he would die. She said, "Why, whatever is wrong with you, Yvette?" But I just kept sobbing; I was afraid I might throw up. I kept running. Once I got in my car I sat there for five minutes, stunned.

I don't know why I dredge all this up now, maybe just to keep myself honest and not to wallow in posthumous idealization. I have to admit he was and will be the only man to touch me in this life; Duke tried, Mercy as a woman succeeded, but Daddy was the only man to enter me and make me pregnant. Lot's daughters may have made their father drunk and raped him to get pregnant and to continue their family line; Noah's son may have seen his drunken father naked and done something to him (whatever it was) that shamed Noah when he took note of it the next day. Fathers and children . . . The Old Testament is rife with incest and family violence. Abraham's willingness to sacrifice Isaac puzzles all of us today, but they say the moment God substituted a ram for Isaac symbolizes the end of human sacrifice in the Middle East. But think of the horror of the father taking his little boy's hand and carrying the firewood and his knife and leading him up the mountain to his certain death. Isaac, puzzled, asks his father where the ram to be burned and sacrificed to God is. The father says, guiltily, "God will provide." But the boy is stripped and bound and only when Abraham raises his knife does he spot a ram, his horns caught in the thorns. And the animal is sacrificed instead of the child.

Of course, God himself was willing to go all the way and to sacrifice his only begotten son, to let him be crowned with thorns and crucified. We say the lamb of God but he was really the ram. Why would God demand a man sacrifice his son to Him? Why did God let me be sacrificed to my father?

The Book of Common Prayer may be Protestant but it says it best.

"Father, I am sore affeared
To see you bear that drawn sword."

The father says;
"Make thee ready, my dear darling,
For we must do a little thing.

Come hither, thou art so sweet.
Thou must be bound both hands and feet."

When a father sacrifices his child, plunges his sword into him or her,
we should say, "For we must do a little thing." Death should be called the
Little Thing. My bishop wants me to go as a missionary among the indigenous people, where I might contract dengue fever. It's not usually fatal,
but I am so frail (some days my only nourishment is the host) that I
fear—and he must fear—that I'll die from it. If the bishop demands my
sacrifice I am eager to make it for him and God: the Little Thing.

Bobbie Jean suddenly arrived here in Jericó! Of course, true to character, her first half hour of conversation was all about the difficulties of
getting here. ("But my travel agent, that nice Dorothy Spiers, was willing
to turn herself inside out for me, she'd like to join the life-drawing
Rembrandt Club, I'm the president, don't you know, but we're not sure
she's qualified, anyway, she gets an A for agreeable, but I must say I was
surprised that the folks down here don't speak much English. What's
wrong with them? Are they just backward? Maladjusted? Retards?")

The second half hour was all about the details of Daddy's funeral—the
black ebony coffin with the rose velvet lining, the telephone he wanted
installed in case he was buried alive; he wanted it hooked up to the police
station. Bobbie Jean pointed out that all his blood would be drained and
he'd be filled with embalming fluid. She also pointed out that he'd just
be a vegetable after all that time in the ground. "And I said that that
sheriff was always drunk and wouldn't hear the phone ringing and if he
did he wouldn't answer it. Daddy looked real nice in his best navy blue
suit with that awful hand-painted Countess Mara tie he liked so much.
They put too much rouge on his face. His part was on the wrong side.
But he looked peaceful and I can't wait to join him. There was only some
old uncle who came and Pinky drove up but stayed in the back away from
the white folks. She always knows her place, you gotta hand it to her. I'm
gonna have a nice marble stone carved for him but I might wait cuz if I
die it's cheaper to put two names on the same memorial at the same time."

Then she wept and I tried to take her in my arms but she shook me
off with a little ironic laugh.

Then she got down to business. I knew, didn't I, that she had to have dialysis every two weeks, her high blood pressure had destroyed her kidneys, and she had to move out of that gloomy, understaffed White House into an assisted-living suite next to Neiman's where several of her Rembrandt pals and other ladies from the four-hand piano club were already living, for all that she would need plenty of moolah to pay for her new apartment and her charities and clubs and Daddy left her only nine million dollars ("With that I'd be pauperized," she said seriously). I told her that she could have forty-eight of my fifty million; I needed the rest for my convent since I'd promised it. She grabbed my hands in ecstatic thanks, but then she began to wonder if I wasn't spoiling these simple South American Spanish-speaking nuns, who didn't seem to have such extravagant needs, and they could easily be corrupted with that sort of reckless, thoughtless Yankee wealth thrown in their faces like an insult.

I told her that I would consider her objections and asked her how I could contact the lawyers in order to renounce my inheritance in her favor.

Now that I had laid to rest her fears of dying a pauper I could see she couldn't wait to return to Dallas. In fact, she'd kept her car and driver waiting outside the convent walls.

"Poor man," I said. "Did he get anything to eat?"

"I told him I'd be gone only an hour." What efficiency! I thought.

"Are these people what you'd call wetbacks?" she asked with real anthropological curiosity.

"I wouldn't."

"How do they think they'll ever get ahead if they don't speak English?"

"And you? Are you hungry?"

"Dorothy Spiers told me not to eat a bit down here if I didn't want to have the most awful diarrhea and not to drink anything except a bottled Coke. Guess you've built up a resistance. She said when I got back to the Hilton Bogatá I could order room service. It's safe there, but she told me to brush my teeth only with bottled water. Imagine that!"

I walked her to her car and she gave me a peck and said, "So long, Sister." By her tone she sounded like a gangster in a '30s film saying, "Kiss off, sister."

I watched her drive away with her overweight mustachioed driver behind the wheel. I went to kneel before the statue of the Virgin. Now I was less devoted to God and more intimate with his mother. She was the great invention of the Catholic Church, our Kali when angry, our Kwan-yin when peaceful, the soft-spoken (or silent) guardian of Baby Jesus, and the desperate, mourning mother of the Crucified Christ. She pitied us all; like a truly gentle mother she knew how to console us. I needed her love. The final curtain had fallen on the great drama of my life.

Last week Bishop Oscar was assassinated! He was coming out of the cathedral after his Sunday morning Mass, surrounded by the faithful and altar boys, when suddenly someone in a passing car opened fire on him. The murderer must have been a good shot, because only one youngster was wounded in the shoulder otherwise, but Oscar was killed instantly. When his body was brought into the convent he was gray, he'd lost his miter, and his robes were soaked in blood. He was dead; he'd predicted his own death.

Just before he was shot he'd delivered a homily about the sufferings of the poor in the village and in the surrounding countryside. His Sunday talks were broadcast and were blamed for the unrest among the tenant farmers and campesinos. His text that day was from Vatican II: "God's reign is already present on our earth in mystery. When the Lord comes, it will be brought to perfection." In Oscar's interpretation: "That is the hope that inspires Christians. We know that every effort to better society, especially when injustice and sin are so ingrained, is an effort that God blesses, that God wants, that God demands of us."

Poor Oscar, though he knew his life was in danger and that the landlords or the government had shot a fellow priest a week before, was willing to be a martyr in his fight for better land distribution and a sharing of wealth. Since Adam sinned, he left Eden as a landless man. But Christ redeemed us from Adam's sin—and with that redemption restored land to the least man or woman. Jesus said that whatever is done to the poor is done also to Him—for that reason the poor are both human and divine. Oscar said God is the one who wants land reform.

We all feel vulnerable now. Thugs could attack the convent at any moment and mow us down. The walls of the convent, which seemed so monumental, now feel paper thin. Of course, we nuns are silent, passive, and the convent is just a warehouse for off-loading unwanted daughters. No reason to slaughter us.

I'm determined to fulfill my promise to Bishop Oscar to go as a missionary among the Embera-Chami. Just because he was assassinated is no reason to disobey him. I doubt he told anyone about my mission and I could do as I please with impunity, especially now that I'm giving two million dollars to the convent (Oscar told me to limit my gift to two million). I could probably be made Mother Superior for such a sum. But I prefer my nearly anonymous life.

We feel so adrift without Bishop Oscar to guide us. He was the good shepherd. That he loved me with a love not entirely befitting a priest made me feel special. I'm only sorry that my passion for Mercy troubled the last weeks of his life. Or maybe not so much. His energy was almost entirely devoted to the people and their struggle to survive.

Anyway, I've cooled off on Mercy since Daddy's death, as if I no longer have to impersonate him, the unwelcome maniac bullying a pure, unwilling victim; now that he's gone I no longer feel the urge to enact his indecencies.

I may not be able to write you for a while, since I'll be traveling through rough country.

CHAPTER 18

A dhéaume prided himself on having reformed French taste and having transmitted it to America. He felt that Americans had been overly impressed by Spain or by Venice previously and that he'd been the necessary champion of French architecture and decoration—and of French culture in general. I asked him what had given rise to this fantasy of his. I told him that Americans paid lip service to their national origins ("Then I discovered I was half Danish and half Montenegrin") and thought of Europe as a mildly diverting but too-distant and too-expensive Disneyland. As for architecture and decoration, there were two styles: "cute" and "expensive." For an expensive look they might like velvet and silk and human-size blue-and-white Chinese vases, but the chairs had to recline and the TV screens had to be huge. The kitchen should be open to the dining room so the cook-wife wouldn't feel isolated from her guests. Unlike the French, Americans liked the smell of cooking food and they felt uncomfortable having servants lurking around. Above all, everything must look new and match and be replaced every two years. Less fortunate people could make do with the cute look: creamers shaped like tiny cows, beanbag chairs, slippers like dachshunds, dishes printed with prewar Coca-Cola advertising, rubber mats twisted and colored to look like daisies. Designers might flip through books of old furniture or decors in search of new motifs, but the customers wanted everything new, unscratched, and comfortable. A Louis XVI La-Z-Boy was preferable to some actual Louis XVI "broken duchess."

Addy had met the shah of Iran and decided to give a *bal masqué* for him preceded by an elegant dinner of *le tout Paris.* The only problem was that the shah was used to dining with the most beautiful, half-nude adolescent girls and he couldn't understand why he was surrounded by old bags and bleary-eyed gents, none of whom seemed capable of belly-dancing for his pleasure or serving him peacock tongues and pistachio sherbet, their eyes lowered respectfully. Instead, they were glowering at him and cackling at their own jokes; in his country he would simply have beheaded them and silenced that awful noise, but here he had to treat these dukes and marquises as equals and pretend to be interested in their squalid lives. The food was in twelve courses instead of the normal sixty-six, in reference to the 6,666 verses of the Koran, and some of the dishes smelled of *pork.* Fortunately, the shah was warned off it by his official taster, who spent the rest of the evening in his room vomiting and reciting spells to undo the dreaded *ithm.*

When Mme de Clermont-Tonnerre asked the shah what he was reading at the moment, he replied, "A monarch has no need to read. His ministers can do that for him. You don't lead the masses with books but with eloquence, prestige, and physical prowess." Her smile vanished.

The Persian Ball went better. No one over forty had been invited. The Princess de Lucinge had a great success in her beaded midriff and harem pants covered with paillettes doing her very athletic sabre dance. I made my entrée with three women dressed as birds in cages carried by blue Negroes. The Princess de Polignac was a white owl. Six bare-chested boys in floppy trousers by Mme Grès pretended to rape us bird-women. It was a big success. Addy came as a sultan and sat beside the shah on a dais fanned by ostrich plumes wielded by young aristocrats. The shah looked absolutely bewildered, especially when Mme de Montargis came in on a bejeweled elephant, which promptly defecated in the ballroom filled with spotlit orchid pyramids ($100,000). About the dinner and ball, Addy said with satisfaction, "This cost me three million and amused me for three minutes." The shah, despite his preference for youth, said, "This smells like armpits. Let's go to the Ritz for champagne."

When I found out Daddy had died I felt there was nothing standing in the way between me and the vault of the night sky. Unlike my sister,

I'd never believed in Heaven and God and his saints and the Holy Virgin. I could feel the absolute bleak emptiness of nonexistence all around me and above me. There was no Daddy to protect me now, to stand in my way, to rebel against, no Daddy to disapprove of or to glory in my accomplishments. No Daddy to ride herd on my expenses. I was all alone in the universe. No relative who was next in line to go to the slaughterhouse and into the grand Nihil. I was the next, or would be. Even my struggles with him now had to be waged with a proxy. He had withdrawn into an impenetrable basalt sarcophagus, his orifices stuffed with oil-softened cotton, his limbs straightened, his skeletal hands folded over the empty balloon of his belly. He was unreachable. His life had vanished.

Daddy's will made me the executor of his estate. I guess he thought Bobbie Jean was too much of an airhead and Yvette too spiritual (or too much under the spell of the Church). But what about my cruel, fortune-destroying husband? The man who threatened to harm my children if I divorced him?

I went to an American lawyer on the Avenue Montaigne whose job, I gathered, was to help his fellow Americans to buy property in France, to sue the French (though the courts here did not reward such huge damages and there were fewer pretexts for clogging the courts), and to arrange their taxes for both countries. With me he wanted to open Daddy's will.

Jim West was an affable, round little man in a Brooks Brothers suit with a rep tie and no hair. He wore a gold wedding ring that was engulfed by his pudgy finger; it would have to be sawed off (the ring, not the finger). He was the sort of Yankee I'd met in white-shoe lawyers' offices in Dallas, reassuring to Texans. He had a big Kiwanis Club banner on his wall under his University of Michigan law degree and an Ohio accent to match ("probably" was two syllables, "coupon" was "koopawn," "route" was "rout," he offered to pour "melk" in my coffee). He'd met a Frenchwoman in Chicago, married her, and moved to Paris. He was a little too chatty for my taste (or for the occasion), but I played along and did my American "act." He reassured me they went once a year to stay with his "ant" in Kal-ma-zoo.

He was affiliated with Daddy's Dallas lawyer. He offered me his condolences and observed five seconds of silence. Daddy wrote of his beloved wife, Bobbie Jean, and his beloved daughters ("Says here your sister is a Catholic nun," Mr. West observed as neutrally as humanly poss-ble).

"Each of you is to receive a third of his estate, minus about five million, which you and your husband charged to your father."

"That was my husband's doing."

"I see. Well, there's still about forty-five million dollars left to you and about fifty million for your sister."

"My sister was talked into giving all but two million dollars to my stepmother, but that will be handled by the Dallas lawyers."

"How odd," Mr. West said.

"She *is* a nun," I pointed out.

"Of course."

Mr. West poured us some more coffee minus the "melk." Then he said, "Another thing that's odd is that though your father trusted you to be the executrix, he's doled out your inheritance in ten-million-dollar payments every ten years over four payments."

"That's to protect me from my husband's profligacy. My husband will undoubtedly try to break the trust and get all the money immediately."

Mr. West shook his head no, as if he were awakening from a bad dream. "He won't be able to do that. Mr. Crawford's will is airtight."

"Can you send me a letter with all the terms?" I handed him my address and stood up. "You will be so kind as to send me a bill?"

"No, all expenses are handled by the estate. I already have your address—that's how I contacted you."

I hurried away.

On the one hand I was relieved by Daddy's will and on the other a bit frightened by what would surely be Addy's rage and violence. I knew he'd been running up enormous bills on the expectation of "his" inheritance. He'd waste another million on court procedures trying to unpick the lock.

I waited until Mr. West's letter arrived and then put it beside Addy's breakfast setting. No comment.

As expected, by noon he was fuming at my father's "treachery" and he'd already engaged an international lawyer, someone he'd met at the

Jockey. "Oh no, *no*, he's gone too far this time, tricking me out of my money."

"I was under the impression he was my father and he'd left the money to me."

"No sophistry, please. It was always a clear arrangement: my title and taste for your fortune."

"I don't remember signing any such agreement."

"But it was always understood. That's the subtlety of the 'unsaid,' the *non-dit* in French."

"Trust me, I've already mastered that expression."

Adhéaume and his utterly predictable greed and vanity made me so weary. Why hadn't I spotted the rotten fruit right away? Because of the fancy packaging? So many bows and so much glitter wrapping?

Every time I went past Addy's door I could hear him on the phone talking urgently to New York, where it was six hours earlier—urgently, no laughter, none of his famous charm. This was serious business. He was probably taking notes and paying for each minute of counsel.

We went back to the castle in the Var. Addy's parents were staying there. They felt so much more at ease, more "natural," inside their ancestral walls than in their shabby one-room in the Sixteenth with its grand entrance and twenty-five square meters. Here they could spread out in the regal boredom of their domain. Days would go by without their ever setting foot outside. They blamed the weather, but in truth it was their age. They felt at once cozy and magnificent beside the electric fire in their vast painted chambers. They seemed to relish the tedium of their empty days, as if on the threshold of eventless death. They'd discuss something or read something and forget it the next day. Every day enjoyed the same featurelessness, which seemed somehow "aristocratic" to them, as though excitement were bourgeois and only people of ancient lineage could afford to be bored. Boredom, they thought, was becoming to people of their age and dignity and fragility.

Mercy sent me a telegram telling me that my sister had died. She had gone on her mission to the indigenous people, caught sick, and been brought back to Jericó by mule, where she died a day later. The convent had a telephone number that Mercy confided to me but warned me should be used only in emergencies. I judged my sister's martyrdom to be an emergency. Mercy spoke English with difficulty and in such a tiny, little girl's voice that I could scarcely understand her, but I grasped that Yvette had died in agony but in the embrace of her beloved Mercy, for which I was grateful.

"Do you think Oscar knew the mission would kill her and that he wanted her to die because she loved you more than him?" I asked.

My question was followed by such a long silence that I thought she'd hung up. At last I said, "She was such a good woman."

Mercy said, "She *una santa*."

"Yes, a saint. You and I—"

"Yes?"

"Let's make her a saint."

"Yes yes yes!"

"We make her a saint," I said in my kind of Esperanto.

"Yes! How?"

"Ask the new bishop to nominate her."

"What?"

"*Nominar.*"

"Yes!"

"*Todo resto hago yo.* I do all the rest."

"*¿Yo? ¿Nominar?*"

"*Si si. Gracias.*"

"*El Obispo. Nominar.* Bishop nominate. *Adios.*"

Lord knows what poor Mercy made of all that. Her Spanish, I imagined, was almost as impressionistic as mine. Tagalog—wasn't that her language?

Neither of these deaths (my father, my sister) affected me as much as they would have once, since neither person was part of my everyday life or woven into my habits. Of course, my sister had been remote from me for a long time. Whenever I thought of something funny that would tickle her I'd had to recognize that by the time I wrote her a letter and she responded the joke would long since have fizzled out.

I loved her as much as myself (which wasn't all that much). I must have nursed the fantasy that someday we'd live together, that she'd give up the Church and I Paris, that we'd live somewhere warm, maybe Hawaii, and we'd spend our old age together, dressed in playclothes to expose the varicose veins on our legs, where we let the hairs grow in. Each of us tolerant of her twin's proclivities toward girls, if we were interested in sex at all in our later years. We'd each have to become more feminine since I knew baby butches preferred older femmes. We'd live in Hawaii, get tired of the sun and surf, ration each other's cocktails, flirt with the native housekeeper, learn to like pop music sung by overweight, round-faced, bare-chested Hawaiians, the sumo wrestlers of song.

I was grateful I'd been able to see her one last time and that she'd met my children, though Daddy had ruined everything with his senile sex obsessions. I suppose we were all oversexed. Now, at least, two of the three were quiescent.

Their deaths had made all human effort seem pointless. At least Addy was concerned with the patrimony, though that concern didn't go along with his vengeful attitude toward the children. As long as he could tap into my millions (money for title), the children were safe, but they would be the first victims of divorce, it seemed (Papa Addy's surprise vendetta).

Yvette had been my ransom paid to virtue. She was living an alternative life, but somehow it was genetically identical. I was never completely alone while she was alive. I was bad, but not that bad as long as she was my double, my frail ambassador. I would often talk things over with her in my imagination. She could be sternly disapproving of me but she always understood me. To understand may not be a guarantee of forgiving, but at least it's a down payment toward it.

Now I felt fragile. Every sniffle, every stomachache, our migraines (now they were just *my* migraines), every scratch seemed foreboding if not fatal.

I thought constantly about how my sister and I had been identical, how for the first twenty-four hours we'd been just one zygote, the fertilized egg, though that extreme, almost suffocating coziness had soon come to an end, how mitosis had split us one from the other, though we remained indistinguishable down to the last atom until fate sent us off in different directions—or rather made us the two very different sides of the same coin, she intellectual, martyrized by kindness, consumed by piety, me frivolous, robust, pagan. But what remained was the intuition that for a long day we'd been a single cell.

I had a friend, a priest, society's priest (*le prêtre mondain*), called the Abbé Pierre Thomas. He was a charming, elderly man who had a big apartment near the Gobelins, which was convenient since it was near one of the few brasseries open on Sunday and I could meet him there after Mass. He had just one plume of hair on his head, shooting straight up, and only two soutanes, both of them shiny and worn. What made him distinct was that he loved literature, including modern poetry and fiction, though his two favorites of the past were Stendhal and Chateaubriand. He became friendly with Chateaubriand's descendants and spent many months in their château, Cobourg, in Brittany. There he could imagine the author as a boy huddled with his mother and sister at the dark end of a vaulted hall while his melancholy father paced the length of the room with the only candle—or that moment as an adolescent when he attempted suicide (and failed because the gunpowder was wet).

Of course, Chateaubriand was ideal because he'd written a brilliant defense of Catholicism, *The Genius of Christianity*, and he hated Napoleon. The Abbé Pierre could quote from memory whole pages of Chateaubriand's rolling periods, an account of when he was living in London as the pampered French ambassador, close to the room where he'd barely survived as an impoverished French teacher in exile after the Revolution and was so hungry, or when, earlier, as a very young courtier, he went on his first stag hunt with Louis XVI and in the confusion killed the animal, although the king was supposed to dispatch the stag. Pierre could also quote reams of Valéry's "The Young Fate" and Baudelaire's lesbian poems and Mallarmé's beautiful nonsense. Every writer wanted to know him, especially the experimental ones. He was friendly with Alain Robbe-Grillet and his sadistic wife, Catherine, who had tortured many chic Parisians in their *château-fort*; she wrote down in a big book which things she'd done to whom, next to the pasted-in label of the wine she'd served them over dinner (no repeat punishments or vintages). Alain,

EDMUND WHITE

the author of *Le Voyeur*, looked on. Pierre knew the poets, too: Yves Bonnefoy, André du Bouchet. He had rare first editions of most of "his" writers. If they weren't given to him, he'd demand them, saying, "I'm just a poor parish priest." Originally he'd intended to donate his first editions to a school on the Côte d'Ivoire, but now it seemed more practical to sell them to a collector and give the proceeds to the school.

He was much in demand among the *gratin*; countesses competed over him as a dinner guest. Every reactionary aristocratic family was proud to have a priest in attendance, but most priests were such dunces and prudes and bores. Pierre was the most amusing of the lot—humble, kind, but witty and so cultivated!

He had so many funny rejoinders, most of them irreverent. When one writer, a talentless and pompous member of the Academy, began to bore everyone with his piety, Pierre said, "Perhaps he wants a soutane. I have two!" Once he was seated next to a famous whore, who had gotten lucky and become a Romanian princess, and he said to her, "Your last lover will be Jesus Christ," and she was instantly converted. But he could be acerbic. When someone pointed out a jeweled crucifix on a woman's bony chest and asked him, "Have you seen the Cross?" he replied, "No, but I've seen the Calvary." People choose (or God chooses) the oddest moments to be converted; the poet Max Jacob was watching a gangster movie when suddenly he had a vision of Christ's head on the screen! The cardinal of Paris disapproved of Pierre's frequentation of the best salons (or was envious) and assigned him to an extremely poor parish in Montreuil with the highest crime rate in France. The Communist Party had a stranglehold on the community. Montreuil's main attraction was a miserable flea market selling unmatched shoes, damaged tires, and charred tinware. The church itself was ugly and recent, unattended and full of plastic hearts of Jesus that lit up from within, half-full of a liquid that looked like cherry soda.

Pierre never complained about his congregation, though they were rude and smelled bad. His own origins were rural and poor in the Meuse and he never felt superior to anyone. He had risen so high socially only because he was witty and literary. It helped that he was tiny and very pious—he felt to others like a piety doll! He was never censorious,

252

although he disapproved strongly of war and was a pacifist, which made the Communists say they doubted his patriotism. He brought two count-esses over to the Church; he was never stern in confession. He considered adultery a form of love. Homosexuality was "a throwback to the Golden Age." His only fault was that he drank too much, mostly brandy and mostly when alone late at night. Someone in moral agony had once called on him at his apartment at the Gobelins after midnight and found him incoherent and reeking, walking on all fours.

He was a valuable ally and of course an ornament to my soirées. He brought the great composers Dutilleux and Messaien to my salon, so much more talented and bearable (and personally charming) than the serial killers. Both men seemed devoted to birds and their cries. And Messaien to Our Lord and angels and saints (years later I attended the premiere of his opera *Saint François d'Assise* with him; he wept throughout). At our salon Dutilleux tried out a cello sonata and sketches for a cello concerto. If I understood right he introduced a major theme first in fragments and hints, just as Proust might mention a character by reputation long before he or she comes "onstage." Of course, as a priest Pierre had a special access to Messaien. My greatest joy was dropping in on Duteilleux at his small Île Saint-Louis apartment. He was always shaved and combed and neatly dressed. A beautiful Corot landscape hung over the fireplace. His wife, the pianist Genevieve Joy, would make me a cup of tea in a cup that didn't seem altogether clean. I never stayed long.

Thanks to these two star composers, our musical salon became famous and Pierre and I became best friends. I knew he was keeping a detailed journal that would be published after his death—it was my passport to immortality, since it was sure to be an indispensable guide to Parisian aristocratic and artistic life during those years. Maybe he'd even say the awful truths he knew about me; that possibility urged me to say them first, from my point of view.

Adhéaume liked him since he thought priests were a good thing, especially one who was *mondain*. I invited Pierre to the castle in the Var along with the prince de Joinville, Addy's cousin (Addy's father's sister was the prince's mother). "Eddie," the prince, didn't much like Addy. The dislike was mutual, but at some point they'd agreed to be civil with

each other. I think Eddie and Addy discerned in each other a superfici-
ality joined to a pretentiousness; since they were French they were
obliged to be cultured, but neither was. When they were teens they'd
gone clothes shopping with each other more than once; they were about
the same age and size.

One night Addy was specially rude to me because I'd never invited
Spanky to the castle, which showed how ungrateful and egotistical I was.
There she was, impoverished, obliged to take in boarders; she was
responsible for our married bliss. I looked to see if he was being ironic.
Oddly, he wasn't.

He wasn't interested in the reality of a situation but only in how it
appeared to others.

I phoned Spanky and invited her to join us in the country. She said at
the moment she had two "guests," but they'd be gone by the end of the
week. Could she come then? Of course. Would she like us to send our
car and driver? Or a train ticket? Car, please.

The Abbé Pierre had titled friends in the Var who came to kidnap
him for a day or two. After one jaunt with some rich Italians he came
back raving about their library. An eighteenth-century forebear had
been a voracious bibliophile and had agents working for him in every
country in Europe. The collector's idea was to buy an illuminated
manuscript of a title and the first printed copy of the same title. Pierre
had had to wear white gloves when he handled the books. Their paintings were dull copies of Renaissance canvases, mostly of Judith cutting
off Holofernes's big, shaggy head with the beard and thick neck (Judith
usually had an openmouthed maid helping with the sawing), but the
books were splendid, the better part of the inheritance (the older
brother had inherited the Luca Signorellis of dive-bombing, rubber-
winged angels).

When Spanky arrived in the castle, we all sat down to dinner
together—Victorine, Eudes, Prince Eddie, Pierre, Spanky, Addy, and me.
The children were brought in by the German nanny to greet Mme de
Castiglione. When the nanny spirited them away, Spanky said, "Adorable.
Like little angels."

"Not for long," Addy said. "Soon they'll be dirty ruffians if Von goes through with her plan to divorce me."

"Let's not go there!" I whispered, but he shouted, "I'll go anywhere I damn want to! How dare you try to censure my conversation at my own table. You've become so *prim*"—he said the word in English—"for someone who started out as a cowgirl."

Eddie grabbed my hand under the table and I was grateful for his kindness.

Spanky and Victorine looked confused and turned to praising the wine, which ordinarily they would never have done. Eudes just appeared bewildered with the perpetually exploratory expression of the hard of hearing. Spanky, not as clueless as the other Courcys and a bit more at home in the real world, gave me her condolences about my sister's death. I was so unprepared for this show of sympathy that I burst into tears. Mme de Castiglione came to my side, put her arm around me, and said, "She sounded like such a beautiful soul—a saint, really."

"Oh, she was so good, kind, self-sacrificing, pious. Father Pierre and I are going to campaign to have her made a saint, a real saint. If I throw myself—my time and prayers and money—into working toward her sainthood, then I might miss her less or at least feel I'm channeling my grief into something productive."

I think Spanky, so quietly religious herself, volunteering day after day at the hospital despite her age, was impressed, or at least soothed, by my Vatican aspirations. She kept patting my shoulder as she'd never done before and even presented me with an embroidered, lilac-scented hand-kerchief she'd hidden in her sleeve. I remembered that she'd opposed the Nazis and that she lived uncomplainingly in respectable poverty, that she coexisted with the most terrifying snobbery and the most Christian charity, that she loved the poor and despised the bougeoisie, respected the rich but worshipped the titled. She was a complex woman, but her kindness to me made me grateful to her.

After dinner I sat in the window embrasure of the great hall with Father Pierre. I explained to him Adhéaume's threat to gain custody over our children and to send them to a gulag of a boarding school, where they'd become little dirty cigarette-smoking hoodlums (or "hoods" as we called them back in Texas, those knife-wielding, motorcycle slim boys and fat girls who smelled of leather, sweat, and tobacco).

The good Abbé held my hand. *He* smelled of Adhéaume's expensive century-old brandy. Normally at night he smelled of chartreuse, perhaps out of loyalty to the monastery (or Stendhal).

"What shall I do?" I asked.

"Murder him," Father Pierre said.

My eyes must have widened. Perhaps I gasped. Pierre patted my hand with his little boneless hand and smiled. "I can't see any other way out."

I swallowed. "You're right." I closed my eyes. "But how?"

He pulled a packet out of his shirt pocket under his soutane. "Put this in his wine, then walk him to the pre-ruined temple, the Hercules Victor, beside the precipice—and push!"

"What if he struggles?"

"He won't. This powder is from a *farmacia* I know very well. He won't be able to resist. His legs will be rubber. It's guaranteed."

"And then what?"

"You'll grieve. You'll mourn. You'll be a very powerful—and respected!—widow."

"But . . . ?"

"The baron's parents won't want their grandchildren to have a murderer for a mother. They'll back you up. There will be no autopsies. In any event the drug is undetectable."

I smiled slowly at my savior.

After a moment, he smiled back. "We never had this conversation."

"What conversation?" I asked.

Father Pierre said he would like to see the temple of Hercules. I accompanied him there, he breathing heavily with his brandy fumes and taking two steps for every one of mine. I slowed down and gave him my arm. I felt very blond and manly.

Once we looked at the temple replica with its circular footprint and Corinthian capitals, three columns artfully fallen whereas the original was intact (the real temple was just beside the *bocca della verità*—the mask in whose mouth a liar risked having her hand bitten off), we walked over to the precipice and looked down at the olive trees gone wild. "Just a little push," Pierre said.

That night I went in to kiss my sleeping babies. When Ghislaine began to fuss, I said, rather harshly, "For God's sake, Ghislaine, don't fret." I suppose I thought I was about to commit a crime for their sake and they should be grateful. I don't know why I was so strict with her.

Then I went to bed, read for a few moments, and snapped off my light with that sinking feeling of disappointment that always visited me when another day had ended and I was about to surrender consciousness. Was the party over? Never going to happen? Is that all there is?

I listened for footsteps in the hallway. I half-thought that Addy might come to me, apologize for everything, make love to me. I wouldn't have to kill him. In my dreams, however, he was nasty and snide. He was also a white rat with an electrode planted in his cortex, an animal running on a moving walkway.

The next night at dinner I sat next to Addy, which made him raise a sealskin eyebrow. I played "vivacious" and "charming" as only a Texas deb can do. I told him his hair looked wonderful like that. He looked confused and touched his hair and murmured, "I used a new conditioner."

"It's like silk," I said, touching it. "You've never looked better. That plain burgundy tie, white shirt, and dark blue jacket—you have such perfect taste."

Now he was wearing a suspicious little smile. "What's come over you?" He didn't actually say that but he might could.

"Isn't this a delicious wine?" I asked, filling his glass; it was a very old Nuits-Saint-Georges grand cru.

"Please, no more, I already had my normal two glasses."

"Let's drink more than usual. It's such a lovely night. We might go for a walk after dinner."

"Where?"

"I want to show Father Pierre the temple to Hercules you're building."

"Hercules? Don't go imagining it's in homage to your Ercole."

Like my Baptist cousin, the one who playfully slapped Adhéaume's shoulder at La Tour d'Argent when he suggested they order wine, I laughed and frowned and pretended to touch his sleeve reproachfully. "Oh, you, I don't ever think of him."

Father Pierre was exclaiming over the view, of the last rays of sunlight illuminating the sudden rain, and begged everyone to come to the window, where he'd pulled back the heavy curtains. To be obliging, everyone joined him and Spanky the Pious said it was like God's grace, the crystal heart of an affliction.

I'd torn open the packet of digitalis and stirred it into Addy's wineglass and refilled it.

"I saw you!" Addy shouted, returning to the table. "You're determined to get me drunk."

Father Pierre said, "If you're really afraid of being hungover tomorrow, just pop this suppository in, it's called Supponeryl. It will give you a perfect night's sleep and you'll wake up feeling refreshed."

"I'm not used to suppositories," Addy said with a troubled look. All of his relatives were reacting to the mention of this novelty.

"I've used it," I said. "Three times. It's heavenly."

"You just take it out of its foil wrapping and pop it in," the good priest said.

"Is it painful?"

"Of course not, it's glycerine and very small. You won't even feel it."

"I'll take it," Addy said, rising to the challenge, "not for a hangover but for a decent night's sleep. I've had terrible insomnia."

"No more," Father Pierre said. "Now you'll sleep like the dead."

"When do I take it?"

"Now. Just duck into the Henri the Third loo. In an hour you'll be floating on a cloud."

"I'm so grateful," Addy said, and absented himself.

Neither Pierre nor I was skilled at winking, but we tried our best, looking at each other.

"It's true," Addy said, reemerging, "I don't feel a thing." I was gratified to see he finished off his wine, saying, "It's too good not to enjoy."

"And now our walk to the temple," I said. "I've promised Father Pierre you'd show it to him, and explain the details. All the details."

"Well, come along, children," and he crooked both elbows, one for me and one for the literary priest.

It was early spring and a gentle rain was falling, more a mist, and indeed there were trails of mist in the valley below us. Good, I thought, the footing will be slippery. Addy was already getting groggy and he kept leaning into me. I could sense his knees were buckling. He was cheerful and unsuspicious, perhaps because I'd been flattering throughout the dinner—his last, one might hope. My strategic kindness had made me see how easy it would be to win back his affections, if I was willing to let him "dilapidate" my fortune, as the French put it. I realized Adhéaume despised me for making money the red line in our marriage, but I wasn't a materialist (certainly not compared to the Courcys); it was just I feared no one would want me without my millions. I had grown so used to wealth as part of my appeal; I suppose it was a bit like fame. One might deplore the attraction of being famous, but one counted on it. TV celebrities outside their range of fame always looked so bewildered. Poor, I'd feel nude. Common. Or old. Stripped of this annoying but all-powerful advantage.

Addy was prattling on about another folly, the Désert de Retz, put together in the late eighteenth century. "The temple of Pan was my model—Roman, rounded—except all the columns are standing. The whole place (it's next to the destroyed royal residence of Marly) is enchanting. Do you know it, Father?"

"I regret to say I don't."

"There you are wrong," Addy said in his bossy, know-it-all way. "Utterly enchanting—must sit down."

"We're almost there. Let's keep going," I said. "The Désert de Retz?"

"Udderly tscarmin," Addy mumbled, stumbling, though Pierre and I kept him from falling.

"But why did you decide to build your temple with prefallen columns?"

"Mo' pitchersque."

"Let's look at the wild olive trees," Father Pierre said.

"Why?" Addy asked. He was drooling on himself now.

"So picturesque," I said, steering him over to the precipice.

"I'm afraid of catching a chill," Pierre said suddenly. Quite right, too, I thought. I should be the only witness.

"But wait! We're going to look ass wild Olivia."

But Father Pierre had rushed off. Addy was leaning heavily into me.

"Point out your favorite olive tree," I said, guiding him right up to the edge of the precipice.

"Thas tall one."

"Which one? Point it out to me, Addy."

He pointed and I pushed. As he fell he shouted and then he hit something solid. Rocks, I remember. There was no light and I couldn't be sure he was dead. But I waited a moment and listened for a groan. Nothing. I started wailing. "Oh, my God, help! Help! Adhéaume has fallen! Help! Help!"

I ran sobbing all the way back to the château. For an instant Victorine and Eudes, who'd moved into the Zodiac Room and their green slipper chairs, looked at me as if I was being a loud Texas woman yet again, but within minutes they understood, a servant with a flashlight was leading us all to the precipice, Father Pierre had given his arm to Spanky, Prince Eddie had his arm around me, Eudes kept saying, "What's happened? Who's fallen? Please, tell me what's happened."

"It's Addy, Eudes," Victorine said.

"Is it serious?" The French word *grave* sounded more tragic than "serious." "It can't be serious."

"Courage, Eudes, courage!" Victorine said, grabbing his hand as they staggered over the muddy ground. By the time we reached the edge of the precipice, the servant was shining his flashlight down on the bloody mess: Addy's broken body and upturned face. "Run down there," Victorine ordered the servant, "and see if he still has a pulse. Hurry! Hurry!" except the *Vite! Vite!* sounded like the blades of scissors cutting the tender air. I was reminded that Victorine was proud to be descended from crusaders. She put her open hand across Eudes's eyes to spare him the sight of his mangled son; Eudes's antecedents were less brave. "He's dead," the kneeling servant shouted up to us.

"How did this happen?" Victorine asked me in a commanding, deep contralto voice I'd never heard before.

"He went to the very edge to point out his favorite wild olive tree, and he must have slipped."

Prince Eddie looked me in the eyes and smiled in the dark; his wink was very practiced.

CHAPTER 19

After Adhéaume's "tragic" death, the château settled down with remarkable ease. Victorine and Eudes must have decided between themselves not to make a "fuss." They reported the "accidental" death to the police, who sent out an inspector to ask a few questions. Our answers must have satisfied him ("heavy drinking," "rain," "no lighting," "slipped," "dead instantly," "widow only observer") because they decided to forego an autopsy, which Adhéaume, as a pious Catholic, would have opposed in the interests of preserving his body, already badly mangled, for the Resurrection. His distraught parents wanted him prepared for immediate burial with his ancestors. ("That was his principal reason for buying the château," Victorine explained, "to be eventually reunited with his forebears. A bit prematurely, in this case. The Courcys have been buried here for centuries," which the inspector, a local, seemed to know already.) "It's good to see the old families back where they belong," the inspector said under his breath, as if embarrassed.

We already had in residence our family priest, Father Pierre, who agreed to stay on two more weeks, to say a Mass for Addy every day in the castle chapel, to play consoler-in-chief, to pave Addy's way to Heaven, and to make all the funeral arrangements (including hiring the parish choir to sing an In Paradisum). The black vestments, the polished mahogany coffin with gold fittings, the flowers, the candles—everything was chosen by Victorine, who was in her element. Father Pierre, of course, was impeccable. He knew that a layman's feet in the coffin should be facing the altar, whereas a priest's head should be in that position. Of course, he knew when this or that should be recited or sung, when the holy water should be sprinkled, and when everyone should be incensed.

Four little bells were rung during the consecration. Everything in those days was recited in Latin, of course, which left me alone with my thoughts and a mild feeling of guilt (or maybe just a fear of being found out and apprehended). When Communion was celebrated I led the parade in my widow's weeds. No one seemed grief-struck; I wished we could still rent professional *pleureuses*. In England, I understood, there was a service, Rent-a-Mourner.

The twins were restless and confused. If the coffin had been open, they might have understood that something had happened to their father, but the disastrous state of his corpse after the fall had made a closed coffin a necessity. Ghislaine kept sliding down from her pew just in front of me, where she was seated with her brother and Frau Dichter, and racing about, inspecting the flowers, touching the carved wood at the foot of the altar. Foulques was tired and sucking his thumb, his eyes crossed with boredom, his short pants bunched unbecomingly around his slumping crotch. In a rage I leaped up and grabbed Ghislaine by the arm: "You will sit quietly beside your brother, young lady. This is not about you, for once, but a very solemn moment celebrating your poor father. Do you understand me?" I hissed in English. All my excitement had turned into anger. Ghislaine looked terrified and ran back to the pew, where Frau Dichter lifted her back up into her seat and then straightened her skirt. In a rare gesture of affection the good lady patted her on the head and Ghislaine turned toward her, eclipsing her face, and hid against her black serge suit jacket, even pulling some of the rough fabric over her features.

A wave of guilt and something like grief broke over me. Why was I so harsh to the little girl? Yvette had asked me that and had instantly picked up on how I was more drawn to my son. Perhaps because most grown-ups had preferred my sunny disposition to my somber sister's bookishness, even aloofness, I was alert to any partiality. There was something brazen in my daughter that alarmed me, an *explicitness*, that compared unfavorably in my mind with my son's *innerlichkeit*, as Frau Dichter called it, one could even say his *mystery*.

I had seen how brutal and decisive I could be; I was afraid that nothing could stop me now. Once the tiger had tasted human blood, she was on her way to becoming a serial killer.

Father Pierre said the absolution at the bier and then the coffin was carried by Prince Eddie, a neighbor, and four footmen out to the cemetery. I was glad my face was hidden by my black veil, as heavy as a beekeeper's mask, to keep out the sting of indiscreet glances and to conceal the buzz of my dry, wandering eyes. Only at the graveside did Father Pierre say a few words in French about the deceased. "His family and intimates will always remember his exquisite taste, his love of tradition, and his way of making traditions live again. He was filial *and* devoted to his wife and now orphaned children, for whom we must pray, since they are fatherless. Let us hope that as the archangels open the portals of Heaven to Adhéaume de Courcy, he will take delight in being rejoined to his noble ancestors, those armored and visored heroes of the Crusades. And may he be permitted to *arrange* things attractively in Heaven, as he did so often in a life that was admirable if too brief. He was unwavering in his faith and has reminded us what a Christian gentleman resembles." I couldn't help smiling; luckily no one could see. The idea that these people were the guardians of our morality was as hypocritical as it was ridiculous.

More holy water and then the precarious descent of the coffin into the family mausoleum.

Victorine, who was determined to be heroic to the end, broke down and sobbed now that the end had arrived. Eudes, looking dazed, tried to hold her but his wife proudly shook off this sign of comfort.

Next there were drinks and snacks in the guardsmen's room. I absented myself a moment to change into my flats out of my heels, which had become cold and painful and covered with wet gravel. I exchanged glances with Ghislaine, who looked at me with real hate, the sort of look that said, Some day I'll make you pay!

After I had exchanged mournful sounds with a few old ladies, I stood with Prince Eddie, who was introduced to everyone as the baron's cousin, which awakened new frowns of condolence. He was looking very handsome in a double-breasted dark suit with padded shoulders, a dazzling white shirt, a blue tie of muted wide stripes, his *chevalière* (gold signet ring), and some sort of enameled black order in his lapel (I'd heard the Swedes had given him the Order of the Polar Star for skiing or something). Imagine traveling with your order *just in case*.

I had constant nightmares, a perpetual sentiment of guilt that sinks talons into the shoulders, a jumpiness that responds nearly hysterically to the slightest unsuspected, stealthy touch. I slept badly and dreamed frequently of Addy, who came toward me with open, imploring hands and a skull split wide open down to the white brain. I wished I could bring him back to life and restore our previous existence, even with all its anguish, as if I could rewind the film and see him borne seamlessly aloft and placed, grinning foolishly and pointing to his favorite wild olive tree, on the edge of the precipice, before turning back to me and retracing his steps in reverse to the ruined temple. When I ate, within seconds I could feel the food rising and souring my mouth. I feared I'd vomit everything, which wouldn't be very attractive. I heard that admonition about *being attractive* in Addy's tone of voice.

I had no idea what Victorine and Eudes thought had really happened to their son (they frequently exchanged burning, meaning-laden glances), and I slid around corners trying to catch them in an anguished scene or to overhear them bad-mouthing me. Perhaps "officially" they'd decided their grandchildren could not have a murderer for a mother. Children of a homicidal mother would never be unaccompanied by gossip in society. Imagine the burden of hearing people whisper behind your back throughout your life! The Courcys had always been above reproach. Whenever I'd catch Victorine darting looks of hatred at me, she'd rush forward and smother me in embraces, murmuring, "My poor Von."

Prince Eddie lingered on longer than he'd planned. So did Father Pierre. Because of this reluctance to move on, we were all obliged to begin and end every dinner pulling long faces, though we were merry enough during the *entrée* and the *plat principal*. I suppose we were aware of Addy's absence to the degree that we were more relaxed and cheerful and that the children were more high-spirited. They would come thundering in, giggling and wriggling with Frau Dichter in hot pursuit; never would Addy have permitted such gaiety, but he was "away," it seemed, on a long trip (maybe for a fitting in London).

I could see Eddie was more and more determined to court me, but though I liked the idea of being the princess de Joinville, I didn't want to rush into another marriage with a fortune-hunting cad. One night, when we were alone in a corridor in the château, the cold coming off the rough-hewn walls, Eddie cupped my ass with his hand and said, "I've been longing to do that."

I said, "Now that it's been done, one hopes it won't be repeated."

"You didn't like it?"

"A widow must be concerned with the proprieties."

"Rubbish."

I looked back instantly to see how seriously dismissive he was. Reassured that he wasn't mocking my grief, I stood my ground and said, "The funeral meats will not coldly furnish forth the marriage table."

"No one has proposed marriage . . . *yet*. Unless you freeze them, the meats will go off by that time."

"I wonder. A widow with a fortune needn't go unbidden for long."

"Unless she's very discriminating."

"Or has many demands."

"For the true lover, his lady's demands are his own fondest wishes."

"But it's exactly that sort of courtly eloquence I distrust."

"Then I will pursue my suit with rudeness—slut!"

"Somehow that doesn't do the trick either."

"I think I'd best take up my cause another day."

"That might be advisable. Or simple friendship might be best of all." Rather fantastically, I got tears in my eyes. "I think I need a friend."

"Of course, of course, she needs a friend," the prince said in that weird way the French have of speaking in the third person *about* a baby *to* a baby ("She wants her bottle, doesn't she?").

Eddie had a short upper lip that always exposed his upper teeth, so it looked as if he were smiling all the time, even when a smile wasn't appropriate. Depending on the circumstances people liked him for his unrelenting good humor or disliked him for his sarcasm—he was someone to whom unearned sentiments were attributed.

He was well informed, like a journalist who knows a little about everything but not a lot about any one thing. He had an old man's habit of reeling off one anecdote after another. If his memory were a closet it would be full to bursting; on some remote hook a joke he heard when he was ten could still be found dangling shapelessly. He had a muscular, "sincere" way of shaking hands firmly and, while looking someone in the eye, saying, "We must get together soon. Very *soon*," though his perpetual, unintended smile added irony to what he said and confused everyone. Most people suspected him of compulsively showing off his erudition, shallow though it might be. The Devil could drag him by the hair off to Hell and Eddie would still be chatting amiably, wracking his damaged brain for his next bon mot. In boarding school he'd translated a poem by Catullus to Lesbia and everyone had praised it, which led Eddie to announce he was going to devote himself to Catullus 65, the little epic about Ariadne deserted on Naxos by Theseus.

But he never made much headway. He would try a very free, slangy version but a friend who was a classicist objected strenuously. Then Eddie went back to the text, which only depressed him; why was he sitting alone in a room with a poem he couldn't even tell if it was meant to be parodic or not? He would tell friends he was nearing the end, but in fact he hadn't even finished a stanza that satisfied him. He had, however, read reams of commentary about the poem and his conversation was lightly peppered with classical allusions. The made-up jobs of aristocrats (Ercole's painting, Eddie's translating, Addy's decorating) began to irritate me. We were supposed to discuss and praise their fine points longer than they actually pursued them. Everyone owed a certain deference to them.

Ercole had been my most satisfying lover. He liked masochism. He understood my attraction to women. He was polite and deferential. He'd even had the wit to reject me (ha! ha!). I doubted he and Helen were happy. Couples were never happy because individuals were never happy. That was their secret. They didn't have sex and they made each other miserable. Of course, they'd sooner die than admit that, since everyone wanted their friends to envy them. Envy was the only viable guarantee of bliss. One could construct a whole life out of being envied. Envy is to experience as petrol is to an automobile.

I was very suspicious of Prince Eddie. I knew his castle on the Marne had been sold, I realized they were related to the Guises from Lorraine (the duc de Guise had become the prince of Joinville), a Catholic family during the Reformation that took terrible revenge on Protestant conspirators. There was a duc de Guise who was the lover of Louis XIV's brother for forty years, though the duke preferred women but wasn't above being the *maître en titre* and appointing and administering the thousand servants of the Palais-Royal. He really was a Guise but out of some sort of reverse snobbery he went under the less impressive name of Joinville, like Proust's Baron de Charlus, who had the right to throw around far more exalted titles but chose a humble one out of reverse snobbery.

Eddie told me that the seventeenth-century composer Charpentier had written a gay opera, *David and Jonathan*, for the king's brother and the duc de Guise—and that it was swooning with love duets between boys and we should stage it somehow. I was amazed how rank outweighed every other consideration. When the king's mistress Mme de Maintenon told him he should banish the sodomites from court, Louis asked wearily, "Must I begin with my brother?" The king loved his brother and allowed him alone to serve him dinner. He also esteemed the duc de Guise, who after all was from a princely family.

My prince de Joinville told me that I was doing my children a disservice by not providing them with a "father figure," which he pronounced in the English fashion, "figger." I turned it all into a joke and began to call him "Dear Figger." He was amiable enough to laugh, but he didn't like me mocking what he no doubt considered his strongest suit.

To myself I argued that if the children would benefit from a "figger," then maybe Eddie wasn't the best example—a man who didn't work except to sigh over his Catullus translation, whose princely title was worth more than his fortune. I began to go out with a rich commoner, Monsieur Delage, the biggest mass producer of women's shoes in France, who was an obsessive collector of the painter Derain and who lived with his mother, once a famous *grande* cocotte and said to be the model for Colette's Léa, in a twelve-room apartment on the Parc Monceau. He was a nice man, very eager to rise in the world, though he had an unfortunate comb-over and a hair color not found in nature as well as exaggerated vertical marionette lines around his mouth from excessive amiability. He owned a few of Derain's great London paintings but also several more recent lifeless works similar to *The Painter and His Family*. I thought it might be amusing to collect the later, uninspired works of painters who had taken a wrong turn, such as Derain and di Chirico.

Then I went out with a Chicagoan who was working for a French international; they were paying him a "hardship" allowance for living in Paris. He's been married twice and divorced twice. I never could figure out what had gone wrong with the marriages. It couldn't have been sexual; he was the best sex of all my beaux. He wasn't against "muff-diving," he had a big dick, and was a slow cummer. He told me that once he'd done a six-month "seminar" on anger management, but I never saw him angry. He listened to those businessman inspiration tapes you see advertised in in-flight magazines and I found that depressing. Once, when stationed in Los Angeles, he'd taken "a course in miracles," whatever that was. His clothes were sloppy and didn't fit; I imagine he'd bought them off the rack. I found that reassuring, after having lived with a Savile Row dandy. I would have dropped him if he hadn't been such a good lover.

Father Pierre came back briefly. He'd become bewitched by an ex-priest, Thomas Mirabeau, a married man who claimed his American wife, Eunice, had introduced him to a deeper knowledge of the godhead than Jesus Christ had ever done. The priest was unusually eloquent, I'd heard, but he'd been reduced to lay status for questioning the doctrines of papal infallibility and clerical celibacy. "That man is a heretic, Pierre, and is predicting an immediate and rather unpleasant Armageddon unless we accept his ideas. He's always in a rage, they say, and will make public your letters to him to show how he has won over an orthodox priest such as you."

Pierre laughed and shook his head, his plume of hair accompanying his movements. "Now you've become my spiritual counsel, and I don't doubt you're wiser than I."

"But I actually need your counsel."

"Yes, my child."

I told him about my Chicagoan, about Monsieur Delage, and updated him on Prince Eddie.

"You don't sound so taken by any of them," Pierre remarked. "You couldn't be so satirical if you really had a crush (*un béguin*) on one or the other."

"But what about the father figger problem?"

"Complete nonsense. In any event they're hardly exemplary—a collector of Derain, a layabout Latinist, a Chicago divorcé. I don't think Foulques could learn anything good from that lot. The wrong painter, the wrong poet, twice the wrong wife."

I felt relieved, though I couldn't dismiss Catullus so easily. "Can I go on just being a widow?"

"No one's suggesting you forego carnal relations. But a long, long widowhood will impress your in-laws. Besides, black is very becoming to you with your pale face and hands and blonde hair. I don't think you need worry about Foulques."

"But about Ghislaine?" I wailed, clutching my hands together.

"I think she needs a different kind of love than the kind you're giving her."

"What do you advise?"

"Prayer."

I examined him to see if he was joking, but he wasn't.

"How often?" I asked.

"Daily. Pray for guidance. The Lord wants to help you."

I thought about that for a moment then said, "Does the Lord love a murderer?"

Father Pierre looked around uneasily. "I alone must hear your confession."

"Agreed."

"And don't forget to pray to the Virgin. She was a mother, too."

He suggested I see a chic Left Bank psychiatrist, a Lacanian. I was having the most terrible migraines, something my sister and I had always suffered from but that now were excrutiating and nearly constant. I gratefully pocketed the doctor's *coordonées*.

I didn't want to spring too much on Father Pierre at one sitting. I could tell he was weary (from his travels but also from always having to say quotable things that stayed within the boundaries of decency). It must be tiring to be a *prêtre mondain*. To be witty *and* pious. I kissed his small, soft hand and he immediately withdrew it like a Moroccan king. "Don't exaggerate, my child," he said, scandalized.

The next day when I found him alone by the Arethusa fountain, which was quietly reciting its rosary to itself, I asked him if I could bring up something serious with him.

"As long as it won't leave frown lines on that lovely face."

"I want to promote Yvette as a saint. I just spoke with Mercy, and the new bishop has agreed to take up her cause."

"Excellent."

"Will you?" I asked. "Would you retire to Rome? I've found a lovely villa for you with large gardens and a staff. You could keep your apartment in Paris and come back on frequent trips. The villa has a Renaissance private chapel. And two guest bedrooms."

"I have a young Norwegian friend named Pal who likes gardening. Could I bring him, too?"

"I've never heard you mention him before."

Pierre blushed, ever so faintly. "He's a ski champion and models ski clothes for a German catalogue. He's excellent company, a hard worker—and, how do you say in English—*easy on the eyes*?"

"How old? Catholic?"

"Twenty-two. I think they're some sort of Lutherans. Non-practicing."

"Of course you can bring him. Where is he now?"

"Oslo."

"Rome sounds much better. Actually, it's an hour away on the Appian Way. Does he drive?"

"Yes. He's almost two meters tall. No Mini Coopers."

"I had no idea you had a special friend."

"He's like a son to me."

"Sounds more like a *nephew* . . . What do we need to make Yvette a saint?"

"Money, first of all. It takes about half a million. No one without rich backers was ever beatified."

"Money. Okay."

"Then two miracles. It used to be four. Almost all the miracles are medical."

"We have one of those. The other one occurred when she lifted a car off a Mexican boy in Texas."

"Any witnesses?"

"Yes, for both."

"Of course, most miracles are posthumous. The Vatican distrusts miracles during the saint's life—that might be the Devil's handiwork. Whereas the Devil is powerless once the saint is dead."

"We've put her remains in a grandiose tomb next to her Saint Catherine of Siena altar. They're already lining up to ask for miracles and there are several ex-votos—those little primitive paintings on tin—to attest to a divine cure for rheumatism and another for an oven fire that went out and that my sister magically reignited."

"That won't do much good with the Curia, I fear."

"But there will be others."

"We must assemble letters and testimonials that prove she led a life of heroic virtue. Letters from people who knew her."

"Spanish is okay?"

"Of course. Most of our postulators know five modern languages and the two ancient ones."

"What else do they look for?"

"The saint's own writings."

"I have countless letters from her, deeply pious."

"But didn't you tell me she wrote about being in love with Sister Mercy? And even passing to the sinful act in Rome? What we call PSA—passing to the sinful act?" His English was an accented Oxbridge way of talking. Where was he from? I wondered.

I thought a moment. "Her handwriting and mine are identical. Always have been. Only a handful of her letters to me would need to be censored and recopied."

"Can we trust Mercy to send us some blank convent stationery? And a bottle of convent ink? I'm good at slightly antiquing paper. The Vatican labs are very thorough at detecting frauds."

"Yes, Mercy will help in every way, I'm sure. Are our chances for beatification and canonization good?"

"Well, since Vatican Two they're interested in servants of God who are somehow relevant and original. Holiness is no longer enough. The causes of lots of holy people are languishing. The fact that Colombia has a recent saint, Laura Montoya, from the very same village who worked with the indigenous—that's not promising. And that Yvette's from North America, not Colombia—that's bad. That she didn't found an order of nuns—traditionally that would have been against her, but who knows now?"

"Doesn't piety count for something? Or good works?"

"That you will establish by editing her own writing. And by the testimonials of those who knew her—her priest in Texas, her sister nuns. And we need to get a local doctor to verify that cancer miracle."

"Of course we must do what we must do. But it does seem to me a proof of her saintliness—her very skepticism, her tormented love of Mercy, her extraordinary way of forgiving our unforgivable father. I realize the *people* don't want flaws in the diamond, but for me the flaws are as beautiful as the perfect facets. She *struggled* to achieve sanctity."

"With the Indians, do we know of any pious acts on your sister's part; did she intercede to cure anyone of a harelip or something? Did she divide her cloak with a beggar? But seriously, medical miracles seem to be better; we may already have one and all we need is one more."

Although Pierre's "official" family name was Thomas, he confided in me, looking at me intensely, that he'd been born Jewish in Alexandria, where his name was Pringsheim, and only after he'd attended Oxford and converted to Catholicism did his name "get changed" to Thomas; he said it as if he'd had no agency in the transformation. He "confessed" his origins as if the Inquisition were still in full swing and he was a converso celebrating Shabbat in the basement every Friday evening. Then it occurred to me that I'd heard the people I was living with mutter anti-Semitic slurs and that Pierre owed his prestige to his continued secrecy. I drew a zipper with a finger across my lips. We Texans could be racist toward blacks and Mexicans, and in the old Klan days we'd opposed Jews and Catholics as well, but we weren't trained to sniff out Jews and our anti-Semitism was more latent than active. I myself was utterly indifferent to people's origins, but I'd learned not to say that. I had a French friend ask about a Madame Cohen, "She's Jewish—from where?" "France!" I exclaimed, indignant. Of course, it was Muslims, not French Catholics, who were desecrating Jewish graves—but we weren't allowed to say that either.

Now that Pierre had told me two "compromising" things about himself (that he had a Norwegian "nephew" and that he'd been born an Egyptian Jew), I felt closer to him. A week later the "nephew" himself showed up, speaking perfect English, of course. He was a giant with a bass voice and a black beard, hands the size of baked hams, neon-stitched trousers, and a leather coat of many colors. He walked strangely, with a wide stance; later Pierre told me that Pal had just had surgery, had added genital jewelry, a "Prince Albert," like Victoria's husband's modification, Foxy's great-great uncle. I asked Pierre if he'd seen the results. "All in good time," he said with a wink.

When I walked past Pierre's room that night, I heard him and Pal laughing and talking (or rather I heard Pal, whose voice was so resonant), a cozy exchange between two friends who could let long silences accumulate . . . I was happy for Pierre, to know he wasn't living a loveless life. They reminded me of Yvette and Mercy.

The next time I spoke to Pierre alone, he said, "It's good that Yvette was a religious. There have been very few married women who became saints. And it's good that the Pope is traveling soon to South America. He likes to name local people as Venerables when he's in their country and to open their cause."

"Cause?"

"There are about fifteen hundred open causes—would-be saints. Some of them date back to the Middle Ages. Of course, the actual congregation must approve of the candidate. Some Burgundian bishop of the fifteenth century is scarcely remembered unless prayers to his relics are answered. But a good woman who helped the congregation—and in Heaven is still interceding for them—is likely to have plenty of advocates. I'm sure your sister will be named a Servant of God, a Venerable, and then a dossier will be opened for her in Rome with the Congregation for the Causes of Saints. A postulator and a relator will be named. The postulator's job is to produce a *positio*, roughly a thousand pages of biography, listing the two miracles and the proofs of heroic virtue. It contains the would-be saint's writings, testimonials to her, observations from doctors, a documented chronology. Usually a postulator will choose a collaborator, a scholar often from the same community. They might find a learned nun from her order."

"If there is one," I said, smiling.

"This will all take decades. Saint Thérèse of Lisieux was canonized twenty-eight years after her death—a real speed demon, mainly because the church and state had been separated in 1905 and the pope wanted to present a consolation prize to the Eldest Daughter of the Church."

"What does the relator do?"

"The postulator's job is done once the *positio* is accepted. The relator makes certain that the cause results in canonization. In your sister's case I'd be the relator. I know most of the cardinals and could grease their wizened palms. But the actual canonization will take place long after we're both gone."

I reached for his hand and squeezed it; I couldn't bear to think of a world without him. My own death seemed unreal to me, though I'd murdered my husband.

I was astonished by how many people Pierre frequented—and how diverse. He was friends with Lou Reed, he'd converted Wittgenstein, he was friends with Dacia Maraini, he'd written the introduction to one of William Burrough's paste-up novels, he'd helped Pierre Bergé deal with Yves Saint Laurent's depressions, he'd proofread Cocteau's *The Difficulty of Being*, he'd helped the vicomte de Noailles lay out his cubist garden. I had to drag out of him all these accomplishments and *connaisances*. Young, he'd been told that nothing was worse than a name-dropper (there's no word for that in French); he took that hint too seriously, which made conversation with him awkward at times ("A physicist of some repute" would be his way of referring to his friend Einstein, "a belletrist of the old Austro-Hungarian empire" would have to do for Milan Kundera, "a regular Corinthian hetaerae" meant Louise de Vilmorin).

I saw Father Pierre's psychiatrist the next time I was in Paris. He was a tall, balding man in his forties dressed in a dark suit and tie, wearing a lovely citrusy English scent, Blenheim Bouquet, which I recognized because it was Addy's favorite. His office was probably his salon, with big bay windows looking out on one of those surprisingly peaceful gardens just a few meters away from Boulevard Saint-Michel. He was very clean and gentle. He sat in a facing chair with his head bent and the fingertips of his right hand touching those of the left.

Maybe it was his attentive silence or that he was wearing Addy's cologne, but just after I told him I had terrible migraines I started sobbing and blurted out that I had murdered my husband. He let thirty seconds go by, stood, and said, "Our session is over."

"What! I've only been here five minutes."

"We've done some very good work," and he escorted me to the door, his arm around my shoulders.

Only later did Helen, who'd seen Jacques-Alain Miller, Lacan's son-in-law, tell me that Lacanians rarely saw patients longer than twenty minutes and could terminate the session after five minutes.

My migraines, magically, went away and never came back. Father Pierre assured me my secret was safe with Dr. Palme.

CHAPTER 20

Today it's a beautiful spring day and I've left the children with their grandparents at Quercy. Ghislaine was quarrelsome and difficult as usual, wondering why she couldn't come up to Paris, too; I always dreaded the day she'd learn the word "boredom." Now she's acquired it and wields it like a weapon. She can say it in three languages, *Langeweile*, *ennui*, and boredom. She's precocious. She pronounces it like a reproach: "I'm so *bored* with these dull, deaf old people living in the past. There's no place on earth as *boring* as this humid old Schloss. I have friends in Paris; in Paris I can take ballet class; in Paris I can go shopping. Here there's no one. I'm so *bored* I could scream." And with that she did scream.

I left the room and closed the door. I ran into Foulques, who was putting together a dinosaur from a balsa wood kit. "What kind of dinosaur is that?" I asked.

"*Tyrannosaurus rex*," he said in almost a whisper. I bent down to ruffle his lovely blond hair, and, a bit annoyed, he patted it back in place.

"Mommy's off to Paris for a few days."

That caught his attention and he looked up apprehensively. "Why?" he asked.

I felt horrible and made up something on the spot: "To buy you that darling border collie puppy we saw at the D'Amours."

Foulques was so delighted that his happiness made him stand up and shift his weight from foot to foot. "Really?"

"What shall we call him?"

"Dan."

"That's a nice name. What made you choose that?"

Foulques, smiling a bit foolishly, just shrugged.

"No, tell me. What?"

"I dunno. I'd like to be called Dan."

"But, darling, you have such a beautiful historic name."

"When are you coming back with Dan?"

"Next Tuesday evening," I said.

He sat back down to construct his dinosaur. I could see how excited he was, though it was beneath his dignity to leap about. He looked back up. "Will Dan be my dog or do I have to share him?"

"He'll be all yours."

The next time I passed him he was humming, which I'd never heard him do before. I imagined Ghislaine would insist I buy her something equally valuable in compensation. Maybe ice skates. And a cat.

As I pulled into Paris off the *périphérique*, it sparkled under the shifting gray clouds. No country has more beautiful clouds than France, another whole upper country of gray hills, gray battlements, gray villages, enormous rose-tinged gray flowers, gray valleys, gigantic gray faces . . . An alternative landscape, a kingdom of memories; horizontal in space, vertical in time—a Cross!

I knew that Yvette would have shed tears over a hint of the Crucifixion, but I was so exhilarated to be pulling into Paris that I couldn't spare a thought for anything tragic. I remembered when I first came here for my junior year abroad.

Everything had been cleaned just a decade before and the whole city was glittering. It was both new and old. Notre-Dame, freshly hatched from its dirt shell, gleamed with optimism and detail worthy of the kings who'd celebrated Mass or coronations or victory here. Later I learned the Hotel de Ville had been destroyed and rebuilt in the nineteenth century, but I took it for Renaissance. The Louvre was new-minted and probably at no point in history had been so peaceful.

But at that time I had no knowledge of history. For me Paris was just sun and shade on unbroken façades, massive stone bridges, ornate monuments, gravel paths, pruned trees, streets radiating out from an arch, underpopulated sidewalks, underpasses suddenly bursting into light and a river view, unfamiliar-looking small cars, cafés with awnings and reed chairs, uniformed guards (some on gleaming horseback, their tack all gold—bits, bridles, girths), the whole indolent parade of a weekday in spring in a city without skyscrapers, green-shuttered book kiosks along the quais, everyone clothed in dresses or suits, a *clean* city, as if it had been thoroughly hosed down at dawn (it had been). To me it was an Impressionist painting (with darker clouds, no children, and fewer flowers). In Texas we'd thought of "old" as poor, due for a face-lift, but here these old stones seemed to be treasured. I thought of cities as rushing places, as solemn streets between thronged avenues, as backdrops, all identical, sliding by on casters, but here the city was nearly silent, immemorial, a sandstone fringe brushed on an immense horizon of bruised-blue clouds, each building unique, prized.

I remembered how rude and unwelcoming Mme de Castiglione had been, how I had sobbed in my *chambre de bonne* smelling of roach spray, how greedily I'd wolfed down my *réligieuse* pastry, then that horrible first meal of Jerusalem artichokes.

Now I was slender, well coiffed, dressed in perfect if not stylish taste (I'd stayed too faithful to Givenchy). Now I knew how to speed fearlessly through Paris in my Mercedes. I left my car with the doorman at the Bristol (I'd sold the Avenue Foch apartment to pay Addy's debts), checked in, was shown by the bellboy up to my room (weren't bellboys called *chasseurs*?), awaited my luggage, unpacked, opened a window, and called Duke Willens, who was on a whirlwind European trip.

"Hello, Duke? It's Yvonne de Courcy, known to you as Why-Von Crawford."

"How's my little gal? Why-Von, you've lost your pretty East Texas twang."

"Yours is still intact. That's not all I've lost."

"What else, sweetheart?"

"My innocence, my husband, and a good deal of my money."

"I never was innocent or had much money and my wife went and died on me."

"Sorry for your loss." We both sank into a respectful silence. Then I said with Texas pep: "What about that drink you promised me?"

"Come on over to the Meurice—that far away from you?"

"Walking distance. I'll be there in half an hour."

When I arrived at the Meurice I called up to Duke's room.

"Doncha wanna come up here, little darling?"

"No, Duke, come on down," I said.

"You're no fun."

"Give me a chance. I remember you called me brassy and forward once."

"I never did no such thing," he sputtered.

"I heard you with my own ears, Duke. I overheard you telling Why-vet that I was brassy and forward."

"I don't think I even knew a word like 'brassy' back then."

I thought he probably heard his mother say it.

He sighed and said in a low voice, "Mighty pretty little ears, I recollect."

"Here you are, sweet-talking me and you haven't even seen me yet," I sighed.

When he got off the elevator he stopped melodramatically in the lobby and looked and looked at me, his face expressionless but his arms extended and his hands open, as if thunderstruck. I smiled and reeled him in.

"Did an angel come down from Heaven?" he asked.

"Don't tell me you've become a day drinker, Duke Willens."

Now that I could take a good look at him, I could see he'd gone to pot but was still sexy, kind of. He'd put on weight and his beer belly was pushing against his mustard-colored button-down shirt; the fat part of his tie was shorter than the skinny part, but hey, he'd made an effort. His face was tan and his eyebrows unruly, the character lines in his face deeply engraved. He must have skipped a couple days of shaving; his beard was coming in gray. His earlobes were hairy in the crosslight. He wasn't as tall as I remembered. I guess he was still rich; these hotels cost a thousand dollars a day.

"Look at you, will you?" he said. "You've become a raving French beauty, so well turned-out, but for me you're still a Texas bluebell. C'mon, give us a hug." He opened his arms and pulled me against his lumpy body. He smelled of whiskey.

When we had ordered our martinis (which we had to specify were the American cocktails, not sweet vermouth), I asked Duke whom he'd married. He seemed confused that I didn't already know his whole story, though we hadn't been in touch for decades, as if we'd been talking daily or as if he was so famous I must have been kept abreast. "What do you know about me?" he asked with an American man's arrogance.

"No more than you know about me," I said.

"You don't even know I wrote and published *The Willens: The First Century in Texas?*"

"Who helped you with that?"

"My wife, Ima. She was a librarian from Lubbock."

"What happened to her, Duke?"

"Cancer. Breast cancer. At least it was quick. She had the best treatment in the Anderson Cancer Center in Houston. Wonderful palliative care. She didn't know where she was or what was happening to her."

"That's nice. Duke, I can't think of you with a librarian."

"Now, she was a real looker! And a good church woman. Lubbock's the buckle on the Bible belt, you know. Baptists."

"Any children?"

"You mean, Why-Von, you don't honestly know about my little Molly, the love of my life?" He seemed genuinely nonplussed.

"How much do you know about my children?"

"You've kept yourself such a mystery, Why-Von."

"Well, I have two. One of each. Twins. The girl is Ghislaine and the little boy is Foulques."

"Too bad you saddled them with foreign names."

"They don't sound foreign in France."

"Ain't you ever coming back to Texas? I could give you one good reason."

"You always were such a flirt, Duke Willens."

He smiled in acquiescence.

"I like Paris," I said.

"How did your husband die?"

"He fell off a cliff."

"Ouch. Drinkin'?"

"Yep. Poor guy."

I'd always told myself that I'd go back to Texas some day, but I didn't see why, exactly. It's true I missed the huge vibrant blue skies, the nosy, shockingly friendly people. I didn't have any relatives there now, at least none I was in touch with, but somehow I'd feel safer, especially as I got old and fragile, with "my own people," whatever that meant. I had put those terrible Texas Baptists out of my mind until Duke reminded me of them. That shallow, bigoted, self-satisfied religion! My children were Catholics, didn't play baseball; Ghislaine would never agree to a debut, at least not in Dallas. She didn't know how to gush and Foulques wasn't prepared to sock someone in the face. They had surrendered to the strong gravitational pull of France. They had no desire to see the world except on an educational tour with other French people. French culture was so hypnotic to the French; no wonder they almost never emigrated, unless they were persecuted like the Huguenots or the Jews. My children spoke in French slang, listened to French pop music, rode English saddle, were embarrassed by my American accent and begged me to stay silent around their friends, knew more about Truffaut than John Ford. Ghislaine understood instinctively how to tie and drape a scarf. They liked museums and trooped through them dutifully but spent more time reading the historical placards than looking at the paintings. They wouldn't eat anything sweet (mint sauce, cranberry sauce, maple syrup) except as dessert; they would hold the waffles till the end of the meal. They made faces and pretended to gag over anything spicy. They peeled their figs, even apples. They couldn't eat tomatoes that hadn't been peeled and seeded. They said "*Excusez-moi*" constantly as proof of their breeding rather than as a sincere bid for pardon. They didn't understand random chatter or anecdotes, the staples of Texas conversation. Instead of matching stories they'd say, "What's your point?" or "Then what?"

"Where are the little kids now?" Duke asked.

"With their French grandparents in the South of France."

"Don't you miss them?"

"Lord, no," I said gaily. "I love them to bits—don't get me wrong."

"They must miss a father figure."

"Does Molly miss a mother figure?"

"She has my sisters. Say, I heard Why-Vet passed. What a shame. How did that happen?"

"She became a nun and died on a missionary trip among the Indians in Colombia."

"Well, I declare. A Catholic nun?"

"Yes."

He thought for a moment and said, "No wonder she was a little funny about making out."

"You tried to get her to lick your penis."

"I did not! I was not brought up that way!"

"I remember it as if it were yesterday. You were studying algebra together and you pulled it out of your pants and asked her to lick it and she said you should try me, that I liked that sort of thing."

A sly smile canceled out his indignation. "I guess I was barkin' up the wrong tree." He actually adjusted his crotch.

I suddenly felt shy and said, "Say, we're well on our way to getting Why-Vet declared a saint."

"Seriously? That's a very big deal, I guess. How does that go, exactly?"

"Well, first her local bishop has to make her a Venerable. Then she's made a Blessed. We've already done those two steps. I've got a very good man working on it at the Vatican. Eventually, long after we're gone, she might make it to sainthood."

"It's sort of like a PhD."

"Except there are very few new saints."

"How do you hurry it along?"

"Money."

"Well, the Crawfords got plenty of that. I heard your dad and his wife—wasn't she named Bobbie Jean?—I heard they passed, too."

"You have a good memory, Duke Willens, and you sure keep up on folks."

"I guess I care a lot about old friends." He raised a reproachful eyebrow.

"I gotta run to have my hair did."

"When am I gonna see you again, you brassy little thing?"

I smiled. "Tomorrow at one. Right here. I can spend the whole afternoon with you."

"That sounds wonderful as a hot bath after a day's ride on the ranch."

"Don't overplay the Lone Star folksiness," and with that I rose, kissed his forehead, and ran off.

That evening I asked myself if I wanted thirty years too late to start up with Duke. Then I said, "We live in different cities, on different continents. It might be fun to see what I've been missing all these years."

The next day I went up to his room and within minutes we were tangled in each other's arms. I guess I preferred men's bodies but I figured I could fall in love only with a woman. He was built large, even with the natural shrinkage of age, but his pubes and chest hairs were gray. I sat on him; luckily he didn't try to rest his weight on me. Then we showered and dressed and ate at a café on the Left Bank. Duke ordered two of everything. Otherwise, he was hungry all the time in Paris, he explained. Now that I'd slept with him, he seemed less attentive and we made no more plans to get together. He appeared surprised I could speak French to the waiter.

CHAPTER 21

Dear Yvette,

Today is our birthday. Thirty-five years and two months after your death. Before he left this world, I told Father Pierre that I missed writing you and he said I should write you a letter and burn it on the altar of Santa Maria Maggiore in Rome and the letter would be delivered intact to you in Heaven. I'm heading to Rome the day after tomorrow. I'll be staying in a house on the Appian Way that belongs to Father Pal, Father Pierre's charming Norwegian "friend" and loyal companion (truth be told, I found the house for them). Pal is a bit feeble now (old ski injuries) but he's still an avid gardener and keeps both a *jardin potager* and a spectacular *jardin de plaisance*. He has a handsome, unsmiling young Norwegian *homme à tout faire* living with him who does all the hoeing and toting.

I'm sure you have lots of activities in Heaven, especially as a saint-in-waiting, but you may have been keeping an eye on your old twin (I suppose people don't age in Heaven—at least I prefer to see you as eternally young). You no doubt know (or saw) that Ghislaine killed herself. She became so disagreeable for a while, then turned eerily docile and anorexic and began to cut herself. We sent her to a sort of boot camp in upstate New York, where she was bound to a chair and force-fed. She came back to France plump and almost comatose. We gave her a giant eighteenth-birthday party and her friends from Rosey, her school, flew in from all over the world. We put them all up at the castle and in adjoining hotels and inns and conveyed them about in a fleet of cars. We had horses for those who wanted to ride. I hired twelve more staff to make beds and cook and serve and iron. The château never looked more lovely (we'd filled in the white quarry spots with new lawn, we'd gotten the Arethusa fountain up to speed, Addy's garish Four Continents fountain was repaired). Ghislaine was happy, I think, or maybe just hysterical. A day after everyone left she killed herself—a gunshot to the head, which they say is unusual for females, who prefer pills. If I sound cold, it's because I've lived so long, with the guilt and constant nightmares, running through alternate scenarios that might have saved her. Some of my friends—Helen and Ercole, Prince Eddie, that old Duke Willens from Dallas, remember him?—were there and had stayed on to comfort me, I guess you could call it that. Foulques, who builds harpsichords in Rome and seems to like boys, drove up for the party and dance. He was just as uncomfortable as you at my debut, remember? How you were sealed naked into that tube of a dress and had had your hair peroxided but still cut short, you looked like a Nordic Saint Joan . . . He's a dear boy but still very shy; he's a whiz at restoring those slender Italian harpsichords and those more complicated, bigger French ones. He even paints little pastoral scenes on the harpsichord lid—who knew he was so talented? Of course, I understand firsthand how devastating it is to lose a twin, although technically you didn't kill yourself. He sits by the Arethusa fountain for hours and has even begun to ask me questions for the first time about his father. I paint a rosy picture, of course. It was a little tricky to get Ghislaine buried in holy ground, but the chaplain is a young local a bit awestruck by the Courcys and he was willing to buy the story that she had had an anaphylactic shock from eating a dish prepared elsewhere, somewhere the cooks didn't know about her peanut allergy. The local retired doctor, a gay English doctor who's a friend, confirmed our alibi. They say the doctor was the model for the gay Jewish doctor in *Sunday Bloody Sunday*, played by Peter Finch (Glenda Jackson was in that, too). Anyway, he's very civilized and Church of England if he's church of anything. He and Foulques are friends, though there's a fifty-years age difference.

Eudes died of a stroke and Victorine a year later of dementia; I was always nice to them and patient with them. They lived in the château full-time and were very comfortable here (the castle has seventeen fireplaces). I gave them a nice allowance, which Addy never did. Of course, they had their suspicions about me, but they were ultra-discreet. Luckily they didn't live to witness Ghislaine's death. Their life was irreproachable, at least by their lights, though I'd say they were useless.

You could say I've been pretty useless, too, most of my life. Rich people in France think that's totally normal. They have no concept of charity and think the state should do everything. Back in Texas we thought you should have a life of service, and big sit-down gala dinners were always, remember, for cancer or muscular dystrophy. In France they're just for fun.

In the last few years I've been doing some good works; I've been raising money for AIDS and even visiting sick patients. Lots of ladies here are afraid of touching men with AIDS, but I'm fearless. I may have always been a spoiled brat, but remember how I was a good jumper on horse-back? I was never afraid. Maybe even reckless. Anyway, now we know you can't get AIDS by touching someone or from saliva or mosquitos, but back then we didn't know anything—that you get it only from blood or sperm. In France we had all these contaminated blood scandals for hemophiliacs, just because France didn't want to pay for a perfectly good American detection system that was already in place.

Why AIDS, you may wonder. I don't think Foulques has ever had sex or if he has he probably left his underpants on, but since he's part of the "at-risk" population I thought I should devote myself to that cause. A gay cause. Don't forget that you and I are a little bit gay around the edges, though lesbians never catch it. In recent years I've spent more and more time with Foxy, Adhéaume's German cousin, the music critic. When she's not covering opera in Orange or Cleveland or Palermo, she's here with me at the château.

When I look back at my life I think I haven't changed that much. And though I've recopied all your letters, leaving out the lesbian or questioning parts, I'm perfectly aware how similar we are. We're both sensualists, you even a bit more than me, I suspect. We both believe in a life of service. Remember how our real mother used to tell us there's nothing more important in life than serving others? You served the Lord and His saints. I served fashion and served men. We both ended up far from Texas but in the end we were good Texas girls.

ACKNOWLEDGMENTS

Michael Carroll and Giuseppe Gullo listened to every word of this book as I wrote it. Richard Bates helped me prepare the beginning of the manuscript. Keith McDermott, Rick Whitaker, and my sister, Margaret Fleming, encouraged me along the way. Paul Halsall gave me some Catholic advice, but the mistakes are all my own. Diane DeSanders corrected some of my Dallas mistakes. Nicolas Gaviria gave me great suggestions about Colombia. Paul Eprile helped me with the French. David McConnell let me use his studio.

I am grateful to my editor, Liese Mayer, and to Barbara Darko, for her careful reading of the text.

I consulted hundreds of books. The most helpful ones were *Making Saints* by Kenneth L. Woodward, and various books by saints and about Saints Óscar Romero and Laura Montoya and about Dorothy Day. The memoirs of Élisabeth de Gramont inspired me.